SABER, WISDOM AND JUSTICE

BOOK 3

MONICA RED

Monica RED

ISBN: 978-1-7328755-6-2

Editing by First Editing
Cover Design: MREd
Art Smimbipi|Pixabay|BookBrush

Map Illustrator: Diego Esperon Rodriguez

Library of Congress

Created with Vellum

TO MY WHOLE WORLD, JOSEPHINE

And my biggest fans,
Gloria and Antonieta.
Thanks for reading all of this.

FREE BONUS

JOIN MY MAILING LIST TODAY AND GET A HOLD TO

FREE EXCLUSIVE PREQUEL NOVELLA

Saber, Seeds of Darkness

I was supposed to die in that fall, but I didn't.

I used to believe my precarious brother and abusive father were my biggest problem, but all changed.

Now, I can't trust anyone and if I don't control the power in me, everyone will be in danger. Especially my Elizabeth.

Discover how it all begins.

Hune
The Verge
Lost Caverns
Northern Forest
Eternal Glaciers
Swamps
Laconia
Tundra
Reign Mountain
Waterfall
Desert
Andromeda
Southern Forest
St. Patrick's Abbey

LAST STAGES OF WAR

Lily half-ran, half-stumbled over the uneven ground of the Northern Forest as she raced to meet the valsings arriving at the refuge.

A few weeks had passed since she'd sent the group to the Soto Forest to find out what had happened to St. Patrick's Abbey and the zhortas. It was one of the first orders she'd given as their new leader, and she had questioned it every day.

A weight lifted from her shoulders when she saw that the four valsings had returned. "Liam," she said, breathless, "did you find it? Is everyone—"

She exhaled and stood still. In the past, she had been a messenger, and she'd hated it when her former monarch had ignored her but demanded he be told what she had learned. She looked up at the group again and, in a steady voice, asked. "Are you all right? I was so worried about you all, and if something might have—"

"It was a long trip," Rusell said without looking at her. "I apologize, your... The abbey is too far away... What we found—"

"We found nothing," said Agnes, the younger one. "Hune is turning for the worst. I have no doubt about it."

Then Anha spoke up. "There are so many things changing that—"

"What are you talking about?" Lily turned to the only valsing she had met before. "What happened, Liam?"

Trust wasn't the problem, but unlike the other three, they had belonged to the king's community. For years, they'd lived in the Soto Forest, which was why she'd accepted Liam's offer to go with the group.

"We should talk somewhere else," he said, looking around. "This goes beyond the abbey, Lily."

She nodded and led them to her shelter.

It didn't surprise her how exhausted Liam looked. When he'd left, open wounds had covered most of his body. The memory of his back, bloody with strips of cloth and skin hanging from it, came to her mind. However, the worst part had been learning it was their own community who had done it while forcing him to kill the members of the queen's people. The human soldiers had to help him because none of the other valsings wanted to be close to him.

She shook her head and brought attention back to the present. At that moment, she became conscious of the laughs from the human children playing with the young ones of her own race. The sound of clashing steel had become as normal as birdsong after the soldiers had volunteered to train any valsing interested in self-defense, proving that the valsings didn't know everything and could learn from others.

There was harmony in the refugee. The heat from the fires kept the place warm, the smell of food traveled around, reassuring everyone that they would not go hungry, and the comfortable shelters created a barrier to the war outside. It was a lie, and they were in danger, making each peaceful day a treasure. A shiver ran down her spine as she thought of the approaching time when they would lose it all.

Anha didn't enter the shelter. Not all valsings liked having Lily as their leader. Though they would follow her orders, they wouldn't do more than was strictly necessary.

Lily hated it the most, though, and couldn't wait to find Donald. The best decision Queen Vanessa had made was leaving him in charge. He would know what to do and how to unite and protect them.

Rusell, Agnes, and Liam entered the shelter and waited for Lily to show them where to stand or sit. The fireplace's light increased the fatigue in their eyes, highlighted the tension in their attitude, and showed the lack of color in their skin. It wasn't because of sickness, though. Lily was looking at the face of fear.

"It was hard to find the abbey, Lily," Liam said. "I did not want to believe it, but, well, after the reisers, St. Patrick's Abbey was not going to be—"

"I have no idea what you were expecting," Rusell said, "but it was a good thing you sent us. That place is cursed! We should mark it as forbidden."

"I told you it is not jinxed," Liam said. "The village is, though. The abbey does not have a poisonous mist around it, and the trees are still alive."

"Barely! We may not have lived in the Soto Forest before, Liam, but that valley is not just disgusting. It is dangerous. No one should go there anymore."

Lily exhaled, containing her desire to demand an explanation. Instead, she gestured to some chairs and waited for them to sit.

"Please, start from the beginning," she said. "Otherwise, I cannot understand—"

"You want to understand?" Agnes said. "You should have gone, then! I do not agree with Rusell. Nothing good will come from this ridiculous tantrum of yours. Your personal needs should not be our priority. Why did you send us there?"

"Agnes," Lily said, "it was not personal. To find out what our priorities are, we need to learn what our enemies have done."

"I did not have enemies until you came to our community and bewitched the head of our Congress!" Agnes stood. "I despise knowing what is coming, and I hate you for making me see all of that." She strode out of the shelter.

Lily struggled to contain her tears and hide her trembling hands.

"Please, forgive her," Rusell said. "I'm old and have nothing to hope for, but for our young ones, this is devastating."

"What is devastating?" Lily said, staring at the valsing, but it was Liam who answered.

"We walked south, right to the edge of the Soto Forest like you told us. Once we reached the desert, we did the same. Just like we did for years, we planned to walk into the Soto Forest after we passed Reign Mountain, but that is not an option anymore."

He rubbed his face, leaned forward, and rested his head in his hands. "The trees moved."

"What you mean they moved?" Lily said. "They are always moving."

"I have never been inside those woodlands, Lily," Rusell said, "but the way the roots dug into the sand and the darkness of the branches were not good or normal."

"They are taking over the desert."

Lily sat back while her body temperature dropped. "The trees are moving out of the—"

Rusell and Liam nodded.

Many years ago, when the war started, Hune lost its beautiful ocean, creating the desert that now rested in its place. As a result, things changed. The great waterfall in Laconia dried out, most of the Southern Forest died, and the swamps kept expanding into the Northern Forest. But during all that times, the Soto Forest remained the same. It had been the only place unaffected by the war until now.

"Did you even find the abbey, then?"

Liam sighed. Though his gaze rested on the other side of the shelter, his mind was somewhere else. Finally, he said, "It took a tremendous effort, but having lived there helped… The valley is just a bunch of massive branches. Pieces of metal and rocks piled on top of each other. Beyond the view, what shocked me was the missing aroma from the flowers… I do not know if they vanished or died."

Rusell stood and paced around the room, scratching his head. "What happened to my community here…what Orson did was monstrous, but that… It wasn't the reisers."

"What do you mean?" Lily said. "They sent the reisers to attack the abbey. Their leader and the sorcerer were talking about—"

"Rusell is right, Lily. I'm sure it was magic, not the reisers, that destroyed—"

"Destroyed? What they left behind!" Rusell stopped and turned to her. "The zhortas, those poor ones. They engraved their remains on the roots. You can see their expression, full of fear and pain, and even the tree that captured them looks…somehow in torment."

Lily covered her face with her hands. She had been right to accuse the zhortas of kidnapping Sara, but they'd also protected her, and they'd died because of it. Sara needed to learn what had happened to them, and she had to hide from those monsters. Everyone was at risk, but her best friend was in even greater danger.

"I saw Zhorta Stuart, Lily… I tried—we tried to get them

down to bury them, but…it has to be magic and not from Hune. If this is the work of the sorcerer you overheard in the forest, I do not believe we can stop him. Neither can the humans."

She closed her eyes, afraid of asking something so ludicrous, but it was important. They needed answers.

"The abbey's library. Is it also destroyed?"

"No," Liam said, but his tone lowered and he stared at her. "The abbey collapsed, along with the scaffoldings. Most of the roots dropped on top of the valley, and although they looked darker and full of moss, their sprouts are trying to reach the ground."

"Those things aren't normal," Rusell said. "I would love to burn them…all the forest with them, too."

Liam sighed. "We tried, but it is impossible. But to answer your question, Lily, the same moss covered all the abbey's ruins. We didn't dare to touch it. However, the dome of the library, the big vault, and all of its windows are intact."

"You cannot send anyone there!" Rusell said, shaking his head and walking towards her. "It is a death sentence. He's right. We should not disturb that thing. It is cursed, I'm sure of it. You can't—"

"I won't." Lily stood and took a few steps away from him. "I understand the danger. I met the monsters who did it, remember?"

Liam put a hand on Rusell's shoulder. Though it startled him, it helped him stop and breathe again.

A knot formed in her throat, and not for the first time, she wondered how Queen Vanessa had kept her composure while facing the destruction of Hune. Lily's hate for Orson grew, and not because of the role he'd played in that madness. Thanks to her former king, she had settled for years in the same place. Unlike the queen's community, she'd had a home, and now it was gone.

"Lily," Liam said, "what do you want us to do?"

She turned and faced both valsings.

Their sagging shoulders and the lack of life in their eyes were things she had no cure for. She was aware she probably looked the same. They needed help, and she had no idea where to even start to find it.

"Just rest," she said. "But please, try not… We can't lie. That's how we ended up here. If they ask, tell them the truth." She inhaled and covered her face. "We have to find Donald and…we need to find them. They need to learn about this."

"Will they be able to help?" Rusell asked.

She lifted her shoulders, and a few tears blurred her sight. "Maybe…but I do not know if anyone could stop the Soto Forest from consuming Hune, our most dangerous threat."

ASCENSION

"Damn it!" Chris said the second he woke up. Although the image in his head was graphic, it was the sensation of Sara's blood on his hands that bothered him the most. He took a deep breath and, with relief, noticed the essence of flowers was missing.

He rubbed his face, hoping he would never have to use a sword like he had in his nightmare, and focused on the chilly night of the Northern Forest, the campfire, and the reiser in front of him. Once again, he wondered if he'd made the right choice by leaving Sara with John and Donald. At the time, it had seemed to be for the best, but it didn't remove the guilt for not talking to her before or for leaving her.

"I guess your conscious is not that clean after all," Hayden said without looking at him.

Chris stood and wandered around the fire. The idea of joining forces with his enemy to defeat Gemli and Murllen was still strange and grotesque to him.

"I wouldn't hurt her, you know?" Hayden said while pushing a branch into the flames.

"No. I don't know," Chris said, staring at the reiser, "and I don't think you can be sure of that, either."

"You don't think I know myself?" Only then did Hayden raise his eyes to Chris's. "I would never attack someone who saved my life. Perhaps you would."

Chris's muscles tensed, and his jaw clenched, but Sara's words rushed to his mind. He groaned and looked heavenward. Nothing could change the past, but they needed to find a way to save their future.

"I believe the reiser who asked for my help in the forest wouldn't, but you are different now."

Hayden narrowed his eyes and rested his back against a tree. "I am still a reiser, Christopher. I may look more like your race, but I'm not one of you."

Chris sat by the fire and let the heat warm his hands. "Are you sure about that? Because I suspect your armor protected you from more than the environment. Now you feel—"

Hayden laughed. "That's stupid. I have always felt! As much as you want to keep looking at me—at us like monsters, we aren't. Pain, hunger, cold...we get all of it."

Chris sat back and crossed his arms. "I may not be an expert, but in all the years I fought your kind, I learned stuff."

"Like what, Christopher?"

"I understand your race protects and fights for the common good and disregards individuals. You don't fall in love with a particular reiser but give your life for the well-being of the majority. Every member is a soldier, and you fight until you die."

It pleased Chris to see the surprise on Hayden's face. "Now you see things differently, and I don't buy that this won't affect your priorities, reiser or not."

He wasn't making it up. During their walk to the refugee, he had observed the reiser. He didn't trust him and was ready to attack if necessary. However, the reiser's behavior seemed off for a soldier.

From time to time, Hayden had stopped to touch the trunk of a tree or the ground beneath them. Their surroundings had distracted him, and more than once, a simple noise from the woods had startled him. Neither the reisers nor his soldiers behaved like that, and it made Chris glad and concerned at the same time.

"What will happen when you have to fight your own?" he asked.

Hayden nodded and leaned forward. "I'll hate it, but killing a reiser is something I've done before..." He gazed into the distance. "The guilt will stay with me for the rest of my life. However, I'm convinced this is the best for my race. I need to save them from an oppressor." He looked back at Chris. "I hope murder is something I can avoid, but I'm not naïve, and neither you are. We have been fighting all our lives. I am ready to do what it takes to finish this madness. I hope you are, too."

For the first time, Chris thought about killing Murllen and what it would mean to him. Whether or not Gemli had changed him, he was still human—the worse kind, but human—and Chris had killed no one of his own race.

"Finish this madness..." Chris sighed. "Not in a million years would I have imagined uniting with your race to end this war."

Hayden nodded and pushed another branch into the fire.

Chris wondered again how it was possible that no one had realized Murllen was an imposter or that the reisers were forced to wear armor that made them look like monsters. He didn't want to accept that it had all been part of Gemli's plan, because that made Gemli too powerful and increased Chris's fear for Sara's life.

"When did you start questioning Murllen?"

"Not soon enough," Hayden replied bitterly. He fixed his eyes on the fire and exhaled. "I'm not sure what made me do it, the change between killing and taking prisoners or that he ordered my reisers to murder me."

"Kill you?" Chris puffed. "I guessed anyone would have to question their leader after that."

Hayden grinned and nodded. "Yes, but it was what Amanda told me about why Murllen wanted me dead that made me wonder."

"Or," Chris said, lifting an eyebrow, "it was Amanda. After all, you saved her more than once."

Hayden rubbed his chin, stared at Chris for a moment, and then chuckled. "Who knows? It could have been Jean."

"Jean?" Chris cleared his throat. He'd purposely avoided asking about his soldiers or the civilians from Tundra. He was aware Hayden had taken them prisoner, but he feared the second he learned what had happened to them, any alliance would die—along with the reiser in front of him.

"Oh, that's right! You know her." Hayden lifted his hands. "Like I told you, I would never hurt anyone who saved my life, and last time I saw her, she did that...or at least, she tried."

Chris narrowed his eyes and pressed his lips together.

"You don't believe me?" Hayden said.

"Oh, no! I'm sure you wouldn't lie about that. I just can't picture Jean doing—"

Hayden crossed his arms behind his head. "Then you don't know her at all. The moment I met her, she sort of impressed me. We terrified her, and still she confronted me, asking if she could help the prisoners and the soldiers. She always argued with me about everything!" A smile spread across Hayden's face. "She was your best fighter... Such a shame you never noticed."

Chris sat forward, resting his elbows on his knees. He hadn't thought about Jean in weeks. The memory he held of her wasn't a pleasant one. She'd made his life a misery in Tundra, always trying to boss him around and pushing their engagement, which she hated just as much as he did. The day he left, she'd ended it by yelling at him, leaving him with guilt and regret.

Before that, she had been the delicate, well-behaved girl his mother had taken care of, the one who invariably had to wear neat clothes and have perfect hair. It was difficult to match the memory with the fighter Hayden described.

"And she saved your life?"

"No, but she almost got killed trying to." Hayden sighed. "I saved her, or at least, I hope I did."

Chris nodded, conscious of the actual concern in Hayden's voice but not ready to ask questions that would lead to answers he didn't want to hear.

"Maybe it was Sara," Hayden said. "After all, she saved my life."

"No," Chris said, controlling his tone. "You asked for my help before you met her."

"Yes, but she is a sorcerer."

"No!" Chris shot to his feet. "She is not!"

Hayden sat up, and his features hardened. "Are you sure? Because I met one of them, and though she seems different, she has the same confidence and certainty…just like that bastard."

Chris shook his head. "I get it. I can see it, too, but she is not. I met the bastard, too."

"Sorry to hear that, but…how did you meet him?"

Chris rubbed his face and stared at the trees. Sara had told him once that they needed to understand their enemy to defeat it. As difficult as it was for him, he had to trust the reisers and their new plan if he wanted to stop the war and

Murllen. After all, they were trying to accomplish the same results.

"All right," he said and sat down. "Let's talk again, but...if you betray us, I swear to you, Gemli and Murllen will look like angels compared to what I'd do to you."

Hayden leaned back. "Fair enough. I'm listening."

Chris told the reiser what he knew. They talked about the prophecy and what Sara had said about it. He told Hayden about meeting Gemli and what the sorcerer had done and then about the encounter with Cielthos. Hayden asked a few questions, and he looked troubled but not shocked when Chris finished.

"Well, that explains why Murllen never cared about you not being with the first guard."

"I suppose it does. Those bastards were planning everything for decades. Even the murder of Sara's family."

"He is waiting for you two." Hayden's tone had changed, and the unease in his voice surprised Chris.

"I'm sure he is. Getting the sword, finding them...that's his plan. However, he can't see my plan or my priorities."

Hayden's face shone with a smile. "I just got an idea."

Chris leaned forward.

"The soldiers in the refuges that we are trying to find aren't your best ones. They must be sick or too old; otherwise, they would be fighting, correct?"

"Correct."

Hayden lowered his voice. "There is no way you—or we—could get past the walls of the fortress with them. However, we could intercept your guard and get your best fighters. Then, once we convince my best reisers, we can attack Murllen."

"How could we get to my men in time?"

Hayden grinned. "Like I told you, half of my squadron is taking the prisoners—your guard and people—to the fortress. I ordered the idiot who failed to kill me to slow the caravan. I'm sure he will. We'll have time to intercept them if we pass through the Netherworld."

"The Nether—no one has ever crossed—"

"Not totally true. There is a shortcut, a secret passage that we use to reach the fortress faster. We still need scrappy soldiers, though."

Chris wasn't sure if he was imagining the flowers' aroma around him or if it was real, but his interest in Hayden's idea grew. "All right, tell me more."

THE CAVE

The sight of the sun was a luxury Sara didn't often experience in the Soto Forest. Still, she missed the massive trees. The open sky, although beautiful, reminded her of the coming dread.

She was sitting on a rock, wrapped in her coat, with Gemli's journal at her side. Her bare feet played in the water, making ripples in the little creek, which surrounded her with its melody. The conversation she'd had with her dad, what she'd learned from the book, and Hayden and Chris's encounter kept her mind restless.

There were many things she didn't comprehend, and the ones she did terrified her. She couldn't deny the magic in her anymore. Small clues pointing to it had surrounded her all her life, but being aware of it made it easier to find—and, thanks to Gemli, manipulate.

She stared at the water, and effortlessly, the waves grew around her ankles, creating a whirlpool by her feet.

She shivered.

Her dad had warned her about her new role, and she had no doubt that it would cost her everything. The same knot that had grown in her throat the night Hayden and Amanda showed up now reappeared, and when Chris rushed through her mind, she had trouble swallowing.

The last time she saw him, it was clear he wanted nothing to do with her ideas, and she feared her connection with magic would make him hate her, too. He'd already left her, even though he'd promised never to do it again. She understood that the demands of his new role would keep him away and busy, but it still hurt that he didn't even say goodbye.

"Sara! Are you decent there?" John said from among the trees behind her.

"I sure hope so." She sighed and climbed down from the rock.

For the last few days, she had stood out of their way. Besides gathering food and collecting water, there wasn't much she could do for them.

John spent most of his time with Amanda, even though she mostly slept. Donald had decided to use his valsing abilities on Hayden's armor to build something to help her walk.

Sara was putting on her boots when she overheard voices coming from the bushes.

"Look, Amanda, I'm trying to be a gentleman here!"

It was hard to ignore how different John's behavior was. Even when he was mad at the circumstances and hated to talk about Hayden, he was calm and cheerful. Nothing could compare with the smile Amanda's presence drew to his face.

"There you are," he said and carefully set Amanda down on the rock where Sara had been sitting. "You see, my sweet wife insisted she needs a bath."

Sara chuckled. "I'll be happy to help. The water is cold, though."

"Wait, what? I was going to do it!" John said, tossing his arms in the air.

The comment brought a shy laugh from his wife, which made him smile as he walked backward toward the trees.

"I'll be waiting around here. Just tell me when you finish, so I…"

He stopped, pressed his lips together, and lowered his eyes. Then he turned and left, taking all his joy with him.

Amanda's gaze was fixed on the ground again, and her knuckles were white around the fabric of her pants.

Sara had heard John say how losing her leg was Amanda's worse nightmare, and she'd had little to say in the decision. Sara hadn't been there when it happened. Amanda was wounded by a reiser's sword, and though Hayden saved her from the poison, the infection was killing her. In a second, he had cut her leg off below the knee, saving her life.

"I don't know how…" Amanda wiped her eyes. "What's the point of surviving only to end up like this?"

As Sara hugged her, she remembered what Chris had told her. "Many things happen that make no sense. What matters is what you do after. In your hands lies the decision of how you want to live the rest of your life. You are still here, and John is, too."

Amanda covered her face as she cried, trying not to be loud, so Sara just sat by her and rubbed her back.

"Any idea what I should do?"

Sara tilted her head and narrowed her eyes. "I suppose, as a soldier, you need to fight? Or you could leave the army, though."

"I don't see…" Amanda sighed and pointed at her missing leg. "I won't be able to fight."

"But you want to?"

Amanda's expression closed. "I chose to save my world, Sara. But now…"

"In that case, I'm not sure if you noticed, but a certain valsing would love not to give you any vacations."

Amanda giggled. "The real question is if our commander will agree with that."

"Commander?"

"I suppose you don't have to call him by his rank."

Sara smiled, and something inside her warmed up a bit. "I tried, and it didn't go well. I'm bad with ranks and titles. John told Chris how important this is for you. He'll find a way."

DONALD WAS WORKING outside the cave with the armor when Sara, Amanda, and John returned from the creek. A lot of valsings lived by the abbey, and none of them made a mess as big as Donald's.

Pieces of wood and metal were all over the ground, and in Sara's opinion, whatever he was making wasn't close to being done anytime soon. She blamed it on Donald belonging to the queen's community. They were used to designing livable spaces, nothing else.

Regardless, Donald seemed very optimistic, and as soon as he saw Amanda, he explained to her what he was doing.

"Now," he said, "I need to take your measurements. It has to match your height and support your weight."

"You don't have to do this," Amanda said.

"Nonsenses! There is no reason for you to stop moving around."

John stared at Donald but said nothing, and although Amanda was a little hesitant, the idea of being able to stand on her own clearly appealed to her.

"Do you think it will be ready by the time the commander comes back?" she asked while John helped her up.

"Chris," John said. "I'm sure he wouldn't appreciate you calling him by his rank unless you were on duty."

"I'm not sure I can do that," Amanda said. "I don't know him. Maybe I should call him big commander like Charlie said."

John laughed while helping her to sit down. "Big commander? That's a new one.

Donald shook his head. "I do not know about this modifier before a rank, or this Charlie, but I agree with John. Chris never forced me to call him by his rank."

John laughed louder.

"Hey!" Donald crossed his arms. "He welcomed me into the army a long time ago! I am sure he will confirm this to you, and I am certain he said I was a major!"

"You just said that because I'm a lieutenant!" John said, still smiling. "Any idea when he'll be back? He said the refuge was only a couple of days from here."

Sara frowned and stared at the trees, which John misinterpreted.

"Nothing to worry about, Sara. He is all right and will be back soon."

"No," Sara said. "He is not coming back, John."

Donald stopped his work and looked at her. "What do you mean? Did he tell you something?"

She shook her head. "No, he didn't talk to me before he left, remember?"

"Sara." John moved closer to her. "There is no way in this world he would leave you. He is my friend, and I'm sure—"

"It's all right, John. I understand. He can't come back. He'll send someone else."

"I don't think you really..." John looked back at Amanda. "I would move the world to be with Amanda, and he is—"

"He is in charge of everything now. Just think about it. He is the only leader alive of all the humans, not only what's left of the army. He doesn't have the luxury to walk back here."

Donald stared at Sara. "How did I miss this? You are—"

"No!" John said. "Listen to me, Sara. He'll come to get you, and maybe us, too.

Amanda touched John's arms and waited until he looked at her.

"Sara is right. Our king is a traitor, and as far as we know, all royalty and the High Council members must be dead. Chris is our last commander, the only one left to keep everything standing."

John shook his head. "No. He took off before. Why would this be different?"

"Well..." Sara exhaled and looked at the trees. "Whether or not I'm wrong about this isn't important. I can tell you Hayden and Chris reached the refuge this morning. I'm guessing they will either come or send someone back immediately, so Donald, you need to hurry."

Donald stared at Sara for a couple of seconds before stepping over to the pieces of the armor.

"Are you just guessing?" asked Amanda. "Or, because you are a zhorta, can you predict the future?"

"I can't predict anything." Gemli's notes came to her mind. "No one can. But there are...elements only I understand." She smiled at Amanda and John. "I'll get some food."

She walked into the forest, hiding her trembling hands and the palpitations of her heart. Somehow she'd figured out that Chris and Hayden were at the refuge. She even knew Lily was there and things weren't going as smooth as everyone had hoped. The problem was, she didn't understand how all of this came to her mind.

From the top of the trees, an owl's hoot made her stop.

"How do you do it?" she said once she spotted it. "How do you—what kept you sane after that—this?"

The familiar black and white bird flew down and landed on a lower branch. It stared at her hands, which twinkled and warmed up. She looked up at her father, and this time, the bird moved its wings.

Sara felt its breeze, but she also perceived the touch of the feathers, stretching and bending with each movement. Around her, the leaves on the trees twirled, leaving minor scratches on her skin, and then the hard surface of the trunk stopped her.

Suddenly she realized it wasn't her hand but the air she was feeling. Without the need for words, she understood how the wizard's power worked—something sorcerers didn't know, not even Gemli.

~

THE NEXT AFTERNOON, a group of five soldiers showed up by the cave with enough horses to take Sara and the others to the refuge.

Even when Sara knew she would have to interact with more members of the army, her heartbeat became hard to control, and she had trouble slowing her breathing.

"John Monder," the soldier at the front said while dismounting his horse. "It's a miracle you are still alive!"

John hugged him. "I could say the same, Joseph, or should I call you Commander?"

"Oh, boy!" Joseph shook his head but didn't lose the joyful tone. "Those times are long gone, along with our glorious army. Once I joined Tundra's forces…those idiots played with our ranks! Now I'm a major."

John laughed and, wrapping his arm around his friend's shoulders, guided him towards the cave's entrance. "Tell me about it! I should be a colonel by now." He sighed. "Instead, I'm still a lieutenant."

"Well, that sounds about right."

John ignored that last remark and turned to invite the other soldiers to follow them.

Sara had a hard time standing still. All her instincts were shouting at her to run into the trees or hide at the far end of the cave.

"Let me see," John said. "These are my friends, Donald and Sara."

"I heard about you two," Joseph said. "It is a pleasure to meet you."

Donald cleared his throat and placed his hand over his heart. "I can only imagine how highly Chris talks about me, but I am certain he talked more about Sara."

Sara's cheeks warmed up. Knowing her voice would fail her, she just smiled and focused her attention on the light outside.

"Sara, yes, of course. But I learned more about you, Donald, and not from my commander."

Donald frowned, but before he could say anything, Joseph looked across the cave and said, "And who is this?"

"Oh." John's features lit up. "This is my wife." He knelt by her and kissed her hand. "You must have heard of her, Major Amanda Belk."

"Of course I have," Joseph said. "It is very nice to meet you, Major. Leading the armament must have been a challenge."

Sara took the opportunity to leave the cave. The other soldiers were helping the horses or resting outside the entrance. As she passed them, she was proud of herself for not running.

When the only things around were trees and the only sounds were the chirping of birds, she allowed herself to crouch and covered her face.

It took a while to control her trembling hands, and the

hard breathing left her exhausted. When Donald pushed his way past a nearby bush, she suffocated a scream.

"It is me," he said and put a hand on her back. "Do not worry."

"I should stay here, Donald. It's a nice place. I could live in that cave, and when you find the saber, I could—no. Just send it my way. Sounds good?"

Donald laughed and sat next to her. "I hate getting lost, Sara. The only thought of it, of the memory of when it happened, made me want to throw up."

She looked at him; though he was smiling, when he showed her his hands, they were shaking.

"See, just the thought. Imagine how hard it was for me to walk through the Soto Forest."

"How did you do it?"

"Eventually I got used to the place, it's darkness and strange movement…and you will get used to these people. Just like you did with John and Chris."

Sara sighed and rested her head on her knees.

"Take your time…and if you need help, I am here."

They walked back to the cave to find the soldiers getting the horses ready.

Donald had finished Amanda's prosthesis. He promised to make improvements on it once they arrived at the refuge. John didn't seem convinced, but he supported his wife, who seemed very happy with it.

"There you are," John said, walking towards Sara. "This beauty is yours."

He pointed to a horse that made the ones the zhortas owned look like ponies. "You think you can ride by yourself?"

"Honestly?" She stood by the animal; there was no way she could climb up without help. "I have no idea."

John nodded and helped her up while giving her some

easy instructions. "This is a very nice horse. It looks big, but it won't give you any trouble...and I'll be riding right behind you if you need anything."

Sara petted it. Its dark fur was rougher than she thought, but it still felt nice to the touch. "Do you think he has a name?"

John lowered his gaze and moved a step closer.

"You didn't hear this, but Major Joseph, the other soldiers, even me...we all have strict instructions to protect you no matter what. I don't know—Chris is worried and...it is only—"

"John, it's fine."

"I didn't—I meant it when I told you that Chris wouldn't leave you. I'm sure he has to—"

Sara's throat closed, and she had to swallow her tears, but she touched John's hand. "I understand... Things changed."

He shook his head. "It's not my place to tell you, but because of my mistakes..." He took a deep breath. "I remember how I offended you because of what I implied about you and Chris. I'm sorry about it."

"John, it's all—"

"No, it isn't. I was a jerk... Please believe me." He glanced at Amanda, who was waiting for him on one of the horses. "I have known Chris for a very long time. Not being here is killing him."

With that, he turned and walked over to Amanda, whose face lit up when he climbed up behind her on the horse.

~

THE REFUGE

The sun was setting when Sara and the others finally arrived at the refuge two days later. From the forest, the smell of wood burning and food cooking reached her before she could see the lights of the camp or hear voices. She wondered if Chris had sent the horses to help her with her fear of soldiers. After riding for so long, she was just glad to be done, swords or not.

Although she somehow knew the valsings were with the humans, the settlement still surprised her. A small village with lighting and defined streets welcomed them. Instead of tents, they'd built sturdy shelters following some kind of hierarchy, where the biggest one was at the far end of a central plaza. Not even the valsing community by the abbey came close.

The humans' presence was visible, too. On their way there, they had found scout groups, and around the perimeter of the refuge, soldiers stood ready to attack.

"Are you all right?" John said, stopping by Sara's side with Amanda riding in front of him.

"Yes," Sara said, and she smirked when she found the

valsing she was looking for. "Watch this." She pointed at Donald, who was dismounting.

The last time Sara had spoken to Lily, the wounds covering her friend's face, arms, and legs were healing. A horrible wound under her eye had just begun to scab over, and her hair had been cut so roughly with a razor that her scalp was exposed and scratched in places.

Now she looked like the valsing Sara had met years ago. Her blond hair rested in short curls on her shoulders. Her skin was blemish free, and all but a scar under her eye remained from Orson's attack.

"Donald!" Lily said, running towards him.

He seemed to have frozen, incapable of moving away from his horse. Then slowly he turned, and Lily threw her arms around his neck and hid her face in his chest. Even from a distance, Sara could see Donald's hand tremble when he touched Lily's head for a second before picking her up and spinning around, making her laughter fill the refuge.

"Lily?" John said.

"Yep," Sara said. "That's Lily Granite."

"Not bad," he said, and Amanda hit him on the shoulder. "No. Not like that. I mean, for him. Valsing stuff...him."

"Right, John," she said, pushing him from the horse. "That's what you—"

"My sweet Amanda," he said, resting his arms on her leg and staring into her eyes, "you are the only angel I have met in Hune, and there is no one more beautiful than you... Sorry, Sara."

Amanda blushed, smiled, and then quickly turned her attention to the valsing couple.

Sara looked at Lily and Donald, who seemed unaware that everyone was watching them. "Well, I guess she finally got it right."

"I wouldn't want to be in that poor valsing's place," a

familiar voice said, startling Sara and reminding her that she was sitting on a tall horse.

"Sorry," Hayden said, laughing. "I didn't mean to scare you."

John's expression changed like day and night, and a palpable tension grew around them. Hayden's smile grew wider.

"Obviously," Hayden said, "you have no idea what all this means." He ignored John's groan and turned to Amanda. "Feeling better?"

"I think so, but…can we talk, you and me, later—if possible?"

Hayden nodded.

John said nothing. Instead, he moved a couple of steps away from his wife's horse.

"John, no…" Amanda said. "I need to—"

"What the hell?" he said while looking ahead of them.

Lily wasn't hugging Donald anymore.

She stood next to him as all the valsings knelt before him. He looked around but couldn't walk away, since his people were blocking him. Lily held his hand and whispered something in his ear that hardened his expression.

John turned to Hayden. "What do you know?"

But it wasn't the reiser who responded.

"Well, a lot has changed for the valsings over the last weeks."

Chris approached them, and Sara's heart sank when she noticed his tense posture and hard expression.

"King Orson joined Murllen," he said. "He also had his half of their community slaughter the other half."

Sara returned her attention to the valsings and noticed the wounds and healing scars on most of them. Their semblance was dark and frightful.

"Queen Vanessa died and named Donald her successor."

Donald and Lily walked into a shelter. Sara found it peculiar how she had known that the valsings and her friend would be there, but not what had happened to them.

"Great!" John said after a while. "Just what we needed. Feed Donald's arrogance."

Sara giggled, trying to ignore Lily's warning of the danger of Orson joining the reisers and what all of them had gone through.

"Can you get down?" Chris said at her side.

"Down? Oh, yes," she said. "I'm sure I'll hit the ground… Actually, accidentally kissing it is more likely."

Chris chuckled. "So, you didn't enjoy Mulsh?"

"Mulsh?

"Your horse. His name is Mulsh."

"Oh, no! Mulsh is great." Sara patted the steed. "I'm glad he came. I'm just not sure if riding anything but roots is for me." Chris's jaw set. "But I could get used to it. The Soto Forest wasn't the right place for this luxury."

Chris looked at her, but his smile didn't come back. "Let me help you."

He reached up and grabbed her by the waist. His hands were steady and strong while she dismounted, and he held her until her feet touched the ground. Unfortunately, she couldn't feel her legs, and when Chris let go, she had to grab the saddle to avoid falling.

His hands held her again, and his deep voice close to her neck made her shiver.

"Are you all right?"

Sara nodded as she clutched the saddle tighter. She feared many things those days, but one of the biggest was allowing the feelings Chris had awoken in her years ago during her vivid dreams to come back. Those needed to stay buried deep inside her soul.

"Yep," she said, not daring to look at him. "Just not used to this luxury."

"It isn't a luxury, Sara," Chris said, letting her go, "and long trips like the one you took aren't easy. I'm sorry I didn't—"

"It's fine… I'm fine." Sara turned her attention to Mulsh, who seemed to enjoy her brushing his fur. "Thank you."

"Sure, Sara." Chris sighed and walked towards Amanda. "Let me help you."

He picked her up. "How are you?" he said while walking to the shelters, not waiting for John.

"Better, sir," she said.

He smiled at her. "Just call me Chris, please, at least while we aren't working."

Sara turned and stopped listening. It hurt how easy it was for them to relate to each other. Even Hayden, who wasn't human, understood them better than her.

"Sara!" Lily said, and like she did with Donald, she leaped on Sara and hugged her, almost making them fall. "I have been so worried about you. There are so many things… But first, I am very sorry for what I said to you the last—"

"No, no. I'm so happy to see you."

Lily turned back for a second and grabbed Sara's arm. "Come. We have to talk now."

"Wait, Lily." Sara's legs were still recovering from the long ride, and she kept stumbling as her friend pulled her across the yard.

"No, Sara. There is no time. I cannot believe I once thought you liked that arrogant human."

"What are you—Lily! You are going to make me fall."

"You need to listen to this, but he believes he owns you! It is ridiculous!"

"Who are you talking—"

"Granite! What the hell are you doing?" Chris said from far behind them, which only made Lily pull Sara harder.

"See!" Lily said. "He believes you should not learn what happened to them."

Sara stopped mid-step. "Happened to who?"

Lily looked back and raised her voice. "I told you a million times, Riddley. I have known Sara for more years than you, and I am certain she can handle this and more. You have no right—"

"I have no right?" Chris's voice grew nearer. "This isn't about the right to do something. It's about the time and its consequences."

"Oh, I listened to all of this, Sara. He is just worried about his stupid reiser and their moronic idea of joining forces. You are the last of his priorities."

"You stupid… How dare you?" Chris said.

Sara closed her eyes and focused her attention on the darkness in front of her.

"This isn't about my priorities. It's about your need to have the first and last word all—"

As Chris argued with Lily, Sara slowed her breathing and blocked out all the surrounding voices. She didn't need to listen to Lily. It was obvious she was talking about the zhortas.

Effortlessly, the abbey from her memories came to her mind. Her heartbeat sped up, and she hesitantly opened her eyes. Instead of the shelters, she saw the massive trees and the fungi and vegetation of the Soto Forest. However, the branches of the roots were too dark, like they had been burned by the cold, and the mushrooms covering them were rotting the trees instead of helping them grow.

She held her breath and raised her eyes.

The abbey, her home, lay in ruins at her feet. The scaffoldings supporting the impossible gardens that had once produced so much food for Hune's people were nothing but pieces of metal on the ground.

She put a hand on top of her heart as her vision found the roots closer to the castle.

A dark magic had entangled the zhortas, her family, leaving pain and fear etched on their faces as they'd suffocated when the trees had claimed them. Screams and rumbles filled her ears, as if they were also stuck in the forest, incapable of reaching the afterlife and peace.

Something touched her shoulder, and the terrifying image vanished. Once again, the illuminated streets of the refugee and the valsings' shelter surrounded her.

"Sara," Chris said softly, "can you hear me? Please talk to me."

His gray eyes were staring at her. He'd told her a long time ago that although she'd lost her family, he was still there. They might have met under strange conditions when they were young, but she wasn't alone. It had been important then, but never as it was at that moment.

He grabbed her by the shoulders and lowered his face so it was level with hers. "Hey, I'm here. Just talk to me."

"Why would she?" Lily said from a few steps away from her. "It should be me who—"

"He didn't destroy her like you just did," Hayden said.

"I did not destroy her. Sara deserved the truth."

"The truth is a powerful weapon," Hayden said, "as dangerous as lies when told at the wrong time."

"I'm all right," Sara said, stepping back, only to realize John was standing there, holding Amanda in his arms. "I saw the abbey… The poison in the forest will be a problem, and I'm not sure how to fix it."

"Sara, I don't care about the forest. It's you who—" Chris moved closer, which forced her to step back again.

"You saw what the reisers did?" Lily said. "You mean, you pictured what they—"

"No, Lily," Sara said, looking at Hayden. "The reisers didn't do it, though. Just one of them did, and it was an act of revenge."

Everyone kept their eyes on her.

"I don't know what your plan is, but...Hayden, if you fail, what happened to St. Patrick's Abbey will look like a child's game compared to what he'll do to your race."

Sara pushed her hair behind her ears and walked away. What she had witnessed scared her, but the rising rage filling her soul frightened her even more.

~

AMANDA HAD WITNESSED many battles and many people get killed. A few had died by her own hand. Still, she had never been so terrified as when John set her down on the cot by Lily.

After Sara walked away, the only reason Chris didn't murder Lily was that Donald proposed to have her check the prothesis he'd made.

"Let me see," Lily said, more like an order, and without waiting, she cut open the leg of Amanda's pants. "How did you keep this thing on?" With no warning, she took the prosthesis from her knee.

Amanda turned away, but it was too late, and the brief sight she got of her leg before Lily covered it with a blanket was enough to twist her stomach and speed up her breathing.

John crouched next to her and caressed her head. She didn't dare look at him and hid her face in his shoulder.

"Lieutenant!" someone shouted from outside the shelter, making John groan.

"Be right back," he said. "I'll tell them to go away."

"You can't," Amanda said. "There is a reason we rode as fast as we did."

"I got this," Lily said. "Unlike Donald, I am an expert on these designs, and she is right. You should go before they come to arrest you."

John looked into Amanda's eyes and didn't move until she smiled at him. Then he kissed her head and walked out of the shelter.

Lily watched John until he left, and a knot grew in Amanda's stomach. Lily's look had never concerned her before, but now everything was different. She couldn't be the person John had fallen in love with anymore.

"Hey!" Lily said and knelt by her. "It will be all right."

Amanda sighed. "How? I have no idea how to—"

Lily stood and moved to a table where she had plenty of tools and pieces.

"I understand your life can't be the same, but that doesn't mean it has to be worse." She placed some things on Amanda's cot but didn't start working. "I am being tough…with you and Sara before, but…what I saw taught me how our lives are hanging by a thread, and I am afraid it will rip soon. The best we can do is grow from it and become stronger."

She cleaned her tools to avoid looking at Amanda.

"And when someone looks at you the way he did… Humans do not judge each other like valsings do. You will be fine, although this is going to be uncomfortable."

A strange pressure made Amanda lightheaded and nauseous, so she breathed slower for a while. "I'm sure," she said. "What if he only feels guilty and pities me?"

To Amanda's surprise, when Lily looked up at her, tears filled her eyes.

"I have the same feeling." Lily chuckled. "About Donald, of course."

Amanda wondered what could make Lily so insecure. She

had just seen Donald kissing her as if no one else was around.

"I'm not an expert, but why would you think Donald…"

Lily went back to cleaning her leg, making her almost throw up this time.

"I am not trying by any means to minimize your condition. I am still learning how delicate human communication is." She looked up. "The scar on my face? It makes me a disgrace to my race."

For a few seconds, Amanda couldn't reply. She had seen the scar before, but the physical violence behind it was more shocking to her. "That's ridiculous!"

"Funny," Lily said, "that is how your race describes mine. Ridiculous."

It wasn't an accusation, but an agreement.

"But Donald would never—"

Lily shook her head. "He is a valsing…and our leader. I love how he has different ideas and principles, but…there are so many things he would have to overlook, things I had done that he will need to ignore. I am going to work on this, and I promise you, it won't hurt anymore."

She grabbed the prosthesis from the ground, folded it in a blanket, and then walked out with it.

Amanda looked down at her leg, and once again, her stomach twisted. Her race might not consider her disgraceful, but she did. She was angry at herself for being so blind and naïve, for not listening to John and hurting him the way she did.

The armament soldiers were her responsibility, and she could do nothing to protect them from Leonard. All her suspicions were worthless because they had come too late.

She threw the blanket back up and covered her face, incapable of stopping her tears.

"Hey, angel, don't," John said. "We'll figure it out." He knelt in front of her, taking Lily's place.

"How can you say that?"

"Because." He grabbed her hand and kissed it. "I can touch your hand if I need to. Because you are here with me."

Amanda shook her head. "Please, don't. I was wrong when I left you, and I was stupid. I didn't want to see what was in front of me. I should have...after the battle, that last one, I should have talked to Chris then, but..."

"Amanda, what Leonard did or not isn't your fault and... perhaps you left, but I never try to—I should have supported your decision. If I had been there for you, discovering what that bastard was doing would have been easier."

He leaned forward and kissed her forehead.

"I became the luckiest man in the world when I met you."

Amanda looked up and found his eyes were filled with tears.

"I have to push my luck." He inhaled and, from the pocket of his coat, took out a leather bracelet.

Amanda's heart skipped a beat, and her hands trembled.

"Why did you leave it?" he asked.

Amanda's voice cracked and wasn't higher than a whisper when she said, "You hated my decision, and I assumed you'd hate me for it. I wanted you to find the happiness you deserve."

John looked at the bracelet and brushed his fingers over the engravings he had made for her. Amanda didn't need to see it to remember all the symbols he had cut on it, or what it meant to her.

"In that case..." He sighed and stared at her. "I have always known my happiness is you." He grabbed her wrist and tied the leather bracelet around it. "Would you wear it again? Would you be my... I never blamed you for anything... I blamed myself, though."

She reached out to touch his face, but then she stopped herself. "I'm—"

He held her hand and placed it on top of his cheek.

Memories of times she had tried to keep deep inside rushed to her mind. She hugged him by his neck and pulled him closer, but he stopped an inch short.

Amanda ran her fingers through his messy hair and smiled like she hadn't done it in many years. His familiar blue eyes stared down at her as he bit his bottom lip and rested his hands on the edge of the cot.

"Yes, John. More than anything, I would love to be your wife."

It wasn't the first time he had kissed her since they'd found each other, but this was different. He wrapped his arms around her waist and pushed her back on the cot, making sure there was no distance between them.

"My sweet angel," he said in her ear, "I love you so much."

"Me, too…so much."

John leaned forward and kissed her again, making Amanda forget whatever was outside or what had happened to her. Instead, she just enjoyed being with her husband.

~

CHRIS KEPT CLENCHING and unclenching his fist as he strode around the shelter.

"What is her freaking problem, Donald?"

"I do not know what to tell you, Chris," Donald said from a chair by a large table. "Lily has a strong temperament—"

"Temperament? I have another word to describe her behavior."

Since the moment he and Hayden had arrived at the refuge, Lily had complicated his life. He had allowed her to ask questions, but that had soon become an interrogation, and she hadn't stopped until Major Baker had confirmed who he was. After that, she'd questioned every decision he'd taken without respecting his authority but demanding that he consider hers.

"She is helping Amanda now and will leave you alone…at least for a while."

"She shouldn't have said anything to Sara. And she doesn't know me. How in the gods' name does she dare to imply what my priorities are!"

"Chris, I did not hear what you are talking—"

"You did not. Well, lucky you! At least someone here won't have nightmares about the Soto Forest."

Donald crossed his arms and sat back.

"What?" Chris said. "I'm right to be mad at that—your girlfriend."

"Sure, but you are missing the important part here."

"Really? What am I missing? Because, two seconds ago, you confessed you had not listened to Lily's detailed description."

Donald stared at the ceiling and took a deep breath.

"Sara is changing, Chris."

Chris stopped moving and looked at Donald as a chill ran down his body.

"You must have seen it," Donald said, leaning against the table in front of him. "I was too far away to hear the conversation, but…Sara was not looking at Lily. She even said it after. She saw the stupid forest, and Chris, this is not the first time she's done—"

"What are you…" Chris lowered his tone as his muscles tensed. "I told you what Cielthos said. She has some relation…connection, I don't know, with the big magician. That's how she didn't get lost in the Soto Forest and got us out of it."

The dreams in which he'd met Sara came to his mind,

along with the way she'd discovered how to open Hayden's armor. She'd seemed to be in shock after he'd pushed Lily away from her, but it was more than that, and it shrank his heart and put all his nerves on edge.

"The Great Wizard, Chris," Donald said, "and if it is his magic on her…I suspect even the smallest of the connections will be enough—"

The door to the shelter opened, and Hayden entered, followed by Major Baker and Sara.

"Interrupting something?" Hayden said as he took a seat. "I thought you'd send for us."

Chris nodded, and another two valsings walked in, along with some of his soldiers.

Donald showed Sara a chair by him, and she sat in it, keeping her eyes on the table and her hands in her lap. John arrived, and without needing an order, he sat at her other side.

Chris was aware of how difficult it must be for her to be there, and he wished he could save her from it, but the last thing he wanted was Lily talking to her again.

Before that evening, he had intended to ask her to stay with the refugees. Walking with the valsings had to be easier for her, but not anymore. Whether she'd heard everything that Lily had described to her or not, it didn't matter. Sara had learned in the worst possible way what had happened to her family thanks to that stupid valsing.

"All right," he said, and the room grew silent. "We don't have too much time, and this is our last chance to save our people."

~

Sara sat in silence, trying to understand Chris's explanation, but too many things kept crossing her mind.

Donald had been right. She was getting used to being around all those soldiers. Now she didn't have palpitations, and only her hands still trembled, although any small noise startled her.

"Wouldn't it be easier not to risk anyone and ride faster to catch them?" Major Baker said. "We aren't that far from the Netherworld."

"We are at least a full day away," Donald said, "let alone walking to the other side of the mountains by it. I dislike the idea of crossing underneath, but I doubt we have an option."

Chris set his hands on the table and looked at Hayden. "We all understand this isn't a perfect plan, but at this point, nothing would be. We need to use what we have before our enemy figures it out."

"So," John said, "we save the first guard, and then what?"

Chris lifted an eyebrow and smiled at his lieutenant. "Well, we get the other part of the reiser squadron to join us. Then we march towards the fortress."

"The other what?" John said.

"Reiser squadron," Hayden said for the first time in the shelter. "It's kind of like your guards, but better."

Sara didn't understand what everyone was talking about. Chris remained quiet, though, and there was a calm about him that made her believe he knew what to do.

After a few minutes, he hit the table and stood up, making her jump in her chair.

"Perfect! Now that you've all learned how everyone feels about this mission, we have to move. Things have changed. We are aware now that, like Leonard the III, the reiser's leader is a traitor, too. Together they betrayed us all, and we need to fight together to recover our world."

"How are we going to talk to them, Chris?" Donald said. "I am guessing the armor they wear will be an issue."

Chris set his eyes on Sara and gave her the same hard

look he had when she'd helped Hayden. She turned away, and a pain in her chest brought a knot to her throat.

"One of your valsings came up with an idea for that, Donald. Liam, please explain what you came up with."

The room became quiet again, and everyone stared at the small valsing by the entrance. Sara recognized him, which meant he was part of their king's community. This explained the hard looks from the other valsings.

"The concept is to break the locks of the armor before the battle starts. By using the correct resonance, the metal will shatter, just like glass with the right tone."

Hayden laughed. "Are you trying to tell me you are planning to scream at my reisers to stop them?"

Liam moved the collar away from his neck, and Sara noticed the sweat dripping from his forehead. "Well, no…not exactly. Kind of. Your armor…it's designed to resist changes in the environment or physical forces, but simple details like vibrations, especially in the precise tone, won't—"

Hayden leaned forward, and Liam stopped and shivered.

"It is brilliant," Donald said. "No one should minimize the damage the correct tone could produce in anything. A glacier, for example, could be destroyed with just a sound, or you could move the whole Soto Forest by talking too loud. Right, Sara?"

All attention turned to her, speeding up her heartbeat. "I guess…somehow. It's a little more complicated, but I'm sure what Liam is doing is also more complex than his explanation."

Liam smiled at her, and he seemed to stand taller.

"Wouldn't the sorcerer's protection stop us from using that…resonance?" John said.

"You'd think so," Chris said, "but Sara opened Hayden's armor."

This time, Sara didn't dare look up.

"Maybe," John said, "but Sara is...Sara. She has—is—"

"We can't be sure whether or not the spell will protect the reisers from something like this," Chris said, "but I'm open to ideas."

Donald put a hand on Sara's shoulder. "Sara could—"

"No," Chris said in a tone that made her look up at him. "I can't put that weight on you. It's already dangerous that you are coming. I won't be asking you to do anything else."

He turned to the rest of the group. "We'll leave right after sunrise. Major Baker, let's work on the plan for the ones staying."

Sara followed John and Donald out of the shelter, but she didn't stay to talk to them. She was confused and mad. If Chris saw her as a danger, why not leave her behind again?

More importantly, she wasn't sure whether or not she'd used any magic to open Hayden's armor. It seemed a lifetime ago, and her memory of it had become blurry. She'd hit the armor with a rock in the right spot, but what if she had used more than that?

THE WISH

The night was brief, but sleeping didn't come, and Sara was exhausted. The light of the sun was barely visible on the horizon, and she was already waiting, away from the soldiers, to depart. Part of her liked to be up when it was still dark. It reminded her of the abbey and the Soto Forest.

The memory of what she had seen made her shiver. No matter how much she loved that place, if it invaded Hune, it would destroy everything, and she had no idea how to stop it.

Just as the sky turned pink and orange, the peculiar song of the bluebirds reached Sara's ears. She found a few of them among the trees, and the sight of them made her smile.

"You can't possibly be happy about riding again," John said as he pulled Mulsh towards her.

"Why do you ask? Did Mulsh complain about me?"

John laughed and offered her the reins, which took the joy away.

"You seemed happy. Where is Amanda?"

"My sweet wife is leading the rest of the group later today." He glanced at the shelters. "I'll miss her, but…she understands why she needs to stay this time. I can't complain."

Sara grinned and returned her gaze to the trees. She shouldn't complain, either.

"Ready?"

"Are we going now? Because the more time I stay on my feet, the better."

"Yeah, Chris had the same idea. That's why he left you alone until the end, but we are leaving now."

She used his help to climb up into the saddle, and only then did she notice that he had changed his clothes. His uniform looked not only cleaner but in excellent condition.

Looking around, she realized all the soldiers wore the same dark blue, almost black coat with the symbols of both armies, Tundra and Laconia, on the side of their arms.

Beyond the more elegant and slightly overdressed look, the thickness of the material, along with the patches to emphasize protection, reinforced the uniforms for battle. It was the first time she had seen that garment, and it made her uneasy.

"Are you wearing valsing clothes?"

John shook his head. Pulling on his collar, he showed it to Sara. "Not valsings, but Lily got them busy working on these."

"You have something new, too," he said. "I mean, under your old coat. How did you skip Lily's supervision?"

Sara giggled. She had found a warmer dress with wool tights on the cot she'd slept on. Now she realized they matched the new uniforms. "I snuck out."

"That helps," John said.

Hayden walked by them on his way to the front line, and he winked at her. He was wearing the same uniform, which made her heart feel at ease. That was a step towards their future, or so she hoped.

At the front, she found Chris's silhouette. She didn't understand his words, but his tone was firm and authoritarian. John must have noticed, because he climbed on his horse and directed it to stand next to hers.

"We better get going. You don't want him yelling at you. Staying back here and away from the mess. It's our priority."

"Don't get into anyone's way and try not to get into trouble?"

"Not try, Sara. Just don't get into trouble."

She was going to answer, but John's hateful glare at Hayden stopped her.

"What is it?" she said.

"Well, he is supposed to be with Chris…guiding the army."

"Is that so bad?"

"I don't… No. I mean, I trust our commander, but…"

"You followed me through the Soto Forest, and I'm a zhorta."

"That's different. You weren't going to—"

"To send you into a trap because the reisers were also chasing me?"

John frowned, but he nodded.

ALTHOUGH THE TRIP from the cave to the refugee had been difficult, nothing could have prepared Sara for this one. The soldiers not only moved faster, but in a very specific order and with no rest time. At her side, John kept trying to distract her. He explained that they rarely used horses, since it was a luxury for them, but the mission had a huge timing issue, and it was necessary to risk losing the animals.

She tried to give him her attention and asked questions, but her eyes became heavier, and her mind wandered back to the bluebirds singing above her. It occurred to her how peculiar it was that they were so far north, and then she remembered the last time she had encountered them.

As her mind envisioned the past, everything vanished, and John's voice became a faraway whisper. Chris stood next to her, and he handed her the bluebirds' nest by the scaffoldings. She remembered the branch where she'd placed it and how she told him to make a wish. He had laughed, and she doubted he'd listened to her, but now she wasn't so sure.

The memory spun, and the dark figure of Gemli stood by an ice block with a sword inside of it. He was trying to get it out, but then he paused for a second and turned, making Sara's heart skip a beat. Instead of finding her, though, he waved his hands, scaring the fowls that stood nearby.

"I got her," someone said, and Mulsh stopped.

She opened her eyes and found the forest trees illuminated by sunlight. The birds' song had also ended, but when she looked up, hundreds of them painted the branches in blue.

"Go to the front and inform me if anything changes."

Sara recognized Chris's voice and turned to see him mount her horse and sit behind her.

"Good morning, Sara," he said by her ear. "I'm sorry I couldn't greet you earlier… You looked exhausted."

He moved her hair to the side and touched her forehead.

"I'm not sick," she said, breathless, and closed her eyes again.

"Try this."

He swung one of her legs so both were on the same side of the horse, and she found herself resting between his arms.

"I wasn't going to fall," she said when he reached to take the reins from her. "Mulsh wouldn't…won't let me."

The way Chris looked at her made her shiver and smile at the same time.

"I trust Mulsh, but just in case, I'll be holding you, too."

Sara wanted to answer, but her mind blurred, and her head found the perfect place to rest against Chris's chest.

"Ready?" he said, and the next thing she noticed was Mulsh moving again. "John and Hayden are worried about you. Should I be, too?"

The bluebirds' song became louder again, and she was back watching Gemli as he used his magic on the ice, and a lot of what she read from him made more sense.

~

LIGHT STILL ILLUMINATED the forest when Sara woke up with Chris still holding her as they rode Mulsh. The galloping of horses and soldiers' voices were all around her instead of the birds' song.

Her hands trembled, and her temperature rose. Witnessing Gemli's work, how everything surrounding him had to suffer in agony, had made her understand the reason Hune was dying, and her desire to stop him burned inside her soul.

"Hi, there!" Chris said, and his voice sounded deeper as she leaned against his chest. "It's nice to see the blue of your eyes again. How are you feeling?"

"Is it noon?"

Chris puffed and shook his head. "I know you don't like riding, but sleeping while on a horse is not a good idea. And, no. It's going to be dark pretty soon."

Sara sat up as much as she could.

The forest looked different. The trees were thicker, and their leaves touched the ground as if they were falling from their branches. The bushes were also fuller, and a few flowers and berries grew on them. The grass had a greener shade in some spots, wild plants grew here and there, and through a break in the trees, the top of the mountain was visible.

"It is beautiful!"

"I thought you might like it," Chris said. "We are getting close to Laconia's lands. It isn't Tundra, but it's not that bad!"

He fixed his eyes on her, and though he tried to smile, his voice had a hint of anxiety.

"I'm fine now," she said.

"You said that to John and passed out for a whole day."

She turned to the trees but couldn't find any birds.

"Did you hear the bluebirds?"

Chris shook his head. "Someone else had all my attention."

Sara looked down and bit her bottom lip. "It's kind of your fault."

"I supposed it is." He slowed Mulsh to a slow trot. "You enjoyed little your previous trip, and this happened too soon after. I just couldn't—"

"Not that." She sighed and fidgeted with her fingers without looking at him. "Did you make a wish?"

"A wish?" He chuckled. "I haven't made one of those since—"

"By the abbey, Chris?" She glanced at him. "After you helped me with the nest? Did you forget?"

He stared at her. "Of course I remember helping you, but I don't…"

His smile vanished, and he stopped Mulsh. "Why did you say it's my fault?"

Sara avoided his gaze. "I didn't mean it as a bad thing."

"Sara, what did I do?"

Her shoulders dropped. She couldn't tell him the whole truth, and she should have thought about that before.

"I don't know what you wish, but I was… Gemli has the saber, and he spent all this time trying to break the curse. He did—used…" She swallowed bile at the memory of the sorcerer's disturbing work. "I'm part of the curse, so I think the magic in the bluebirds protected me from all of that."

"You aren't part of…"

Chris pushed his hair back, and his movement forced the horse to pace, and Sara had to grab his arm to stay in the saddle. He held her again and took a couple of deep breaths.

"I know Cielthos said a bunch of…stuff, but you aren't cursed, and you shouldn't have anything to do with Gemli."

"I saw him before, when he was torturing you, but then he noticed me. This time, he didn't. Thanks to your—"

"No, Sara! I did nothing, and you can't think like this. No wishes can stop that monster."

"You can't dismiss—"

"If my wish is so powerful, why are we still at war? I'm positive I have been hoping to end that for years."

"I don't know, Chris." Sara bit her lip again. "You saved their nest, and they granted you the wish you made."

"You don't even know what I wished for!"

"No, I don't, but I thought… Maybe I'm wrong about this, and you did nothing." She sighed. "Gemli has the saber, and he'll try—"

"Listen, Sara. I'm not a fan of using Hune's power or magic, but…" Chris lowered his voice. "I know there are things you are not telling me. Just like when we talked in the hallway of the abbey. Only this time, it's your secret and your decision to keep it from me."

She took a deep breath and held her fingers tighter on her lap.

"I hope you realize by now that you can trust me," he said.

"I'm trying, but—"

"Tell me everything, then."

Sara shook her head and covered her eyes for a second.

"Why should I? You don't trust the magic in Hune. You

called me a danger, and you were forced to bring me with you."

"What? That's not what I meant, and it has nothing to do with—"

"With me? Because Cielthos told us that—"

"That asshole? The one who showed you what happened to your mother with no mercy?"

Sara turned to him. "Yes, him. Because he also trusted me to help save my world and mentioned part of the—"

Chris shook his head and pushed his hair back again. "He said some of the huge magician's wizardry had infected you, not that you were a sorcerer."

"The Great Wizard, Christopher! And I'm not infected with anything. I'm not sick or dying, and we need the magic of Hune to stop this madness."

After a deep breath, Chris looked back at Sara. "Listen to me, please. I met Gemli, and he is a bastard, Sara. I was his prisoner, and I'm only alive because he wanted it. Your power…Hune's power is beyond my understanding, but… you aren't even close to doing anything against him. Don't you see how weak you are?"

He turned away for a second and then, in a somber tone, continued. "It isn't normal to sleep for hours on a horse ride… You have no idea how many times I feared you were dead. I had Donald check on you at least every hour…and last night? When Lily… I thought I lost you then, too."

"But I'm not dead, and I wasn't in shock or panic yesterday, either. To save Hune, you need my help."

"Sara, you are not a sorcerer. Even Cielthos agreed with that."

She was going to reply, but he shook his head.

"You aren't a danger; you are in danger. That's why I can afford to leave you."

Sara pushed her leg to the side and sat back on the saddle with her back to Chris.

"Are you trying to make me fall?" he said in a friendly tone.

"As if I could do that. After all, I'm so weak, infected, and have nothing to do here but be a burden."

Chris dismounted the horse, and the heartache only increased her frustration.

"Sara, I don't think you are weak, but what Lily described must have hurt you, and if you saw the aftermath…" His gaze dropped. "It's something that changed us—changed you. You were right about the reisers and Hayden, and now we are fighting for something I would have never imagined, all thanks to you. Will you consider that this is all you have to do in this war?"

"If you truly believe it, you should have left me. Why am I here, Chris?"

He rubbed the back of his neck and turned towards the trees for a few seconds.

"Well, that's not a simple answer, and I didn't decide lightly. I promised you I wouldn't leave you—"

Sara shook her head, and her hands trembled again. "I never thought of you as a hypocrite. Maybe Lily is right."

Chris moved closer and stared at her. "I'm not a hypocrite. I made a promise—"

"You left me before! And you didn't just leave. You took off without talking to me, making sure I felt like an idiot."

He took a step back and let Mulsh's reins fall from his grip. "Sara, that isn't—"

A horse approaching interrupted him.

"Damn it! What is it?" he yelled at the soldier.

"Commander, we reached the bottom of the mountain."

Sara kept her eyes on the last rays of light on the horizon.

"We need to set up camp. Send the explorers to check… The passage should be—" Chris stopped and whispered to her, "We really need to talk, but…I have to go. I wish—"

"You should stop making wishes, Chris," she said, avoiding looking at him. "Just go."

After exchanging a few words she couldn't hear, Chris mounted the soldier's horse and rode out of sight.

INCONVENIENCE

Murllen's mood darkened with the sky. Orson's valsings had arrived at the fortress with the saber and disturbing news. The stupid group had fallen days behind. All of his reisers had been killed, and they'd lost their prisoners, among them Orson's daughter.

According to the idiots, a woman and a reiser ambushed them in the Northern Forest, something hard to believe since three members of his personal guard had died. For a while, he tried to stay optimistic. After all, they'd brought the saber. However, after hours of watching Gemli perform disgusting tricks on that block of ice, both had given up.

It was nighttime, and life crowded his swamps like never before. The valsings set up a camp inside the fortress, covering half of the patio. They lit the place up, increased the temperature as much as possible, and even cooked outside, allowing the aroma of their food to block the rottenness of his home.

"I'm wondering," Gemli said, catching up with Murllen, "how the valsings came up with the idea of a reiser working with a human?"

Gemli's voice sounded paternal, and his face displayed a welcoming smile. "I just can't imagine such a useless bunch making up such an amazing story."

Murllen frowned. The sorcerer had ignored an important detail. "They wouldn't dare lie to us," he said. "This is revenge against me."

Gemli stopped walking and narrowed his eyes.

"Come on!" Murllen said. "It's not so hard to despise me. You always do."

"You really can't understand how big this problem is."

A familiar and unwanted force pushed Murllen towards Gemli's tower. He didn't fight it; in fact, he was relieved that the valsings wouldn't witness what the sorcerer would do to him. The last thing he needed was for those little invaders to lose their fear of him.

Too soon, they reached one of Gemli's chambers. Murllen was grateful that it wasn't the one on the lower level. In those days, he only feared that dark basement and the sorcerer's vault in Reign Mountain. Both brought memories of a time when his humanity allowed him to feel pain, when losing his brother weighed on his soul.

"My dear Murllen," Gemli said.

His knees lost strength, and the impact of his fall rushed up his spine.

"I am amazed by your level of stupidity. It requires a certain talent to mess up this part of the plan."

Murllen's face hit the ground, and a weight pushed his skull against the floorboards.

"You see, the reason we chose this race is their blind, borderline insane obedience and loyalty." Gemli sat in the chair at the head of the table. "Reisers don't question their leader. They don't think twice about their personal well-being or have attachments to others. By nature, they can't desire revenge."

The sorcerer stopped and allowed Murllen to sit up.

"Murllen, if you assume they despise you, it's because you don't understand them. However, if you made one of them hate you..." Gemli shook his head. "Sort of amazingly stupid."

The light of the valsings' camp shining into the chamber made him groan, and he switched chairs at the table to get away from it.

Murllen couldn't blame anyone but himself; what had happened in the forest was his fault. He didn't need to investigate it. Colonel Green had killed his guard, and the woman must have been a prisoner.

"I ordered two reisers to ensure that Green never returns —at least alive."

The sorcerer didn't seem surprised, but Murllen was when the force pressing him to the ground suddenly let up.

"Is that all?" Gemli said, crossing his arms.

Murllen grew concerned, more than he had been in decades. "Yes...I asked Major Dunstan and Sargent Paul to kill him."

Gemli stood and walked around the chamber, which put Murllen's nerves on edge.

"That shouldn't be enough for a reiser to betray their race," Gemli said after a long time. "There has to be something else. Think, Murllen. Every day you send reisers to kill or get killed in battle. Even if Hayden abhorred you, he should have just escaped. He should never have attacked his own."

"What about the human?" Murllen leaned forward. "Green may have been protecting her. Many stupid things are committed in the name of love."

Gemli turned to him but said nothing.

"Ridiculous!" Murllen said. "But we have to think about everything."

He looked out the window. The joyful valsings at camp didn't matter. The dark stone fortress stood as a testament to the reisers' will to survive. Its asylum was an example of their intelligence, dedicated to raising warriors to kill for their existence but kept a secret. The only reason for that race to attack anything lived inside there.

Murllen wondered if it had all started before he sent Hayden to find the humans.

"Listen," he said, staring at the asylum. "There was a peculiar incident that may have caused this." When he turned to face Gemli, his smile was wide, and he lifted his hands. "But this is not my fault."

"I don't see how something would ever be your fault, innocent Murllen."

The day Alleta Riddley had arrived at the fortress, he had been so excited by the future pleasure she would bring to him that he'd forgotten his encounter with Genevieve.

"I left the commander's mother in the asylum so they could cure her and get her ready for her son. Something you approved of, and you even seemed proud of my patience. Well, I learned that day that the ruler of the house had died."

"Oh, no! Did the event traumatize you that much? I mean, Estela had a special place in your heart, right?"

Murllen just kept talking, hoping the comment and memory wouldn't haunt him later. Her kindness towards him had almost changed his mind. He'd even thought about helping them against Gemli for a while, but like his brother, she'd betrayed him and only wanted to use him.

"The point is, her stubborn daughter took charge, and more peculiar is that she is with child."

Gemli's mocking expression vanished. "Pregnant? That is ludicrous. You know they don't really—"

"Well, it has been years since I saw a pregnant woman,

but I still remember how it looks. And yes, she is...just like a human."

Gemli moved to the window and stared at the asylum.

"Not only that, my dear sorcerer." Murllen put a hand on Gemli's shoulder. "She told me who the father is, and she suspects he is their rightful leader. It was curious, but since she believes in her heart that leaving without armor will kill her...I thought I'd set things straight after the bastard's birth. Way more fun."

An evil light crossed Gemli's eyes, a spark the sorcerer rarely revealed, but Murllen understood its meaning.

"I'm thinking it's about time we remind the reisers in the asylum what happens when someone breaks our rules."

Murllen smiled. "I'll do it myself, but...she is a great fighter, and she's protecting a baby. Uff!"

"Have you become so comfortable as a leader that it scares you to fight?"

"No, no, Gemli. On the contrary, I know my limitations. I won't deny who is the more suitable opponent for this battle."

THE ASYLUM SEEMED different to Genevieve. Before meeting Alleta, the only human she had met was Murllen. Because of him, she'd concluded all their kind were monsters and needed to be stopped. However, in just a few days, the new human under her care had changed her mind.

Murllen usurping the reisers and betraying the humans should unite them against him. She had hoped to be able to walk outside and talk to the other reisers. However, she couldn't abandon her responsibility to the young ones under her protection, even though the similarities between the two races now made her doubt that they needed armor. Still, she couldn't risk her baby.

Thinking about her baby always brought a smile to her face, and thanks to Alleta, now she enjoyed the little one moving inside of her—even though their rules prohibited it.

The reason they avoided real pregnancies was the attachments they created between mother and infant, mother and father, and probably father and baby.

Those bonds were against their belief of protecting their race without prioritizing the individual. She understood the value of this but couldn't imagine anything more magical than her baby.

She needed to be careful, though.

The reisers ignored that she wasn't just carrying an infant sack. She wanted to talk to them. In the end, they would approve since there was nothing more valuable than a reiser's life, but it would bring problems in the future.

They would become curious and want to try it. Considering their circumstances, her race would face a genetic disaster, not to mention Murllen's reaction. She couldn't risk it.

"Genevieve," a reiser said, "someone is approaching the asylum."

The tone of the reiser matched the growing concern inside of her. It wasn't normal to have visitors late at night, which meant it had to involve Murllen. Most likely, he would demand to take Alleta.

"Let's see what they want," she said as she walked to the stairs. "Keep everyone alert, though."

Not for the first time, she thought of lying. Murllen knew Alleta was sick, wounded, and old, so dying shouldn't be a surprise. Alleta had told her not to do it, though. She didn't want to put them at risk. Genevieve appreciated this, but she hadn't made her mind yet.

A reiser was waiting in the dark by the entrance as usual, but instead of a knock, the door flew open, slamming him against the wall.

Genevieve skipped the last three steps and was ready to fight whoever was breaking into her home. A sudden light illuminated the room, blinding her.

"Well, my dear Genevieve," Murllen said. "There you are."

Something she couldn't see held her arms and pushed her against the wall so hard she lost her breath.

"I didn't want it to be true," he said, taking his time to walk into the room. "Such a horrible crime against us…and from you."

Murllen shook his head and halted a few steps away from her. All the other reisers stopped what they were doing and listened.

"What are you talking—" she said, and then it felt like nails were scratching the inside of her throat, blocking the air.

"There is only one punishment for betraying our laws." Murllen put a claw over his chest and looked down. Behind him, a tall, dark figure walked towards her.

She hadn't seen him since he'd brought Murllen to the asylum. She was only a child then, but he'd left her terrible nightmares. At that moment, all her muscles tensed, and her heartbeat pulsed in her ears; still, her hands shook as she fought the force trapping her.

Gemli smiled wider, and a soft touch crept up her arm and stopped at her neck. The sorcerer stared at her like he had his mother years ago, and she understood that the visit had nothing to do with Alleta.

"You alluded to Estela's death," Murllen exhaled and sat down. "I exonerate you of that. But this…it breaks my heart. I can't even imagine forgiving such an atrocity!"

The reisers in the asylum and even herself lost all importance; the only one who mattered was the helpless baby in her womb. Fear filled Genevieve's soul, making her eyes wet.

"Listen up, everyone!" Murllen shouted. "When I heard the rumors of what the new ruler of the house had done, I denied them. I fought to clear her name, but the details, those horrifying specifics, were too clear to be a lie."

Genevieve bit her lips hard, trying to block her tears from falling.

"This thing," Murllen pointed at her. "This supposed protector used this sacred place to experiment with prohibited practices, ones that would destroy our race." He inhaled and stood taller as he stared at her. "She is with child, and not like you, my devoted reisers, but like those disgusting humans. She tricked one of our best warriors into—" He touched his forehead and looked down. Only Genevieve saw his brief smile. "In her perverted desire, she did the unthinkable, and now...we will have to lose a great warrior, too."

Murllen stepped forward and ripped open her coat, allowing the reisers to look at her swollen abdomen.

She closed her eyes, hoping to wake up from a nightmare and incapable of facing her own mistake. The force holding her stretched her arms out, making them crack.

"I have to do something." Murllen moved out of the way, letting Gemli close the last two steps between them.

Genevieve used all her strength and fought to move away, but it was impossible. She tried to ask for help when she noticed the blade in the sorcerer's hand, but her throat closed, and a voice inside her mind almost made her pass out.

"I have a message for our beloved Colonel Hayden Green...and whoever is with him."

As soon as the pounding in her head stopped, the cold metal crossed the skin from her side to the middle of her stomach. A second later, ripping and burning pain blocked her mind. An atrocious heat filled her wound as if a hot, muggy liquid were being poured inside of her, and the moment it touched her baby, the infant moved like never before, and all her insides seemed to be grabbed by large claws.

She heard herself screaming, but it seemed strange to her, and the pain was so severe that she didn't notice when she hit the ground.

The voice shouted inside her head, "You'll survive until you find him. Then and only then will you die. Your dead bastard will be your poison."

Genevieve felt Murllen pick her up and carry her to the exit of the asylum.

The exclamations of horror behind her and the cries of the little ones made her tears fall.

"My poor reisers, I don't know what to tell you," Murllen said by the door. "I was hoping it was a lie, but the blood and this full abdomen...this compromises the devotion of our race. She has to die, along with the atrocity."

Alleta tried to move towards her, but the reisers blocked her, and none of them attempted to help her.

Genevieve didn't blame them. She hadn't betrayed them the way Murllen had said, but in the end, she did betray them. She hadn't told them the truth, and now she was leaving them at the mercy of those monsters.

"Now, my dear," Murllen said, and she perceived his warm breath in her ear. "I need you to scream...loudly, please."

He stepped out of the asylum, and her voice seemed to rip from her throat when her back cracked backward, tearing all her nerves.

Still in his arms and incapable of moving, Genevieve noticed the reisers outside in full armor, moving closer. To her surprise, valsings were inside their fortress, something also prohibited by her race.

The air smelled of death and putrefaction, and the cold humidity of the swamps reached into every bone in her body. Still, it wasn't deadly, which increased her hate for herself, for she had been so blind and stupid.

"Listen up!" Murllen yelled, and he let her fall from his arms. Her back hit the ground, emptying her lungs.

"The corruption in our race tried to reach us. Here is the evidence!"

He pulled her up by her hair and forced her to kneel.

The skin of her abdomen ripped, and a weak scream escaped her. She covered her mouth, trying to mute her sobs, when she felt the motionless weight inside her.

"I found this human in the asylum." Murllen said, "most likely, poisoning our future legacy."

The reisers moved closer to their leader and stared at her. Murllen's and Gemli's cleverness impressed her. None of them would ever suspect she was one of them. Without armor, she was a human to them.

There was no point in fighting any of it, and she closed her eyes. She didn't want to see her own race wrongfully killing her. If she paid attention to them, she would recognize them. Most of them had either grown up with her, or she'd helped raise them. They would follow Murllen's orders.

The first kick took her thoughts away and forced her down on the ground, but after that one, she didn't notice the difference. Physically, her body had given up, and mentally, she was too weak to fight her growing hope of dying soon.

"Enough," Gemli finally said. "She is dead."

Genevieve heard the reisers cheer and celebrate.

"I will take care of this…thing," the sorcerer added.

SHE REALIZED from the change in the air that they were outside. The wind had become bitter, and the humidity denser, but the smell had cleared up. For a long time, something carried her away from the only place she knew in Hune. She had no means of knowing how far she was from the asylum or where they were going. Most likely, she had been falling in and out of consciousness.

The gentleness with which whatever was holding let her down put her nerves on edge once again, and the feeling didn't go away when Gemli's wicked smile appeared in front of her.

"Very well," he said. "You are as strong as I thought you were—at least, more than your mother."

She tried to sit up, but her arms gave out, and she stopped trying.

"I'm curious. What bothers you more, realizing there is no poison or having fallen for that trick for so long? I was in a rage when I figured it out...so stupid and still effective way to imprison..."

Genevieve stared at him, disgusted by what he said and hoping it was the high fever making her hear things.

"No answer... Oh, well...let's get back to business, then. I need you to deliver my message."

Something forced her to sit up, taking her breath away and speeding up her heartbeat. She glanced down, and her womb looked as it had in the morning, so she rested her shaky hands on top of her stomach.

The heat emanating from it, along with its hardness, made her cry out, and she lifted her hand and covered her mouth.

Gemli tilted his head. "I told you it was dead, and I'll

suggest you find Colonel Green soon, or your agony will become worse every day."

He touched her cheek and pushed away a lock of hair from her face.

"It is romantic, Genevieve. Your lover is the only one who can stop your suffering." He chuckled and stood up. "Amazing! You are my first love curse!"

The ground seemed to slide out from underneath her. She hit her head on a rock behind her, and then everything went dark.

~

THE SUN WAS high in the sky when Genevieve opened her eyes. The fog covered parts of the swamp, and its humidity dampened her clothes, making it easy for the cold to freeze her body.

She pushed herself up, and the effort turned her stomach, making her throw up, which brought a sharp pain in her abdomen and blurred her thoughts for a while. Once she calmed herself, she looked around. She was relieved when she couldn't find the fortress, and that made her sad because the place she loved and lived for had become her worst nightmare.

She tried to stand up, but the effort weakened her legs, and she tumbled down and lost her sense of her surroundings again. After a while, her eyes adjusted to the light above her. She didn't move, though.

Gemli had made the mistake of letting her know Hayden was alive. She knew he was their rightful leader, and if Murllen hated him so much, it must mean something. The last thing she would do was look for him. She had already lost her baby. Putting Hayden's life in danger wasn't even a possibility.

She held her breath and turned around, and although the movement almost made her throw up again, this time, she was expecting it. She moved her hands over the mud, not caring how cold it was or what lay beneath it. As she slid on it, she didn't stop until she found a long stick.

The effort weakened her again. She groaned but let her head down and rested for a while. Once her arms felt stronger, she used the stick to stand up. The way she moved was too slow, as she could only take one step at a time and had to drag her other feet. And after every step, she needed to stop and breathe to contain the burning sensation inside her.

Still, she had a plan.

Somewhere in Hune was the human army, and now she not only looked like one of them, but she knew who to talk to. She would find Alleta's son and make sure he and his soldiers stopped the monsters in the fortress. It weighed on her soul that it could mean the death of many reisers, but she needed to do what she had been born to: protect her race's future. Hopefully, she would give them a very different one.

NETHERWORLD

The Netherworld was where Hune's magical foundations sprouted. Geographically, it was where the mountain systems of Laconia and Tundra merged. From both cities, the outside of the system was, although long, an easy climb. Once on top, the power lying between them became visible.

Chris had climbed the Tundra side of the mountains when he was in training. A vast valley opened at his feet, where half shone like pure light while the other was covered in pitch-black darkness.

Most people believed that the heat in there would melt anything. However, the Eternal Glacier had convinced Chris the Netherworld had to be a frozen hell.

After Chris commanded his soldiers to set up camp, he took Hayden and Donald to find the passage. Hayden mentioned it was almost invisible to everyone, and he was right. The opening among the trees would have passed unnoticed if he hadn't been looking for it.

They hadn't gone far before the path stopped in front of the mountainside. The massive rock stood tall, blocking passage. Almost at the bottom, a short but wide cave opened, letting Chris see inside the formation. Even from where he stood, he could see how its path dropped underground and curved along the outer line of the mountain.

"It took us a couple of hours to cross it," Hayden said.

"Hours?" Donald said from a few steps behind. "It would take days to go around the mountain!"

"I know. We have taken that route, too. This passage doesn't move around, though…and I'm sure walking is easier than climbing some sections of the one you are talking about."

Donald raised his nose as he explained how it would be impossible to cut down that much time. Chris wasn't in the mood for a discussion, especially when they ignored the reisers' faster pace.

He stepped inside the cave and let his eyes adjust to the darkness. The passage was taller than him, and as far as he could see, it didn't shrink. He exhaled and walked a little more confidently. He didn't want to crawl under a mountain ever again.

The path would fit two soldiers side by side, but the grade was too steep for the horses. The idea of losing them twisted his stomach and made him groan, even though he had thought about it before. He would have to send the animals around with the valsings since he couldn't risk any soldier. Those morons walked slowly, and he hoped they wouldn't need the horses to outrun the reisers.

"Chris!" Donald said from the entrance. "Are you all right?"

Chris growled and spun around. Donald should have come inside to check on him. If something had hurt him, answering would have been impossible. No, the valsing was a coward, and he would learn his lesson. He would punch

Donald until he broke his nose. After that, he'd go back to the important business of checking the safety of the path.

The idea of safety stopped him, as he realized the danger. His anger wasn't normal, and he felt out of control. Sara had once called him a dangerous person, and at that moment, she was right.

He forced himself to slow down, and his hands trembled with the energy that wanted to get out. Before his next step, he inhaled, and only then did he notice how cold the air was. He glanced at his palms, and they looked blue, like Sara's hands when they'd gotten stuck on the glacier.

The second the wind from outside touched his face, he took a deep breath.

"Hey, you were not answering—" Donald said, but then he stopped.

Chris shook his head and stepped to the side of the tunnel's entrance. A huge part of him wanted to punch Donald just for the pleasure of doing it. A smaller part just wanted to break anything, but when the trees seemed an appealing target, he feared it would take breaking his hand to stop himself from punching things.

After a few minutes, he regained control of himself.

"What happened?" Hayden said.

Chris dared to look at them.

Hayden was covering Donald's mouth.

"Hey! He would not remain quiet for this long!" Hayden said, letting him go.

Chris laughed, and relief washed over him, improving his mood.

"You freaking bastard!" Donald said. "You were not helping. You are—"

"Right!" Chris said, getting Donald's attention. "I was ready to kill you." He tried to sound casual, but he knew how close he had come to murdering his friend.

Donald stared at him, opening and closing his mouth but incapable of making a sentence.

"Not that I blame you, but why?" Hayden said.

"Well…" Chris pushed his hair back, and pieces of ice, like frost, fell from it. He shook his head, and a cloud of white dust billowed down.

"The cave…" he said, and a chill ran down his spine, leaving him exhausted. "What the hell?" He sighed and sat down.

"First, I was fine, but then anything enraged me. When Donald called me, I was going to kill him for interrupting me, and then, when I walked back, I—I don't know. I hated myself for…abandoning everything."

There wasn't a point in mentioning their problem. If Chris had almost lost control of himself within minutes, something he hadn't only trained to avoid but had worked all his life on, there was no way they could walk for hours inside the tunnel.

"Not ideal," Donald said. "Do you think Sara—"

Chris's muscles tensed, and he pressed his lips shut while shaking his head.

"Oh! Come on, Chris," Donald paced around. "Accept that she is more than—"

"She knew we were coming to the Netherworld. If she had known something about it, I'm sure she would have mentioned it before."

Donald crossed his arms. "What you want to do, then?"

Chris lay on the ground and stared at the sky. His head pounded, and his exhaustion blocked his thoughts.

"Tell me, how was it inside there?" Hayden said, sitting against a tree.

Chris sighed. "Well, I'm freezing now, but I wasn't inside."

"Did it seem like Gemli's—?

"No, more like being trapped," Chris said. "Did you ever feel anything when you were crossing it?"

Hayden shook his head. "No, but I had armor."

"The armor…". Donald said. "Did your armor protect you from Gemli's magic?"

Hayden looked at him and frowned. "Of course it didn't! Also, it was his spell, the one protecting us. I am sure it affects us!"

Chris smiled. "That's good."

"If you say so," Hayden said.

"It is because, if the cave didn't affect you, it means that whatever is inside there is related to the environment and not—"

"Magic!" Donald said, standing up. "Of course! The magic would have affected the reisers. More importantly, if the issue is the atmosphere, there has to be something we can figure out!"

Hayden narrowed his eyes. "What about the possibility that I'm a reiser with or without armor, and that's why it didn't affect me?"

Chris looked at the cave. "The question is if Gemli's spell was what protected you from it and not the armor."

Hayden smiled. "That isn't the case. I have crossed the passage without his stupid spell plenty of times."

Donald moved closer to the cave's entrance and searched around, which seemed like a good idea. After all, analyzing was the valsings' strength, so Chris closed his eyes.

"Chris, when you were inside, did you touch anything?" Donald said.

Chris shook his head. "No, and I didn't eat or lick anything, either."

Donald returned and took a seat next to the others. "In that case, I am certain whatever the problem is has to be in the air. Since it is not affecting us out here, I suppose it is deeper or lower."

Chris sat up on his elbows and looked at the cave while Donald continued. "I am not positive how much it will affect you without your armor, Hayden. Considering your race is the weakest one when it comes to the environment, I suggest you wear extra layers or stay behind."

Uncertain of how he did it, Chris moved fast enough to grab Hayden by the arm before he could jump on top of Donald. "We have more important things to do."

Hayden narrowed his eyes, but he stopped fighting him.

Donald turned and smiled at them. "You did not notice how cold you were?"

"Not until I was coming out. Why?"

"Well, your hair was full of frost, your face was red and had signs of frostbite, and you were trembling. Not to mention the ice all over your clothes. It could not have been comfortable."

Hayden puffed. "Valsings, always concerned about the most important details."

Donald was about to answer, but Hayden didn't let him.

"When we crossed, there was a section that always reminded me of nighttime at the swamps, freezing cold, but it didn't last long. Most of the time, the passage felt like the weather here. It happened almost at the exit on the other side, too."

"Any idea for how long?" Chris said

"It varied, but I'd say around half an hour. An hour seems too much."

Donald threw his arms up. "Great! We just need to stop breathing for an hour while running as fast as the reisers."

Chris stood and walked towards the cave. "At least this time, you considered the reisers' speed."

"Where are you going?" Donald said.

"Well, if the problem is the air, we may have something to protect us against it." He took out a scarf and put it around his neck. "We use these when we burn the…around the fire so we aren't affected by the smoke."

"So, you just run through it now?" Donald said.

"Of course not." Chris tied the fabric and moved it up to cover his face. Then he closed his coat tight. "Walk taking slow and steady breaths…and as shallow as possible."

Hayden puffed, still leaning against the tree. "So that's how you got away after burning the battlefields. Interesting… Didn't you just leave some of your soldiers behind?"

Chris turned and strode towards Hayden.

"Chris!" Donald said, standing in his way.

"You can't go back there," Hayden said. "Obviously, whatever the hell is in there is still affecting you."

"I'm fine," Chris said, "but what you said was—"

"I agree with Hayden," Donald said. "You have been falling asleep now and then."

"What?"

Hayden laughed. "See, you didn't even notice. You could fall asleep the second you walk inside that dark, cozy place."

Chris knew he was tired, but he didn't realize he had fallen asleep.

"I'll go," Hayden said, reaching for Chris's scarf.

"No, it can't be you or Donald." Chris sat down again. "None of you are human. We have to be certain this…thing, whatever it is, won't affect most of our group."

"What about the other valsings?" Donald said.

"Yeah, about that." Chris stared at the cave. "The horses won't be able to walk in there, and we'll need them. The best thing to do will be to send your people with them around the mountain. We'll meet them on the other side.

Donald kicked the ground. "What if they get lost?"

Chris took a deep breath. "I care about your people, and I

need their help with this. The priority of this mission is to stop the caravan. But then we will—"

"Fine." Donald waved his hands at him. "We still need to test this fabric."

"We need John here," Chris said after a moment, and Donald jumped up and walked towards the camp.

"I will get him, but if this stuff does not work, I will be the one knocking him down."

Chris chuckled while Hayden said, "In case you haven't noticed, John is taller and stronger than you. If he comes out in rage, how are you going to knock him down?"

Donald cleared his throat and while walking away replied. "There is more than brute force in a fight, Hayden."

Hayden sat on a fallen trunk not too far away. "By the way, what I said about the fires was to prove you are still affected." He shook his head and looked at the sky. "If I believed you had abandoned anyone, I wouldn't have asked for your help."

Chris nodded and wondered how it was possible that in such a short time, he found himself comfortable with Hayden's company. Lily's annoyance had helped, but despite that, for years, they had been enemies. They had blamed and hated each other's race for their own destiny.

"Do you think it will work?" Hayden said, looking in the distance. "I hope so, but what if…"

"We don't have much of a choice, but like I said, I'm open to ideas."

Hayden just chuckled. There was no time for changes; in fact, they needed to hurry.

"Speaking of wrongful things. What do you think of Liam's stuff and Gemli's spell?"

"Honestly?" Chris picked up a small stick and played with it. "I hope your people get angry and decide to finish us instead of taking prisoners."

Hayden looked at the ground. "What about Sara?"

Chris felt a knot in his stomach that grew bigger when he remembered what his father had sent him to do in Tundra. Luckily, Hayden interrupted his thoughts.

"Could she do something?"

Chris shrugged. "She isn't sure about it, either, and like that, I won't be putting her in danger."

Hayden nodded. "This is a reiser's point of view, so don't get offended. Isn't the slightest chance of help better than nothing? I mean, it could improve our chances of winning this battle."

The question didn't upset Chris. It had crossed his mind before. "Would you send someone who wasn't confident about her skills to fight in a battle like this?"

The nightmare he'd had days ago came to his mind. He opened and closed his fits, getting rid of the sensation of blood after cutting Sara's body with a sword.

"She told you this, or you guessed? Because when she saved my life, she had no doubts about herself."

Donald returned, pushing John through the bushes, and as expected, John wasn't taking him seriously.

"What is the matter with you?" John said. "I was working on something."

Chris stretched and stood up, struggling to send Hayden's question to the back of his mind.

"What happened to you?" John said when he saw Chris. "You look like crap!"

"Don't worry about me," Chris said, smiling. "It's your turn!"

In short terms, they explained to John what had happened and what they were working on.

"John, you have to walk in there, slow and steady, like when we crossed the battle fires. Give it a quarter of an hour and come out." Chris took a rope from his sack. "We better tie you…just in case."

Chris had been giving John orders, but he wished he didn't have to. After all, there was the possibility that John would not make it out of the cave. No one mentioned it, but they were all aware of it.

John tied the rope around his waist, closed his coat tightly, put the scarf around his neck, and covered his mouth and nose to stay as warm as possible.

Chris held the rope while John walked inside, and soon the line became the only sign he was still alive. After a few minutes, though they seemed like hours, from the dark distance, they heard a soft yell: "Coming back!"

The rope went slack for a second until Chris and Hayden pulled it towards them. John came out of the cave with frost on his hair and red cheeks and nose, but he didn't look tired or upset.

"I guess it'll be fine. It's cold, though. It reminded me of the refuges by Laconia."

Chris exhaled while he coiled the rope.

"But was it cold all the time or just for moments?" Donald said. "And did it smell different?"

"Well, I didn't smell—"

"What about the humidity? Did it change? Was it too dark, or could you see? How deep do you think it is?"

"Can I answer a question before you ask another one?"

"Sure," Chris said, "you can do it at the camp. We need to go back and get ready for our next move."

"What is the next move?" Donald said.

Chris, already a few steps ahead of them, called back, "We are resting tonight. Tomorrow we'll cross this freaking place before sunrise."

CHRIS SAT BY THE FIRE, enjoying the valsings' food and the momentary peace around them. His thoughts were a mix of concerns about the coming battle and the passage and how much he wanted to see Sara.

"There you are!" John said. "Nice way to hide from Donald's questions. I need to learn how to do that…faster."

Chris chuckled and looked around at their camp. Most of the soldiers were still up, enjoying their meal or laughing and talking. It reminded him of the last time he saw Charlie in the tavern. Their options had been very slim then. Now he was fighting a different war, and his first move was to recover his people.

"I have to say, though," John said, "the tents these little people have are amazing! How did we survive without them for so long?"

"I can't believe we are working with them at all."

"Right! Their princess incident." John whistled. "That was some gossip!"

Chris shook his head, but instead of remembering what had happened with the valsings' princess, he thought of the times he'd enjoyed Sara's company in what he'd thought were dreams. A pinch in his heart stole his smile. He needed to face the fact that she possessed some kind of magic, but he dreaded what it would bring to her life.

"Speaking of gossip, Chris, did you hear your new rank?"

Chris turned to John, frowning.

"Hey! It's all over the camp. I have no idea how that happened, but Charlie and Amanda named you big commander."

"Big commander? You'd have thought they'd have a better imagination." He smiled at himself. "Someone called me admiral not too long ago."

"Admiral?" Donald said, taking a seat next to them. "That

is a difficult position considering our ocean's situation. But in all seriousness, you need to change your rank."

"And mine, too," John said. "Since we are moving stuff in the army, it's about time to promote me."

"John, this is not the moment for nonsense. Chris needs to move up because he can't be in a lower position than Hayden."

Chris had thought about that before. The rank of colonel already belonged to him. He'd just stopped Leonard from using it when his father had died. He couldn't take his place.

"Sara is right," John said, losing his joyful tone. "You haven't realized how much you mean now to us…to everyone. Look around you."

Hayden came over and sat by the fire. Behind him, some valsings were training with a few of his soldiers. All wore the new uniforms, and at a glance, they seemed to be a united army.

It had been months since the last time Chris had talked to his soldiers, but the moment he stood up, his confidence as a soldier and leader guided his words.

"Listen up!" he said, silencing the camp. "We are going to leave before sunrise. The passage isn't far, and it'll take only a few hours to get to the other side. There is some danger, however, and I need you to be aware of it. We'll be wearing everything we need to stay warm. It is important that you remember this while walking through it. Keep in mind that you need to be in control. Don't let yourselves believe you are more powerful, impatient, or frustrated. Anger must be the last thing on your minds."

Chris walked around the camp as he continued. "Tomorrow we'll find the reisers, and we'll look at them with fresh eyes. Our real enemy has put their lives in danger, too. However, they are unaware of this. It is our duty to help them and protect them, not only because we have a common enemy, but because the human army's mission is to save Hune and its inhabitants, whether they are humans, valsings, or reisers."

He stopped in the middle of the camp and raised his voice. "I am not asking you to forgive our former aggressors. I'm urging you to give us a chance to live in peace once and for all. Without the reisers' help, we won't be able to stop this war and defeat Murllen and the traitor Leonard. This is when we take our destiny into our hands and get rid of the lies and traps of our ancestors. We are going to recover our home and save everyone in Hune!"

He wasn't expecting a response. He hadn't meant to give an encouraging speech, just an informational one. The soldiers and valsings needed to know what was coming and what they were fighting for. Still, when he sat down, it felt good to hear cheering and clapping.

"Not that bad!" Hayden said. "Although, not my style."

"How come?" Chris said. "You don't talk to your reisers?"

"Oh, I do! But I just yell something like, 'Let's kill those bastards.' It works."

Chris laughed and nodded. In any other circumstances, that would have worked, too.

THE PASSAGE

The sun's rays peeked over the horizon when Sara saw the cave entrance. The passage had been tricky to find, but the opening wasn't, and the rock of the mountain above it just made it look more dreadful and massive.

"Sara!" Donald said as he ran back to her.

She had been waiting as far away as possible, just like the day before, when she'd only overheard Chris from behind the trees.

"I looked for you yesterday to tell you about this place."

"You didn't stay with the valsings," she said.

"No." Donald shook his head. "I do not—no, no… They will be fine, and Chris needs me here. So, where were you last night?"

Sara shrugged. "Reading, resting. Staying away from…everyone."

"I see. Still worried about the army."

She smiled and didn't correct him. Although the soldiers' presence still affected her, it was Chris she was avoiding.

"Did you hear Chris's speech?"

"It was hard not to."

She had never heard Chris talk like that, and it had impressed her. With a couple of sentences, he'd gotten his men ready to defend their lifelong enemy. It took her weeks and a life-changing discovery to convince Chris to learn about the reisers.

"What do you think of this place?" Donald asked.

"The Netherworld? No idea," she said, looking at the mountain. "That entrance? Dark, cold…scary?"

Donald chuckled, but he seemed nervous. "You heard what the deal with the cave is, right?"

"As much as anyone could have gotten from that explanation."

"Donald," Chris said as he approached them. John trailed behind. "You are traveling in the front."

Donald nodded, but when he turned to Sara, she noticed his trembling hands. "I will see you later," he said to her, smiling.

"Don't say that…at least not to me…unless you are going to die." Sara looked at her hands. "'I'll see you later' is the way the zhortas say farewell."

"We can talk bad about Chris later. Is that better?"

Sara grinned but didn't look up. "Take care, Donald."

He didn't have time to answer, as Chris touched his shoulder and signaled him to leave.

"Sara," Chris said, "this is for you." He handed her a scarf. "Do you know how to use it?"

She looked at the piece of fabric. "For the cold or poison? Or was the cold a side effect from the poison?"

"What?"

"There are a lot of poisonous mushrooms in the Soto Forest. They grow in dark places, like underneath roots, and you can be killed just by breathing close to them. Some medical ones grow around them, so we need to collect them." She looked at him, and his straight face hurt her. "What you said last night about the changes and the cold…sounded like the side effects of these mushrooms."

"Did it occur to you to ask her about this?" John said.

Chris ignored him and moved closer to her. "This rope is for your safety," he said without looking at her as he tied it around her waist.

"Too tight?" His eyes met hers, making her cheeks warm up, so she only shook her head. In response, he tied it tighter. "Wear it at all times."

He didn't wait for an answer before walking to the cave.

The moment Sara covered her mouth with the scarf, Chris's essence calmed her down.

"Hayden told us the cold doesn't last long," John said while checking that his coat was closed again. "Like an hour at the most! What a joke!"

He and Sara were the last ones to enter the cave.

The first steps were hard, but she was used to climbing on roots, and the rock wasn't more slippery than the moss on some trees.

A few soldiers had torches, but the tunnel was still dark. As Sara's eyes adjusted, she bumped into John. When he turned, his hair sparkled in the torchlight. It took her a moment to realize that he was shivering and covered in ice.

"Are you all right?" he said, pulling his scarf down. "I'm hoping it'll be done soon…if Hayden is correct, of course."

He put his scarf up and pulled it tighter.

Sara looked at her coat, and it had frost on it, but when she shook her head and pulled her hair to the side, it had nothing on it. She looked at her hands, and they seemed normal, too.

"Do you feel that?" John said, half-turning. "Much better now, right?"

She pulled her scarf down and inhaled. Thousands of aromas reached her, among them the glacier orchids and the mushrooms from the Soto Forest. She concentrated, and the texture of the tree bark brushed her fingers. Amazed, she focused, and the steel of the scaffolding made her palms cold. Then the soft rumble of Hune filled her ears, similar to a river muffled by the mountain on top of it, and the surrounding energy told her how close she was to the foundations of her home.

For the first time, she understood and accepted who she was. The Great Wizard was her father, and unlike any other wizard or sorcerer, the power of her land ran through her veins. She had the responsibility to protect it from any menace, even when her human half weakened her, and the option to choose to live neither dead nor alive, like the sorcerers didn't apply to her.

Her surrender seemed to be a part of herself. If she concentrated, her breathing could teach her about the environment, and she could manipulate it. Her fingers touched the rock walls, and the marks on them moved as if she were painting with light and shadows.

The abbey and the Soto Forest were the first things she drew, but her fingers couldn't trace the zhortas' faces, so she thought about them, and they showed up on the wall.

She visualized the places she had seen, and they appeared in front of her. She stopped for a second and, with more detail, remembered her father's face, which appeared on the rock. Then she thought about her mom, who, instead of dying on the ground, stood happily by the man she loved.

As Sara brushed her fingers over the image, a growing heat filled her heart, and all she had drawn vanished. She took a step back and Murllen and Gemli manifested in front of her. She let her anger and thirst for revenge to draw what she would do to them if she had the opportunity.

"Sara?" John said at her side.

He looked pale and cold, but it was the fear in his eyes that made her step away from the rock.

"Don't touch it," she said. "It's very hot."

She moved past him, thinking how ironic it was that only she understood what was happening, thanks to Gemli's journal.

As they continued, she tried not to get distracted. She couldn't see the soldiers, and she didn't want to jeopardize their mission. However, when the light from outside illuminated the cave, the influence it had on the men became apparent and dreadful.

Some tried to untie themselves and walk back, yelling that they could do everything by themselves. Others fought with each other, not caring who they were. Almost none seemed to want to leave the tunnel.

"Would you move faster?" John said, pulling her by the rope around her waist. "This is the last time I take care of you. I'm not a babysitter. I'm a freaking soldier from Laconia's army, which didn't deserve to get killed the way it did. It was all Chris's fault. Like right now. If he cares so much about you, he should be the one staying behind, making sure you stay out of trouble."

John grabbed Sara's arm. "I should teach Chris a lesson. Next time, he will be more careful with his girls."

Sara tried to pull her arm free, but he only tightened his grip, digging his nail into her.

"John," Sara said, touching his face and hoping she wouldn't have to hurt him. "You are hurting me." Her voice was only a whisper, but his eyes cleared up. He let her go, took a step back, and shook his head.

"Sara, no—I'm so sorry. I didn't mean to… Are you—"

"It's all right, John, but we have to stop them." She walked to the first soldier, and her muscles tensed. "We need to get them out. Now."

She picked up the rope and pulled it just enough to confuse the soldier, and when she pointed at the exit, he left without questioning her.

As she walked to the next one, someone pulled the rope on her waist, and when she turned, John picked her up and tried to get her out. Once she touched his hand, he stopped.

"Stay close to the exit," she said as she untied herself. "I'll push them your way."

"Sara, I can't let you do—"

"We don't have time for nonsense. Get them out."

She strode back into the cave, and one by one, as gently as possible, she pushed the soldiers towards the exit.

A few minutes later, the confusion had turned into chaos, and she wished she could use the magic to protect them. However, using any power in there would be devastating. In that section of Hune, balance sustained the land.

"That's it!" she said and, a little more joyfully, pushed another soldier toward the cave exit.

Now she knew how to stop Gemli's spell and release the reisers.

~

THE LAST PART of the cave was the problem. The scarves didn't protect them that long, and Chris hadn't expected the increased heat at the other side. Anger piled on him, but when he started to question Hayden's wiliness to help them, he knew he had to get out of there. Behind him, the soldiers lost their formation, and voices grew angry. In no time, a fight would break out.

He strode towards the exit, breathing as slowly as possible, not to avoid the poison but to control himself. Once he climbed the last rock in the cave and the full sun welcomed him, he heard someone crying.

"All this is my fault, Chris!" Hayden said. He was in tears and down on his knees. "I won't live with this on my conscious… I can't—"

"What are you—?"

"The spell won't fall, and all the soldiers are going to be killed by my…my…reisers…or taken prisoner. Murllen will laugh while torturing them."

"Don't be stupid," Chris said, unsure that he could control his temper.

"But I…I won't live with something like this. I'd rather die here and now."

Hayden walked towards the cave, but just when Chris was going to pull him back, Donald jumped on him and grabbed him by the neck.

"This is your fault! It is a death sentence, and still you allowed my valsings to join this madness. They are not warriors! They will get killed!"

Chris didn't have time for this nonsense. He reached behind him and, with one hand, grabbed Donald and tossed him to the ground. Then he dragged Hayden out of the cave by his coat.

"You two morons! It's the freaking cave! You better get your heads together, or I'll be kicking the sense right back into you!"

It didn't pull them back to normal, but it confused them enough, and Chris released some anger.

He walked to the entrance and noticed only a few of his men were coming out, and they did not look like they were in the best condition. After taking a deep breath, he pulled his scarf up, strode inside, and began to push his men out.

A little more than half of the soldiers were outside when it was his turn to get out of the cave before he started killing them.

The light hurt his eyes, but he soon got used to it. His

men outside were still angry and not in total control of themselves. The tiredness hadn't touched them, but he wasn't sure he should be thankful for that or not. He didn't need a bunch of sleepy soldiers, but the other option didn't look more promising.

Hayden took his place in the cave, and Chris stood by the entrance, as close as he dared, to keep helping. After a few more minutes, most of the soldiers had made it outside, and Hayden decided it was his turn to come back up again.

"I can't see anyone else," he said with tears in his eyes.

"What do you mean?" Chris walked to the entrance, but Donald held his arm.

"You cannot go in there, Christopher. You have a responsibility out here, and you look angry already."

Donald was right, but Chris would not leave the rest of his soldiers, and especially Sara. He pulled his arm away, but two other soldiers came out, blocking his way, and Donald used the opportunity to pull him back again. He lost his balance and hit the ground.

"Hayden, help me!" Donald said, and together they pulled Chris farther from the cave.

"Gods be damned!" Chris said at the same time he saw John walking out of the cave. "John, get these idiots out of my way."

John stepped closer but didn't help him. "Look around you."

Chris shook his arms, and Hayden and Donald let him go. He stood up, ready to kill them, but John grabbed his shoulders and turned him towards the forest.

All his soldiers were arguing and fighting. Their voices were loud and incoherent, just what the reisers would love to hear as they approached and discovered their ambush. Hayden had shown Chris on Hune's map that the main road wasn't far from the entrance on that side. The forest wouldn't cover all that noise. He needed to stop all the madness.

He opened and closed his fists, but after sighing, he found himself walking towards the cave. Sara was all that mattered. He would not risk her life, especially now that they were doomed to lose the battle.

Donald held his leg, preventing him from moving.

"If something happened to her, I swear, Donald, I'll kill you very slowly. I'll make Gemli and his dragon look like—"

"Chris!" Sara said, running out of the cave. "I got it!"

Chris got loose and strode towards her. She showed no signs of anger. In fact, her smile was wide, and she seemed to be skipping instead of walking.

"Are you all right? Did anyone hurt you? If they did, I'll kill them."

He held her by the shoulders and looked her up and down. As far as he could tell, she wasn't injured. No bruises or marks, not even a scratch. But then he stopped. She also wasn't wearing his scarf or the rope.

"What were you thinking?" he said, taking a step back from her. "It was for your protection. What are you trying to do? If you don't want to be a danger, stop—"

"I'm fine," she said and walked farther out. "No, I'm better than fine. I don't think I've felt like this ever in my life. It is...delightful."

"Delightful?" Chris's concern grew, and he shook his head as he followed her. "Sara, this has to be the cave—"

"Well, of course it is the cave, Chris." She turned and touched his face. "I could see it! Something almost impossible to identify according to—the book, the journal. Anyway. I know what to do, Chris!"

She sat on the ground and untied her boots. "Listen, we have little time. You need to make everyone quiet."

"What are you doing?"

"I need to feel Hune, and I can't walk on my hands, so… here, take care of them. I don't want to lose them… No, wait. Don't worry about them. I'll find them after the—"

"Sara, no." Chris crouched in front of her. "What are you talking about?"

She stopped and looked up and him. "I know how to get rid of Gemli's spell, and you may not even need Liam's stuff."

She put her ear to the ground and signaled for him to move closer, which he did. Then she whispered, "The steps of the reisers…humans, too. They are walking toward us. There is something… heavy, like…wagons. Yes, it must be that, and horses. There aren't moving fast, but they will be within hearing distance soon."

She stood up with no problem.

Hayden stood nearby looking guilty and sorrowful, as if everything around them was his fault.

"Listen," she said. "The caravan is less than a mile away. I'm going to get—"

"No, you are not," Chris said, grabbing her arms and pulling her close. "The last you'll do is get close to—"

"Christopher Riddley!" Instead of moving back, she stood on her toes and stared at him.

He was so close that he noticed the dark lines in her eyes again, and the knot in his heart grew.

"That is enough," she said. "As the daughter of…the colonel…yes, the colonel of the…the army, I inherited his position, so…" She cleared her throat. "This is an order. Get your soldiers ready and wait for the signal."

Chris let her go and rubbed his face. "You know it doesn't work like that, right?"

"Wait for the signal."

She turned and ran towards the forest, yelling back, "I don't remember if I told you this, but anger is powerful. Use it this time."

"Sara, no! I can't let you."

A hand touched his shoulder, and it surprised him to find John standing next to him.

"She'll be all right, Chris. I mean, Commander."

Chris glared at John, who looked pale and shaken.

"She can do… I saw her… I'm more afraid of her anger now than anything else in Hune, sir."

~

CHRIS STARED at John for a moment, but it wasn't the time to ask. He turned to his soldiers. "Enough!"

His voice echoed against the mountain rock, emphasizing his authority.

"The caravan with our people is close, and we are their only hope. I understand the frustration and desire to destroy whatever is in front of you. We'll use it to free our people, our friends."

He made them get in formation, and the forest became quiet. A few minutes later, everyone was kneeling by the edge of the road, ready to attack. After one last check, Chris took his place.

The plan was to wait until the leader of the caravan reached where Chris was waiting. That way, they'd cover most of the reisers, preventing an escape. Once they jumped out, Donald and Liam, the only valsings there, would use the resonance.

The reisers were going to fight with or without armor. Hayden had explained that their nature was to survive, and he'd shown the soldiers a few of their techniques. The plan was to trap them and, after everything calmed down, talk to them. However, their first priority was to break the prisoners free. If they needed to kill, they would do it.

Sara walked to the middle of the path, catching Chris's

attention. From where he was kneeling, she seemed fragile and oblivious to the coming danger. Of everyone there, including the valsings, she looked the least like a soldier.

Her hair, though braided, was more ready to have flowers in it than to be in a battle. She was wearing a dress appropriate for the weather but had no protection for a confrontation and no weapons. On top of that, her lack of boots only emphasized her weakness.

"Listen, Chris," Hayden said at his side, "I just thought about this while looking at Sara. Jean may be in the front, too, not with the prisoners."

Chris turned and stared at him.

"I ordered Paul to protect her," Hayden said. "That would be the best way to do it."

Chris nodded and went over to the valsings. "Donald, there may be a woman at the front line with the reisers. After you use…turn on, or whatever you do with this…stuff, I need that you and Liam to get her to safety."

Donald frowned, but he didn't question the order.

"Her name is Jean."

As Chris slid back to his position, Donald asked in a very low voice, "Who is Jean?"

Hayden whispered something in response.

"The commander's fiancée?" Donald said loudly.

~

DONALD'S WORDS echoed in Sara's mind, but she didn't have time to think about them. The shapes of the reisers appeared in the road ahead of her, getting all her attention, as she had to fight the memory of her first encounter with them by the abbey. Wilson and Daniel had been with her, and she had lost everyone shortly after.

A knot grew in her throat, and her hands trembled, but

she concentrated on who the real slaughterer was and allowed her desire to murder him replace her sadness.

Her plan was simple. Because of the closeness with the Netherworld, it would be easy to perturb the surrounding balance. She only needed to try using her magic. It would be enough to wake the foundations of Hune, which would notice the large amount of power from Gemli and negate the sorcerer's spell.

When the reisers were close enough, she took a deep breath and interrupted them.

"I'm afraid I can't let you go through."

Only then did the reiser at the front notice her, and he laughed as he slowed his horse to a stroll.

"Should I bow to you as well?" he said. He sounded like Hayden, but it was the smaller figure next to him that stole her smile, tensed her muscles, and made her fist tremble.

"You don't have to," she said, staring at the king. "If you give me the bastard behind you, the path is all yours."

"What did you call me, stupid girl? I am your king. I will... Just get her," Leonard said to the reiser. "I'll deal with her later."

"Like you did with my mom? Bastard!"

Leonard sat back and positioned his horse behind the reiser's. "Kill her."

Sara tilted her head. "Are you sure that's smart, Leonard? I assume my uncle won't be too happy with that order, and Gemli...well, isn't he your real monarch?"

Leonard's face lost all its color, and he grabbed the reins so tightly that his knuckles turned white. "Sara. How are you —you look just like your mother."

"Only, I'm not lying on the ground, wounded and dying while you kick me."

She took a step forward, and the reiser blocked her.

"Did you ever wonder why you have to protect this moron?"

The reiser looked around, but he did not get out of her way. "Right. You are following Murllen's orders. But don't fear. I'll do something about it."

"You are just a spoiled ignorant!" Leonard said. "Your mother was—"

"If you think I'm going to listen to your stupidity, you are wrong."

Sara moved her hands up. In response, the wind blew from behind her, towards the end of the road, touching all the reisers and prisoners. The trees lit up for a second, the ground shook, and the roar of an explosion shook the forest.

Most of the reisers lost their balance. The ones riding fell, and their horses ran, escaping towards the forest. All the wagons turned over, and the prisoners helped each other out of the wreckage or ran away.

From the sides of the road, the soldiers charged, and the silence was replaced with screams, shouting, and the clang of metal. Only a few seconds later, a second loud noise rumbled through the forest, making the ground vibrate and sending all reisers tumbling down.

Sara wasn't paying much attention to that, though. Her eyes were fixed on Leonard, who had fallen from his horse during the first explosion. She walked towards him as he lay on the ground, and when he noticed her, his eyes opened wide, and his lips trembled. First, he tried to push himself back, but then he gave up and crawled away from her. However, the many pieces of metal and reisers trying to get up blocked his path.

She found a sword lying beside its owner, who was having trouble moving with his armor cracked open. She ignored him and picked up the weapon.

"Please, Sara, you can't," Leonard said. "You aren't evil. Your mother—"

The sword remained steady in her hand and felt impossibly light. She held it up and swung it in the air, amazed that she did not fear it.

"At least let me stand up."

"Why? Did you let my mother?"

Her father had told her that he'd used his anger to kill the soldiers who'd hurt her. At the time, she didn't understand what he meant, but now she got it.

"Gemli. He forced me to—"

Sara wasn't there to listen to lies or explanations. She put the tip of the sword to his neck, and though Leonard's flesh resisted the metal, she quickly calculated how much weight and strength she'd need to slit his throat.

"Sara," Chris said beside her.

His hand covered hers gently but firmly, and he pushed the sword down and away from Leonard. After crawling and sliding away, the king got up and ran.

"I won't let you lose your soul."

Sara turned to look at Chris. His gaze was fixed on her eyes, full of understanding and concern.

"But he deserves it." Her eyes filled with tears, but Chris didn't let her cry. He tightened his grip on her hand and touched her cheek.

"Yes, he does, but not like this, and not by your hand… I'll explain it to you later, but I need you now."

Sara sighed and nodded.

"Help me free the prisoners before they get hurt by mistake." He threw the sword away and looked at her for a second. "Please."

Then he turned and chased Leonard, who was running up a small hill, towards the forest.

CHRIS WASN'T IN A HURRY. Leonard couldn't run fast, and he would be easy to find.

A reiser wearing broken armor tried to block his way. Chris swung his father's sword and knocked him down. It had been a long time since his last battle, and even more since he'd had no trouble fighting. His confidence was growing, and that was good. In the last few minutes, he'd gone from having a lack of possibilities to a certain victory.

Nevertheless, all the changes had come with consequences. He'd never considered the presence of Leonard in the caravan, and he should have.

For a second, he thought that Sara's attitude had changed because of what Donald had yelled. It was almost too late when he realized what was happening. From the edge of the forest, he couldn't see her eyes, but he was certain they looked like Gemli's, because she sounded a lot like him.

Hayden had even risked exposing the ambush to tell him she sounded like Murllen, and Chris was positive the reiser hadn't pushed her to the side because of it.

Still, he'd had to wait for her signal. Thankfully, an explosion was easy to recognize, although he was afraid to find out how she'd done it.

Liam's resonance had worked with no trouble.

Chris had been the first to jump out, but he'd had to stop a reiser before he could reach Sara. His heartbeat had sped up when she'd grabbed the sword, because she would never have done that before, and the ease with which she swung it had only confirmed his fears. Part of him wanted to believe it had been the cave's effect, but he knew deep inside it wasn't, and he dreaded losing her.

He couldn't let her kill Leonard. In reality, he didn't even know if he could kill another human or how it would affect him.

He breathed again when he reached her just in time and felt relief when he didn't have to fight her to get her to stop. The best option would have been to take her away from there, but there was no time. Instead, he'd given her a task, and he hoped she understood why he had done it.

Another reiser attacked him, and he blocked the blow. He was about to bury his sword in her chest, but her armor was open in the middle. He kicked the reiser's sword away and pushed her to the ground. Her helmet opened, and Chris saw the more human-looking person inside, confused and afraid. One of the soldiers from the caravan moved towards them, and Chris barely had time to block his thrust.

"No!" he ordered. "They are not our real enemy. If they stop fighting, we take them captive."

He realized he had reached the end of the caravan. The soldiers there were the ones from his guard, and they looked as confused and tired as the reisers, which was a good sign. It would be a brief battle.

From the corner of his eye, he saw Leonard again. The little bastard was almost in the forest, so Chris ran after him.

Sara had a lot of reasons to hate Leonard, but Chris's list wasn't short, either.

The stupid king had betrayed everyone in Hune, sold the humans to Murllen, made sure their armies were destroyed, and murdered his father. Leonard's expression when Chris had informed him that their colonel was dead came to his mind. This time, he realized Leonard's strange look had been that of a man trying not to laugh.

He swung his sword at Leonard's feet and tripped him.

"Your highness!" he said. "I didn't have a chance to tell you what happened on my mission."

Chris grabbed Leonard by the front of his shirt and

pulled him up. The king was so short that only his toes touched the ground when Chris lifted him to eye level.

"Freaking bastard! You thought no one would realize your treason! You really believed everything would end up good for you?" Chris pulled the fabric tighter around the king's neck, making it harder for him to breathe. "I am just curious about one detail."

He threw the king against a fallen tree, and his head hit the trunk so hard that for a moment, Chris thought he had killed him. But a few seconds later, Leonard tried to scramble away, so Chris grabbed him by the neck again.

"Did you think Murllen was going to protect you? Or that Gemli would give you a part of Hune? You were their prisoner, too." From the little man's expression, Chris knew Leonard hadn't seen it like that.

"You idiot! It would almost be worth it to see what Murllen would do with you!" He dropped the king.

With the help of the trunk behind him, Leonard pulled himself up. "Why don't you just kill me?"

"No, your highness!" Chris smiled. "You will face your people. They will give you a sentence."

Leonard smiled, too. In the distance, Sara's voice was filled with despair as she yelled out, but it was too late. Cold steel penetrated Chris's back.

Chris's legs lost their strength, and he fell to his knees. He knew the warm liquid dripping on his lower back and legs was his blood, and then an agonizing pain and pressure made breathing difficult.

A reiser approached Leonard, who was laughing, and kicked Chris. He collapsed onto his back and stared at the sky. It was bright blue, like Sara's eyes the day he met her.

Chris smiled. Dying while staring at that color couldn't be bad, but a second later, the same thought broke his soul. He wouldn't be able to protect her anymore. He would never tell her what she meant to him, and he would leave her alone. His eyes filled with tears as he realized that he had failed her.

"Give me your sword," Leonard said, and although he was standing nearby, his voice sounded far away. "I will finish this bastard. I'm going to enjoy this as much as I did when I finished your freaking father's life."

Chris waited for the blow, but the sword didn't strike him again.

"What are you doing?" Leonard's voice had turned higher.

"You are only in my way," a deep voice said. "I'm sure Murllen will love to receive both of your bodies."

Leonard screamed, and then Chris heard a loud snap, followed by silence.

A breeze crossed his face, and he thought he heard Sara's voice. But his eyes had closed, and he didn't have the strength to open them.

He imagined her wearing one of his favorite smiles, and he envisioned another life, one where they could have been together.

For a second, a nice warmth embraced him, and then everything turned black.

ROYALTY

Even when Amanda's family had lived on a farm outside of Tundra, before the land became a desert, she was familiar with the Northern Forest. She joined the army at a young age, and most of her training took place in those woods. Her family didn't take her decision well, and they forced her to train as far away from them as possible.

Otherwise, she would have trained with Chris and Charlie. She might have attended her parents' funeral and seen her brother again. Instead, she got a letter from him months after the event and another one from the city council informing her of her brother's passing.

"Will we find them soon?" Lily asked again.

"Well, at this pace, I doubt it. Maybe tomorrow night or the next morning."

Lily kicked the ground and frowned. "Do you suspect they found the caravan already?"

"I hope so...or it will be too late."

Lily nodded and sighed. "How are you?"

Amanda looked at her leg. The prosthesis that Lily had made couldn't be compared to Donald's, and it felt better than her own leg while she walked with the prisoners. It wasn't the same, but at least she hadn't needed to use her horse yet.

"I am good. I can never thank you enough for—"

"For that? I am so ashamed of it! Once we have more time and the right supplies, I will work on a new piece. That one is only for this trip."

Amanda smiled, and her cheeks warmed up. Lily filled many of the valsings' stereotypes, but she was also kind and concerned about her. She had no doubts as to why Donald loved her.

"The worst thing is that Chris was correct!" Lily said, shaking her head.

"What do you mean?" Amanda said. Chris had been right about many things.

"That we would delay them... I just hope they are safe."

Amanda put a hand on Lily's shoulder to comfort her.

"How do you do it?" Lily said.

Amanda looked up and pressed her lips together. For years, she had tried not to wonder if John was dead or alive, healthy or wounded. In her worst nightmares, she saw him at the hospital but didn't reach him in time, and he died alone.

"I try not to think about it," she said. "It will drive you insane."

Lily frowned again and pushed her hair back.

"Tell me how you met," Amanda said, and Lily grinned.

For the next couple of hours, Lily talked about Donald. In the short time Amanda had met him, he'd seemed a decent guy, but through Lily's eyes, there was no one remotely close to him. The conversation didn't annoy her, and it helped keep her mind somewhere else. After all, John was with that group, too.

The birds in the forest stopped singing, and the breeze brought a strange sound with it.

"Wait," Amanda said.

Chris had left her in charge, something she appreciated because, even though she had the highest rank after him, it was in the armament, the worse part of their army to most soldiers.

She ordered two scouts to move into the forest and took her sword out. Everyone else got ready to attack.

"Stop it," a girl's voice said. "Let me go!"

One of Amanda's soldiers came out of the woods, dragging a valsing with him. Not long after, the other one appeared, leading four valsings at sword-point. Two of the valsings each helped a wounded one.

"How many?" Amanda said to the soldiers, but the valsing girl interrupted her.

"You are no one to hold me like this, human."

After working with Leonard, Amanda had no trouble recognizing the superior tone of royalty.

"Right now, I'm your captor, and it depends on which side are you"—Amanda pointed her sword at the valsing's face—"whether or not I let you live.

"It is you!" the girl said, trying to free her arm from the soldier. "You tried to stop those bastard deserters in the forest!"

Amanda narrowed her eyes and stared at the girl.

"You were with that reiser." The girl stopped fighting and turned to the soldier. "She is a traitor, working with the reisers and now holding valsings prisoner!"

"For the gods above!" Lily said. "Only you can be so stupid."

The girl faced Lily, and a wicked smile crossed her face.

"Lily! Why am I not surprised to see you with these...humans."

"These humans are the ones who saved your people from your awful father. Did you miss that part? Or do you only like the humans who fool around with you, Princess Cassandra?"

Cassandra managed to pull the sword from the soldier's scabbard and threw it at Lily, but Amanda stepped forward and blocked it.

"Enough!" Amanda said. "Tied her hands behind her back."

"Mother should have killed you the second you stepped into our tent, bitch," Cassandra said. "Stupid Orson's spy. Too bad my mother never listened to me."

"Your mother took your crown away," Lily said. "We are not your valsings, and we won't follow your idiocy around Hune."

Amanda noticed that the soldier had to use all his strength to stop Cassandra and that the rest of the valsings had gathered near them. She didn't have much time. Most of her group belonged to that race, and though Donald had left Lily in charge, as a princess, Cassandra was their rightful ruler. It wouldn't take much for the situation to change for the worse.

"Lily, that is enough!"

Amanda stepped close to Cassandra.

"I'm not a traitor, and I'm not forcing anyone to follow us, either. However, if you are working with your father—"

"That freak monster should burn in hell! Do not call him my father again." Cassandra took a deep breath and stopped struggling. "Where is my mother?"

Amanda didn't need to answer. The valsings turning away said it all.

"Oh, no!" the princess knelt, and her shoulders sagged.

Lily exhaled and paced.

"Lily," Amanda said, "she just—"

"She is an actress! She doesn't care about the queen!"

Amanda wasn't falling for those tears, either. She already

had a good idea of the princess's personality. If she were telling the truth and Amanda had met her in the forest with Hayden, then many valsings were missing from her group of prisoners.

"What happened to the others who were with you?" Amanda asked.

"I don't know," Cassandra said. "The bastards injured some, and they stood behind… Dead by now."

"Did you just leave them?" Lily said.

"I am not a medic! I was not helping them. Besides, they seemed more peaceful…resting."

Amanda noticed the horrified and disgusted looks the soldiers gave the princess, and the valsings' faces held similar expressions.

"I have no time to waste," Cassandra said. "I must reach St. Patrick's Abbey."

"Why do you need to get there?" asked Amanda.

"How do you plan to reach the abbey if you keep leaving your people behind?" Lily said shaking her head.

"I do not have to answer to you. As I see it, you not only stole my fiancée, but you may as well have been sleeping with my father."

Lily pushed Amanda to the side and tried to attack the princess, but two soldiers held her back.

Cassandra didn't flinch, and after shaking the curls from her face, she stared at Amanda.

"To answer your question, I am looking for…hope." She glanced at the other valsings. "I ignored why my mother waited so long to realize how outrageous Orson was. She should have known better or listened to me. I do not care who oversees our people now, but I promise you Orson will pay for what he did to us."

The group of valsings responded with cheers, and Amanda's fear grew as she witnessed what could become a rebellion.

"Let's camp here," she said to her soldiers. Then she turned to Cassandra. "How many valsings were with you today?"

The princess looked confused, so one of the two valsings answered, "Five more."

"See if you can find them," Amanda said to both soldiers.

She pulled Cassandra up and forced her to sit away from the others while they got the tents ready.

"Who in the gods' name are you?" Cassandra said.

"Major Amanda Belk, and as of now, you are a prisoner."

~

LILY GROANED AS SHE PACED. She knew it was wrong, but she was disappointed that Cassandra was alive. Of all the valsings, she was the only one who deserved death. Even her mother, Queen Vanessa, detested her. Now, along with all the other problems they had, Amanda and the others would have to keep an eye on the princess and her games.

"Lily!" Amanda said while walking towards her.

"Yes?"

"What the hell is going on?" Amanda almost whispered. "Is that your princess? Is she still the rightful—"

"Of course not! Vanessa saved us from that!"

Amanda touched Lily's arm. "Don't let her see how much she bothers you. That's her best weapon against you, and right now, you are in charge of the valsings. I need you to focus here."

Lily took a deep breath and nodded. "We need to learn what she wants. As far as I am aware, she's never cared for anyone but herself. I hope she won't want to deal with us, but...I just do not know... If she figured something out about the abbey and Sara, she may be dangerous. Orson could be aware, too."

Amanda agreed with her and came up with a plan. Although Lily was hoping to persuade Cassandra to talk or abandon her in the forest, Amanda's idea wasn't bad.

Once the fires were lit and they'd set scouts around the perimeter, Lily and Amanda walked to the princess's tent.

Cassandra smiled at them from a chair full of cushions. She looked almost sincere, as if she were thankful to have shelter and a warm place to sleep again, but manipulation was Cassandra's master's ability. Lily recognized the bruises on the princess's face and arms gave her a pathetic look.

Even in an oversize human uniform, the princess looked regal. The new dark blue color contrasted with her curly auburn hair, and ridiculously long eyelashes framed her big, dark eyes. Her hairstyle seemed to have taken hours to style, and her posture was one that she used to intimidate her court.

In the past, it had taken an immense effort for Donald to convince Lily he didn't like or care about the princess. Now that the scars on her body disgraced her, she couldn't stop wondering if he might change his mind.

"I hope you are feeling better," Amanda said.

"Stop the act, Cassandra," Lily said. "What in the hell do you want from the abbey?"

Amanda rolled her eyes and sat in a chair.

"Yes, please," Cassandra said, "make yourself comfortable."

"Of course I will," Amanda said. "This is my camp, my shelter."

The tent was purposely small, and it seemed even smaller with all the valsings that had arrived with the princess. They belonged to Cassandra's personal escort, and unlike her, they seemed exhausted and sick.

"Things have changed in the past weeks," Lily said. "When the queen died, she gave Donald the—"

"You told me this before." Cassandra waved her hand at her. "And in case your memory is so short, I already stated to the major, who is in charge of this group of…soldiers, that I do not care who leads the valsings."

Lily threw her arms in the air and turned around.

"I understand you all were prisoners of the reisers and Orson," Amanda said, "but I'm not sure I can trust you, and… I won't take any chances."

She leaned forward and stared at the princess. "You are free to go, but…the valsings with you stay with me. Their new ruler may want to see them"—she turned to the valsings behind her—"and they don't look healthy enough for such a trip."

"No, you cannot take them from me!" Cassandra stood. "You are nothing to me…to us!"

Amanda sat back. "If you want to, I'll prove to you how much I can take away from you."

The day Lily met Amanda, she had been in Chris's arms, looking fragile and exhausted. Lily hadn't realized she was a soldier until John mentioned it to her. She wasn't a weak woman, but Lily had seen her cry in pain and fear.

At that moment, though, Lily understood how Amanda had survived for so long in her king's court and led the humans' armament. She was glad she hadn't met that side of her before, because she would have judged her to be like Chris and would have missed making a good friend.

"You won't get too far with me," Cassandra said. "I am not your—"

"But you are, Cassandra. I told you before. You are my prisoner. Unless you want to be alone and walk out of here by yourself. Then you are free. Understand?"

Cassandra exhaled, and she almost growled as she said,

"Still, until you talk to Donald, you cannot take them away from me."

Amanda smiled. "Well, whether or not I talk to Donald about this, it's up to you."

Lily wasn't sure if Amanda could remove Cassandra's escort, but the princess believed it. Her expression was somewhere between upset and worried. Probably for the first time in her life, someone was threatening her royal privileges.

"I do not understand how my plans interest you."

"Well, Cassandra," Lily said, sitting by Amanda, "we need to learn what your business in the abbey was and what you know about that place."

"Nothing and no one!" Cassandra crossed her arms and turned her back to them. "Like you, I learned this by living there."

Amanda shook her head. "That doesn't make sense. It's a long journey to make, knowing nothing or no one."

Cassandra looked back at her escort and sighed. "I understand your need to trust me. But even this moron"—she pointed at Lily—"could tell you how little I care about this war."

Amanda turned to Lily, who simply nodded. "If that's the case, you should have no trouble telling me the truth."

Cassandra's voice trembled. "It is personal… I had no idea what my father…Orson… Not in a million years would I have thought he could… I have hated him most of my life, but that…" A few tears escaped her eyes, and she wiped them away. "I will do whatever I can to help you stop him, but… unfortunately, I do not…"

Amanda sat back and nodded.

Lily sighed. Most of the valsings had always disliked her and thought her stupid. Her parents had never cared for her, and now her future had been taken away. They'd left her with nothing.

"The reisers destroyed St. Patrick's, Cassandra," Lily said.

Cassandra covered her mouth and shook her head. Her shoulders dropped, and she turned away from everyone, sobbing.

"Cassandra?" Amanda said after a brief moment.

"Are you sure?" Cassandra said. "Everything and every... everyone is dead?"

Lily looked at her for a second. "I am sure. What the valsings I sent described to me is horrifying. The reisers made a point with that massacre."

Cassandra stared into the distance, not trying to hide her tears anymore. "In that case, my plan has changed. I need your help to find someone."

Amanda crossed her arms but didn't need to say anything.

"I understand, in my situation, I have no room for demands, but...there is always some advantage to having me on your side." Cassandra wiped her face. "Like I said, I want Orson to pay for what he did...along with whoever is working with him. I just need to find a soldier."

The confusion was general, as her petition surprised even the valsings in her escort.

"Your highness," one of them said, "I am not sure you have thought this through—"

Cassandra stared at her, and she fell silent.

"I met him years ago, and he owes me...a favor."

Lily didn't like where the conversation was going, and neither did Amanda. "Finding a soldier in these times is very difficult, Cassandra. I don't think we have the time to—"

Cassandra smiled. "I assure you, he is alive and won't be hard to find. I have not met as many... Let's just say, during the incident, he was very good at his job. At the time, he was a captain. Last time I met him, I did not ask for his rank. Riddley, I believe…"

Lily shook her head and touched her forehead. Of course, it had to be him.

Amanda shifted in her chair. "Commander Christopher Riddley?"

"See!" Cassandra said. "I told you he was good and not that hard to find."

Lily had heard about the princess's interlude with a human soldier. She'd never liked Chris, and now she disliked him even more. And the idea of him owing something to Cassandra was wrong.

"Is he still alive?" Cassandra said. "He left with Donald, so I am guessing he is."

Amanda stood and moved to the tent's door. "I can't promise you anything. Whether or not Commander Riddley owes you something is none of my business."

"Is he with…" Cassandra smiled. "No, he is your commander, and you have to bring me to him."

Amanda left the tent, and Lily followed her. She had nothing to say to Cassandra.

"Amanda, wait!" Even with a prosthesis, Lily had to run to catch her. "Is it true? Do you have to bring her to Chris?"

Amanda stopped. "Yes, I do."

"Why? She is—"

"She is a lot of things, and I dislike her, too, but…she is your former monarch. I can't ignore that… She is royalty. I have to bring her to my superior."

Lily closed her eyes and shook her head.

"Did you know any of this?" Amanda asked.

"Only rumors. I tried to stay away from her and her messes."

"But you heard?"

Lily groaned and looked up. "A long time ago, Cassandra

had a personal encounter with a human soldier. That's when Orson sent her to be with the queen."

Amanda looked at the ground. "How... Define personal encounter, please?"

Lily chuckled. "The kind where you lose part of your clothes and—"

Amanda shook her head and walked away, but then she turned back to Lily. "Really? I would have never believed it from Chris... I guess she is pretty."

Lily hated the idea of Cassandra having some kind of power over Chris, who, whether or not she liked it, was in charge of everything. Even Donald, or at least, that's what he told her before he left with the soldiers.

"All right," Amanda said, "let's think for a moment. Cassandra claims to know Chris."

Lily nodded. "Claims? I am sure she knows him quite well."

Amanda frowned. "Fine, they've met, but...she didn't know he was our commander, and those are many years she ignored about him."

"That is a good thing, right?"

Amanda shrugged. "The past is a skilled teacher, but when it comes back to you, it could turn into a horrible friend."

WOUNDS

Sara stopped listening to Donald.

He could have been saying the storm had passed and the sky was opening, or the stars were getting blocked by dark clouds. She didn't care. It had been at least two days since the battle.

She couldn't remember whether or not she had eaten since then, and she hadn't slept more than a few hours, scared of her nightmares or that she might miss something.

It was funny how everything had changed in just a few minutes.

After her father had explained who she was and the reason she was part of the curse, Sara understood what ending the war could mean to her life. She'd never imagined Chris wouldn't be there.

Now she didn't care if Hune fell under Murllen's hands or Gemli took control of its foundations. Her only concern was to figure out how to stop her heartbeat once Chris's heart failed him.

Everything had happened too fast and a second ahead of her. She had been about to kill Leonard, but at the last moment, Chris had stopped her. He'd been right, but if he hadn't arrived then, no one would have hurt him.

He told her they would talk about it and asked her to help with the prisoners. She didn't have time to answer before he raced off after the king.

She looked around and found Donald kneeling by the device. A woman was with him, and they were moving something. John shouted to another soldier while he tried to stop a reiser. She started to help him, but then a muffled groan got her attention.

During the battle, a wagon had fallen sideways, pulling a soldier with it. The wheel had gotten stuck with the chains around his wrists underneath it, and he couldn't stand up. His forehead was bleeding, and he had a dark patch in one eye. The worst was the big purple bruise on his side.

She found the key to his chains on the ground, and within seconds, the soldier was free. He nodded and ran to help John.

An overwhelming alarm inside of her made her turn.

To the south of the road, a small prairie framed a short hill, and beyond it stretched a forest. The sunlit landscape was full of wildflowers. On top of the hill, Chris pushed Leonard down and grabbed him by his collar.

A few steps ahead of her, a reiser stood. His armor had only a small crack in the side. He stepped towards John and the other soldier, but then he saw Chris and, with his sword ready, ran to catch him.

It only took her a second to react, but it was a second too late.

A soldier tried to stop the reiser, but he cut the poor man in half and kept running up the hill. Sara chased after him, yelling at Chris, but her voice couldn't reach him.

In the back of her mind, she kept telling herself that Chris would be all right. He was a commander in a horrible war and had survived all these years, but the distance between them seemed to grow as she ran.

Her heartbeat pounded hard inside her head, louder than the battle outside, until the moment she saw the reiser raise his sword. Then everything went silent, and she screamed Chris's name so loudly it hurt her throat. He heard her, but it was too late. The reiser struck him in the back, and he fell to his knees.

Leonard laughed, but then the reiser grabbed him and ripped his head off. The reiser turned, but he stopped moving when he noticed Sara racing towards them. Instead of attacking Chris, he ran away.

Sara knelt by Chris.

His blood was already pooling beneath him, and his eyes were closed. She had helped sick and injured people before, but none of them had looked as bad as Chris. She leaned down and tried to listen to his heart, but her sobbing was too loud and blocked any other sound. He felt warm in her arms, but the only movement was the trembling of her own body.

"Let me see."

Hayden knelt and touched Chris's neck. Then he put his hand on his chest.

"Sara, he is still alive. Barely, but alive. I can help him, but you have to—" He exhaled and looked down the hill. "Listen. Only you can save him now."

Sara shook her head.

He touched her hand. "I'll try to heal him. We'll need Donald, a lot of the antidote, and a shelter, but only you can make that happen."

Sara heard footsteps, and then a soldier grabbed Hayden by the arms and pulled him up.

"You thought I wouldn't recognize you!" the man said, pushing Hayden. "You bastard! Where is Amanda? What did you do to her?"

Understanding dawned on Sara, and a colossal weight fell on her shoulders.

She stood and shoved the soldier so hard he almost fell backward. "What the hell are you doing?"

"This monster is a reiser! He is the one who took us prisoner!"

Sara noticed that several soldiers had gathered around them. Their uniforms and swords made her shiver, but in their eyes, she saw the same fear she had of them. Maybe under other circumstances, she would have cared, but not now, and she took advantage of it.

"I know who he is." She stared at the soldier. "He's also the only hope we have to save Chris, and I won't let you get in his way."

"This man is my best friend," the soldier said in a louder voice. "I won't let anything bad happen to him."

"If what you say is true," Sara said, with no need to raise her voice, "you should get back and let Hayden save him."

"If this reiser hurts him, I'll make you responsible—"

Sara stepped forward, and the heat rising inside her must have been visible, because the soldiers all took a step back.

"I'm just guessing here, but aren't you the one who was in charge of this guard before? And didn't you lead them to become prisoners?" Sara narrowed her eyes. "Yes, I'm taking my chances, and I'll be personally responsible for what happens here. Is that clear, soldier?"

When he hadn't replied, she'd added. "Make yourself useful. Find our valsing medic."

Now she was sitting inside a tent, watching the time escape from Chris's life, and she had no idea how she had taken control of everything.

Major Baker and his men had found a good place to build a camp and had set scouts around it, something, Donald had informed her, that had happened under her orders. He'd also informed her that they'd lost Liam.

The device had needed to be set close to the reisers for it to work. When their armor had broken, a sharp piece of metal had hit Liam in the back of his head, killing him. Donald had gotten a deep cut in his arm and leg.

Later, during the first night, the group of valsings had arrived on horseback, and she'd made sure they helped with the fires and food for everyone.

No one questioned her authority, and the idea made her shiver. Maybe she had inherited some of her uncle's skills, since she knew they all followed her orders due to fear.

For the last two days, Chris had been unconscious. Hayden had used all the antidote they'd found and assisted Donald in closing the cut on Chris's back. The sight of it had frozen Sara's soul. It was long and deep, and she couldn't imagine how he would heal.

In truth, the second she'd looked at it, her hope had vanished, and she'd begun to wait for his suffering to end. He had proved to be strong, and though he wasn't conscious, from time to time, he mumbled. He also had a high fever, and each shiver made him frown.

"Hayden, can I talk to you?" John said, and then he stepped outside the tent.

Hayden walked out, but he stood right by the entrance so Sara and Donald could hear them.

"We can't wait any longer. You have to explain the situation to them… I'll try to convince Charlie again, but he isn't—"

"It won't work if the soldiers aren't on board anymore, John."

Sara stepped out, and the darkness of the night surprised her. She couldn't imagine another day had gone by.

"Can I ask what the problem is?" she said, brushing a lock of hair behind her ear.

John looked at her, but it was Hayden who answered.

"The reisers are in the camp, guarded by soldiers. Major Baker and Donald have assured them they aren't prisoners and something else is happening, but no one… If Chris dies, I doubt Charlie will follow his plan."

"He may," John said. "He just needs to understand more about it."

Sara pulled her hood up and walked towards the camp. "Let me do it."

"You don't have to. You have done more than—"

"Will it hurt if I do it?"

John shook his head and smiled. Dark circles had formed under his eyes, and his arm hung in a sling, but the deep bruises and cuts on his face were finally healing.

"I'll go with you," Hayden said, "to talk to the reisers, of course. I will make things worse with Charlie."

The reisers were at the far end of the camp. They had food and a pleasant fire, but they still sat away from everyone else, and the soldiers nearby didn't look friendly.

"It's a shame, you know?" Hayden said. "Christopher's plan, although Amanda's idea first, was ingenious."

"It's both your plan… It won't work anymore?"

Hayden sighed. "Christopher was my prisoner, and I asked for his help when I met him. There are too many things between Abbott and me to just… The second Chris falls, Charlie will be in charge."

"Yeah, I hate that."

Hayden stood in front of her. "What are you going to do if Chris… Would you still help us?"

Sara looked away. She heard an owl hoot in the distance, which made her grin. "I love this land, Hayden. I'll die defending it from those monsters. I may just get there by myself."

They had reached the reisers, so Hayden didn't ask any more questions.

Most sat by the fires, just like the soldiers did. They wore the humans' old uniforms, which made Sara breathe easier. Lily had thought about that detail.

Aside from the reiser that had attacked Chris, none had escaped. The missing ones must have been dead somewhere on the road or in the field. Hayden had told her that he'd lost at least a quarter of his squadron, and the weight of it was visible in his eyes.

"Good evening," Hayden said, getting their attention. "I'm sure I look different, but—"

"Colonel?" one of them said, and a few stood and saluted him. However, most turned away, and their anger charged the atmosphere.

"I'm sorry about all the…misinformation," Sara said. "The plan isn't going well, as you can imagine."

"What will happen to us?" a reiser said. He stood, which made Hayden step closer to Sara. "Will we be killed or—"

"No one is going to kill you," Hayden said. "You have my word on that."

The reisers puffed and groaned at this, so Hayden took a step forward.

"If you have a problem with me, let's settle it now. I may not look the same, but I can kick your ass the same."

That got the soldiers' attention, and they fell silent.

"Colonel, it is hard to see beyond your treason," said the reiser who was standing.

"Which is why you are here," Sara said. She walked to the middle of their camp and sat down between two of them, and they shuffled uncomfortably.

Hayden chuckled. He crossed his arms but remained standing.

"My name is Sara White, and I'm a zhorta...among other things, I guess." She looked at the fire for a second. "My uncle killed my father before I was born. He left with Gemli, and they invaded your asylum."

As she expected, that put the reisers around her on edge, including Hayden, who asked, "How do you know about the asylum? I never—"

"I read it in Gemli's journal."

Hayden sat down and stared at her.

"As I was saying, those two invaded that sacred place. The ruler of the house could do nothing, as they believe going out will kill them. Just like you did before. Gemli took advantage of it and forced him to train my uncle, who became Murllen."

The reisers' reaction was what she had expected. Following Chris's example when he'd talked to the soldiers back at the refuge, she let them yell, swear, and protest for a while.

"As you can see," Sara said, "there is a traitor, but it isn't Hayden. He is the one leading you to save the rest of your race." A hush fell. "You all have seen what Gemli is capable of. What will he do to your race when he is done with mine?"

"And we should believe this from you?" a reiser said, "Aren't you a zhorta? Didn't your kind betray the humans?"

"You should believe her because it's the truth," Hayden said, "and you all know it as well as I do. We have noticed the peculiar behavior of our leader, and we knew it was wrong. Now we know the reason for it."

For a few minutes, everyone remained quiet. Although they were strong and in better shape than the soldiers from the caravan, their pale skin and somber expressions made them look sick. Only a few were injured, but all had bruises along their arms and face.

"And the plan is to work with the humans?" one of the reisers said. "I don't see them liking us much."

"I don't think you like them, either," Sara said, "but isn't peace what we are looking for?" She sighed and stood. "If you want to walk out of here, no one will stop you. I'll make sure of it."

Hayden narrowed his eyes.

"I'm not a soldier," she said, "and have a limited idea of the war, but it's my understanding that your help is crucial to finishing this nonsense."

At the far end of the group, a young reiser said just loud enough for the others to hear, "General Murllen sent us to kill Colonel Green. I know this because he ordered Mayor Dunstan and me to do it." He looked at the ground. "I'm very sorry, Colonel. I should have told you but—"

"I get it, Paul," Hayden said. "I should have done something about it long ago."

"Even if the soldiers have accepted our presence," another reiser said, "what about the people? We trapped them and kept them prisoner. They won't understand this agreement. Most of them will want revenge."

"Revenge, right," Sara said. "People don't follow the rules, but they fall for superstition." She smiled at them. "Some stories can teach powerful lessons. I'm sure they have been talking about me and what happened on the road… I wouldn't worry about them. They know I would stand to protect you all."

~

SARA WAS GOING BACK to Chris's tent when she noticed a group of new people arriving. It took her a second to remember Amanda and Lily were leading the refugees to find them.

"Sara!" Lily said, walking towards her with a smile on her face.

"For the gods above!" Amanda said, rushing to her husband.

"I'm fine, Amanda," John said, and he managed to hug her with one arm and kiss her. A few people cheered, which made Sara chuckle.

Lily hugged her for a second and then stepped back and looked around.

"Donald is all right," Sara said. Her friend's shoulders relaxed, and her eyes focused on her.

"What the hell happened? How are you?"

Before Sara could answer, Donald was standing next to her, and Lily threw herself at him.

"Finally! Our new monarch shows off!"

Sara didn't recognize the valsing who'd spoken, but Donald did, and he wasn't happy to see her.

"What are you doing here, Cassandra?" he said, grabbing Lily's hand and keeping her close.

The valsings nearby moved closer or stopped to look at them.

"I thought you would want to check on your former fiancée," said the valsing. "Also…I need to talk to an old friend."

"You have nothing to talk about with Chris," Donald said, surprising Lily and Amanda. "Aren't you supposed to be grieving the death of Queen Vanessa, your mother?"

Charlie approached the group, his jaw set and his arms crossed. The patch over his eye only emphasized his seriousness as he stood by Donald in front of Cassandra.

"Well, I am not sure if I want to grieve her," Cassandra said. "After all, she gave away my birthrights to an…you."

Sara stepped aside and walked to Chris's tent. She didn't

need any more drama. She'd heard enough about their princess from Lily and the gossip around the abbey.

Memories of a long-ago story came to her mind.

The only time Sara had left the abbey had been when the valsing's princess had left her father's community and gone to live with her mother. News of the worsening war reached the Soto Forest, and Sara wanted to help more. Rafael didn't agree, so she left.

Sara found Chris's dad, and her vivid dream led her to Chris. Things worked differently than what she'd thought, and after a while, she moved back.

The valsings had whispered then how the princess's interlude with a human had outraged and humiliated Orson, so he had sent her to live with her mother. Now Sara could put things together, and she wished she could ask Chris about everything. But even if he'd been awake, it wasn't her past, and it wasn't her place to inquire about it.

Hayden was checking Chris's temperature when she entered the tent. "How did you make it here faster than me?" she asked.

"I didn't stop to greet anyone." He stood and rubbed his face. "Listen, Sara. I'm very thankful for what you said to my reisers, but…I'm worried about you."

"About me?"

"Yes." He exhaled and tilted his head. "We haven't known each other very long, but when you saved my life, I thought… you were different."

Sara sat on the ground and looked at her hands. "I'm tired. Nothing else."

"No, it's not just that. You…you kind of… I'm not sure how—"

"Are you afraid of me?"

Hayden looked at Chris and then back at her. "Should I be? I mean…how do you have Gemli's journal? And when…

Chris told me that you have some connection with magic, but that… I have seen Gemli's work, and what you did—"

"We were too close to the netherworld." She pushed her hair behind her ears. "I just asked for a breeze. All of that was Gemli's spell falling apart."

Hayden nodded, but he didn't move. Instead, he exhaled and crossed his arms. "As long as you know what you are doing."

"Does anyone here know what they are doing?" Sara chuckled and shook her head. "Before we met you, we got trapped in the Eternal Glacier. Cielthos gave me the journal. You and Chris left, so I had time to read."

She didn't want to talk about something she couldn't explain without lying, and she was too tired to avoid questions with half-answers, so she got up and went outside.

The fresh night air cleared her mind as she sat by a fire. She was alone since everyone was watching the discussion between Princess Cassandra and Donald.

She wasn't sure how much time had passed before Hayden called to her.

Her heart dropped, and all the warmth seemed to leave her body. For a second, she doubted her legs would sustain her, but they did and took her all the way to the tent. She held the door for a moment and tried to breathe.

"Why did you assume the worse?" Hayden said, and she turned to look at Chris.

His gray eyes were looking back at her with a weak smile. Sara wiped her tears away, and for the first time since they'd brought Chris into the tent, it seemed to be too big.

"Chris." As she knelt by him, Hayden walked outside.

"My lady," Chris said, almost out of breath. "Did I worry you too much?"

She held his hand and rubbed it with her fingers. She wanted to say many things, but the knot in her throat didn't let her, so she bit her bottom lip and tasted the salt of her tears.

"No..." He moved his other hand up and touched her face. "Don't cry, pretty. I promised you I wouldn't leave you."

Donald ran into the tent, and between laughing and jumping, he pushed Sara out of his way.

"You bastard!" he said, hugging Chris. "You terrified me!"

"Hey," Chris said, smiling. "That hurts."

Donald jumped back. "Of course! I am so sorry!"

Sara heard people talking, and almost immediately, Charlie walked in, too. His smile vanished the second he saw Sara, and he stopped until she stepped back.

"Why am I not surprised at you making all this drama? Always getting everyone's attention!"

At the sound of Charlie's voice, Chris beamed, and he even tried to sit up. "Charlie!"

Charlie stopped him. "You better stay there. We don't need you to get you broken." Then, laughing, he added, "Like I always knew, you are too fragile!"

"Chris?" a girl said from the entrance.

Sara had seen her over the last few days, usually around the soldiers or helping people.

"Jean!" Chris managed to rest on his elbow. "Please, come in."

She walked inside, holding her hands in front of her and looking from the ground to Chris.

Sara hadn't thought about it until then. Before the battle started, Donald had said something about the commander's fiancée. Jean knelt and, unlike Donald, gently hugged Chris, and a smile illuminated his face.

Sara's throat closed, and tears came back to her eyes. Jean, or the commander's fiancée, looked different from her, more like the valsing princess. Her dress, although ripped, still held the elegance of what had once been a fancy piece. She looked tired, but her walk was graceful, like it belonged to someone from an important family.

"I'm so glad you are awake," she said, blushing. "I was worried about you."

"It's all right, Jean," Chris said, and Sara walked out.

She had been aware of how bad it was to let some feelings come back. It had been hard enough to deal with some of the memories from her vivid dreams. Now she would have to face them again.

The camp seemed too bright and crowded. The looks of people, soldiers, valsings, and even reisers bothered her more than before, making her pull up the hood of her coat.

She strode into the trees, allowing the darkness of the forest to guide her.

"Sara!" Amanda said, catching up with her. "I'm so glad to see you."

"You look good," Sara said, but she kept walking until Amanda stood in her way.

"Is it Chris? I thought Hayden... Wasn't he getting better?"

"He is...I think."

"So, what happened to you?"

In the distance, Sara noticed an owl flying towards the forest. Its white and black feathers were hard to hide in the dark sky. She didn't care about Gemli; she needed her father.

"I'm...sorry. I have to go."

"Go? Where?"

Sara didn't wait and didn't care to answer. She moved fast, looking for her father.

THE GREAT WIZARD

Moonlight illuminated Sara's path. The voices from the camp had disappeared long ago, leaving the bugs and the wind to fill up the night. She had followed the owl deep into the forest when the ground under her feet changed.

After they had taken Chris to the shelter and gotten settled, she'd found her boots inside the tent. Donald told her that Chris had asked him to take care of them since she would need them. They were now in her hand because they blocked her from feeling her world. However, she didn't like the wet, dense sensation of the cold ground she was walking on.

The owl landed on a nearby branch. Sara crouched and discovered the forest was turning into a wetland. She had been walking for a while, but not enough to have reached the swamps.

Inside her mind, she heard her dad laughing. "Are you concerned about getting dirty?"

She looked up at the bird, and her heart felt at peace. The voice of her father was a delightful sound. She found a dry rock and sat on it. From the path she had followed, she heard footsteps and branches moving around.

"Sara?" Amanda said from behind the tall grass. "What are you doing?"

Sara glanced at the owl, who stood on the branch. "It's getting moody around there. Be careful."

It took Amanda more time than it had Sara to reach the rock, but the couple of times Sara offered her help, the major shook her head.

"The Northern Forest collided with the swamps," she said when she sat by Sara. "This is probably the beginning of them."

"There is no way we are that closed. It has to be..."

"It has to be what?"

The owl puffed his feathers and stretched his wings.

"Sara! It has to be what? Are you feeling all right? I followed you for more than an hour before you sat here. Where were you going?"

Sara smiled at her. "I'm not sure, but we are about to find out."

The owl flew off the branch at the same time that Sara jumped down from the rock.

"What are you doing?"

"Would you wait here for me here?" Sara said, leaving her boots by Amanda. "I need to check on someone." She pointed at the owl, which Amanda hadn't noticed until then.

"What, an owl? I don't understand. What is—"

"More like *who* he is, but that doesn't matter right now. I'll be back. If it gets too cold, go back. I don't want you to get sick."

Sara turned to her father, who was waiting on a branch farther away.

The mud was freezing, and it hurt Sara's feet while its

density obstructed her legs. The uneven ground didn't help, and thinking about falling into the muck made Sara shiver.

"It's not a good idea, Sara!" Amanda said.

In her mind, Sara agreed.

"In that case, what is the plan, little wizard?" her dad said in her head.

"What can I do?"

Behind her, Amanda asked Sara what she had said, while her father answered, "So far, you have surprised me so much. I'm impressed by you."

She felt her cheek warm up and took another clumsy step.

"I want to teach you a useful tool for wizards: traveling. We need to reach Laconia tonight, so tell me, are you swimming or flying?"

Sara frowned and looked down, unsure if there was running water in that mud. She turned to the sky, and her hope set on the branches above her, just like she had traveled in the Soto Forest.

"Nice choice, although we won't move these trees. People would freak out." The owl landed on her shoulder, and its claws were so soft that she barely noticed them.

"You need to feel the way you did before. Remember in the forest? The moment you change your perception of things, it will come as easily as moving your arms."

Sara closed her eyes and exhaled.

It sounded similar to how she had moved the soft breeze before the battle. The cold mud on her feet got her attention, so she tried to focus on her surroundings.

She heard the noises of the forest and Amanda shuffling while waiting for her. In the darkness, she felt the surrounding air, and she turned up her palms, letting them feel it. Then it changed. She recognized the sensation of wind hitting her hands and sliding by them.

She inhaled and perceived the forest covering as her weight lightened and expanded, leaving everything below her. All kinds of shapes moved past her on her way, but they didn't hurt her, and in a few tries, she learned how to interpret them.

The first thing she focused on was the owl flying in front of her, and she allowed the joy of freedom to fill her heart.

The different shades of green, brown, and yellow under the moonlight made the woods look like clouds on the ground, and the mountains ahead seemed to be dark monuments. She distinguished the sand of the desert flying up in the breeze.

A knot grew in her stomach when she saw the massive trees of the Soto Forest. They had moved farther into the desert than a few days ago, and the swamp underneath her, spreading into the forest, had already reached the top of Laconia's waterfall.

A few minutes later, the owl descended into some ruins and landed on one of them.

Sara followed and circled the owl for a moment, feeling its feathers moving and the flaps of its spotted wings. The moment her feet touched the ground, she got dizzy and lost her balance.

Her hands and knees became cold when they pressed into the snow. It looked clean, like it had fallen only hours ago, but it had already frozen. Still lightheaded, she turned around. The snowy blanket covered everything, giving a serene look to the city, Laconia.

Its streets were lined with pieces of wood that must have been a dock, and a few broken ships lay half-sunken in the icy sand. The houses didn't look any better, and the rusted streetlights on the corners had fallen or were tilting.

Dry weeds covered all the walls. Everything was silent,

and the lack of sound felt unnatural to her. Nothing lived here, not even bugs.

She stood and looked back at her father, but he remained quiet. He flew ahead of her, so she followed him on foot.

At the end of the dock, the imposing rock structure that had once been covered by the flowing waterfall had turned into a colossal piece of ice.

The street where she was walking was divided. One path moved along the shore of the missing ocean. The one her father took climbed up the protective wall of the city.

Once at the top of the stone stairs, she noticed signs of a fire on the walls, and the smell of smoke hit her, making her cough.

Not much was left of the once-magnificent palace. She had seen paintings of it and read about it in the abbey. It may look better than the castle she grew up on, but still, it was impossible to believe that these burned piles of debris had been once a crystal and marble building.

"It was years ago, Sara," her dad said in her mind. "You won't find any signs of the slaughter. I'm sorry you saw what happened in the Soto Forest."

Sara nodded and bit her lip. "Can we do something about it?"

Her father flew and to the top of a fence she recognized. Cielthos had shown it to her. It had been in better shape, but it's white color, the swing on the porch, and the flowerbeds in the windows were still there.

Sara grabbed her pendant and looked at it. Like Chris had told her, it was a map, one she now understood. She opened the fence but then stopped.

"It's all right. I'm a regular visitor to this house. It's the only thing I have left from your mom."

The door squeaked when Sara pushed it, and the wooden floor creaked when she stepped inside. Only the moonlight from a window illuminated the room. The smell of fire and smoke was stronger inside, and for Sara, time had destroyed everything. Still, she could imagine how wonderful it would have been to live here.

She walked upstairs and found two rooms. The owl flew straight to the last one in the hallway. As she passed the first door, she saw burned boxes and broken chairs inside the room.

The second door led to a bedroom. The bed, although full of dust, was still intact, and a tipped-over crib rested at its side. An old painting stood on the nightstand. It was dusty, but when Sara blew on it, she recognized the city, only it was full of life and color.

"You mom worked with flowers."

Sara sat on the bed and looked at the painting.

"Well, with glacier orchids. She and her grandfather found, collected, and used them to decorate all kinds of joyful events here and in Tundra. As you know, she also picked them up afterward to prevent horrible cuts. That's why I thought you didn't..."

"I didn't what?"

A soft, cold breeze crossed the room, making Sara cover her face. She felt the bed bend next to her, and she opened her eyes to find her dad sitting there. Without wasting a second, she wrapped her arms around him and hugged him tightly.

"I miss this, too, Sara," he said and pulled her closer.

After a moment, they let go. She sat, resting her head against his shoulder, while he spun a hat in his hands.

"Like I was saying," he said, "you got stung by one of those flowers."

"Mushrooms?"

Her dad chuckled. "Right, Elizabeth would have corrected me, too, but she called them all sort of things."

"Why is it important that I got hurt? I shouldn't have been playing with—"

"Well, you didn't know it then…but they never hurt me. My power protected me from them. When you got injured, I thought you didn't have magic…or not as much."

Sara sighed and looked at her hand. The only scar on it was the one from the sword.

"I wasn't happy about that one," her dad said as he covered her palm with his, "but Xander was a great man. He and Alleta would have taken great care of you…although that would have put your life in more danger, considering how much magic you have."

"Cielthos told me the Great…you passed some of it to me. I guess since you are—"

"It's more than that, sweety. Your mom got pregnant after I took back my role as the Great Wizard. It's in your blood, as you already figured out. But as long as I'm alive, you won't have all of it."

Sara turned to him and shook her head. "I don't want it. I want you here, with me."

Her dad hugged her and brushed her hair. "I know you do, but…" He exhaled. "If I stay, Hune will suffer, and everyone will pay for it. I can't let that happen." He stared at her. "And I'm sure, neither will you."

He took the painting from her hand.

"The waterfall used to bring to the surface the magical foundations of our world. Its waters spread them around our world. Without them, I'm afraid Hune will continue to change for the worse."

"Why are the trees moving?"

"They need to reach the foundation to survive. They sense it's north of them. Those massive trees will destroy so much."

Her dad chuckled and gently bumped against Sara.

"Elizabeth was obsessively in love with the Soto Forest. She thought it was the most amazing thing in Hune. Even though she knew who the Great Wizard really was and married him, those roots were more impressive."

Sara giggled, but something in her heart hurt.

"You want to see her?"

"My mom?" Sara raised her eyes, and like the drawings in the cave, she saw a girl smiling at a younger version of her dad while picking up a bunch of glacier orchids and putting them in a basket. Too soon, everything vanished, and only her dad's face was in front of her.

"I met her by accident." He looked into the distance and remained quiet for a moment. "I knew what she meant to me not long after, and I kept bumping into her accidentally. My life was a mess, and she always tolerated everything with me. My favorite was surprising her during her dreams and taking her to places like the Soto Forest. The day she told me she loved me, she also asked me to leave her alone." He sighed. "I was trying to figure how I was going to live without her when she yelled what an idiot I was and how much in love she had been with me for years."

Sara pictured that in her mind and treasured the memory in her heart.

"If I can offer you one bit of advice…don't forget to live no matter what is happening around you. I know you are mad. No, you are in rage, and rightfully so, don't let hate take over everything."

"How?"

Her dad hugged her and whispered, "Remember that being fair isn't about making someone pay for their actions. Nothing can take away the pain in your heart but you. Being fair is allowing others to face the consequences of their actions."

She moved back and wiped her eyes. "How am I going to do it without you?"

Her dad smiled, but tears filled his eyes, and instead of answering, he embraced her once more for a longer time.

Sara stood at the edge of what had once been the lake that had created the waterfall. Her father, at her side, smiled as he looked down at Hune.

"I told you it wasn't as impressive," he said. "It's so high that the clouds are the only thing you can see."

Sara still thought it was magnificent. From there, the distance to the Soto Forest didn't seem so far. Part of her wished to fly there and hide. Her dad had explained how everything would change after this night, and she didn't want to go through with what they were about to do. They had no other option, though.

"I don't know if we can fix the city," her dad said, "but we'll start fixing Hune. Everything will be easier after."

He put a hand on her shoulder. "I wasn't going to try, but…it's amazing what you can already do. I'm sure this will work. I wish I had been the one to teach you, though."

Sara looked down and played with her fingers. "Is it wrong to have read his…"

"Gemli's journal?"

He grabbed her shoulders and turned her around. "Cielthos gave you that book for you to understand more about Gemli. I don't think he imagined you could learn magic from it, but you are a wizard, like me, so we have more…um… It's easy to get a hold of the power…and you are more careful than me."

"But Gemli is the one destroying—"

"Yes, he is, but he is also an outstanding sorcerer, and the way he simplified magic..." He shook his head. "Cielthos is great but has a few too many dragons on his mind. Gemli is focused. It's a shame he wasted it all on revenge." He stared her in the eyes. "Learn from that mistake. But I'm proud of you, Sara. I know Hune will be safe in your hands."

She had to swallow a hard knot.

"Now, to business." He turned to the drop ahead of them. "Gemli stopped the waterfall from getting down here. That destroyed the city and dried up the land below. The water here is overflowing the top of the mountain, making the swamp expand."

"Why would he do that? Isn't that like destroying your own home?"

"Yes, but he doesn't care about a home. He cares about unbalancing Hune to the point where he will be the only one capable of returning it to its natural order. That's why he killed all the other sorcerers, made sure I found his journal, and sent Thornton to kill Landford. He believed Landford White was a close friend of the Great Wizard and couldn't risk anyone trying to find him. He never got that we were the same. Thank the gods for that."

"He used me because I'm Landford's daughter? The curse isn't more powerful because of my relationship with Thornton? He just wanted to get back at you?"

Her dad nodded.

"For reasons only you understand, the Great Wizard seemed to favor Landford in many things. Gemli likes to hurt his enemies deep in their souls before delivering the final blow. I think that's the reason he chose Thornton and you, but your family relationship doesn't affect the curse. That needs nothing else."

Sara turned and looked at the swamp. The darkness about them, the rotten smell, and the lack of life weren't natural.

"The power of Hune over the swamp allowed Gemli to gain more power for himself," her dad said. "He fed his powers by sucking up what should have been Laconia's waterfall. The sorcerer consumed any life that tried to live here."

Sara shivered and wrapped her arms around herself.

"This step is simple. If you can correct the course of the water, Gemli's power will return to its normal state, and then I have no doubt that you can stop him."

Sara shook her head. "I don't like what it entails, Dad."

"I know, Sara." He stepped closer to her. "I know, but I once chose to die so I could live with your mom. Even if none of this had taken place, if you had grown up with us, one day we would have had to say goodbye…at least for a while."

She started to reply, but he said, "Remember the danger now. Gemli will sense something has happened, and he'll come to check it out."

She nodded and stopped her tears from falling. "How can I change this?"

"Well, what I would do is call the water down the cliff. But you do things differently. That's a compliment, my sweet girl. I'm not being nice because I'm your dad. You surprised me before. Just do it again."

She chuckled, took a deep breath, and looked at her surroundings.

The ground was as dense as it was by the forest, but she concentrated on finding the water in it. The mud bubbled and opened, letting a clearer liquid rise.

"Just remember. This time, you'll be the only one getting rid of Gemli's magic. I'll help you as much as I can, but it may be uncomfortable."

Sara closed her eyes, and it took less time for her to feel the mud and dirt pushing the small polls of water. Holding on to that, she called the wind and pushed the clay towards the cliff. It hadn't moved more than a few inches when a strange resistance stopped her, like the wall of a dam, and something sticky grabbed her arms. Within seconds, it became too hot and burned her.

The mud crawled up her body, and she was drowning. Suddenly a fresh breeze flew by her, and the water dropped. She took a deep breath and, allowing the frustration inside to come up, moved her hands, sending a massive wave of mud and water down the edge of the waterfall.

A loud explosion filled the valley, and Sara opened her eyes just in time to see the swamp's water rushing down the cliff. She chuckled, and the water followed her thoughts, destroying what was left of the invisible barrier.

The force of the water pushed down, gaining speed, and Sara felt as if she was part of it, ready to run down the mountain. At the bottom, the mud reached the rocks of the dry riverbed and got stuck in it until the water hit it, cleansing it all.

The foundations of Hune ran freely over the land, filling her heart with the rush of joy from her world.

Sara turned from water to wind and flew past the streets and houses of the city, dropping parts of Hune's magic on top of everything. The snow remained on the ground, but now it healed the foliage under it instead of killing it.

The grass and plants would grow back, inviting the fauna to live there again. Once the war ended, her mother's city would be ready for the races of Hune to inhabit it.

When Sara reached the ruins where they had arrived, she turned back into her normal form. This time, she didn't fall, and the dizziness was minimal. Right behind her, the owl landed on a stone wall.

"Unbelievable!" she said.

The bird shone, and then her dad stood in front of her

once again. "I couldn't agree more." His eyes were full of tears that shadowed his smile. "Gemli will be here soon. He didn't… His magic didn't hurt, right?"

Sara shook her head and hugged him. "You moved it away, Daddy."

He wrapped his arms around her. It was the last time they would hug one another in this lifetime.

"Good. I was happy to use all I had left to protect you."

He explained to her that Gemli had to believe that he had used all his power to break his spell. Otherwise, the sorcerer would suspect someone had helped him, and it wouldn't be long before he found out it was Sara. More importantly, according to her dad, by breaking that spell, they had weakened Gemli's powers, and it would take time for him to recover.

"What if I stay and help you?" Sara said. "You just told me you didn't know how much power I have. You don't have to die anymore. I can—"

"Sara." Her dad touched her face and smiled. "You understand there's a lot more to be done than just stop Gemli. Let me do this for you. Everything else will be easier after."

"Dad, you don't even have a sword."

"A sword won't work with Gemli, sweety. He is a coward and won't come close enough." He stared at her for a moment and took a deep breath. "You look so much like your mom."

"What if Gemli recognizes you?"

"Um…I guess Gemli doesn't know that much about wizards." He smirked. "A sorcerer's magic dies with them, but wizards don't. Anything you do, everything I have done, remains intact unless you take it away. The spell I used in the past to protect me will do it tonight."

He grabbed her by the shoulders again, but this time, both had tears rolling down their cheeks.

"Now, remember, just like I can feel your mother's presence around all the time, I will be with you, no matter what. I trust you, Sara White. I know you'll be all right. You are in excellent hands, even though you haven't realized it yet." He closed his eyes and rested his head on top of hers. "I'm going to miss you, sweety...but I'm eager to see my Elizabeth. I have missed her so much for far too many years."

He kissed her forehead. "Now, you must go, and Sara...I hope I'm wrong about the curse and you figure it out."

"I love you, Daddy."

Sara took a deep breath and stepped back. He was smiling, and it was easy to picture her mom at his side. Although she couldn't stop crying, she knew he would find her soon.

She closed her eyes and kept them shut until she found Amanda waiting for her. She knew that if she caught even a glimpse of Gemli, she would fly back to help her dad.

~

AMANDA WAS DUMBFOUNDED. It wasn't until Sara had finished tying up her boots that she was finally able to talk.

"What happened? Where is the...the owl?"

Sara shook her head and stood. She pushed her hair behind her ears and exhaled. "Let's go back."

It seemed to Sara that they reached the camp too soon. "I'm going to sleep." She stopped at the edge of the forest. "Thanks for waiting for me."

Amanda put a hand on her arm. "Of course." She sighed. "Whenever you want to talk... Just one question. Did you just turn into...?"

Sara grinned, and as she walked away, she answered, "Yes, of course. Best way of traveling."

~

FORECASTING

The morning fog covered the camp, blurring the surrounding forest. It was cold and humid, but voices filled the place with life, making Chris feel better.

"I told you it was a bad idea," Donald said when Chris groaned while he helped him sit by the extinguished fire outside his tent. "You can barely move. If you are not careful, your wound will open again."

Chris shook his head. It was true that he needed time to recover, but they didn't have that luxury. "Did you ask the others to..."

He noticed Hayden coming from one side of the camp and Charlie from the other. After a second look at the settlement, he found the reisers sitting at the far end, while the humans were just wandering around. This was something they'd have to work on, maybe for years to come.

"So, what's going on?" Charlie said. "Shouldn't you be taking a morning nap?"

Before Chris could reply, the four overheard a discussion between Lily and John as they approached.

"Are you kidding me?" Hayden said, sitting close to

Donald and as far away from Charlie as possible. "Did you have to invite her, too?"

"We had an endless night," Donald said. "I will not argue about her presence here. She is the only one who can make Liam's device work…now that we've lost him."

Chris frowned and sighed. He had just learned about losing Liam, and he felt responsible. The poor valsing shouldn't have been there, even though he had offered to help.

"You don't care where Sara has been all this time?" Lily said to John, who rolled his eyes and sat by Charlie. "Last I heard, she was with your wife."

"I don't have to give you an explanation," John said. "Maybe she didn't want to talk to you."

"That is ridiculous!" Lily said, walking over to Donald. "Why would she not?"

Chris could easily think of over ten reasons for Sara not to talk to her. However, he also wanted to know where she was. The night before, he noticed when she left the tent, and she didn't come back. For sure, he was glad to find Charlie and Jean safe, but like he told Hayden, the only person he wanted to be with was Sara.

"Where is Sara?" he asked John.

"Honestly, I have no idea."

Chris's muscles tightened. If he could have, he would have just gone to find her.

Amanda approached with Jean, putting him at ease.

"The last time I talked to her," Amanda said, "she was going to sleep."

John stood and, with one arm, helped Amanda sit down. Although she still had trouble bending, she seemed much improved since they'd left the refuge.

"She had a long night," Amanda said.

"A long night?" Lily said. "Where? How come? She

wasn't—"

"Is she all right?" Chris asked Amanda.

"Well..." Amanda shrugged. "She seemed tired, quiet, more or less how she was when I met her at the cave."

"After all she's done here," Jean said, "she looks great. All these days, she has been dealing with us, the valsings, the reisers, the camp...I think."

Chris nodded and smiled at Jean. She was right. According to what Donald, Hayden, and Charlie had told him, Sara had taken control of everything.

"See, John," Lily said, pointing a finger at him. "I was correct. You knew where she was!"

Jean sat by Charlie, and Chris remembered what Hayden had told him about her, which was still hard to believe. She looked out of place among all the soldiers. Part of him would have liked to watch her confronting Hayden.

"Are we waiting for Major Joseph?" Hayden said, more uncomfortable than Chris.

"No. Since Charlie is here, I'll have Major Joseph stay with the civilians, the injured ones, and the valsings who aren't fighting with us.

"Colonel Green?" Jean said. "I didn't recognize you. You look so—"

"Jean, it is a pleasure to see you again...and well."

For the first time that morning, Hayden smiled, turning Jean's cheeks red.

"And who is this?" Lily said, frowning. "What is she doing here?"

"Lily!" Donald said.

"Why is she here? What if—" Donald's look made Lily stop talking, which impressed Chris.

"This is Jean Walker," Chris said. "She had been negotiating with the reisers to keep my people and soldiers in the best possible shape during their time as prisoners." He looked at Jean. "I also heard you saved Hayden's life?"

Jean seemed to sink behind Charlie. He smiled at her in a way that confirmed Chris's suspicion from back when he'd left Tundra.

"And unlike you, she is here because I asked her to come. I'm sure you have an issue with that because you have a problem with everything and anyone, but with what you decide. Nevertheless, I'm pleased to remind you that since I survived, I am the one in charge."

Lily crossed her arms and looked away.

Chris turned his attention to the rest. "Is everyone familiar with the plan?"

"I explained it to Charlie," John said, "about going back to Tundra to intercept Hayden's squadron."

Charlie shook his head and rested his arms over his knees. "With all due respect, that not only sounds dangerous but...unlikely. I understand why the reisers may want to get rid of their leader, but as far as fighting with us...I'm not sure. I've walked with them, and we still aren't even at the level of acquaintances. Pretty sure they feel the same."

Chris turned to Hayden. "Is that correct?"

Hayden shook his head. "You can thank Sara for it. She talked to them last night, and...she has a way to make people change their ideas."

"Yes, she does," Chris said, smiling. "Will they stand with us?"

"Yes. They won't call you commander or anything, and... Sara promised them they were free to leave if they wanted to. So far, nobody has tried, but—"

"She is right," Chris said, making Charlie rub his face. "If they don't want to fight, they are free to go. They aren't our enemy."

Charlie crossed his arms.

"Do you trust me?" Chris said.

"Of course I do," Charlie said. "I just… I told you. You weren't his prisoner. You can't understand what we went through."

"I wasn't his prisoner, that's right. But deep down, you can imagine how, if they had been our prisoners, things would have been worse."

Jean put her hand on Charlie's back as he looked at the ground and nodded.

"There is more," Hayden said. "They informed me the squadron left Tundra already. Murllen sent for them a few days ago. I'm not even sure if we are still—"

"We have to try," Chris said.

Donald took out the map of Hune and calculated where the reisers could be. It was clear they'd have to leave immediately.

"If they've reached the swamps," Hayden said, "we'll have to find another plan. That is Murllen's territory. We better be ready for an ultimate battle when we step on that land."

"Look at the positive," John said. "We won't have to walk all the way to Tundra!"

FOR THE REST of the meeting, they focused on planning their next move and all the details they needed to figure out. Chris was very conscious of his army's condition. They might not be going to a battle, but the possibility of a confrontation was imminent, and those reisers were some of the best.

Not for the first time, he noticed how thin and tired Charlie looked, and though he didn't ask, the patch over his friend's eye gave him a good idea of what they had gone through.

"Are you out of your mind!" Lily said, turning from

Donald to Chris. "Do you realize how long it will take me to figure out how Liam's device works? Not to mention the time it will take me to fix it…or build another one?"

"Don't you pride yourself on your intelligence?" Hayden said. "I thought you might enjoy the challenge."

Lily groaned and turned back to Chris. "I am not stupid, but you do not understand what it takes to create something like that."

"Right," Chris said. "And I'm not expecting you to fix it or build a new by yourself. In case you haven't noticed, there are more valsings to help with that."

"That is your solution? What kind of leader are you? You are not even going with them!"

Chris moved forward, and a stabbing pressure in his side reminded him of how bad his injury was.

"I'm in a good mood, so I'll explain myself, something I don't usually do." He stared at Lily. "I won't jeopardize this mission by being a burden. The fact that I can't go bothers me to a point I'm sure your egocentricity doesn't allow you to understand. If I had even the slightest chance of making this work without your involvement, I'd take it, but Donald assured me you are my best bet on this matter."

Lily lifted her chin.

"Do not fail!" Chris sat back and frowned. "And I suggest you stop complaining and start working. Prove you are worth it, because, to me, you are a lot of talk and nothing else."

Lily stood and walked away from the group.

"She may be difficult," Donald said, rubbing his face, "but believe me, she is our best option." He exhaled. "I will make sure she works on it."

Donald followed Lily, and for a second, Chris felt bad about what he had said. After all, she had a tremendous responsibility for the mission.

"What about Sara?" John said. "Is she coming to remove Gemli's protection?"

Chris sighed. "I need to talk to her, but John, regardless of what she says, you are not going."

"Excuse me? I can't just stay—my arm is fine."

Amanda, at his side, shook her head. "Fine?"

"Before you two fight," Chris said, "let me finish."

They looked at him, and he said, "Amanda will take the front with Charlie."

John groaned and tried to throw his arms in the air, but he had to stop them midair. Swearing, he walked away.

Amanda stood and said to Chris, "May I?"

"Sure," he said. It wasn't a formal meeting; otherwise, John would have been in contempt. "Just be nice to him, please. This mortifies him, and I'll have to listen to his complaints here."

Amanda smiled and left.

"Nice commanding skill, Christopher," Hayden said, and to Chris's, surprise Charlie laughed out loud.

"You, too?" Chris said.

"The reiser has a point. Even I controlled them better."

Chris shook his head, but he let them mock him for a while. It was going to help in their near future.

"Hey, when you finish being an idiot," he said to Charlie, "can you help me here? I need to find Sara."

"Wouldn't it be easier to ask her to come?" Hayden said, and Charlie nodded, but when Chris got up, his friend moved to assist him.

"It'll be good for the people to see me. Alive and moving," he said, although he just wanted to find her.

While Charlie helped Chris down the hill by the camp, Chris was aware that his best friend was carrying most of his weight. Every uneven step was like hammering his back, and the skin around his wound burned and felt like it could rip apart at any second.

"At least you should have let me find her first," Charlie said. "It isn't an enormous camp, but for you, it's like crossing the desert."

"I did that before," Chris said, a little out of breath. "Besides, I know where she is. The far side of the camp, away from everyone, closer to the forest."

Charlie stopped and narrowed his eyes.

"What? She is there!"

As Charlie led them towards the woods, in a mocking tone, he asked, "Care to tell me what happened that brought this out of you, Chris?"

Chris chuckled, but he had to stop and touch his back while controlling his breathing again. "Care to tell me what happened to you after I left?"

"I wanted to talk to..." Charlie stopped walking. "You almost die, and now we don't have time to... It wasn't my intention... She didn't want to do anything until we talked to you. It didn't matter that you two were done. I agreed, but... things changed. Your horse showed up, we found the reisers in the desert, and...I couldn't allow more time to pass between us. But it was never my or her—our—purpose to—"

"What are you talking about?" Chris said.

"Jean! Who else would I be—"

"The patch on your face!" Chris puffed. "That happened after I left, too, right?"

Charlie shook his head and sighed. "I guess so, but—"

"It was you!" Chris said, clapping Charlie's arm. "Hayden was talking about you and Jean! The commander's fiancée. Wait, that was fast."

Charlie chuckled and scratched his head. "I guess, if Hayden said it, it must be true. Although, I should check with Jean before sending—"

"But why are you worried about it?"

"She was your fiancée." Charlie shrugged. "Like, for real, not because a reiser got it wrong, and I don't want you to—you two were done, correct? I mean, she told me she broke off the engagement before you left, but..."

Chris thought about joking, but Charlie's expression was almost painful.

"She was very clear about it. It hurt my pride, of course, but it was the right thing to do. I am happy for you, although she can get bossy."

"Hey! She is a sweetheart!"

Chris didn't answer.

In the distance, among the trees, Sara was sitting by a small creek. She had a book in her lap, but her gaze was lost in the water.

"You were wrong," Charlie said. "She is in the forest near the camp, not in the camp by the forest."

Chris didn't move, though. He just watched her for a moment.

Even from that far, it was obvious something was wrong. His chest tightened, and his jaw set. It seemed from the second he'd met her that her life had fallen apart. She might have been part of the war from the beginning, but he should have done more for her. For instance, he could have explained to her what she meant to him.

"Are you all right?" Charlie said.

Chris rubbed his face. "You have no idea how much I hurt her."

"Hey! I told you before. She almost killed me just for trying to help you."

Chris raised an eyebrow and frowned at him. "Um, I

thought you were trying to get rid of Hayden, who was trying to save my life."

Charlie waved his hand. "Details, just details, but...you cared about her."

Chris nodded and then glanced at his friend. "No, I don't just care about her, Charlie. I love her." He turned towards Sara. "I want her safe, away from all this madness, especially the next part, but...we have—I have no options." He pushed his hair back. "I'm asking because I hope she'll say no, but... she won't. And it is killing me, having to send her—"

"Hey," Charlie said, "we have been friends for years. At some point, I accepted your stupid idea of not caring for a future of your own, for not having a reason to fight. When you left Tundra, I thought your wish might just come true. I never imagined this would happen. You have my word. I'll do whatever is in my power to protect her." Charlie looked at Sara. "Let's just hope she lets me. I'm pretty sure she hates me."

~

SARA SLEPT LITTLE. Her dreams were full of happy moments being destroyed by the monsters in her life: Leonard killing Chris, Gemli slaughtering her father, and Murllen laughing at it all. However, the worst was when she did something to them. A shiver ran down her spine, and she shook her head to push the memory away.

She also wanted to forget what had happened to her dad. She realized he had died before the sun rose, when a tickle in her hands and strange but welcoming heat woke her up. It didn't last more than a few minutes, but it changed her.

Now her senses became more acute.

She distinguished sounds from hundreds of miles away, and if she wanted, the conversations by the camp would be easy to understand. The smells of fires and food around her were a combination of culinary aromas and dreadful odors that made her apprehensive about eating. The best part was the sensations in her hands as the wind, water, and ground sent pictures to her mind of places miles away.

But besides the waterfall running once again, nothing had changed in Hune. This made her wonder how long it would take for things to improve and how great Gemli's damage was.

"I'm sure you are wrong," Chris said, taking her away from her thoughts.

She looked back and found him standing with Charlie. In the last few days, she'd gotten used to the uniforms and weapons, so it got her attention that Chris wasn't wearing his. His shirt was loose and half-open, letting her see the bandage around his torso. He hadn't tied his boots all the way, and he was wearing a thick cloak over his shoulders.

Although his skin remained pale and couldn't stand without Charlie's help, a hint of healing was visible in his eyes, and his smile was a joyful one.

"You should be resting," she said without getting up.

"Sees, she bosses me around, too," Chris said to Charlie, who helped him sit down. He took a moment to catch his breath and then said to Sara, "I heard you met Charlie."

"I don't think we have been formally introduced," Charlie said, and for the first time, his gaze wasn't hard or accusatory.

"Well, in that case," Chris said, "Sara, this is my best friend, Charlie Abott. He may look and act like an idiot most of the time, but—"

"Hey!" Charlie gently pushed Chris. "You should stop after 'best friend.' Unless, of course, you are going to talk about my good looks and excellent sense of humor."

Chris pointed at Charlie. "Like I was saying, an idiot, but he is a great guy. You can always count on him."

Sara grinned while pushing her hair behind her ears. "I'm sure he is a wonderful friend of yours." She cleared her throat and looked at Charlie. "I apologize for being so rude when I met you. I'm sure you wanted the best for Chris, too, but…" She turned to the water. "Without Hayden, Chris would have died, and we didn't have time to explain a lot back then."

Chris put his hand on top of hers, and although her heartbeat sped up, she didn't look at him. There was only so much pain she could take. She needed nothing else to break her.

"I'm not sure what to say," Charlie said. "I mean, you were right, and I should be the one apologizing."

Sara shook her head. "No need for that." She turned to Charlie, using that as an excuse to move her hand away from Chris. "Being right doesn't matter. What is important is that you allowed us to help him. You've tolerated me for the past few days and remained open to new ideas, even when, by your rules, you were the one in charge. So, thank you for that."

"I told you she was amazing," Chris said.

"Oh, I was aware of that," Charlie said. "Sara and I go way back."

Sara narrowed her eyes.

"Really?" Chris said.

"Of course!" Charlie smirked. "Minutes before you took a break from working, she rescued me. Thank you for that, Sara. That wagon got too heavy too soon."

Before Sara could say anything else, Charlie stood.

"Anyway, I better get ready. You see, Sara, my commander is not a big fan of resting…except when it comes to himself."

He bowed his head at her and patted Chris's shoulder before walking away.

Chris watched his friend leave. "He is a good guy. You are going to love him. Wait." He turned to her. "Don't love him."

Sara chuckled. "I won't. I thought I should love John instead, but it turns out he married someone already."

"Hey! What about falling for the really handsome one?"

"Donald?" Sara put a hand over her heart. "That is mean, Chris. I know you don't like Lily very much, but she is my friend."

Chris shook his head and smiled, but after a couple of seconds, his expression darkened.

"I'm sure a lot happened since the last time we talked. And I'll understand if you don't want to talk to me about it, but…what is bothering you?"

Sara sat up and avoided his eyes. She forgot how he had a way of knowing things, but this time, she could say nothing. She would not let her father's sacrifice go in vain.

"All right, then," Chris said, "but I meant it before. You can trust me."

"It's not about trust, Chris." Before he could reply, she added, "And you aren't here to ask what is happening to me? Just tell me what you need. That'll make things easier."

Chris lowered his eyes and rubbed his face. "Sara, it's not… You saved my life, and everyone else's. Donald and Hayden told me what you have been doing, and…I'm not expecting that you—"

"It's my job to save Hune, too. How do you expect me to trust you if you don't want to see that? Just tell me what I need to do."

A deep silence fell between them, during which she avoided looking at him. It was hard enough to keep her tears back. The night before, when she had seen his eyes open, she had been a different person. Now who she had become was what he hated the most, not to mention Jean and all his additional responsibilities. He was right. A lot had happened, and it was worthless to talk about it anymore.

"What are you reading?"

Sara looked at her lap. Frowning, she patted the journal. "The book that Cielthos gave me."

"Did you learn how to—to remove Gemli's protection from it?"

"Um…" She shook her head and handed the book to him. "I learned a lot from it."

Chris opened it and turned the pages, but he didn't read them. He closed it while staring at her. "I'm not sure how to ask… You have done so much already, more than what I could have even imagined." He tried to move closer, but then he groaned and touched his side.

"Are you all right?" Sara reached for his wound to check it, but he grabbed her hand.

"Believe it or not, sometimes I listen, and I remember very well what you told me before we reached the Netherworld."

Sara felt her face warming up as she remembered the fight they'd had a lifetime ago.

"A reiser told Hayden his squadron left Tundra days ago. We have to move right away if we want to get them on our side."

"You need me to be there." A crazy idea made Sara shiver. "Please tell me you are not planning on leaving with—."

"No, I won't go, but…" He tightened his grip on her hand. "I have to break my promise, Sara."

She shook her head, but he slid closer. Her new senses perceived his scent, and warmth surrounded her, making her heartbeat pound so loud she feared he could hear it.

"I promised I wouldn't leave you. I understand why you believe I already broke my word, but I didn't. That time, you were safer with John and Donald than with me, and in a matter of days, you were going to be with me again." He rubbed her palm with his thumb. "I didn't trust Hayden then, and I wouldn't jeopardize your life around him. Now things are very different."

He looked down at their hands. "Without you, we have no chance to… I have to ask you to put your life in danger, and I won't—I can't—be close to you."

Sara swallowed hard and moved a few inches away from him.

"Why didn't you tell me you were leaving then?" But before he could answer, she shook her head. "There is no other way. You can't go, and you need to recover. I'll remove Gemli's spell, and I'll be fine." She grinned at him. "It is not like the zhortas never put my life in danger. Did you see those scaffolds?"

He tried to smile, but his concern didn't allow him to look sincere.

The movement of the soldiers getting ready and the valsings helping with the horses got her attention.

"We are leaving now?"

He looked at the ground and nodded. She had never seen him like that, not only weak but as if he were holding the weight of the world by himself.

She reached out and put her hand on his knee.

"Please don't worry about your promise. I understand." She leaned forward, looking for his eyes. "Besides, I'm glad you aren't coming. You need to get better. I don't want to go through what I did the last few days again. Never."

Chris grabbed her hand and kissed it. "You have no idea what sending you there means to me. You are—"

"Well, there you are, handsome!"

Chris looked exasperated at the valsing, and he squeezed Sara's hand for a second before letting her go.

"Cassandra. I had no idea you were here," he said in a bitter tone.

~

ALTHOUGH CASSANDRA HAD LIVED in the Soto Forest with her father, Sara had never crossed paths with her. The princess seemed to never step inside the abbey or wander around the trees.

"To the disappointment of many," Cassandra said, "I survived and found my way here…just to see you again." She tilted her head and stared at Sara. "I haven't seen those coats since…" She sighed. "You must be Sara."

"Nice to meet you, your—"

"Cassandra, please. Between you and me, there shouldn't be any titles."

Just like any other valsing, Cassandra looked Sara up and down. But unlike most, even Lily, her next comment differed from what Sara was used to.

"You are actually pretty. Not an overstatement by your friend. There must be some valsing blood in you." She giggled. "And I know your brain works well, too."

Chris shook his head, and his tone grew angrier. "What do you want, Cassandra?"

The princess moved her weight from one foot to the other and patted her mouth with the tip of her finger. "Nothing with you…at least, not right now, honey…or in that condition. I wish to have a word with Sara before she goes and will probably find her dead."

Sara laughed, but Chris didn't think it was funny. "You have nothing to say to—"

"What is it, Chris? You are sending this cute little human into battle against reisers but are afraid of a little girl talk? Is it the past you regret?"

Cassandra walked a few steps away and stopped with her arms crossed, staring at Sara.

Sara grew curious about what the princess wanted to say to her. She smiled at Chris and stood up, but he held her by the arm.

"You don't have to talk to her. She is an irritating, spoiled, and rude…woman."

"Are you concerned about what she is going to tell me?"

He started to shake his head, but then he stopped, nodded, and frowned at the ground.

"Chris, I'm aware of what happened between you two. I'm not dumb."

He tried to get up but couldn't, so, holding his side, he sat back.

"Chris." Sara knelt and, without permission, moved his cloak. "You need to be careful. It isn't just a cut that you got."

Chris touched the side of her face and looked into her eyes. "Sara, I'm not sure who told you what happened between us, but please believe me. If there is something I regret in my life, although I met you because of it, I would never—"

Sara slipped his hands down but kept looking at him.

"I don't need or want an explanation, Chris. No one told me anything. It wasn't hard to figure it out. Everyone was talking about what had happened. Back then, the valsings by the abbey and now…" She shrugged. "Yesterday Donald implied you had met her, and Charlie looked concerned. I just put things together. I would say it was peculiar timing in my life and yours."

Chris opened his mouth, but Sara covered it with her hand.

"No, your past is yours. I'll never judge you for it."

Behind them, by the camp, Sara recognized Jean walking

towards them with Charlie, and she stood. "She may want an explanation, though."

Sara would meet her one day, but using Chris's distraction and Cassandra's growing impatience, she jumped up the creek and walked to the princess. For a slight second, she was tempted to look back and smile at Chris, like she would have done before, but Jean was there, and she didn't need another painful image in her mind.

"Can you walk faster?" Cassandra said. "You need to go soon, and I need to...want to ask—talk—to you."

~

CASSANDRA DIDN'T WANT to hide the fact that she was talking to Sara.

She found a place where no one could overhear them, but they could see the camp getting ready to leave.

"I am sure your friends, especially Lily, have told you I am a terrible person," Cassandra said, "but I hope that what I heard about you is the truth and you will at least consider answering a question."

Sara sat down, and her expression reminded Cassandra of the peaceful nature of the zhortas, how their personalities were different than those of the valsings, humans, and even reisers. She took a deep breath and sat next to her, hoping not to betray the memory of the one she had loved—still loved.

"What I had heard about you," Sara said without looking at her, "isn't enough to define a person. Also, it's ornamented with details from many voices. As for your question..." She turned to her. "I'll do my best to answer it."

"Did you know Wilson?" Cassandra shook her head. "What am I saying? Of course, you did, but did you—"

"Zhorta Wilson?" Sara's face brightened, pinching

Cassandra's heart. "Yes, I did! He was a great Zhorta, smart and very kind. Always working on something and trying to help the older ones. Why do you ask?"

Cassandra's sight blurred, and her voice shook. "Did he love you?"

"I loved him because he was my family. He wasn't too much older than me." Sara chuckled. "I'm sure I annoyed him as if he were my brother, and he saw me as his little sister."

Cassandra felt a couple of tears escape her eyes. "Wilson told me you were special, and I…I thought it was his way of telling me he was in love with you."

Sara shook her head. "He had a secret. He never mentioned her name, but he was in love and not with me. Very peculiar for a zhorta, since we are supposed to leave our lives behind. You can imagine the gossip around the abbey if they had known."

"How did you know?"

"Well, I saw him once, writing a letter while humming. So, I harassed him until he told me he had fallen for someone. Once, he confessed to me he was going to leave the zhortas."

"Yes…" Cassandra sighed and looked into the distance.

Again, she wondered if she should ask about him, afraid to disturb his memory. However, her need to get closer to him in any possible way was bigger than the truth she protected.

"He asked me to go with him," she said, wiping her eyes. "He always suspected you were more than a child that Rafael had saved. He was not sure who you could be."

Sara tilted her head but didn't interrupt.

"You see, he wanted to protect you, to take you with us. I told him that if he loved you so much, he should stay with you."

Sara's eyes shone, and she looked away.

"Please, don't!" Cassandra said and held her hands. "It is not your fault. I was the one who used you as an excuse for being a coward. I chose to live as a princess instead of having a normal life with the man I love." She cleared her throat. "The abbey and that damn forest. Is it possible, just a slim chance, that they—he—could have escaped?"

Sara shook her head, and the pain in her eyes erased any hope Cassandra had left. She covered her mouth and cried. The warmth of Sara's hand rubbing her back only made her guilt pile up even more.

"Do you think he forgave me?"

"Wilson never stopped talking about you," Sara said. "He treasured your memory and love. He never talked bad about you...unless you count when he complained how hard it was to give you a compliment. Now I understand."

Cassandra chuckled and looked up at the bright morning sky. "Did you know Wilson was a reiser?"

Sara's eyes opened wide, and she shook her head.

"Amazing, right?" Cassandra said. "I was wandering by the desert, close to Andromeda. I left my escort, as I often did. I remember it was so hot. I sat for a while, waiting for the day to go by... My father...I hated his company. The wind picked up, and the sand moved around me. I couldn't see a thing, and when it stopped, I saw a few reisers lying on the ground."

Cassandra smiled. "I stood and ran, but I tripped over one of them. This one was different. Someone had broken his armor, and a hand was poking out underneath it. I thought it was a trapped human. My idea was to get the poor man out, but to my surprise, I pulled a reiser out of his armor."

"Why didn't you say something?" Sara said.

"Well, I tried, but who were we supposed to talk to? My parents? This was before Chris and his stupid guard crossed paths with us. And when they did, I would not give them Wilson."

Sara nodded. "So, I'm guessing you left him with the zhortas?"

"Yes, I did." Cassandra let some happy memories cross her mind. "He was a little too tall to pass for a valsing, and the zhortas were so oblivious of the world, but kind."

Sara laughed while standing up. "I have to go. I don't want to get in trouble with this group."

"Thank you, Sara."

"Thanks to you. It was nice talking about my family with someone."

Cassandra stood and hugged her. Now she understood why Wilson cared so much for "that little human," as he so often called her.

~

SOON AFTER THE soldiers left the camp, Chris entered his tent. He didn't want to worry anyone, but under his shirt, blood had stained the wraps around his waist, and the pain in his side made breathing difficult.

He sat on the coat and rested his head in his hands. The wise thing to do would be to sleep, but he knew it wouldn't happen. All their chances to stop Murllen were out of his reach, and he had never been good at letting others handle what was his responsibility.

Sara came to his mind, and he rubbed his eyes and groaned.

John had mentioned that she had changed a few times, and he had seen signs before, too. Still, he didn't want it to be real. He kept hoping that whatever the Great Wizard had passed on to her wouldn't go beyond finding her way around or looking for things.

After the passage, he had been so concerned with Leonard's presence and how she was talking to him that the magic had taken him by surprise and frightened him. Now he couldn't deny how much they needed her to finish the war, and protecting her would be almost impossible for him.

He also seemed to have lost her trust. He hoped it was just the confusion about Jean and the commander's fiancée, but he knew Sara. What was bothering her was beyond the stupid misunderstanding.

From the moment she'd tried to explain to him the reisers history, she had been right. He shook his head and smiled. She had the ability to make him act stupidly.

"What are you smiling at?" John said as he entered the tent.

"It's a bad sign, realizing you were right."

"I am always right! What are you talking about this time?"

Chris sat up, holding his side. "Well, I need to change ranks in our army."

"So, admiral for you?" John smirked, but after a second, he sighed, and his tone changed. "Did you really have to send her with them? She can't even walk or ride that fast yet."

The decision hadn't been an easy one, and Chris understood John all too well. Still, Amanda was one of the best soldiers, and she was in a better condition that many others, including John.

"You know she can do that and more."

Chris moved to the side and, by accident, allowed John to see his wraps.

"For the gods, Chris. That looks terrible."

"It's not that bad." But from John's expression, he knew it was worse than he had imagined.

"I better get Jean." John left the tent.

Only a few seconds had passed before Chris heard a very annoying voice.

"I can check you up if you want me to?" Cassandra said, walking towards him.

There was no doubt that she was a valsing. The arrogance and beauty, along with her posture and movements, were everything a human could expect from that race. She was also a little dangerous. She had her own ideas and didn't like to mess with them. In the past, it was her slight evilness that had convinced him to follow her plan.

The skin around his wound seemed to rip away from his muscles when he stood up. "What do you want?"

Casandra smiled. "Why are you so upset at me? It was you who lied to me."

"I lied to you? What are you talking about?"

She sat on his coat and took her time arranging her dress.

"You went to the abbey. You saw the zhortas, and you let them die."

Chris frowned. He'd forgotten the last time he had seen her. She'd also invaded his tent, but that was in the desert, when he'd met Donald and Queen Vanessa. She had asked about the zhortas, but back then, his idea of them was the one he'd learned during the war.

"I didn't lie. The plan changed, and we ended up at the abbey. And I didn't let them die, either."

She crossed her arms, and the peculiar light in her eyes softened her features. "You told me you wanted nothing to do with them. You hated them, with no right or reason, and now—"

"I… no, we had no option, Cassandra. If I had stayed, the reisers would have killed us, too."

"So, you saved your life? How heroic!"

She half-turned, and although Chris couldn't see her face, he could hear her crying.

He could have asked her why she hadn't sought her mother's help or helped the zhortas herself, but he didn't. She didn't need to explain her anger and tears; it was obvious to Chris that it involved a broken heart.

She cleared her throat and pushed her shoulders back before looking at him again.

"I know you owe me nothing. Our deal brought what each of us wanted it, but…" She closed her eyes and breathed a few times before continuing. "My father massacred my people. He murdered my mother and took me prisoner. He joined the bastards who attacked the abbey. Do you remember your original plan?"

Chris's muscles tensed as the memory came back to his mind. "You want me to kill your father?"

Cassandra shook her head, but the shadow that crossed her eyes didn't make Chris feel any better.

"No. I wish… I know you, and if you win this stupid war, you will catch him." She stood and took a step towards him. "I am asking you to keep him alive."

"That wouldn't be up to me," he said. "It's Donald's place to deal with—"

"Sure, let Donald run a trial or sentence him to wear mismatched outfits the rest of his life. I don't care. What I wanted is something only someone as good as you can do."

Chris narrowed his eyes and crossed his arms.

"You are a great warrior. Maybe not right now, but you are."

He shook his head, walked past her, and sat on the cot. "What do you think I can do?"

Cassandra knelt in front of him and put her hands on his knees. "I need you to make sure my father's life will have to depend on another's compassion. My compassion. That he becomes incapable of sustaining himself. That he learns how to beg and supplicate, because I want to teach him the real meaning of mercy."

Chris's principles and values conflicted with that. He

knew how to do it, but he wasn't planning on mutilating anyone. He wasn't even considering attacking Orson at that point.

"I understand why you… I can't make you live with that in your—"

She stood and stepped back. "Just so you know, Christopher, I am not out of my mind. I saw my father, and he was proud of what he had done; what he made all of them do." She took a deep breath. "I was correct when I asked you about the zhortas. I am not wrong now, either. Orson's plan has to extend beyond his stupid alliance with the reisers' leader."

"Cassie," Chris said, purposely using that name, "I get he is a monster and needs to be stopped, but I can't do that to you, to whoever's memory is so painful to you. I just—"

Cassandra covered her face and slowed her breathing. Behind her, John and Jean entered the tent, and they stopped the moment they saw her.

"Just keep it in mind," she said, and a shy smile stole part of her pain away. "We aren't that different, after all. We both fell for a zhorta."

ALLIANCE

The dark, cloud-filled night seemed dreadful without a moon. It was hard to hear above the hush of the wind and the tree branches hitting each other. Hayden didn't say it aloud, but he was almost out of hope. They'd traveled faster than he thought humans could, but still there were no signs of his squadron. If someone had asked, he would have bet his reisers had already reached the swamps, and he was certain Charlie and Amanda believed the same.

"Let's send a scouting group and see if they find anything," Charlie said, and he ordered two of his soldiers to go ahead. The rest dismounted for a moment.

"Is it possible something delayed them?" Charlie said to Hayden, "or that your sergeant wasn't that accurate on timing?"

Hayden frowned. His squadron wouldn't be late, but Paul might have been wrong.

Donald approached them. It was easy to distinguish the valsing since he was the loudest of all. "Are we staying here tonight?"

"I'm not sure yet," Charlie said.

"I do not get it," Donald said. "We need to have rules for when we are stopping to rest or just to fool around."

Charlie rolled his eyes. "I told you before. We are not fooling around. It's different when we are chasing the tail of a group than when we are trying to intercept the head. That one bites."

Donald shook his head and turned to Hayden. "Would you say your people are coming, or are we late?"

Hayden didn't answer.

Sara walked over to them with her boots in her hand. Charlie had asked her to stay with the back. He may have been right to do so; she didn't know how to fight. Still, Hayden would rather have had her with them.

The moment he looked closely at her, a knot formed in his gut, and it had nothing to do with his reisers. She seemed to have the same darkness and strange confidence he had seen in Gemli.

"Sara," Amanda said, "what is going on?"

"They are here," Sara said.

Charlie turned to face her. "What makes you say that?"

Hayden knew better than to ask such a stupid question. "How far away?" he said.

Sara knelt and touched the ground slowly and gently while closing her eyes. "It's hard to say... They are moving fast and silently... Half an hour, maybe less."

Hayden knew his reisers, and without a shred of doubt, he turned to Charlie and Amanda and said, "Quarter of an hour, less than a few miles from here."

Charlie narrowed his eyes, but Amanda nodded, which made Hayden smile.

"In that case, we need to get ready," Charlie said, and he gave the order.

When they'd left the camp, all had agreed that the best approach was an open one. Soldiers and valsings would remain visible to make clear that this was not an ambush. It would already be close to impossible to make his reisers stop and listen, but their slight chance would vanish if Major Dunstan suspected a trap.

"Sara," Hayden said, and he crouched next to her while she put on her boots. "I'm sure you need to do whatever you do, but an explosion will put Dunstan on edge. So, as soon as you finish, I need you to run and hide."

Amanda stood by them and touched Sara's back. "I'll cover you."

Sara grinned but in a way that made Hayden concerned. "You are not planning something stupid, right?" he asked.

She tilted her head. "Not stupid, but I'm sure I can make it work without an explosion. We don't need to scare your friends."

"Scare my friends? I didn't say they would get scared. I mean… Wait, why won't there be an explosion?"

She shrugged. "Leonard upset me the other day."

Hayden laughed, and Amanda shook her head and smiled. "Remind me not to be close to you when you are angry," he said.

Charlie approached them and looked at Sara for a moment. "Is there any way you can stay behind?" he asked her.

She turned to the road, and her joyful expression vanished. In the distance, the scouts were running back, giving a signal to Charlie. He turned, and without a word, the soldiers got ready.

Hayden took a deep breath and moved Sara behind him while Amanda stood at her side. It occurred to him that this was the first time in his life that he'd feared death, and ironically, it was because of his reisers. He leaned down and whispered so only Sara and maybe Amanda could hear him.

"No explosion, please."

She nodded and closed her eyes. If she hadn't been so close to him, he wouldn't have noticed the warm breeze crossing his arms and the beautiful smell of flowers surrounding him.

"It's done," Sara said.

It happened so fast that it took him a second to understand. Then he gave Donald the signal.

Lily walked behind Donald and set a small device on the ground. The silhouettes of the reisers appeared in the distance. Donald looked back at them, and his eyes were wide open, and his face was pale. Lily kept moving pieces in and out, but nothing seemed to happen.

The raisers' view cleared up, and the moment they saw the soldiers, they took their weapons out, ready to fight.

"Donald!" Lily screamed, and that was enough to set the reisers off.

"Major Dunstan!" Hayden yelled, gaining seconds as his old friend hesitated when he recognized his voice. "You won't attack your colonel."

From behind, he heard Sara moving towards Donald.

"Who the hell are you?" Dunstan said, slowing the squadron.

"I told you. I'm your colonel, Hayden Green, and you better follow my order. You don't want to mess up with me."

Dunstan laughed, which was what Hayden would have done in his place. "I see humans are in despair. Are you trying to personify us?"

Around him, Hayden heard the soldiers taking their swords out, getting ready to counterattack. He realized it would be a massacre. The one positive was that he wouldn't have to worry about telling Chris how the reisers killed Sara. He put his hand on the pommel of his sword and shook his head. It was ridiculous that he would die like Murllen wanted, by his best friend's hand.

"Lily, focus!" Sara said. "Tell me what it does."

Charlie strode over to her and picked her up.

"Stop!" Sara said. "I can fix this."

Hayden didn't hesitate and moved towards her.

"Let her go," he said to Charlie. "I'll never put her life in danger. I owe her my life. Believe me, if she says she can do something, she can."

Charlie stared at him, but he let Sara down.

"It won't work," Lily said. "I told Chris he should not rush me to… I am sorry. It is useless. I am useless."

Sara turned to Hayden and, holding his hand, closed her eyes. He didn't move away, and when he noticed how little her palm was, he wondered if he had been mistaken.

Dunstan moved his claw up, and the reiser squadron got into formation.

"This will be uncomfortable," Sara said to Hayden, "but I promise you, I don't want to kill you or them."

"It's not you who will—"

Hayden perceived a soft buzz, and the pressure in the atmosphere changed. Within seconds, it sounded as if someone was screaming at a high pitch inside his brain, and all the weight of the clouds and the trees was pushing him down.

His legs shook, and his eyes involuntarily shut. Around him, pieces of metal cracked, and heavy things thudded to the ground. His knees gave out, and he fell. He tried to concentrate, but nothing made sense until the only recognizable sounds were the screams.

In a second, everything stopped, the pain, the pressure, and the weird noises. Hayden opened his eyes and realized he was still holding Sara's hand. He let go immediately, afraid he had been grabbing her too tight.

"Sara." Hayden had to clear his throat. "Did I hurt…? What the hell? How did you…?"

"Here." Charlie offered him his hand, and although he didn't yell, it sounded like shouting to Hayden's sore mind.

Hayden stood and almost lost his balance. His knees were shaking, and he had to fight the need to throw up.

"Are you all right?" Charlie said, still holding his arm.

Only then did Hayden realize that the only sounds were confused voices and painful groans. He looked around to find the dark road and the wind still blowing, but no one had a sword in hand. The reisers' armor lay shattered in pieces, and the valsings and soldiers were helping them up.

"No!" Lily's scream echoed around them. "You killed him!"

Hayden had to look to find her, and when he saw her, she was kneeling over Donald. He clutched his abdomen, trying to stop the flow of blood that pooled around him.

"Lily," Donald said with a whisper.

Hayden didn't wait. In two steps, he was kneeling by the valsing, checking his wound. There wasn't much to do, though. A reiser's claw had cut half of his stomach open. In Donald's case, the poison wouldn't be a problem. He was going to die within minutes, if not seconds.

Lily stood, and though shaking, she grabbed a sword and took a step forward.

The reiser looked different without his armor. Then Hayden recognized Dunstan's eyes and part of the armor at his feet. He was leaning against a tree, holding his side, not moving and bleeding faster than Donald.

"Stop," Sara said, blocking Lily.

"This bastard killed Donald!" Lily said between sobs. "How can you protect him?"

"He is dying, too," Sara said.

"He is a monster!" Lily covered her mouth, and the sword fell from her hands as she crouched by Donald again.

Hayden didn't understand until he saw a small knife by

the fallen valsing. He had stabbed Dunstan, and if Hayden had to guess, the reiser had tried to stop them from using the device.

Lily turned to Sara. "You can do it.

Sara shook her head, which only made Lily raise her voice.

"Sara, use your power. Save him!"

"I can't—"

"Of course you can. You got rid of the protection and then defeated all of them. Save him. You have more power in you. It is possible. It has been written that sorcerers and wizards, or whatever the hell you are, can heal and save lives."

Charlie stepped closer to Sara. He knew what Hayden was thinking, and he got ready to grab Lily if it came to that.

"If that was real, don't you think I would have done that for Chris?"

Lily looked down at Donald, and her hand trembled when she tried to touch his. He smiled at her, and his eyes closed. Lily sobbed louder and looked back at Sara.

"No, you would not. You have always thought of being so righteous. That is why you let the zhortas die, even when you claimed they were your family."

"That's enough," Hayden said, grabbing Lily, which made her madder.

"You would not have saved Chris, like you never tried to understand the stupid prophecy. You owe Donald so much, and you do not care. I know you, Sara, and you are hiding something." Lily shook her head and frowned. "This is your fault. You should have been the one removing their armor. Then none of this would have happened. You killed both of them, and the zhortas, and almost let Chris—"

Sara's eyes turned black as her hands trembled while she

kept moving her fingers at her sides. “Shut up,” she said without needing to raise her voice.

Hayden hesitated, unsure if he should protect Lily instead of Sara or if he needed to protect everyone else from Sara. She had just told him the explosion had happened because she’d been mad, and back then, she hadn’t looked like she could scare Gemli.

“If someone could have avoided all of this, it was you, Lily,” Sara said, walking over to Dunstan. “But you preferred to run, figure it out by yourself, to prove how smarter than everyone else you are…just like you did with the device. Your fault.”

Sara knelt by Dunstan, and her tone changed. “Let me see.” She moved his hand from his side. More blood dripped out, and he gasped for air. She looked at him.

“His name is Dunstan,” Hayden said, unsure why his throat seemed so tight. “He is my friend.”

“Dunstan,” she said. “I need you to fight for a few more seconds. Don’t give up yet.”

She moved to Donald. “Get out of the way,” she said to Lily, and when the valsing shook her head, Sara jerked her hand up.

Just like when Gemli moved reisers, Lily flew a few feet away from Donald, and she screamed.

“Donald,” Sara said, touching his hand. “I need you to breathe…one more time.”

The wind stopped, and the atmosphere heated up until the air seemed to be thicker. The ground shook, and the branch where Dunstan had been leaning on fell while the dirt nearby turned black.

Hayden realized Donald wasn’t bleeding anymore, and his chest moved up and down with a steady rhythm. He turned and found Dunstan looking at his side, his eyes wide open, shaking.

Sara stood, and the storm and cold came back. She smiled at Dunstan and turned to Donald. "Are you all right?" she said, but he only nodded.

Without an effort, he sat up and touched his stomach. His fingers got lost inside his stained and ripped shirt, but he was whole and healthy.

"You saved him!" Lily said, and she tried to hug Sara.

"Do not touch me!" Sara said as she pulled her hood up. "And stay away from me. The gods lost two souls tonight. I'll be happy to send one to them."

Sara walked down the road, and she had no trouble passing the soldiers, valsings, and even the reisers.

"You think I should…?" Charlie said.

Hayden shook his head. But it was Amanda who spoke.

"I'm sure she needs…space. I'll check on her soon."

Donald was standing next to Hayden. There was no sign that minutes ago, he had been bleeding to death. Lily moved towards him and tried to hug him, but he stopped her.

"We need to talk," he said and walked into the forest, away from Sara.

"We should set up a camp," Charlie said, shaking his head. "What just happened? Amanda, are you sure she—Sara—will be all right? I can't lose her. Chris will kill me."

Hayden patted Charlie's shoulder. "It's great to see that you are always in control."

Charlie growled and walked towards his soldiers. Hayden crouched next to Dunstan.

"Are you really Hayden?" his friend asked.

"Yes, Major, you are talking to your colonel…and we have a lot to discuss."

Donald wasn't sure where he was going. The surrounding forest was unknown to him, but he needed to talk to Lily. He couldn't believe the things she had said to Sara. He might have been dying and missed some details, but the general conversation was clear. She had to stop pushing people to their limits, purposely hurting them.

Afterward, he would check on Sara. He didn't understand how he was alive and feeling so good. He wasn't even tired. However, what she had said about the gods losing souls worried him, as had the way she'd looked, just like Gemli.

"Donald, please," Lily said breathlessly from behind him.

"Why?" He turned and said in a raised voice, "Lily, why did you have to talk like that to her? To everyone!"

She wrapped her arms around herself and shook her head. The tracks of tears on her face made his heart sink. There was a misery in her he couldn't reach, and it was killing the person he loved.

"Why did you not ask for help to fix the device? Did you feel the need to prove something? Talk to me...please."

Of course, she didn't answer. Over the last few weeks, every time he'd asked what had happened to her, she'd pressed her lips together and looked away.

Donald threw his arms up and paced around.

The night they had arrived at the refuge seemed long ago, but he remembered her embrace. He'd wanted to stop time and hold her forever. However, the second he let her go, she was different.

Lily told him where she had been, about the attack on the valsings and how she had ended up at the refuge, stating everything as though they were facts that had no effect on her. After that, she'd only looked at him when it was necessary, and if he had to guess, she had tried to avoid him more often than not.

"I am sorry," she said, "but I told you—I warned you I was

different. Orson hurt… Everything changed. I am not an exception."

He didn't know what Orson had done to her, but he had a good idea. However, if she didn't let him help her, if she didn't want to heal, he could do nothing, and that was killing him.

He hated that it was his fault that she'd ended up in Orson's hands. She had sacrificed herself to save him. They'd forced her to run away from her community and witnessed a horrible massacre. He wasn't blind, either, and although he didn't mention it, he was aware of the scar on her face and was sure she had more over her body.

"Lily, I tried. I did, but I cannot—"

"I understand. You cannot stand me anymore. Like everyone."

"What?" Donald raised his voice. "I cannot… I have been trying to be with you since I found you! You do not want me here, though."

"Well, you made a great job of keeping me out of the plans and ideas. If Liam were alive, I would not be here. And even then, it was Chris who ordered me to come."

"Who do you think told Chris who to trust with the task? And thanks to your behavior, it was difficult to convince him."

"Well, I am sure you won't have that problem ever again. After this, Chris will just kick me out, and you will agree with him, which is fine. I have learned how to take care of myself."

Donald groaned and took a step back.

It was the first time he had seen her that vulnerable. Her tears left trails in the dirt on her face, her short curls fell loose and tangled, and her body kept trembling as she tried to stop crying.

"No, Lily, you have not taken care of yourself."

He cupped her face in his hands and rested his forehead on hers.

"You may know how to stay unharmed, but you are not protecting your heart and soul," he whispered. "Lily, I am losing you."

There was a time when Donald wouldn't have hesitated to kiss her. But now, even when she was so close, her arms stayed away from him, more ready to push him than hug him.

"Can you tell—no, you cannot," he said. "Every day I look at your scar, I long for the day I will make the bastard who did it pay."

Lily took a step back, but when she tried to turn, he grabbed her arm and pulled her closer.

"Every time I look at you, I witness how the girl I fell in love with is suffering."

"I told you I have changed. I am not the same."

Donald closed the small gap between them, making her stop. The warmth of her body so close to his made it hard to fight the desire to hold her in his arms.

"I am sure you have changed. I did, too. But…" He moved his hands away from her arms and held his breath, staying as close as possible. "Is this the person you want to be? You do not have to fight everyone. You do not have to keep your guard up and expect everyone to be against you. I am not, and I won't hurt you." He sighed when she looked at the ground. "I am sorry I put you in danger. I should have known better, but…if you let me, I will give my life for you."

She looked up at him. "Is that what you were doing?"

Donald nodded, remembering how it had all happened.

Lily had been closer to the road. The second the reisers moved, Donald jumped up and pushed her to the other side. The reiser at the front saw him and walked towards them. He saw a blade on the ground and picked it up at the same time the reiser raised his sword.

The ground shook, and metal pieces cracked. The reiser lost his sword but moved his claw up, so Donald raised the knife. Everything seemed blurry after that. He felt his weapon digging through the reiser and his abdomen on fire. He'd fallen and watched his blood stain his shirt.

"You tried to protect me?"

There was fear in her eyes, which Donald didn't understand, but it was better than her silence.

"Yes, Lily. And if I must do it again, even if Sara does not save me, I won't hesitate." He reached over and brushed the top of her fingers with his. "I am begging you. Please, I will not force you to talk or stay with me, even when it breaks my soul apart. All I am asking you is to at least believe how much I love you."

Lily remained standing in front of him, her arms locked at her sides and with the same expression he had such a hard time reading—or maybe didn't want to understand.

Donald's shoulders dropped as he exhaled and looked down. There were scars in her heart and soul that he could never heal, although he would die trying. He just needed to find a way through them.

Lily took a small step forward and reached his hand, but then she stopped herself. He didn't need more than that, and without hesitating, he took her hand in his, kissed it, pulled her closer, and hugged her tightly.

"I love you, Lily. Please do not forget that."

Lily turned to the side, avoiding his eyes.

"I am so angry. It is all my… I should not…"

He kissed her head, but whatever he was going to say got lost in his mind when she looked up at him.

"I could have killed him." She sat on the ground, and he sat facing her. "All those deaths… I could just…"

Donald put his arms around her, and he exhaled when he felt her head resting on his shoulder.

"It crossed my mind…after he sent the valsings away and it was only me." Lily shivered, and his blood heated. "I knocked him down, but—"

"That is my girl," Donald said in her ear.

"He was there, unconscious and alone. I hate him enough… I did not even care if the others killed me after. They had already condemned me."

Queen Vanessa's death came to his mind, and for the first time, he thought she deserved it. One day, he hoped Orson would pay, too, but by his hand.

"If I had done it, if I had killed him, all those valsings and the queen would be alive." She hid her face against his shoulder. "I think I hate myself, Donald. I have committed many mistakes, and now…I cannot live with—"

"Lily, no." He cupped her face and made her look at him. "I need you to listen to me. Although that freaking bastard deserves to die, killing Orson back then would have been a mistake." She shook her head but didn't interrupt him. "That crime would have crushed you, and Murllen would have killed the queen and the others after. What about the soldiers at the refuge? Who would have helped them? Or the valsings, as a matter of fact?"

"I never thought…" She rested on his shoulder again, only this time, she wasn't crying. He was about to put his arm around her when she sat up. "But now I have failed. The device did not work, and Sara—what happened to her… I mean, I know I hurt her, but she scared me."

Lily moved away and hugged her knees. "I wanted to help, but Liam…he was wickedly smart. I could not figure it out, and…I never asked… Gods, Sara is right! And it is my fault. Again."

"Please do not think—"

"I almost lost you, Donald. I did not mean to yell at her like that, but I—I cannot live knowing you are not…."

He knelt in front of her and kissed her forehead. "I know Sara. I am sure she will understand."

Lily whispered as her face became wet, "She is my whole family, and I am about to lose her."

"Lily, she will forgive you."

She shook her head. "I do not believe I have the time for that. Have you not realized it? All that power, all that magic…it will destroy the curse and free the saber, but she won't survive it."

He sat on his heels, frowning.

"She has no way out of this. She knows it, too."

He pulled her into his arms, but he couldn't argue.

It hadn't crossed his mind before, but she might be right. There was not enough information about the curse and what would happen to Sara or Chris. He might not survive, either.

"For the sake of everyone, let's keep this to ourselves. I still have the parchments and books that Sara brought from the abbey. We will find something."

He grabbed the back of her head and ran his fingers through her hair. "And Lily, I would appreciate it if you considered me part of your family, too."

He wasn't expecting her to kiss him then, and he barely had time to move his arm behind him to slow their fall, but once they were lying on the ground, he pulled her close. In response, she held him tighter and allowed him to kiss her.

Too soon, she moved back and said breathlessly. "I love you so much, and I am so sorry—"

Donald didn't let her finish before eagerly kissing her.

THE PRISONERS

Knowing the reiser had murdered the human commander and their stupid king, Leonard, should have made Murllen's day. However, the circumstances were far from ideal, and he only believed it had happened because the reiser had brought Leonard's half-rotten head with him.

The information forced him to call a meeting of all the high-ranking reisers, an inconvenience.

"With all due respect, General," a reiser colonel said, "we need to consider the possibility that this a deception by the sorcerer."

Murllen stared at the reiser holding Leonard's head and ignored the question.

"Can you imagine how long I waited to kill this human?"

The reiser shifted his weight and moved the head away from him.

"Decades!" Murllen smirked. "This moment should have been memorable, one of the happiest ones of my life—our lives—and now...you've ruined it."

Murllen walked to the window and stared at the asylum.

"If what you say is true, you also executed the other

human I was looking forward to meeting." He turned. "What would you do about it?"

The reiser looked at everyone but at Murllen. He had seemed so proud when he'd reported killing those two, and now he couldn't stop trembling and mumbling. Murllen's anger rose, but he had more questions.

"Enlighten us with your story one more time, and please—"

The chamber doors flew open and crashed against the wall behind them. Gemli smiled at them from its frame.

"Yes, tell us again what happened, and do not spare any detail."

Murllen did his best to smile, but he also wondered about Gemli's involvement.

A few days ago, Gemli had killed the Great Wizard, or so he claimed. This surprised Murllen, since he remembered that the wizard had disappeared years before the war, even before he'd joined Gemli's plan.

The sorcerer had also informed him that before dying, the old man had restored Laconia's waterfall, which had weakened his power. But with time, Gemli would regain his strength and destroy the waterfall for good. Something Murllen had a hard time believing.

"Did you really have to destroy my doors?" he said, trying to sound normal.

"I didn't want to miss this." Gemli stepped into the room.

"Well, you shouldn't be late, then." Murllen turned to the others. "Everyone but this…informant, out of my chambers."

Unlike with humans, there were no arguments or questions. The reisers believed their leader's purpose was to look out for their well-being. Murllen pitied them and wondered how many other leaders had actually acted under that philosophy.

In silence, he waited for them to leave. Then he said, "You

were marching with the prisoners by the Northern Forest. Then what?"

The reiser looked afraid, and when he talked, his voice sounded reluctant, which seemed ridiculous, considering his size.

"I wasn't at the front of the line, General, but I heard the human king talking with someone. Then there was an explosion."

Gemli faced the reiser. It didn't matter how much taller and stronger the reiser was; the sorcerer had the advantage of fear on his side. "Now, tell me. What, exactly, did the explosion sound like?"

The reiser looked at Murllen, who shrugged. "Answer the guy. He knows what is important."

"Did it come from the ground? Was there a brilliant light? How much smoke surrounded you?" Gemli asked.

Murllen noticed with interest that Gemli didn't use his power to read the poor reiser's mind.

"I think…it seemed to come from the trees…and there was a light, and then the ground moved. We—most of us—lost our balance and fell."

Gemli chuckled. "Brilliant!" He turned to Murllen. "Nothing to be concerned about here."

"Of course not." Murllen hit the table. "The humans killed half of my squadron, recovered their first guard, and saved the Tundra's survivors! Why should I be worried about it?"

Gemli's smile grew wider. "Well, that's all very inconvenient and unfortunate, but they just got lucky."

"I wish I had that luck," Murllen said, but Gemli ignored him and turned his attention back to the reiser.

"Tell me what happened after."

The reiser kept his eyes down and spoke slower, carefully choosing his words.

"I was closer to the trees when the explosion happened. A

tree branch knocked me down for a couple of seconds. When I woke up, humans were running around, their soldiers were attacking us, and... reisers—pieces of them—lay everywhere."

Murllen had heard the description before and hated it. If someone was going to slaughter his adoptive race, it should be him. Whoever had taken charge of the humans had a sanguinary taste like him.

"Interesting," Gemli said. "And then what?"

"The human commander ran after their king, and I followed him. By the time I caught up with him, he had Leonard. He killed the king and charged me."

Murllen sat forward and looked at Gemli. They didn't need to discuss it. He was lying.

"That's unimportant, irrelevant," Gemli said.

"Irrelevant? He may be hiding something important." Murllen turned to the reiser. "He murdered his king, you killed him, and...no one followed you? That's strange."

The reiser stepped back.

"Did it occur to you that you should have claimed the battle and the war? The two humans in charge of their race had died." Murllen lowered his tone. "Why did you leave?"

"General, I didn't think. I have no idea. The soldiers were killing all of us. You needed to—"

"Tell me the truth!"

Murllen smashed the table and stood. Startled, the reiser dropped the head, and it rolled to Gemli's feet.

"General...the commander didn't hear me approaching. I cut his back." The reiser raised his voice and looked at Murllen. "The humans slaughtered our race. He was responsible. I was in a rage—it was dumb. I should have brought him to you, but I just...I couldn't spare his life."

Murllen pointed at the head on the ground.

"The human king," the reiser said. "That bastard had been

a problem since we trapped them. It was his fault that we lost Colonel Green. He ordered me to give him my sword, but…I would take none of his orders. I killed him and brought you his head."

Gemli stared at Leonard's head. "You cut it off after you killed him?"

Murllen put his claw on his forehead. "Aren't you listening? This poor guy went through a lot, and you are concerned about when Leonard lost his head?"

Gemli grinned. "I'm curious. How did you kill him?"

Murllen looked back at the reiser and waited.

"I picked him up by his head and ripped it off."

Murllen smiled. Leonard deserved more suffering, but having him die the same way a farmer would kill his dinner was amusing.

"And then what happened?"

The reiser's hesitation took the smile away. "Along with the humans…there was a sort of sorcerer. She created the explosion. I saw her running towards me." He lowered his eyes. "I escaped so I could inform you of this."

Murllen's concern grew. In their plans, his niece did not have powers. She was just cursed.

"It's so sweet!" Gemli said, using his feet to play with the head on the floor. "Murllen, she wasn't running to this idiot. She was rushing to the commander's body."

Murllen's joy returned, and a hint of nostalgia with it. Love was a beautiful thing that made humans suffer more. Now he had learned his niece had a very strong weakness.

"Captain," he said. "You witnessed a horrible incident. I give you my word they will pay for it."

The reiser stood taller and nodded, but then Murllen grabbed him by the neck and pushed him against the wall.

"Nevertheless, your cowardice and lack of judgment are a hazard to our race."

He pushed his claw through the reiser's neck, and both head and body tumbled to the ground.

"Do you want this one, too?" he said to Gemli.

"Did you really have to make such a mess?"

The sorcerer picked up Leonard's head and stared at it. "This one is different. There is a special power in the fear of dying. You didn't frighten him. I assumed you like torture."

Murllen kicked the reiser's head away. "Let's talk. What the hell happened? I understood Sara wouldn't be a problem, and now this?"

Gemli kissed Leonard's cheek, making Murllen groan.

"I can't decide what is worse, Gemli, you kissing that rotten thing or that you just kissed Leonard's remains."

Gemli walked to the window. "Leonard was a friend. I can only wish him an afterlife full of...discoveries."

Murllen shivered. The last thing he wanted to believe was that Gemli had some kind of claim over death.

"As for your question, like I told you, pure luck! Did you notice where they were ambushed? Right by the Netherworld. There, the foundations of Hune are too powerful. Think about it. Sara met Cielthos, and he talked to her. Now she believes herself to be some sort of sorcerer, which she is...at a low level."

Murllen shook his head, but Gemli continued. "She either tried to protect the soldiers or blocked my spell. Either way, it was Hune who made the explosion. The balance in such a powerful place is very delicate. Anything can trigger it. It was the Netherworld that stabilized everything."

The sorcerer sat down and examined the head in his lap.

"The important thing is that she is mourning her loved one. She will either want revenge or be devastated." Gemli looked at Murllen. "Also, without Christopher, it's going to be harder to free the sword. It'll give you more time to bond with your niece."

Murllen sighed. After all, the death of his enemy wasn't bad, and Leonard being gone was a relief. He stared at the asylum. "I guess I'm in the mood for a visit. It's time for me to introduce our prisoners to one another."

He walked to the now-destroyed doors and shook his head at them.

"I'm not that weak, Murllen," Gemli said.

A force grabbed Murllen and pushed him against the wall. The air became too heavy for him to breathe, and he felt as though his arms and legs were being ripped off.

"Like I was saying, there is a hidden power in the fear of death."

Murllen collapsed to the floor. Slowly he stood and filled his lungs again. The sorcerer walked past him, and from the hallway, he yelled back, "Enjoy your toys. I will surely enjoy mine."

Then he left, holding the head between his arms and brushing its hair.

~

WHEN MURLLEN STEPPED inside the chamber at the top of the tower where he held Rafael, he found Orson practicing his new skills. The brief time the valsing had spent there had taught him a lot. The little guy's cruelty impressed Murllen, although it was also concerning. Orson was a lunatic, and that always made him a risk.

"For the gods! What are you working on?"

"Murllen!" The valsing smirked and took two steps away from a body hanging upside down. "I miss you! I was getting worried about you. Is everything all right?"

Murllen paced around Orson's victim and whistled, nodding at the job. "One of the ones who lost your daughter?"

"Exactly."

The valsing was a mess of body fluids and stained clothes. Orson had even shaved the guy's head, a sort of torture for that race.

"Well, I'm sure he will think twice before attacking an innocent woman in the woods."

Murllen turned to his own prisoner. At the other side of the chamber, Rafael was still alive, although he looked nothing like the day he arrived, and back then, he hadn't looked that good, either.

He had severe dark circles under his eyes, and his face had slimmed down, making the skull behind his skin easy to visualize. His hair, whiter than gray, hung below his shoulders and he had grown a thick beard. Bruises and scars covered him, and he would never be able to get up on his feet again.

"Well, I guess one of my guards gave you a cape so you don't disgust us with your presence."

Rafael didn't even try to look up at him.

"Not interested in talking to us?" Murllen crouched so he was at eye level with Rafael. "Disappointing. I want to introduce you to a lady."

Orson approached him. "A woman? What do you have in mind?"

"Nothing sick, you pervert!" Murllen said, chuckling. Orson smiled and blushed.

The tower below was filled with screams. A moment later, they moved up the stairs.

"Like I told you, Rafael. A lady."

Not too long after, a reiser showed up holding Alleta Riddley.

"Very well! Just leave her by this…hanging fellow here. I'm so glad you are looking much better."

"Where is Genevieve? What did you do to her?"

Murllen touched his chest. "Well, well. Look at this. My reisers worry you?" He turned to Orson. "My dear friend, I have some business to work here. I hope you don't mind?"

Orson froze for a second and then shook his head. "Do you want me to leave?"

Murllen just smiled.

"Oh. I apologize. Of course, Murllen." Orson walked towards the stairs. "I am disappointed, though. I was looking forward to seeing you in action."

Murllen laughed and put his claw on the king's shoulder. "Do not worry, Orson. I will have a blast telling you everything over dinner later."

Then he ordered his reiser to take Orson's victim down and bring him back to the dungeon. Once they had left, he closed the door to his favorite room in the fortress.

He took his time approaching Alleta and Rafael, enjoying the sickness and dread on her face as she stared at the zhorta, who was oblivious to her presence. Murllen grabbed a chair and made sure it scraped the stone floor, making a high pitch sound.

"It's so nice to have you both here. I have delicate news to share with you." He sat down and leaned forward. "I guess I should introduce you first since, under other circumstances, we could have been a happy family."

Alleta looked at him, her eyes full of hate.

"I'm thrilled about this. I just learned my sweet niece is in love!"

Rafael looked up, and in a harsh voice that startled Alleta, he said, "Leave Sara alone!"

Murllen shook his head and giggled. "Like you can do anything about it." He stopped. "But wait a second. You taught her about being careful with boys, right? I mean, the human commander's reputation with women precedes him."

Alleta lunged at him, but he just pushed her against the wall.

"Oh, no! Did I hurt your maternal feelings? I've never quite understood that. I don't think my mother would defend me if she were alive. My father certainly didn't." He shook his head. "Never mind that. Like I was saying, the commander's reputation with girls is not the best. Alleta, I guess we can question your parenting skills."

He lowered his voice to a whisper. "Remember the poor guy who was hanging here? He witnessed how your child broke his friend's nose, and the valsing was only defending the honor of a girl your son played with one night. And I know she wasn't the only one!"

Alleta looked away, but Murllen saw shame in her eyes.

"Anyway, back to the romance, which I'm not sure is reciprocated. Irrelevant detail, though. Like I said, we almost became a family." He touched Alleta's shoulder, and she pushed away from him. "You lied to me, but I forgave you. I knew it then, and I confirmed it now. As a loving mother, you had to defend your stupid and dishonorable son."

He paused, letting the notion sink into Alleta's mind. "I know he is dead."

Her eyes filled with tears, but she refused to cry. Shaking her head, she yelled at Murllen, "You are lying!"

"Oh! I'm not. Why would I do that when the truth is worse than a lie? However..." He touched his chest. "It's a loss for me as well. I won't have the chance to see you two reunited. One of my faithful reisers killed him in a field, along with Leonard."

"That is not possible," Rafael said. "You wouldn't have allowed it!"

"Even you knew that! I'd rather have done it myself, but what's done is done, and both are dead. And...Rafael, Sara is heartbroken...looking for my...consolation, I guess?"

Rafael tried to stand, but his legs twisted, and he screamed.

"Oh, Rafael! Haven't you figured it out? You can't walk anymore. Maybe you are in too much pain to have noticed it." Murllen smirked. "But you can creep like the snake you are. Do you want to see if there is mercy in my little niece?"

Murllen turned to Alleta, ignoring Rafael's vain threats. "My dear Alleta, since I won't have the chance to enjoy the company of your son…" He sighed and moved closer to her. "We'll have a party for two."

~

One thing Murllen enjoyed the most was the stubbornness of certain humans, and Alleta was one of them. He knew now how much he would enjoy spending time in her company. The woman was strong and fought his tortures.

"I'm guessing the screams around the fortress paid off after all," Gemli said. "You looked thrilled."

"And I suppose you are going to change that?"

Gemli's face shone as he walked with him. "Well, that depends on your point of view."

"So, what is it?"

"Um…I think we should bring our oldest prisoner to embellish the next battle."

Murllen stopped and made sure no one was around. "Who are you talking about?"

Although the dungeons were full, the captives there were new. The ones they had taken when the war started were now dead, and they had stopped taking prisoners for years. They had murdered the human royalty and the members of the High Council, and aside from Rafael, no zhortas were still alive.

"Don't worry, Murllen, I won't touch your toys," Gemli said, making the hairs on Murllen's arms stand up.

"So, who is it?"

Gemli's pupils looked to be on fire, and Murllen waited for the darkness to drown him, but then he saw shades and figures in the sorcerer's eyes.

"The Great Wizard had good friends that I tricked into siding with me. I'm sure you will enjoy our new ally's power."

Gemli passed the protective wall and walked into the swamp outside the fortress. "Are you coming?" he said, looking back at Murllen. "Or are you scared to come out into the world?"

Murllen frowned. It wasn't the world he was afraid of.

"Oh, come on!" Gemli smiled. "Do not ruin my fun now!"

Murllen groaned but followed the sorcerer until he found himself standing in the middle of the swamp. The fortress was barely visible behind them. The mud was almost as high as his thighs, and the smell of putrefaction was strong, nauseating him even through his armor.

"Right before we started all of this," Gemli said, "I thought we could use an extra hand one day." He pointed into the darkness near the trees in front of them. "I tricked him into protecting me. Although it is true that to keep the balance of Hune, you need a sorcerer."

Murllen narrowed his eyes and crossed his arms.

"It's necessary to have someone capable of manipulating the magic of our land. Otherwise, Hune would destroy everything."

"Isn't that why you never killed Cielthos?"

Murllen fell in the mud, and the familiar lack of air and burning sensation reached his lungs.

"I told you not to mention it."

As soon as Gemli let him go, he jumped out of the mud and took a deep, painful breath.

"I won't kill you," Gemli said softly, "even though I know you chose to betray my confidence and friendship with Orson."

Murllen ignored the comment and moved toward the trees. "Should I guess who this is, or do I need to introduce myself?"

"No. Just as you enjoyed watching Alleta's pain, I want to see your reaction to this sight."

Murllen threw his arms up, but then he saw it, and he couldn't stop the wide smile that most likely made him look stupid.

"Well, well...welcome to my fortress."

~

For days, Genevieve had walked south to where, she had learned long ago, the swamps collided with the Northern Forest, that dreadful part of Hune.

She hadn't eaten since Gemli had left her outside the fortress. Her arms and legs felt heavy, but she was still able to move. The little sleep she'd gotten had been full of nightmares that had woken her with a start. Her thirst was intolerable, and she couldn't stop herself from drinking, even when she knew the water was mostly mud. Every time, the pain afterward forced her to lie down for hours.

She hadn't understood Gemli's curse then, but now it was clear. Death seemed like a peaceful end to her suffering. Her dead baby would keep poisoning her until she saved her race, because the last thing she would do was find Hayden.

Things had changed, though.

As the days passed, Genevieve felt more tired and less angry. The pain in her body was more present than the one of losing her little one, and she believed it had been for the best. She missed the tiny kicks in her belly and kept crying for the infant, but that was easier than witnessing her baby's life as a reiser. She wouldn't have been able to protect the little one from Murllen or Gemli.

Her mind seemed to play with her as well.

When she was conscious, she understood that Hayden would be the one to end her life. A pain in her chest made her wish she could stay alive with him. In her dreams, she kept seeing him saving her, not because he was their rightful leader but because he wanted to be with her, too.

Alleta had tried to explain what love was, and Genevieve wondered if that was what she felt. It was stupid, considering what her life would have been, but it was a pleasant distraction that helped her go on. At least until something inside made her bend in pain or the surrounding reality brought her back from her thoughts.

Her steps became easier. Looking down, she realized the mud was lower; it only covered the tops of her feet. The air smelled cleaner, more like plants than mud, but it was cold, and she shivered in her wet clothes. This woke a new pain in her stomach, one she couldn't handle, and she collapsed.

The sun was still visible on the horizon when she got up.

As she adjusted her eyes, she saw a line of trees marking the end of the swamp. They were far away, and in her condition, it would take a whole day or two to reach them. She rubbed her face and focused again. Then she noticed the strange trail of smoke drifting in the sky.

She covered her mouth and, for the first time since Gemli and Murllen's assault, cried from happiness. Although she didn't know who was camping or how far away they were, it didn't matter. The sight of their smoke gave her the strength to keep walking and reinforced her decision to save her race.

~

SILVER LINING

Although everyone was tired, only a few got a good night's sleep, and as soon as the sun was up, they were ready to leave. The storm had worsened overnight, and rain had poured down on them. Hayden had never been so thankful for the valsings stuff before. There was no question how much better their equipment was.

"How are you doing?" Amanda said, moving her horse to his side. "How are they doing?

Hayden looked at the group behind him again. Unlike the ones by the camp, these reisers had learned the truth from him and were ready to attack Murllen. Still, he'd told them Chris would have to answer some of their questions.

"All is good," he said, "by a miracle, but good."

Amanda nodded. "I talked to her last night. She wasn't… I saw her before, by the camp." She shook her head. "Sara vanished into the air and left for a while. When she came back, she was… I'm not sure how to explain it."

"She looks the same," he said. "You are looking at her differently."

Amanda chuckled and remained quiet for a moment. "That's a deep thought, Hayden."

"Here is another one. Do you still want to talk?"

She let her eyes focus on the distance. "I do, but..." She sighed, and he had to move closer to hear her.

"You said I saved your life, but...why did you do it? In the cave. Why did you—"

"Donald said you would die, and Chris put his sword in the fire. I'm not an expert on humans." He chuckled, but when she didn't smile, he said, "I was the best one to do it."

"Because of how you did it or...?"

"Both." Hayden cleared his throat. "I was as good as dead. You told me how much you'd fought for your leg. If you were to survive, you were going to need those three. Who cares if you abhor me?"

He looked down, and a strange heaviness pressed against his chest. "Do you hate me for it?"

She reached out and touched his hand. "No. And I'm glad you survived, too, but...I asked because, if it wasn't for Sara... Your armor, did you...?"

He shook his head. "I had no idea the poison would—"

The image of a smiling woman with curly hair like Amanda's but dark red flashed in his mind.

"Are you all right?" Amanda said.

Hayden shook his head, but the sensation he had forgotten something important rushed back to him. It had followed him during the last mission, when they'd taken the humans prisoner. This time, it seemed stronger.

"I don't... I'm fine." He looked at her and shook his head. "I knew what I was doing, Amanda. And all of this"—he waved at everything around them—"it was your idea. You were right. It was worth a shot, with or without me."

Amanda's face turned red, and she looked down. "Well, I'm glad it worked out and that you are here, too."

Hayden laughed. "I'm happy about that, too."

"Why did you save me the first time?"

The question took away the light humor. The woman's face returned, this time in more detail—too many for not being real. She had freckles on the top of her nose and cheeks, her eyes shone, and her hands were soft and gentle.

"You remind me of someone," he said, "someone I'm remembering."

Amanda touched his hand, and only then did he realize that he had stopped riding and the group was ahead of them.

"Is she all right?"

Hayden's heart sped up. He rubbed his face and stared at her, shaking his head. "But I don't know who she is or where to find her."

"That's easy."

He frowned. "How is that—"

"She has to be a reiser, and she is at the fortress."

He felt a knot in his stomach as his muscles tensed. She was right. Still, he didn't remember who the woman was, and he hoped Murllen didn't either.

"Hey, if someone can save her, it's you," Amanda said. "I'm sure of it."

~

CHARLIE LEFT the front of the line and moved back, looking for Sara. He had listened to Amanda and given Sara space, but now he needed to talk to her to make sure she was fine. He owed it to Chris.

Most of the reisers and soldiers were ahead of him when he found her. She was riding as close to the trees as possible, hiding under her hood. He had never seen a zhorta before, but if they looked like her, he was certain that he had been wrong about them all those years. There was no danger in her.

He made sure she noticed him approaching before riding up next to her.

"Good morning...Cap—no. Commander?"

"Just Charlie...or should I call you Zhorta Sara?"

Sara giggled, and Charlie exhaled with relief.

"No one has ever called me that, Charlie."

He rode in silence, unsure of how to talk to her. They'd started on the wrong foot, and that had improved little.

"How...is the ride so far?"

She petted the horse and pulled her hood down. "It's not bad. I suppose my relationship with Mulsh is growing, and I won't fall asleep on him."

"Um, I guess that's good?"

She looked at him. He was glad to see her blue eyes instead of the strange black from the day before. They still had some dark lines that he could swear had increased, but he wasn't certain. Chris would know, though.

"Interesting," she said, returning her gaze to the road.

"What's interesting?"

She shrugged and shook her head. "You taking John's place."

"What?" Charlie shook his head, but he understood what she meant. He changed the topic. "Did Chris tell you how we met?"

"I don't think so."

He smirked and sat taller, making sure she noticed. "Of course he didn't. He was such a lousy boy. He is embarrassed by it.

Sara chuckled, and it seemed to him she looked less concerned.

"So, my parents sent me to the training camp to somehow become useful to our race."

"You didn't want to go?"

Charlie tapped his lip with his fingers a few times. "Not exactly. You see, I wanted to help my people, but I wasn't sure about the fighting part. My family was certain of it, though."

Sara tilted her head and nodded. "I guess it was a way to save your life."

Understanding dawned on Charlie. "I never saw it like that. I assumed they wanted me out of their… I like this thinking more."

"Yep, parents do what they can to protect their kids… even when it is strange and confusing."

She wasn't only talking about his parents, but he didn't want to ask. Nothing good would have happened if she'd ended up in the Soto Forest by herself.

"So, you were in the training camp," Sara said.

"Right. I had been there for almost a week, teaching all the others immature boys how to become useful men, when, one morning, this snob walked in swinging his sword like a fairy!"

Sara looked at him and raised an eyebrow.

"Yes, moving the thing like a magic wand, pretending to have mastered the moves, and…well, showing off."

"Taking your place?"

"Yes. No!" Charlie laughed and let the memory play in his mind. "I walked up to him and politely asked him to stop. As you can imagine, it's dangerous to play with weapons, but he punched me! Just like that!"

"He punched you?" Sara said. "Just like that. So, you had to…?"

"Well, I had to defend myself. See! I knew you'd get it."

Sara leaned forward and stared at his face, narrowing her eyes. "He didn't break your nose. I guess this…snob wasn't that good of a fighter, either?"

Charlie snorted and clapped his leg. "You are good... Wait, you heard about that?"

Sara sat back. "The one with the broken nose lived by my home for years. But that doesn't matter. What happened? Did you teach him a lesson?"

"No, we both learned one." Charlie rested his arms on the saddle. "See, they prohibited us from fighting each other. So, they sent us to a tiny cell and left us there for days...no, weeks! They forced me to live with this snob!"

"And you became a snob, too?"

Charlie smiled and nodded. "I guess you could say that. It was a great way to meet my best friend." He sighed and looked back at her. "How did you meet him?"

"It was a big deal," Donald said as he approached them. "Sara tackled Chris, saving him from a huge root that was about to smash his head."

Charlie's eye opened wide. "That must have been something. I hope he didn't attack you." She looked down, and her semblance hardened. "Oh, boy, did he hurt you?"

"Of course not!" Donald said. "Although he could not see Sara's face yet. He looked like an idiot when he saw her, not knowing what to say and all. The zhortas moving around them confused him more."

"Is that so?" Charlie kept looking at Sara. "He is very accurate with girls."

Donald chuckled. "How many of those saved his life?"

Sara smiled, but it was more polite than joyful.

"I suppose that could be a factor. Did he get better after?" Charlie said, but when she didn't answer, he moved closer. "Sara?"

"Oh, sorry." She shook her head. "I was... What did you ask?"

Charlie looked at Donald, who had also noticed the change.

"Sara," Donald said, "could I… Can we talk?"

Charlie nodded and breathed easier. Most likely, what had changed her mood was Donald and nothing else.

"Um…sure," she said, but he didn't move.

"Could you please give us a moment?" Donald said to Charlie, who shook his head. "Why not?"

Charlie ignored him. "If you don't want to talk, Sara. I'll stay here."

She smiled, for real this time. "Thanks, but it's all right."

Charlie bowed and turned to Donald. "I'll be close…just in case."

Donald rolled his eyes at him and waved his hand. "Sure, we will yell if we need some food."

Charlie swore under his breath and rode farther up, but not too far. After what had happened the day before, he might have to rescue Donald.

~

SARA KEPT her hands under her coat and tried to look normal. She had been sick and restless all night. Nightmares of her loved ones dying kept haunting her. Her fingers and wrists cracked with any movement, and their skin was sore and burned. The screams in her dreams had been so loud that they had woken her up. Her head had been pounding, and she'd found blood dripping from her ear.

The sunlight had improved things. Her head and ears had recovered, and only her hands kept shaking. She blamed it on the swollen veins of her palms and fingers—or that's what she thought until Charlie asked her how she had met Chris. She remembered nothing.

Her mind was blank. She was used to the memories of her vivid dreams with Chris being full of holes, and she understood the reason. She wasn't expecting to not remember when she'd met Chris or Donald, though.

It must have happened at the abbey, but whether in the library or outside, like Donald had said, she didn't remember. The first clear idea she had of talking to Chris was in the hallway, but from the conversation, it was obvious they hadn't met then.

"Sara, I understand you may not want to talk about this but..." Donald said at her side, and she inhaled with relief at having something else to worry about. "Thank you. I owe you—"

"You don't owe me anything. How are you doing? Did you have a good night?"

He stretched and lost his balance, but he got a hold of his horse before falling. "Yes...yes. Just like a baby, and you?"

Sara bit her lip and asked, "Aren't babies always crying and don't really sleep for long?"

Donald laughed and rode in silence for a while before restarting the conversation.

"I am not sure how to ask this, and please do not make fun of me. Yes, I am a valsing, and I am also a diplomat. Still, I have a problem getting into this."

"I won't say anything to anyone about this confession. It'll be our secret."

"Sara! Well, thanks, but—" He exhaled and avoided looking at her. "When you saved me, you said something about taking away souls from the gods. Did you—"

Sara shook her head. "I said that so Lily would leave me alone. You can't take anything away from the gods. Before you ask, I didn't bring you back to life. You and Dunstan were alive, barely, but alive. I just...accelerated your healing process."

"Just that."

It hadn't been that simple, but it was the truth. She'd only helped both to live instead of letting them die. It had given her another glimpse of Gemli's life and the reason he acted the way he did. It wasn't only revenge; his memory had holes in it, too.

At that moment, she decided healing herself was out of the question. If helping others took away who knew how many dear memories from her, the selfish act of preserving her life would turn her into a monster.

"Sara?" said Donald. "Um...Lily did not mean what she said to you."

Sara sighed and closed her eyes. That wasn't the first time Lily had hurt her, and just like Wilson had warned her, she knew how to break her heart and soul.

"She told me how you are her family and she does not want to lose you."

"She won't lose me like that," Sara said, "but I don't want to talk to her right now. I'll do it later."

Donald opened his mouth to say something, but the voices of Amanda and Hayden stopped him.

"We are getting close," Hayden said. "I can see the smoke from the fires."

Sara let them ride to the front to do whatever they needed to do before they arrived at the camp.

The silence was enjoyable, and for a moment, she entertained the idea of turning around and getting lost in the forest. The next part would be harder, and she had never been so lonely in her life.

A few bluebirds flew by, and she wondered why they were so far north.

~

JEAN SAT CLOSE to the fire and held her hands near it to warm them up, but it wasn't the weather that kept her so cold. For days, she had been worried about Charlie. Not knowing when he would be back was killing her.

She stood and tried to find something to do: check the food supplies again, make sure the fires had enough wood for the third time. It was nighttime; otherwise, she would have checked on the injured and sick. She wanted to do anything but stay still, anything that would keep her mind from telling her how horrible things could be, how so many days of no news could only mean the worst.

"Jean," John said, holding a bowl of soup. "You need to relax. Just sit down and have some food. Did you eat? I bet you haven't."

"John is right," Chris said from where he sat by the same fire. "It won't make you any good to worry so much. And you are only upsetting John."

Jean nodded and sat down. Both were right. She hadn't eaten, and she needed to stop worrying. It had been easier when they were prisoners. Sure, they'd had problems, but she'd known where Charlie was and how he was doing. Now her heart sank every time he crossed her mind, which was too often.

John said something that made Chris laugh, and she felt ashamed of her behavior towards him. She grabbed a bowl of soup and blew on it. For years, they had been engaged, and she'd never worried about his safety. It wasn't until the last few days that she'd gotten to know him.

During the years of war, she'd seen Chris only a few times. Colonel Xander had visited more often. She loved his visits. He was easy to talk to, always welcoming and funny. The best was how he made Alleta so happy. Now she noticed how Chris and his father were similar, not only in their features but in their behavior, too.

Although Chris had a million things to do, he had kept her busy. He would answer questions about Charlie and reassure her when she needed it, just as his dad had done for Alleta when she was concerned about her son.

He had no problem talking to the people of Tundra, and with more patience than Charlie ever showed, he answered their questions about the reisers and the war and confronted their accusations about his personal performance as commander. Like Colonel Xander, Chris never let them question his authority or decisions.

Jean had no doubts as to who would take charge once the war was over, not only of the humans but the other two races, and she wondered if he had realized it.

"Yes?" Chris said to her. Blushing, she realized she had been staring at him.

"Sorry…nothing." She closed her eyes. "Are they truly all right?"

"They better be," Chris said, and John raised his bowl in agreement.

Jean nodded, aware that both had the same concern and not just for their responsibility.

She liked Amanda, and she considered her a friend now. She hoped one day the same could be true with Sara, though she doubted it. Chris didn't realize how much importance he'd given her when she saw him in his tent, but she did. She also noticed how Sara had left at that moment.

John said, "How many more days would you—"

"The waiting is over," Chris said. Holding his side, he stood as two soldiers approached them.

Jean held her breath and closed her eyes.

"Commander," a soldier said, "the guard is back. Half an hour."

"Thanks, Captain." Chris looked at John. "Lieutenant, get the soldiers ready."

A hand touched her shoulder, and when Jean looked up, Chris smiled at her. "Want to come? I'd rather meet them before they arrive at the camp, for…" He tilted his head a few times. "Logistic issues, but you can come if you want to."

Jean stood. "Thanks!"

Less than fifteen minutes later, she was waiting somewhere in the forest. It made sense that Chris didn't want to discuss anything in front of the people of Tundra or the other reisers. After all, the news could be bad.

The road ahead seemed to move, and a few seconds later, Jean realized it was the horses riding towards them. A knot grew in her stomach, and she pressed her hands together. Chris had asked her to stand behind him, close to the trees, just in case, but he didn't seem worried. He just stood there with his hands at his side, not even wearing his scabbard or sword. They were still too heavy for him to hold.

Once the riders were closer, the soldier at the front yelled something, and the horses stopped. She recognized Hayden, who dismounted first, and then she saw Charlie doing the same. Her heart jumped inside her chest, and an immense weight lifted, allowing her to smile again. She wanted to run to him, but she waited.

From behind the soldiers, a large group of tall men walked towards Chris. Jean's smile vanished when she noticed John step closer to him with a hand on his sword, and the other two soldiers did the same.

She held her breath as the surrounding tension grew into a strange silence.

"Commander Riddley," Hayden said in a tone that brought no happy memories to Jean, "I'm glad to see you are getting better."

Charlie stood still in front of Chris, behind Hayden, and then Jean understood. If Chris wanted to, he could order his men to capture Hayden and the reisers. A shiver made her wrap her arms around herself. A simple sign could change the war's development once again.

"Colonel Green," Chris said, "it's good to see you again."

A man stepped forward and stood by Hayden. She guessed he was a reiser, but she didn't recognize him; his olive skin and green eyes were strange to her. She hoped that was a good thing for their future.

"Commander," Hayden said, "this is Major Dunstan Miller, my second-in-command. He wants to ask you something."

Chris just nodded.

"Colonel Green told us you want our help to finish the war, to remove Murllen from his position," the major said. "I understand our leader is a usurper who needs to be eliminated. What do you plan to do with our race after the war is over? Would you consider us as your servants or slaves?"

"Major, my ideal is to live in peace and share it with all the races of Hune."

Only then did Jean see that Donald was standing nearby, guarded by a few valsings.

"I'm not naïve," Chris said. "It'll take time and effort from every race to accomplish this. They informed me that even when you took over our cities, Murllen just abandoned them. My preference is to share them among the races. However, I'm open to a discussion with the three races. In no way will you become some sort of lower race and serve any of the other ones." Chris grinned. "Despite what the valsings might think, there is no superior race in Hune."

Hayden nodded. "Any other question, Major?"

The reiser shook his head.

Hayden smiled. "Now that that's settled, we'll be pleased to fight with you against Murllen and then build our new home. It's my goal to live in peace as well. It will be nice to do it along with the valsings and humans."

"I blame neither of you," Donald said. "Who does not want to settle by us?"

Chris dismissed his soldiers, and Hayden led his reisers to the camp. Jean felt a pair of arms around her waist, and she squealed when Charlie picked her up and kissed her cheek.

"Did you miss me?" he said, replacing the seriousness with a wide smile.

Instead of answering, she kissed him and hugged him tightly until she heard Chris.

"How did it go?"

Amanda, standing by John, lowered her eyes, and Donald put his arm around Lily's shoulder. Jean realized then that Sara wasn't there, and she stepped away from Charlie.

"I messed up everything," Lily said.

"No, you did not," Donald said. "The device did not work. It was Sara who broke the armor."

"Where is she?" Chris said. "Is she—"

"She is all right," Charlie said, "but something else happened."

Chris's jaw set and crossed his arms.

"When that thing didn't work," Charlie said, "the reisers got ready to attack. Sara held Hayden's hand, and then all hell broke loose. Chris, I mean, pieces of metal, branches, leaves, everything shook back there. I thought—no, I was certain she had killed everyone. But she didn't, and two seconds later, everything went silent, until—"

"I thought he killed Donald," Lily said in between tears. "I was going to kill him."

"Who?" Chris said.

"Dunstan, the reiser. Sara..."

"She saved both of them, Chris," Amanda said. "She seems fine, but it was strange, and..."

Chris turned to Donald. "Are you all right?"

Donald lifted his hands. "Better than ever."

Chris nodded and turned to Charlie. "You are in charge

while I come back." Then his tone changed, and he added while walking away, "I'm done with this."

~

SARA SAW the soldiers stop and overheard voices at the front. The smoke from the fires was still more vivid in her nose than in her eyes, but she dismounted and walked by Mulsh. Her hands kept trembling, and this night promised to be as bad as the last one. She didn't want to see anyone and pretended to be fine.

She heard loud footsteps approaching, and a few seconds after, the familiar scent of his scarf gave him away. Chris was holding his side, and the moonlight granted him a mysterious look. From the heaviness of his steps, she understood he wasn't happy, and she prepared herself for another fight.

"Sara," he said, "we need to talk."

She shook her head. "No, we don't. I have to take Mulsh to the camp. He should rest and drink water."

By the time she finished her explanation, Chris was standing by the horse.

"No, you don't."

"He is tired and—"

Chris took the reins from her and slapped the horse's leg. Mulsh ran three steps and then kept walking down the road.

"Why did you do that?" she said. She started to go after Mulsh, but Chris blocked her. "He will get lost," she protested.

"No, he won't. He will find the camp. Now, explain to me—"

"How do you know?"

Chris raised an eyebrow. "What do you think everyone told me?"

"What? No, Mulsh! How do you know he won't get lost?"

"Believe me, Sara." Chris crossed his arms. "He can find his home. It's in his instinct. Now, tell me. What happened?"

Sara turned and walked into the forest, away from the road.

"Where are you going?" Chris said.

"Hopefully, my instinct will take me home."

She pushed a branch out of her way and crouched to get past another one. There was a reason she stood behind the group, out of the camp, and away from everyone. She needed time and space to not be questioned. Still, when Chris's hand touched her shoulder, she couldn't keep her heart from beating a little faster.

"Keep going," Chris said.

More upset at herself, Sara shook his hand off and walked deeper into the forest. She didn't slow down, not caring if he could move that fast or even if he was still following her.

She came upon a river, and its sound took her away from her thoughts, slowing her down. She crouched and touched the water. With surprise, she noticed that it helped stop the trembling and cleared a pressure she hadn't been aware of until then.

She smiled, knowing it came from Laconia's waterfall.

"What happened to your hands?" Chris said.

Sara stood and hid them behind her back.

"Really? What are you, a child."

"Just...what do you care. Everything worked out. The reisers will fight with you. They won't have a—"

Chris puffed and leaned against a tree. He looked pale, his forehead was beaded with sweat, and he kept touching his side. Sara concentrated, and the metallic smell of blood reached her.

"You should rest," she said. "You are bleeding again."

"I'm bleeding. You are changing the subject. Again!"

"Changing the—what subject?"

Chris pushed his hair back. "Tell me what happened, Sara. Why are you hiding your hands? I told you, you can trust me!"

She shook her head. "Can I? Why should I trust you if I don't even know you?"

"What—you know me. Sara…we have known each other for years. How old were you, fifteen, when—"

"For years?" She rolled her eyes. "I didn't even know you were engaged."

Chris puffed. "I'm not. Is this what has been bothering you? Because I'm not. I was engaged, and Jean broke it off. Now she is with Charlie. I'm not—"

"And she broke it off when I was fifteen?" She pushed her hair behind her ears. "We met that many years ago, but you never mentioned it? Ever! And you realize you should have mentioned it because some things happened between… Never mind. I shouldn't… It doesn't matter."

"Maybe I never spoke about it because it wasn't important to me. Or because I broke the engagement but my father never gave the message to my mother, who held onto that promise all those years. Maybe—"

"Oh, this is great! Next time you ask me something, I'll just tell you it wasn't important to me."

Chris sighed and stepped closer to her. "You are right. I should have mentioned it, and I have many excuses now, but—"

"It doesn't matter anymore, Chris." She rubbed her eyes. "I can't remember how I met you."

"What? I thought that after we left Cielthos's cave, you started to—"

She shook her head. "Those memories are still blurry. No, I don't remember how I met you back at the abbey. I don't even remember the names of some zhortas and… In fact, it's not a bad idea. Let's get rid of the rest of those memories. They hurt too much."

Without warning, Sara closed the distance between them and touched Chris's side.

This time, it was easier. The heat came to her palm as fast as her thoughts. Her fingers glowed, and the bloodstream in his body responded to her will. She closed her eyes and let the essence of Hune pass through her, healing and closing his wound until she felt his strength return.

She stepped away, waiting for the pain in her hands and the pressure inside her head to hit her, but none of that happened.

"What did…? How did you…?" Chris grabbed her shoulders and looked her straight in the eyes. "Are you all right?"

Sara moved his hands away. "Don't touch me." She rubbed her face and crouched, trying to think. "I don't understand. The last time…it hurt me, but now…"

He knelt in front of her, keeping his distance but not his eyes away from her.

"Tell me…please, Sara."

"I don't—" She cleared her throat and sat on her heels. "I noticed nothing until… Before, when I saved them, my hands burned and felt like they were being ripped apart."

She put her palms up, and although her veins looked as though they had been painted on in blue and dark red strokes, they didn't seem about to explode, and the trembling remained the same.

"Dear gods, Sara," Chris said. He reached out to her, but his hand stopped an inch away. "What else? Are you in pain now?"

She looked into his eyes. Their gray color was familiar, but the missing memories were a dark hole that brought a knot to her throat. She shook her head and swallowed.

"It wasn't until Charlie asked me how I met you that…

Donald told him how, but I…A root, my jumping on you? Nothing."

She bit her lip and pushed her hair behind her ears.

"I thought then, and… I see faces of zhortas, but I can't, for the gods above, remember their names… I'm not sure how long you and Donald were there before the reisers arrived, and even then, I only remember being in the Soto Forest…trying to go back."

Chris rubbed his face. "Do you remember healing my hands from the glacier orchid?"

She shook her head but couldn't speak.

"All right. What about the bluebirds and the nest?"

"No. Do you know why there are bluebirds this far north?"

"I don't—no, Sara." He slid close to her. "We talked in the hallway."

Sara nodded. "I have parts of that."

"I don't think Gemli's journal said anything about this… maybe at the end. I haven't—"

"You read it?"

Chris smiled. "Of course I did. It's important for you."

"And it didn't bother you?"

His jaw set, and he exhaled, but before he could answer, she stood and walked a few steps away.

"Of course it did, but don't worry. I'll keep enough memory to remember what I'm doing here. It'll be hard to forget, anyway."

Chris stood. "And why is that?"

She turned her back at him, letting the sound of the water calm her heart and take away the tears filling her eyes.

"Come on, Sara," Chris said. "Tell me what is so hard to forget, what you think about me. You can't hide behind that hood all the time. Tell me why—"

"I'm not hiding." Sara groaned and pulled her hood down.

"I never have. It's how all of you look at me...at all zhortas that made us put that on."

"Well, it seems convenient of you to wear it while we are talking about difficult—"

She took the coat off and tossed it to the side. "Happy now?"

Chris leaned against a tree. "Well, if you think I'm going to stop you from taking off your clothes, you are wrong!"

Sara narrowed her eyes and turned away again.

"All right," Chris said. "I read the journal because I need to understand what is happening to you, and you aren't telling me anything."

"And why would I tell you? You won't like it. It involves magic and me being infected with it."

"I never said you were infected, but I'm not apologizing for being worried about you. I need—"

"No, you don't. I'm fine. And I'll be there to free the saber, remove Gemli's protection, and open the reisers' armor. Unless, of course, you prefer the valsings' stuff." She crossed her arms. "I'm aware of my role in all of that. I'll help you save your dear Hune."

Chris said nothing for a while, and she wondered if he had left. She dared not look, though, as confirming it would hurt her deeply.

"So," he said, and she exhaled with relief, "you believe that what I care most about is Hune."

She nodded and couldn't contain her tears. She bit her lips and covered her mouth, trying to be as quiet as possible.

"There is a problem with that. If what I care the most for is Hune, how do you explain my hesitation in asking you for help? Obviously, you have the—"

"You hate magic, Chris!" she said, facing him and wiping her eyes.

"Right, I hate magic." He took a step away from the tree.

"So, Sara White, how can I love Hune and hate magic at the same time? How is it possible that I love and care for something that is founded in what I hate the most?"

Sara shook her head and fidgeted with her fingers.

Chris grinned at her. "You are right. I care about this world. For years, it has been my priority to protect it, and I would have given my life for it, but things changed. I'm a soldier, the last commander of what they left of our army. I have a lot of responsibilities."

He stepped closer and moved her hands down. "Still, if you don't want to find the saber, if you are done with everything and just wish to live your life, I'll take you away, and believe me, no one would ever find us."

Sara's heartbeat sped up, and she couldn't look anywhere but into Chris's eyes, which seemed to move closer with every word.

"If you tell me you want nothing to do with this war, I'll give my life protecting you." Chris caressed her cheeks with his palms while his fingers brushed her neck. "I love you, Sara, and whatever else is happening isn't as important as you are to me."

Sara's world became smaller, contained in Chris's arms when he kissed her. Just like he'd said, nothing else mattered, and she let herself fall into that conviction.

Chris moved away an inch and looked down at her. Both of his hands were still on her face.

"The second we left Cielthos's cave, I have been a coward around you. I should have told you this then…or many, many years ago."

He kissed her again, and her heart fluttered until he stopped.

"However," he said, resting his forehead against hers, "I think I know what you are going to say about running away.

Or am I wrong, and you really want to leave? Would you leave with me?"

Sara had to catch her breath before answering. "I would leave with you… I did already…" She touched his face, and he rested his cheek in her palm. "But if we do that, you will hate yourself. Am I wrong?"

Chris didn't answer. Instead, he kissed her again. This time, Sara hugged him tight, and it seemed that time had stopped.

Sara moved a few inches back, and Chris ran his fingers through her hair. He kissed her hand and then walked over to her coat and picked it up.

"If you are serious about going to the camp, we should leave now. Otherwise, I'll just kidnap you." He stopped moving and said without looking at her, "I still want to know what happened to you, that you are all right, and then I'll be happy to tell you how we met… I'll help you remember. If you want to."

Sara froze as understanding dawned on her. Everyone in Hune depended on them stopping Gemli and Murllen, and the growing feeling her dad wasn't mistaken set in her mind. She couldn't survive the curse. She thought about how horrible it would be to live without Chris. If he loved her only half as much as she loved him, the last thing she wanted was for him to endure that torment. Not to mention, he would need a clear head to save their world.

"Chris," she said, unable to move.

"My lady." He turned to her.

"I can make you forget me."

"What are you—"

The second he saw her, he rushed back and stood in front of her.

"I don't want you to suffer because of me." Her voice was a whisper, and her tears had made her face wet again. "If you don't remember, if you don't have any idea how we met and I'm here just to stop—"

He shook his head. "I know there is something you are not telling me."

Sara closed her eyes and almost inaudibly said, "I can't—"

He held her face between his hands again, making her look at him. "I am not asking..."

She rested her hands on his.

"Sara, I lived a long time without being happy. Until I met you, I had no hope for living, and I was an idiot when I didn't believe you were real."

She tried to say something, but Chris shook his head.

"The moment I saw you outside the abbey, my world changed. I know how it is to live without hope. Please don't take this happiness away from me. Don't take my reason for fighting and living again away."

Chris's eyes shone when he rested his head on her forehead. "If I can ask you one thing..."

She nodded.

"Promise me you'll let me try to stop Murllen before you have to—before you even get close to that saber."

Sara felt almost sick because nothing would work, but Chris didn't allow her to answer.

"Just promise me you will let me try." He grabbed her hand and enclosed it in his. "Just one second. I'm begging you, Sara... Please, one second."

"One second..." She wasn't sure if Chris heard her, but she did not want to say anything else, so she pulled him close and kissed him.

He slid his hand to the back of her neck. The softness of his lips and the safety of his embrace woke thousands of sensations in her. It was easy to hear his increasing heartbeat and the shortness of his breathing, but it was his hands that took her attention, the ones warming her up as they caressed her.

Chris brushed her collar bone, sliding away the top of her dress and exposing her shoulder. He kissed his way to her neck and tenderly pushed her hair away from her ear.

Sara shivered as he whispered, “I love you, Sara.”

DARK MAGIC

Sara woke to the sound of the moving water and the smell of burning wood. It was still dark, but the light of a fire and the moonlight made the night less obscure. Chris's coat was wrapped around her, protecting her from the cold, and he was sitting by the fire, not far away from her.

She put his coat on and walked towards him. She wasn't sure how long she'd slept, but in comparison with the night before, even a few minutes of dreamless rest were precious.

He looked at her with a soft expression and a smile on his face.

"What are you doing?" she said. "Aren't we supposed to go back?"

He shook his head and smirked.

Sara wrapped her arms around herself, unsure of what to do because, at that moment, if he told her he would leave the army and the fate of Hune in other hands, she didn't have the strength to fight him.

"It's not very often I can say this." He reached for her hand. When she gave it to him, he guided her to sit in front of her and wrapped his arms around her. "I know what tomorrow holds for us. We have to pick up camp and send the people from Tundra and whoever can't fight somewhere safe."

As he rubbed her arms, she leaned against him.

"We'll have to walk through the swamps, and I'm hoping to find the fortress as quickly as possible. Then we either camp again, get ready for a battle, or both. However..." He brushed her hair to the side and kissed her cheek. "I don't know what tonight holds for us, and I'd rather stay with you."

She turned and looked at him. "That is why you built a fire?"

"I wasn't expecting you to fall asleep, but...I thought you might get cold."

She felt her cheeks warming up and glanced at the fire in front of her. "And what if I get hungry?"

He cleared his throat. "I'll never try to cook for you. I love you, and I won't force you to go through that."

Sara laughed and rested her head in his arms. "I love you with all my heart." Her tone became more serious. "I don't think I have ever loved anyone like this before."

Chris lifted her chin. "You don't think?"

She chuckled and shrugged.

He kissed her, but something in the distance caught her attention.

"What is it?" Chris said, and all the joy and happiness vanished from his expression.

Sara shook her head and stood. Beyond the pain and suffering, it was difficult to understand.

He stood, too, and looked in the same direction.

"Did you hear that?" she said.

In answer, the same noise reached her, and Gemli's magic put her on alert. She closed her eyes and found the poor victim. Without waiting for Chris, she ran towards her.

Soon the forest turned into a swamp, and Sara's boots filled with mud.

"Sara, wait!"

She heard him yelling, and he seemed farther away than she expected, but before she could answer, something gripped her leg. She barely had a chance to put her hands in front of her before hitting the ground, hurting her already sore hands. However, she didn't have time to yell, as something flipped her over and grabbed her neck.

She grabbed the pair of hands, unsure how she knew the red-haired woman was a reiser.

"I won't hurt you," she said, gasping.

"Of course you won't," the reiser said, but her voice sounded weak. "I have—"

The reiser let her go and, with a groan, bent over and clutched her abdomen. Only then did Sara realize she was pregnant.

"Let me help you," Sara said, kneeling beside her.

The reiser rolled on her side and looked at Sara. "You look like him. I won't—" She screamed and rolled over again.

"Sara," Chris said behind her. "Don't listen to—"

"I'm not like Gemli," Sara said. "I have—"

"Not Gemli," the reiser said, "Murllen. Is he your father?"

"No," Sara said, and without permission, she touched the reiser's abdomen. "He is my uncle, and I'm nothing like him, either."

Everything around Sara disappeared. Strange and overwhelming images filled her mind: the lifeless presence of the unborn infant poisoning her body; the agony of her mortal wounds and the curse forcing her to live through them.

Sara stood and stepped away, bumping into Chris, who caught her and kept her from falling.

"We need to help her."

He didn't ask questions but crouched down to pick her up.

Sara looked at her hand and noticed a dark liquid on it. Then her mind got lost in the things Gemli and Murllen had done to the reiser. Horrified, she understood the reason the baby was still inside of the reiser and she was still alive.

"Sara!" Chris said, and she realized it wasn't the first time he had called out to her. "Put my coat on top of her and push the branches out of our way."

She rubbed her eyes and took the coat off. The cold of the night reminded her that she needed to find her own coat, but that wasn't important at the moment.

"Hey," Chris said in a softer tone. "I'm right here. Don't get lost in whatever the hell you were looking at before." He stared into her eyes. "My hands are busy, and I can't just drop her to get you back. Please?"

Sara bit her lip and walked ahead of him. She wiped her hand on her dress, cleaning them as best she could, and tried to focus on their surroundings. Though it seemed an eternity, a few minutes later, she saw the first tent.

She didn't hesitate before stepping inside, followed by Chris. It was one of the bigger tents, which explained Princess Cassandra's presence.

"I need your help," Sara said

Chris moved towards the bed in the middle.

"Get more blankets!" Cassandra said to one of her valsings.

Chris turned and stared at the princess, but she ignored him and said to Sara, "What can I do?"

"We'll need a lot of wraps, water, and some of your medicine."

"You heard her," Cassandra said to the rest of her escort.

Sara turned to Chris, who was standing by the bed.

"Donald and Hayden?" he said. "I'm guessing you'll need the antidote, too."

"Please," she said, and after a deep breath, she moved towards the bed.

Chris touched her shoulder when she passed by his side. "I'll be right back. Do whatever you can, but...be careful." He kissed the side of her head and left the tent.

The reiser was unconscious when Sara knelt by her. She took Chris's coat away and took a closer look at her wounds. There were bruises on the reiser's face, arms, and legs, and judging from the color of her side, she had broken ribs and maybe other bones. She wasn't bleeding, but that wasn't necessarily a good sign. The most painful part for Sara was looking at the bump on her abdomen and knowing she couldn't save the baby.

"What in the—" Cassandra stopped mid-step.

Sara turned, and the valsing looked not only disturbed but almost sick. "You don't need to stay."

Cassandra closed her eyes for a second and took a deep breath. "I'll help you until the others get here."

Sara touched the reiser's forehead, and the reiser opened her eyes and looked at her.

In the dim light of the tent, Sara realized the reiser couldn't be much older than her, and imagining everything she had gone through pinched Sara's heart.

"I don't think I can save your baby," she said.

Tears rolled down the reiser's cheeks. Then, a moment later, her expression changed to one of alarm, and she looked around the room and grabbed Sara's arm.

"This is a safe place for you. No one will—"

"No—" The reiser inhaled and tightened her grip. "Hayden...he can't—not him. I beg you..."

Sara rushed out of the tent and collided with Chris. Donald and Hayden were closed behind.

"You can't see her!" she said to Hayden and turned to Chris. "He can't see her."

Chris grabbed Hayden's arm and pulled him back.

"What the hell?" Hayden said, and Sara noticed how hard it was for Chris to hold him.

"It's part of Gemli's curse, Hayden. She'll die if you go in there."

"Gemli? What the...? Christopher, let me go, or I swear—"

Donald strode past them and into the tent. Sara saw the change in Hayden's eyes when he caught a glimpse of the bed inside. This time, he fought harder to get loose, and Chris had to push him to the ground.

"Let me see her!" Hayden said. "I wouldn't stop you from—"

Charlie and John raced towards them, and Sara ran back inside.

Donald was kneeling by the reiser, looking livid and confused. "What could do something like this?"

Sara moved to the bed. "Gemli"

"I'm sorry, Sara," Cassandra said while handing the medicine to Donald. "I cannot handle... I will be outside if you need something else." She placed more blankets on the floor, and one of her valsings left wraps next to them. Then they hurried from the tent.

"This is beyond anything..." Donald stared at the reiser. "What can I do?"

"I'll take the curse away, but as I do, her wounds will become real." Sara pushed her sleeves up and knelt by the bed. "You have to save her life."

He grabbed her arm. "She won't survive this. I mean, look at her. She should be—"

"Dead," the reiser said. "I know."

Donald's eyes opened wide, and he tightened his grip on Sara's sleeve.

"Peace would be—" She rolled on her side, groaning and clutching her stomach.

Sara slid his hand off. "I'll remove the curse. You keep her alive while I do that. Then I'll do my best to save her."

Donald shook his head, but she ignored him.

She put one hand on the reiser's head and the other on her abdomen. Then she inhaled deeply and closed her eyes. Although the images didn't surprise her, they still perturbed her: the reisers in armor kicking her, Gemli moving towards her, amused and proud.

"I need you to send a message," the sorcerer said.

The message was for Hayden, but Sara learned the reiser had been looking for a human. She concentrated on the reiser's abdomen, and her heart broke as she learned who the little one's father was.

"Sara, this isn't working," Donald said, and when she opened her eyes, she discovered the reiser was convulsing and he was trying to protect her head.

Sara exhaled and looked around. Her father had told her that as a wizard, Hune's magic was connected to her, all of it, good or bad. She needed to call forth Gemli's spell. This was a curse, a poison inside the reiser's body.

"I need a knife," she said.

"A knife? What are you going to do?"

She pressed her lips together and held her open hand out to Donald.

"I am not sure it will work," he said.

"The curse, it's poison has to come out."

Donald groaned, but he pulled a short knife from his boot and handed it to her.

Sara closed her eyes again and placed both of her hands on the reiser's abdomen.

The same dark picture came to her, and she put herself in the reiser's place.

In her mind, Gemli pushed her against a wall, and his dark eyes stared at her. She learned the reiser's name was Genevieve, and the fear that filled her heart also reached Sara when Gemli stabbed the baby.

Sara forced her mind back to the tent and ignored the screams when she pushed Donald's knife into Genevieve's abdomen. She kept her eyes closed as a thick and hot liquid dripped down her hands. She had known it before, but whatever was inside of the reiser wasn't an infant.

Her hand burned with cold, and she bit her lip to avoid screaming. Then she inhaled and forced the knife to open Genevieve's abdomen. In her mind, she saw a dark form decomposing, and with an immense effort, she ignored the thickness of the liquid and the potent smell of rottenness while grabbing it.

"For the gods!" Donald swore, pushing her hands away from the reiser.

Sara opened her eyes and found Donald trying to stop the heavy bleeding in the wide-open body. Genevieve wasn't conscious anymore, and her breathing had become sporadic and short.

"What the hell is that?"

Sara moved as far away from them as possible, holding the dark curse between her hands. As the form dug into her palms, the surrounding air heated, and each breath scratched her lungs and throat.

She coughed as her strength gave out and exhaustion threatened to take over. In the back of her mind, she remembered how her father had protected her from that, and the pain of losing him to that monster made her resolution stronger.

She pressed the form she held again, and it squealed and burst into dust. The air cooled, and breathing became a pleasant feeling once again. In her mind, she saw a little light moving towards the sky. It left a mark in her heart, losing the soul of an innocent baby, and with tears in her eyes, she looked at Donald.

"I am losing her!"

She cleaned her hands on her dress and stepped over to the bed. Then she knelt and took a deep breath to settle herself down.

"You came all this way." She touched Genevieve's head. "Don't give up now."

The power filling her felt warm and kind, like when she had healed Chris. Her hands still hurt, though, and, afraid to contaminate Genevieve, she stopped once she became certain Donald could handle it.

She sat on the ground, not caring about the blood or the dark liquid in it, and let her hands rest on her legs.

Genevieve's breathing normalized, and Donald stopped panicking. It took her a few minutes to stand and look down at the reiser.

Bruises covered the reiser's body, the wound in her stomach would leave a big scar, and all signs of pregnancy had vanished. Donald was still working, giving her some medicine and cleaning the small wounds.

After her head stopped spinning, Sara walked to the door. "I'll get Hayden."

"You do that, and take a break." Donald barely moved his eyes from Genevieve. "I have this, but if anything were to happen to you, I do not know how to help you."

Sara smiled and stepped out.

The light blinded her, making her conscious of the stabbing pain between her eyes. Her knees and hands were shaking, and her dizziness made her nauseous. The breeze and the warmth of the morning sun helped her.

"Sara! What did you—" Hayden stomped towards her, but he stopped short when he got a good look at her.

"She is alive." She sighed. "I tried, but there was nothing… I was too late, but at least—"

"Please, don't—Sara," he said. "I didn't mean… I'm sure you did more than anyone here could, but… I have so many—"

"You can see her now."

Without another word, Hayden entered the tent.

Someone wrapped a soft fabric around Sara's shoulders, and when she turned, Chris was standing there.

"I went back and got it for you," he said, helping her to sit down. "Although you still shouldn't hide behind this hood… at least not from me."

Sara leaned into him and kept her eyes open, afraid of the dark.

~

ONLY A FEW HOURS had passed between the time Chris had been with Sara in the forest and that early-morning event. However, there was a world of difference in Sara's appearance. Her skin was pale, and blood, mud, and a black liquid he didn't recognize covered her dress and hands. She kept trembling and was freezing.

"Hayden is right," Chris said. "Whatever you did in there is more than any of us could have done."

She hid her face against his shoulder, and he hugged her and rubbed her back.

"Charlie," he said, "stay here while I take Sara—"

Hayden walked out of the tent, looking both horrified and furious. "We need to talk," he said, and Chris knew it couldn't wait.

Amanda stepped over to Sara and sat at her side. "I'll stay with her."

"Everything is different," Hayden said, not bothering to

wait for a more private place to talk. "Those freaking—" He groaned and threw his arms in the air. He tried to talk a few times but kept changing his mind. Finally, he inhaled and forced himself to stand still.

"Inside the fortress is a place, the asylum."

Chris saw Dunstan and the other reisers moving closer, but Hayden didn't seem to care.

"It's there that we raise our offspring until they are capable of wearing armor and fighting." He shook his head. "It is all too complicated…even for us, but…once we leave the asylum, they delete all our memories of the place and what happens in it. Don't ask me how. We have no idea what is inside it… The reiser you just saved…she is—was—the one in charge of the asylum."

"The ruler of the house?" Dunstan said, and Hayden nodded. "Why is she…? Did Murllen destroy the—"

"No," Hayden said and turned to Chris. "I didn't remember. I sort of did, but… I think that's why I questioned Murllen… Still, I'm not sure… It wasn't until I saw her that I realized where I had seen her before."

The tone of Hayden's voice was something Chris understood well, and an icy shiver ran down his spine at the thought that Sara could end up like her.

"Gemli and Murllen are aware that I'm working with you. They sent her—" Hayden cleared his throat. "Those bastards sent her to us like this to let me know they will destroy the asylum if I help you."

Chris didn't need to hear any more.

"I gave you my word, and I believe this is—was—a brilliant plan, but I just can't—"

"Hayden," Chris said, "there is nothing to explain. You have no options. We'll figure out something else."

"Gods by damn!" Hayden said. "At least I can promise you I won't fight against you. None of us will."

Chris nodded. Though it was a tremendous deal, there was no way he could challenge such an explicit threat.

Hayden crouched in front of Sara and, in a broken voice, asked, "Did that monster, that asshole, kill my—" Her eyes filled with tears.

At that moment, Donald came out of the tent, supporting the reiser they had saved as she shuffled next to him, capturing their attention.

She looked much better, though she was still weak and pale. Because Chris had carried her, he knew how small she was, and he wondered how long it had been since she'd eaten. Like Sara, her freckles made her look sweet, but the hate in her eyes didn't match her innocent appearance.

"You are going to fight," she said, looking at Hayden and ignoring the rest of them. "In case you forgot our conversation, you are our rightful leader, not that bastard."

She had to stop between breaths, but she didn't have to raise her voice to make her point.

"My mother fell for that threat, and we ended up in a worse situation. I made the mistake of doing nothing… If you don't stop him now, he'll kill everyone." A few tears rolled down her face. "I lost my baby already. I won't let those monsters murder or terrorize my other little ones."

Chris doubted Hayden was their leader, because, even in her poor condition, it was clear she had more power than anyone there. Deep inside, he was glad she had never fought in the field against his army.

"I'm not an excuse," she said as Hayden moved closer. "I walked all the way here looking for someone to save my race, not—

"Genevieve," Hayden said. He stood in front of her, and Donald moved to the side.

As she looked up at him, her severe expression softened.

"Don't let the death of your—our—baby be in vain. You have to fight."

"We will." He pulled her between his arms. For a second, she just cried against his chest, and when her legs lost their strength, he picked her up and carried her into the tent.

It was a tough conversation to witness, and everyone looked around uncomfortably.

Chris stared at the ground as he considered their situation. The news wasn't all good. The reisers would fight with their army, and they had saved Genevieve, but the young reisers were in danger, and learning that his friend had lost his baby was hard, especially when he was certain Hayden hadn't known about it.

He turned to Sara.

"She is now very hot," Amanda said.

Donald stepped closer and touched her forehead. "I don't know what happened, Chris…or how to help her."

Chris crouched in front of Sara and brushed her face. She opened her eyes and smiled at him. "My lady, what do I do now?"

"She needs to get clean," Lily said. "That horrible black thing can't be good."

Chris and Donald nodded in agreement, but when Chris turned back to Sara, she was already unconscious.

THE STORM

It didn't surprise Chris to see the dark storm clouds covering the camp almost as soon as Sara lost consciousness. It reminded him of the Northern Forest's storm, when she'd found the cave. It seemed a lifetime ago, though only a few weeks had passed.

The pouring rain and the sound of thunder made it difficult to hear anything.

"Are you sure Murllen didn't want anyone there?" Chris said to Hayden.

Like he'd told Sara, the civilians and injured soldiers and reisers needed to get to a safer place while the rest of them marched to the fortress.

"I told you a thousand times, your idea is good," Hayden said. "Murllen has never cared for any of the cities, and as far as I know, he mentioned no desire to use them. And remember, my reisers are going, too. Laconia is a good place for everyone."

Chris nodded. He hoped the city wasn't in worse condition than the abbey. The reisers had taken it decades ago, at the beginning of the war. It could be dangerous just from the state of the buildings. Still, it was better than setting up camp halfway to the fortress.

"When will your reisers be ready to leave?"

"As soon as your people are finally ready." Hayden smirked. "Who are you sending with them?"

"Lily, of course!"

"Lily?" Hayden shook his head. "In your dreams."

"I'm actually following your advice," Chris said, "and taking a tremendous risk with it."

Hayden frowned. "If it's my advice, it isn't a risk at all."

Both laughed for the first time that day.

"How are you doing?" Chris said.

Hayden stopped walking. "I'm not sure. I hate the idea of putting the asylum in danger, but…" He looked at Chris, his muscles tensed and his fist closed tight. "Do you have to kill Murllen yourself?"

Chris crossed his arms as his temperature rose. "According to our findings, Murllen was to be destroyed by the saber. Only Sara can set it free, and if we are correct, I'm the only one allowed to use it." He tapped his fingers on his forearms. "However…I'll be more than happy if you kill him first."

"What can I say?" Hayden said. "I wish you are extremely happy once we finish this madness."

They walked in silence the rest of the way.

Chris knew that his decision would jeopardize everything, but he couldn't deny his priorities had changed. At that moment, he wasn't sure he would let Sara be part of it. It was better to have a plan in place, and Hayden had the right to get rid of their oppressor.

Charlie approached and said, "The caravan is almost ready. Some people are having a hard time walking again."

"I had no problem moving them before," Hayden said with a smirk. "You should use some of my techniques."

Charlie rolled his eyes. “Sure. I’ll just tie them to the wagons.”

Hayden chuckled. “Only if you want them to fall and break their bones.” His smile vanished as he added, “I’ll send the reisers to the line now.”

Chris narrowed his eyes at Charlie.

“What? He started it!”

Chris shook his head. “You are such a baby! He started it? Really, Commander?”

“Speaking of,” Charlie said, walking by Chris. “What are you doing about our ranks?”

Chris ignored the question. “You know I’m sending Jean with them, right?”

“Yes, I do.” Charlie’s gaze dropped, but his tone remained calm. “She’ll be safer there than here. I could volunteer to—”

Chris stopped in his tracks. “You can’t do that. Charlie, you are my second-in-command. If something happens to me, I need you in the battle.”

Charlie sighed. “I understand, Commander, but…Chris, this is exactly why I never wanted to be part of the army. My parents never got it, but—”

“I get it, Charlie.” Chris put a hand on his friend’s shoulder. “I was there, and I remember how it was for you when you lost them.”

“I won’t be there to defend her if—”

“Right, but I need you to see my point… Where is Jean?”

Charlie pointed at her. She was getting ready in the middle of the line. Amanda was talking to her.

“Jean,” Chris said, approaching her. “You are in the wrong place.”

“What do you mean?” she replied. “You told me I was leaving with—”

“Yes, but you are going on the front line.” Chris wrapped his arm around Jean’s, and it seemed strange, considering how many times his mother had asked him to do just that.

"Remember how, when they left to find Hayden's squadron, you stood with me?" he said while he led her to the front, aware that Charlie and Amanda were following close behind. "I confirmed something then."

Jean slid her arm away and stared at Chris the same way she had many times back in Tundra.

"You remind me of Mom," he said.

She shook her head and took a small step back. "Your mom? She is amazing, and strong, and kind... I'm nothing like her."

"I think you are," he said. "She raised you to be like her. I never got why you never call her Mom. I'm certain she would love it."

Jean touched her heart and had trouble talking. Chris used her reaction to lead her the rest of the way to the front line.

"Major Baker," he said. "You remember Jean?"

"Of course, Commander."

"Good. She is in charge of the civilians. They will listen to her, and I'm positive she'll be a great help for you and the soldiers as well."

Jean's eyes opened wide, and Charlie put his arm around her shoulders and nodded at Chris.

"In the past, she kept them alive in the worst of the circumstances," said Chris. He turned to Jean. "Hayden told me how you confronted him, and Charlie confirmed how strong you are. I need you to keep them safe, all right?"

Jean stared at him. "I'll do it, but I'm not a soldier. I won't be able to—"

"Don't worry about them, Jean. Major Baker will work with the soldiers and make sure the path is clear. You need to help with the people. They gave us a hard time since we arrived at Tundra, and I realize it was you and Mom who stopped them from doing stupid things. Just do the same."

Jean smiled at him. "I'll do my best."

"I have no doubt you will."

He walked away with Amanda to give space to Charlie to say goodbye. Jean's safety didn't worry him, but he couldn't be that sure about Charlie's.

"What's next, Commander?" Amanda said.

"I hope you are back in shape, Major. We have a serious battle ahead."

~

THE CARAVAN DEPARTED with a few hours of light left in the day. Not that it mattered much in that storm. Lighting and rain pounded the forest. Chris just hoped that Sara was the one behind it and not Gemli.

"Can I talk to you?" Lily asked him on his way to the meeting to explain the plan to everyone.

"Donald didn't ask you to leave?"

Sara hadn't told him what Lily had said to her, but he'd rather not know. It was hard enough to deal with her already.

"He did," she said in a calm tone that Chris had never heard from her. "I asked him to let me talk to you. I will leave after if you want me to."

Chris gave her a second look.

Her eyebrows were drawn together, and dark circles hung underneath her eyes. She kept twisting a curl of her hair between her fingers, and like Sara, she bit her bottom lip.

He noticed a resemblance between them that went beyond their height and structure. Now that Lily wasn't yelling, her voice was soft like Sara's, and although their eye color was different, there was a familiarity to them. He agreed with Cassandra. Even though Lily was pretty, Sara was far more beautiful.

"I understand why you dislike me," Lily said. "It is my fault, but…" She took a deep breath. "I am having a hard time trusting people now these days."

Chris stepped into one of the empty tents, and Lily followed him.

"I told you before, Sara is my family. She is the only one who ever cared for me…before Donald, of course." She glanced at him. "I want to help her."

Chris sat on a cot and rested his arms on his knees. "I'm guessing you have an idea of how…while also keeping it a secret from her?"

Lily twisted her fingers the same way Sara did when she was upset. "I am sure she does not wish to talk to me, and I do not blame her." Sitting next to Chris, she touched his arm and looked into his eyes. "After what she did, I realize she must be part of the next battle but…going against the sorcerer and Murllen…I saw them, Chris. When Orson killed… Let me take her place."

Chris put his hand on Lily's. "I don't think you can."

She shook her head. "No. I do not mean that."

She stood in front of him. "Many have said it before, Chris. We look alike. We are almost the same height and shape, and if I cover my head, no one will suspect I am not her. I can be at your side and keep her safe somewhere else… or until she has to be—"

"You want to pretend to be Sara when we reach the fortress?"

Lily nodded.

"If I stand by you, who will know I am not Sara? I thought about it. If Gemli could find her, he would have done it before, from the moment she broke the first of his spells.

Why would he jeopardize the rest? He has the saber; he just needs her."

Chris rubbed his face, wondering if Lily could be right.

"Lily, you shouldn't..."

She opened her mouth, but Chris raised his hand. To his surprise, she stopped and listened.

"If I know something about you, it's how much the battle you witnessed affected you. This one won't be any different, and being at the front won't improve the sight."

"I have to do it." She wiped the tears from her eyes. "I owe it to her."

Chris looked at his hands for a moment. "Did you talk to Donald about this? And I'm not asking if you talked to your leader."

Lily tilted her head. "Well...not as my leader. He does not have too much to say to me. But I understand your question, and he knows I need to do something. Though he is not happy about it, he agreed to it. Of course, if you agree to it, too."

Chris paced for a moment. It was a tempting offer. Sara could be safe, and if Hayden killed Murllen, there was no reason for her to be close to the battle. Nevertheless, he was sure Donald would hate him for it, and he suspected Sara would feel the same way.

"This isn't up to me," he said. "Sara is the one who should make that decision."

"But Sara won't even talk to me! You can—"

He shook his head. "Just like Donald, I don't have authority over Sara's decisions. And even though she is mad at you right now, I know she will hate me if I allow anything bad to happen to you, especially in her name."

Lily sighed and left the tent, so Chris continued to the meeting. However, footsteps made him turn back just in time to hold Lily when she hugged him. A second later, she left again.

AFTER THE CARAVAN LEFT, their camp was half the size it used to be. It was a relief, though. It was still hard being around civilians, even though the situation was better than it had been in Tundra.

Chris inhaled and entered the tent for the meeting.

Charlie was explaining something to Donald by the table, and Hayden was sitting in a chair by Dunstan. He kept his eyes on the other side of the room, where Genevieve sat. Chris wasn't expecting her to be there, and by Hayden's look, he hadn't been, either.

Although she seemed stronger, it was easy to see how devastated she felt. Her shoulders sagged, her eyes were focused on her hands, and the strength in her expression was gone.

John got everyone's attention when he almost bumped into Chris.

"Oh, boy. Sorry, Chris—Commander."

"Where is—"

Amanda walked into the tent. If it wasn't because Chris knew what had happened to her, he wouldn't have notice her slight limping, which was a relief. He will need her in the battle. "Commander," she said and sat next to Genevieve.

Chris moved to the table and saw the map of Hune lying open on it.

"According to Dunstan," Hayden said, "and I agree, we are a couple of days away."

Chris nodded.

"Murllen and Gemli are waiting for you," Charlie said. "It will be a trap."

"I'm thinking he may be waiting for you," Chris said.

"Why would he—"

"The reiser who killed Leonard escaped. I'm sure he was certain he killed me, too." Chris narrowed his eyes. "We have to assume they are aware of everything, and yes, it will be a trap."

Chris let his words sink in. It was important to understand the danger they would be walking into.

"So, the plan is the same?" John said. "We get there, break the spell, destroy the armor, and take over the fortress?"

"I'm sure there will be some complications on the—" Chris said, but Genevieve interrupted him.

Her tone was perfect for the job she had, caring and sweet, with no place in the war. "The most dangerous thing in the fortress are the reisers in the asylum. We trained the reisers outside to give their life for our race but prepared ourselves to hunt any danger that might threaten our offspring. If you attack the fortress without them knowing you are trying to save us, I'm certain they will destroy everyone."

Charlie and John looked at each other with narrowed eyes, but neither Hayden nor Dunstan seemed to doubt what she was saying.

"There is a reason we were never concerned about an attack on our home." Genevieve sat a little taller. "You would never make it."

"And you did not think to mention any of this before?" Donald said.

"I thought they would be like us," Hayden said, "wearing armor for Sara to break! How could I imagine—"

"Sara broke the armor?" Genevieve said, but she didn't let anyone answer before asking Chris, "Hayden...Colonel Green says you are going to fight Murllen with a special sword?"

"A curse protects Murllen," Chris said. "We believe the only way to defeat him is with a saber."

Genevieve touched her head and inhaled with some difficulty. "My mother used to be in charge of the asylum when Gemli arrived at the fortress with Murllen," she said, and Chris realized not even Hayden had heard that before. "Gemli threatened my mother and forced her to train Murllen so he would fight like a reiser."

She exhaled and brushed her forehead. "When I met him, he wasn't wearing armor. They expected me to be the next ruler, so we trained together. It was easy to overpower him until Gemli finished the job." She looked straight at Chris. "Besides being an excellent fighter, he is clever and patient. Murllen only got me because of the mistake I made. Let me help you defeat them."

Chris wasn't expecting that.

"Genevieve," Hayden said, "you can't fight. You almost died, and you aren't—"

"I'm aware I can't fight, but I still can help. I have to." Genevieve turned to Chris.

He had no doubts she had been making hard decisions all her life and had carried an immense responsibility on her shoulders. Still, when she'd asked, she'd sounded nervous, which made her more dangerous.

"Can I propose something?" she said.

Hayden crossed his arms.

"I am listening," Chris said.

"If I get to the asylum," she said, "the reisers inside will discover Murllen's betray. I'll make sure they fight on our side."

"How many reisers live there?" asked John.

For the first time, Chris saw her smile. "More than enough."

The idea of having a front inside the fortress was tempting, but Chris had to ensure everyone's safety, including the reisers inside the tent.

"I'm more than thankful for your offer," he said, "but the last thing I want is for you to get hurt again. As long as you—"

"You are just like your mother," Genevieve said.

"My mother?" Chris asked without thinking twice, and when she nodded, he wasn't sure if he should be relieved or worried.

"Alleta is kind and strong. I'm here because of the way she talked about you. I wasn't supposed to take care of her, and she ended up helping me much more." The easiness in Genevieve's expression vanished. "Murllen took her to the asylum, and we treated her. She was sick and had a few deep cuts. However, by the time they forced me to leave, she was doing fine."

She slowly stood. "Just consider what I told you, please." She waited a moment before moving, although Chris wasn't sure if it was because of her pain or the tears that filled her eyes. "If you don't mind, I need to rest."

Hayden tried to stand, but she placed a hand on his shoulder and shook her head.

"I will be fine," she said.

He took her hand in his and kissed it while looking up at her. All her features softened, showing again the fragile but lovely girl she must be.

Before she left, she turned to Chris. "Is she Murllen's—"

Chris exhaled. "Yes, like she told you, she is his niece. Her name is Sara."

Genevieve nodded. "How is Sara?"

Chris shrugged and smiled. "She is asleep."

~

It had been months since Sara had experienced a vivid dream, and this was the first time she wasn't in charge of it. Her heartbeat sped up when the idea that she had been captured crossed her mind. She tried to walk, but her feet slid on the smooth floor, and when she touched it, she realized it was ice.

A dim light illuminated her surroundings, and soon she could distinguish the strange walls with the frozen dragons of Cielthos's vault. That only made her breathing erratic while she strode around the place.

"Sara, thank the gods you are here," a familiar voice said. "Just concentrate a little more so you can see me."

She shook her head and tried to find a door. Then she stopped. If this was a dream, she was going to wake herself up.

"No, Sara," the voice said again, "Don't wake up. I can't follow you. I'm not a wizard, but I must talk to you; otherwise, I wouldn't have summoned you. I need to tell you Gemli's plan."

Sara looked around, concentrating on the voice. It didn't take long before a silhouette took shape, and soon she recognized Cielthos's smiling face in front of her.

"Dear gods! You are so much powerful than I thought."

"Cielthos? What is going on? You…did you kidnap me?"

He laughed and shook his head. "Kidnapped you? I couldn't even if I wanted to! My child, I have been trying to talk to you for days… I have no idea what happened out there, but just this morning, I found your magic. Still, it was so hard to."

Sara's body trembled, and it had nothing to do with the surrounding ice. If Cielthos had found her, Gemli could, too.

"He can't find you," the sorcerer said.

"Are you reading my mind?"

"Of course not! You'll know if someone is invading your

mind. It's like getting your brain ripped apart. Your fear is too obvious, my child."

A large piece of ice fell, and she jumped to the side to avoid it.

"It will come down soon." Cielthos looked up. "That, he'll notice." He held Sara's arms and stared into her eyes. "I should have seen it before."

His smile was so big and sincere that she smiled, too. "Seen what?"

"Your father. That stinker! He tricked me for…well, all his life! I should have realized his lunatic behavior was just his young inexperience. Landford! He was the Great—"

She shook her head and grabbed Cielthos by the shoulders. "No, he wasn't. He was a good friend but—"

"It's all right, Sara." His expression clouded. "These are my last minutes in Hune."

Sara looked around and noticed the cave was collapsing and melting and Cielthos's skin was scaling.

"We have to get you out of here," she said, "and the dragons. They need to—"

"Do not worry about them, my child. They will survive, but I won't, and that is fine. This time, I can do my job."

Cielthos exhaled and sat on the icy ground. "You understand who you are, right?"

Sara sat by him.

"Good. Did you read the journal?"

"Yes, I did."

"Even better." His face softened, and his muscles relaxed. "I thought your heart was good enough to tolerate some dark knowledge. Just monitor your mood. If you are angry, things will get out of hand. Sure, it'll be powerful, but dangerous. If you act with logic and a cool head, things will work out. If you are happy, we may end up in a nicer place one day."

Another rumble broke a piece of the wall behind them,

and this one tilted and stopped at a steep angle. It wouldn't stay there for long.

"Gemli has Brutus, Sara." Cielthos shook his head. "My poor dragon believes he needs to serve that bastard, and it will do what he asks."

"Can I—"

"Yes, but not now. When you meet Brutus, tell him all of this. Tell him how much your father appreciated him. He's smart. He'll get it."

"A sorcerer's spell usually dies with them." His voice sounded weaker. "However, Gemli's curse over Murllen is different."

Sara nodded. Her dad had explained something about it. "It's tied to the gods' weapon."

"Yes! Smart girl..."

He held her face between his hands, and his eyes turned red. His forehead touched hers. It burned her for a second, like touching a candle and images of dragons and strange languages entered her mind. When he moved back, he had aged. His skin was pale, and he had no strength to stay up.

She did her best to help him lie down on the ice.

"No." Her eyes teared up. "Not you, too... I can't do this."

"My child, you can do this and more." He closed his eyes. "Your father was amazing, but you...you'll do way more. Sara...there is a powerful protection...you. That's why I couldn't reach you before. You may even... Take care of my babies, please."

Cielthos's head hit the ground, and with his last breath, the dragons on the wall roared and growled, making the rest of the walls crumble down. Sara covered herself, waiting for the wall to hit her, but it never happened. Instead, the sound of a storm sent her mind into a deep sleep.

THE STORM outside only made the night darker, and Chris's tent would have been pitch black if it hadn't been for the one candle he kept lit. He didn't want to disturb Sara, but he wanted to make sure he could see her in case she woke up. He arranged a few blankets on the ground by her bed and got ready to sleep.

The meeting had been prolonged for a few hours; instead of being able to rest, he'd had to deal with Cassandra's presence in the camp. She had accepted Donald as their new ruler, but she would not follow his orders. Her escort and a few other valsings had stayed with her to make sure Orson got what he deserved it, which didn't please Donald.

He wasn't excited about it, either, but he preferred to know where she was instead of getting surprised in the middle of the battle. Her petition kept creeping into his mind from time to time, as well as Sara's words. He was a dangerous person, and his priority was very clear. She was lying right there.

Sara looked the same, but her breathing was more peaceful. He pulled her blanket up, conscious of how worried he was for her and amazed he had done nothing stupid yet. Gemli's journal had been enlightening, not because of the magic explanation, which Chris understood little of, but because of how easily a few poor decisions had created such a monster.

The lack of wind and thunder got his attention as the storm reduced to a soft rain. He looked at Sara, but her eyes were still closed, so he decided that if nothing changed by dawn, he would do something. He wasn't sure what, but something.

He lay on his back and stared at the ceiling of the tent. It had been a long day, and sleep was a good idea. He looked at Sara again, and this time, she was looking at him.

Even more dark lines ran across her bright blue eyes. Her

skin was pale, and she felt as cold as when they had been in the glacier. It took Chris less than a second to be kneeling by her, and he brushed her face.

"Hi, pretty. How are you?"

Sara smiled and bit her lip. "Did you move the camp and send every injured person somewhere safe?"

He rested his forehead on hers and sighed. "Almost. We had a heavy sleeper, so moving wasn't an option."

She moved her hand but stopped before touching his face and stared at it.

"Donald thought it would be better to wrap them," he said and touched the tops of her fingers, which had escaped the bandages. "Do they hurt?"

Sara turned to lie on her back and looked at the tent. He was aware of what she had done with Genevieve, but her deep silence and vacant stare told him something else had happened.

"Are you sleeping on the floor?" she said.

Chris glanced at the blankets under his knees for a second, and instead of answering, he squeezed his arm under her neck and slid into the bed with her. "Only if you push me out."

Sara rested against his chest and hugged him. "Good. I didn't want to sleep on the ground."

"What?" Chris said, brushing her hair. "It wasn't that bad...not the last time—"

Sara chuckled, and he felt a soft push, so he kissed her head and rubbed her arm. For a while, she didn't move or say anything, and he wondered if she had fallen asleep again. The thought made him shiver, and he hoped this time it would be normal.

A few minutes later, she turned and looked at him. "Are those bluebirds?"

Chris listened, and after a while, he overheard the song of

birds in the distance. "I hear birds, but I don't know if they are blue or not."

"I wonder what there are doing so far north." She looked at him. "They can grant wishes."

He felt a knot growing in his stomach. It had been hard to realize she'd forgotten all about their time together in the vault. Although he'd accepted it, a tremendous relief washed over him when she'd told him parts of that time were coming back to her.

Not too long ago, she had asked with no hesitation about his wish. It hurt, knowing she had no idea what they had done with the nest in the abbey, and he was certain that telling her would be the worst thing for her.

She laid her head down.

"Sara, don't worry." He hugged her close. "We will finish this, and then…"

He had to stop. The last thing he wanted to do was lie to her, and he wasn't so sure about their future.

THE MARCH

The last two days had been the scariest time in Chris's life, and it had nothing to do with the coming battle. The overwhelming desire to run away with Sara filled his mind in the mornings while she rested in his arms.

During the day, although he monitored the soldiers, he spent most of his time riding at her side. Part of him wanted to be done with everything, but the other dreaded the idea, because their chances of ending up fine and together were slim.

"What do you want to know?" Sara said.

Chris moved ahead and pulled a dead branch from their path. He wanted to talk to her away from the soldiers and the reisers.

"I want to understand how it works. How all this…magic supports Hune. I want to learn how you…"

He exhaled and rubbed the back of his neck. It was difficult to explain because, although the magic intrigued him, he only wanted to protect her from it, something she wouldn't like much.

"I'm just curious. I never had a chance to ask before."

"Right." Sara narrowed her eyes but kept walking.

"Oh, come on." He blocked her path and leaned down so they were at eye level. "What if I say please?"

The smile on Sara's face made him want to kiss her, but he was on a mission. Instead, he grabbed a curl of her hair and twirled it around his fingers.

She shook her head but grinned at him. "It's difficult to explain it. It's like…like feeling beyond yourself."

"What is that supposed to mean?" He crossed his arms. "That doesn't make sense. You can do better than that."

She sighed and sat down by a pond, careful not to touch the water. "I told you it's hard to explain. I'm just understanding how it works."

Chris sat by her. "Just tell me what you are going through. What do you do?"

She stared at the water, and he saw her relax, almost as if she were at peace. Around him, the cold of the swamp warmed up, and the weird smell became weaker. Chris wondered if Sara was aware that she was doing something or if it only happened because of her presence.

"All right." She looked at him. "Imagine you are touching—"

"Imagine?" He grabbed her hand and kissed it. "Why would I imagine if I can touch you? I mean, I can, right?"

"Do you want to listen or not?" She sounded upset, but her smile was one of Chris's favorites, and she closed her fingers around his hand.

"My apologies, my lady. Please, go ahead."

Sara blushed like she did every time he referred to her that way.

"You see how your fingers touched the skin of my hand? With magic, it's like I'm the heat between our palms, the light breeze of the space that goes through them, the humidity flooding around, the water moving below hiding the dirt, the wind being blocked by the branches of the trees."

"Interesting. Can you get what I feel?"

She shook her head. "Not that, but…my senses are more acute than yours. If I want to, I can hear your heartbeat and your breathing." She closed her eyes. "I perceive your scent and warmth even when you are—"

He leaned closer and moved her hair away from her neck. "How is my heart now?"

Sara looked up at his eyes, and the shimmer in hers encouraged Chris to pull her close and enjoy the soft touch of her lips on his. He pulled her into his arms until his concern called him back to the present. Without letting her go, he asked a question whose answer he feared.

"Does it scare you? Or hurt you?"

"No, not most of the time." She lay her wrapped hands in her lap. "May I ask you something?" She rested her head on his shoulder.

"Anything."

"Are you… Facing Murllen and Gemli and fighting…does it…?

"It's terrifying, Sara."

She moved back and touched his face.

"It isn't that different from what I have been doing all my life, trying not to get killed while stopping our enemy or rescuing our people, but…now more lives are under my command, and that's always a heavy weight to consider. There is also you."

"I'll help you with—"

He shook his head. "I don't doubt it, but it's you I worry about the most."

"There you are," Charlie said from the bushes. "What the hell? We have things to do."

Chris rolled her eyes and kissed Sara's hand before standing and helping her up.

~

THE REASON CHRIS stopped their march in the middle of the day and sent John with an advance group was the fog of the swamp. It had increased since the ground had become more mud than dirt and was now so dense that it was impossible to see very far. According to their calculations, they were getting closer to the fortress, and he didn't want to get ambushed.

He was relieved, though, that John wasn't there to add his opinion to the others.

"We need to fix this once and for all," Charlie said. "And I know who will force you to do it."

Donald slapped his leg and laughed a little too loudly. "A brilliant idea. Even though it was not mine."

Both of his friends were looking at Sara, who took a small step behind Chris and grabbed his hand.

"No worries, Sara." Charlie put his arm around her shoulder. "I promise you, it's nothing bad. In fact, it's something that will help Chris and—"

"And he deserves it," Donald said.

"Chris needs a higher rank." Charlie took her hand and led her away from Chris and towards Donald. "He can't stay as commander. First, I don't want to lose my rank." He stole a smile from her. "Second and more importantly, he needs to have at least at the same rank as Hayden."

"The reisers will not respect a human with a lower rank than their current leader," Donald said. "To them, it only means Chris is not as good a soldier and warrior as Hayden."

Charlie stepped between Sara and Chris. "Under any other circumstances, I'd propose a battle to prove the point, but…" He turned to see Chris's wide smile. "That won't help our cause."

It was a brilliant way to ambush him. Sara would only need to say it, and he would change his rank in that second.

"Do you want to do that?" she said from behind Charlie.

Chris couldn't help but laugh at the other two. None of them expected she would ask for his opinion first. Donald threw his arms in the air while Charlie grabbed his face and growled.

"What is the problem?" Sara said.

It was a silly situation. His friends meant well, and their point was right. However, he remained hesitant to change his rank. It wasn't just that he didn't want to take his father's place. It was wrong to do it without permission, or at least with the common approval of his race.

"I'm not choosing not to do it," he said, "but I don't believe I should."

"Come on, Chris." Donald ran his hands through his hair. "Your race's king is dead, and whether or not you like it, you are their leader now. You must do it yourself."

There was no need to remind Chris about his new responsibilities. He was aware of them and concerned about being in charge of every human's fate. However, just as he was about to argue with Donald, Sara grabbed his hand.

"I don't think you have to change your…" She bit her bottom lip.

"Rank," Chris said, filling in the blank.

"Yes! Your rank, thanks. It would be ironic if you defeated Murllen with a lower… Oh, no! I didn't mean… I don't consider you to be less or lower than he is."

Chris moved closer to her and touched her face.

"As ironic and fair as that would be, the problem will come after," Donald said. "If you really want the races united, you have to be in charge. That calls for a leader, one with a proper and respectful rank for the other soldiers, humans, reisers, and even valsings. I am not implying that you are less than anyone, either, but as sad as it is, everyone will think that for sure."

"Oh…" Sara shrugged.

Chris took a step back. "Now you, too?"

She lowered her eyes, and her lack of a smile made Chris realize he needed to finish the discussion once and for all. He moved closer to her and kissed her hand.

"All right, then. I'll do it, but I won't do it myself. You want to change it? Find someone who will do it."

"Come on, Chris." Charlie paced around. "That's stupid. No one else can do it. It has to be a leader from our own race or a superior one."

Donald cleared his throat, but a noise from the fog behind them interrupted him.

"See, Amanda, we got here just in time," Hayden said. "I think all humans and reisers are on my side here. We don't believe the valsings are superior to anything."

"You mean anyone," Donald said, crossing his arms.

"Well, I'll do it," Hayden said. "I'm the higher official here, anyway."

Of course, Charlie and Donald complained about that while Amanda just laughed.

"It could be Amanda," Charlie said. "She was in charge of—"

"She can't if Chris is her commander now," Hayden said and turned to her. "No offense."

"None taken," she said, still smiling.

"Who is or was the superior race?" Sara said.

"Well, it could only be the higher leaders of Hune," Charlie said and sat on the ground. "You know, the members of the old High Council. Gone for decades, by the way."

Chris liked his resolution. After all, if the reason they

wanted him to raise his rank was to be approved by the races of Hune, him naming himself would not be enough. He knew very well how easily they'd question his position the second they found themselves safe and free.

"That's interesting." Sara smirked and titled her head. "In that case, I could do it."

It wasn't what Sara had said but the slow and wide smile on Donald's face that alarmed Chris.

"Of course you can." Donald slapped his forehead. "How did I not see that before? We are wasting time."

All faces turned to Sara. "Well, I have said it all along. I'm a zhorta, and—"

"Zhortas aren't superiors," Charlie said.

"Right," Donald said, pointing at Charlie, "but Sara isn't only a zhorta. She is the only one left, which puts her in charge and makes her their representative for the High Council."

"Funny," Hayden said, "and here I thought the magical power would prove you superior to us anytime."

Charlie jumped up and patted Donald's back so hard he almost fell. "I told you she could do it."

A peaceful relief washed over Chris. Zhorta or not, Hayden was right, and he had known for many years. This was his time to ask.

"Are you willing to name me?" He chuckled when he remembered how she had changed his rank before. For sure, it hadn't been in the direction anyone had wanted her to take. "I'm ready to start over as a sailor from an unknown sea."

Sara smiled at him, and her face lit up for a moment. However, she kept her distance from him and fidgeted with her fingers. Chris ignored the others' laughs and stepped closer to her. "I would love the change if you are the one making it."

There was nothing to wait for. He didn't want a ceremony, and he was sure Sara didn't either. He took a step back and put his hand up while unsheathing his sword out. Sara took a deep breath and stepped back.

"Here," he said and handed her the sword by the pommel. She took it with some hesitation.

"What are you…?" she said, but Chris didn't wait and knelt in front of her.

Everyone became silent.

In his life with the army, Chris had seen their former king name a few of his superiors. All such ceremonies were obnoxious. Usually, they consisted of a very long, narcissistic speech that said nothing about the soldier and everything about the magnificent Leonard III.

This time was different. He loved the person in front of him and wasn't embarrassed to humble himself at her feet. It wouldn't be a lie to swear his life to her.

Sara cleared her throat, but her voice was even and sure.

"Christopher Riddley, it is my privilege to have met you and an honor to be with you on this journey. I have no doubt that with you as our leader, Hune will be saved and restored. With your guidance, one day, everyone will be glad to call this place home. Your convictions and values will lead our races to create a world that will shine in peace and joy."

Sara smiled and tapped his shoulders with his father's sword. "With the power of Hune in my hands, I name you general of the human army and leader of Hune's Alliance."

She bit her lip and turned to Hayden.

"I'd have appreciated it more if you hadn't given him a higher rank than mine, but that was pretty nice," he said.

She exhaled as she offered her hand to Chris and helped him get up.

"You have no idea how much this means to me, Sara," he

said, and he would have picked her up and kissed her if it hadn't been for Charlie, who grabbed him by the shoulders.

"Finally, man." Charlie turned to look at Sara. "I agree with you. This is our leader. I just wish we could celebrate it."

"We may do it pretty soon," Hayden said, and Donald nodded.

Sara handed Chris his sword, and when he took it, her hands trembled slightly—and it wasn't because of the blade.

"We will," Chris said as he stared into her eyes and tried to convince himself as well.

~

SARA WAS SITTING by a fire with Amanda and Genevieve when Chris and Hayden came back from checking around the camp. It was nighttime, and the fog had only grown thicker. She was certain it wasn't natural, but she didn't want to do anything about it, afraid that Gemli could perceive her now.

"You have no idea what the hell you are talking about!" Chris said as he stomped by the firepit.

"I know what I'm talking about, Christopher," Hayden said, not too far behind. "This...Hune's Alliance and everything would never have happened with Colonel Riddley in charge."

Chris turned and stood in front of him. As his fist closed, her breathing grew fast. "My father was an excellent soldier. He guided our army and people—"

"I didn't say he wasn't a good soldier. In fact, he could have been the best warrior among us. Even so, he wouldn't have taken the chance you did. And that makes you better than him."

Chris rubbed his face and turned away. Though his eyes crossed with Sara's, he said to Amanda, "You knew him. You worked with him for many years. Tell this idiot, please, how wrong he is."

Amanda fidgeted uncomfortably, and her voice wasn't convincing as she asked, "What am I telling Hayden?"

"You are telling me," Hayden said, "that I'm an idiot because I told this moron he was a better leader than his father. We wouldn't have gotten this far with the colonel in charge."

Sara looked down and wished she had been wearing her hood up. Chris hated to talk about his dad.

"I'm sorry," Amanda said. "I—"

"You can't possibly agree with him."

Charlie approached them, and from his expression, he was ready for something to happen. But Hayden just sat next to Genevieve, who seemed as confused as Amanda.

"Look, Christopher," Hayden said. "I'm glad you got to be general, and I don't care if you skip a rank, but you have to accept that you are a better leader. You stopped John from killing me outside the cave, and I was wearing armor then. I doubt your father would have."

Chris shook his head and looked at Charlie, but his friend's expression didn't help.

"You, too?"

"I don't get what the big deal is, Chris," Charlie said, "No one is saying Colonel Xander wasn't good. We are just..." Charlie rubbed his face. "This is an unorthodox move, and I doubt any of the other high-ranking soldiers would have made it. Maybe Commander Daniel, but he left the army years ago."

At the name, a knot grew in Sara's stomach, but she wasn't sure why and didn't have time to figure it out. Chris threw his arms up and walked away from them. Hayden might be right, but the two shouldn't get into an argument at that moment.

Though Chris walked into the fog and away from the camp, Sara had no trouble finding him. He was sitting on a large rock with his sword out in front of him. Its tip rested on the ground, and its pommel lay in his hands. His shoulders were down.

Sara walked over to him, but it was only when her shadow blocked the dim light around them that he looked up.

"I'm nothing like him," he said, and there was peculiar light in his eyes.

Sara crouched in front of him. "Do you trust me, Chris?"

He let his sword rest at his side and leaned forward to hold her hands. She covered his mouth before he could answer.

"I met your father when we used to bring food to the people. He never told me, but I'm sure it was him or his guard who saved me when the other soldiers…when I was a child."

She took a seat next to him.

"When Cassandra left her father's community, I wasn't living in the abbey."

"What?" Chris turned to her. "I thought you always…or at least you grew up there since you were—"

"I think three. If you can believe Rafael…" Sara swallowed the hard memory of that zhorta, the only one she remembered by name. "I was young, and the war was getting worse. Even we knew about it in the Soto Forest. I had to do more than just hope our food got to the right people."

Sara stared into the distance, amazed at how clear that memory was against all the blurry ones that now flooded her mind.

"The soldiers at the camp petrified me, but your father was there, and he welcomed me and was always nice to me. I suspect now, it was because he met my parents. I told him I wanted to join the army. Maybe I couldn't fight, but all soldiers eat and need their injuries healed."

Sara unwrapped her hand and showed it to Chris. "He told me I needed to pass a test first."

Even with the swelling of her veins, the scar on her palm was still visible.

Chris brushed his fingers over it. "He made you do—"

"He put his sword in front of him just like you had it before and let it go. I—"

"You tried to grab it?" His eyes opened wide, and he looked from her eyes to her palm. "Sara, you could have lost it."

She nodded. "You know the rest. I wasn't adequate to be a soldier. He offered to take me to Tundra. He seemed excited with the idea of me living with your mom…"

"Why didn't you?" he asked while wrapping her hand again. "I'm sure it would have been fun to see you there…in real life, of course. We were there before."

Although she wanted to talk more about that, she had to finish her point, and she prepared for his reaction.

"You let me come with you."

Chris puffed and kept looking at her hand. "That's one way of putting it. It was more you saving us from the reisers, jumping all around the Soto Forest, and—"

"No, Chris…" She noticed the change in his mood as he tensed and kept avoiding her eyes. "I know it hasn't been easy, but at least you gave me the chance to—"

He stood and pushed his hair back. "Sara, I'm no better than he was. I never will be. The reason I ended up meeting you is because I did something stupid that almost cost us the war. Cassandra saved the situation, but…I'm not…"

"Hayden is right," she said, afraid to look at him. "You are a stronger leader, and your dad believed it, too. He sent you to Tundra with the king because he believed you could save everyone."

"My father sent me to Tundra for another reason, Sara." Chris rubbed his face and turned away from her. A moment later, he faced her again. "He sent me to make sure my mother didn't suffer at the reiser's hands."

"Or he chose you because he wanted you to survive and save—"

"Stop it!"

A memory came to her mind. Zhortas kept running and screaming away from soldiers and people who kept chasing and killing them. Her eyes filled with tears, and she held her breath, trying to control the familiar tremble in her hands and the loud pounding of her heartbeat inside her head.

"You may have met my father a few times, but you didn't know him." Chris said. "I understand why he sent me to Tundra, and I get why he didn't let you stay with the army. You would have been likely to sacrifice your life, thinking it was for the best. He would have had to protect you and everyone from your own decisions. It's a simple principle, and it doesn't mean he didn't give you a chance. I never had that option, so I had to—"

Sara walked past him, and when he touched her arm, she moved away.

"Sara," he said, and the anger had dropped from his voice, "I didn't mean..."

She just kept walking.

There was no point in talking to him. For a few days, she had thought he understood her role in that war. Now she knew better, and she wasn't sure if her tears were because of her broken heart or her rising hate for herself for having been so stupid.

AMANDA AND CHARLIE had left a while ago. Neither had said anything, but they'd seemed to agree with Hayden. He regretted having brought it up. In his mind, he thought he was reassuring Chris that they were doing the right thing. It didn't work out as planned.

Genevieve was still sitting by the fire. She'd wrapped herself in a thick blanket and kept her sight on the flames. They really hadn't talked. The day Sara saved her life, she'd informed him of what had happened to her in a tone just like one of his reisers giving him a report.

Hayden's hands were sweaty despite the cold, and his heartbeat accelerated when he realized no one else was with them.

"Is this how it has always looked?" he said.

"I don't know." Genevieve looked around for a moment. "I lived in the asylum, but..." Her lips trembled, and she pulled the blanket tighter. "It looks and smells better than the night I left."

Hayden nodded and changed the topic. "Can you feel?" She glanced up at him, raising an eyebrow. "I mean, sort of like humans. Do you have feelings?"

"They designed the armor to make sure no one gets attached to anything, to keep your senses under control to avoid preferences. Whether you like the wind or the rain, soup or bread, or more complex feelings...without preferences, it is easier to follow orders. Now that you don't have armor, you perceive things differently." She turned to him. "It must confuse you. However, I never wore armor. They raised, trained, and educated us to not jeopardize our race over minor things. It seemed right or...or so I thought."

"You thought?"

Hayden stared at her, and like every time he did, something happened to him. The amazing memory he'd recovered the moment he saw her in Cassandra's bed, along with an urgency to protect her from everything and make her happy, overtook his mind.

"I have to ask," he said while studying her. "Which mistake were you talking about? What was it that Murllen took advantage of?"

"You," she said, looking away from him.

He rubbed his face and tried not to raise his voice. "How the hell did he use me?"

"To break me." Tears filled her eyes. "I care too much about you, and…I shouldn't. He was aware of it."

She sighed and pressed her lips together, not looking at him. From what he remembered, her confidence and humor were missing, along with the color in her skin and the spark in her green eyes. She was heartbroken and fragile, but still beautiful.

"Murllen always broke our rules," Genevieve said, "and the day he brought you to the asylum wasn't an exception." She shook her head. "Because I was in charge, I shouldn't have been helping the reisers when they visited us. But when you were there, I was the only one available."

Genevieve covered her face with her hands for a second before wiping her eyes. "I should have let you sleep in the vestibule and sent you out. You wouldn't have known any better… I just couldn't take your rights away." She finally looked at him. "It's your right and privilege to create a legacy for our future. Anyone who stands in those walls deserves the opportunity to improve our race."

"Since I can ask now," Hayden said, "what the hell happens there? Another reiser takes your armor off and—"

"No! It's prohibited. The only reason I did that was because your life was in danger. The sedative was suffocating you. You were dying, and I couldn't let that happen. I wasn't thinking straight, though." She sighed. "I found the answer to our problems in you, and I stopped being careful."

Hayden tilted his head and smiled.

"It is more like a plantation." Her tone sounded formal. "Reisers cannot be fertilized or gestate. Thanks to an amazing design, obviously from the valsings, there is no need for us to get pregnant. Because of this, we avoid maternal attachment."

He had never given too much thought to the asylum. In fact, he'd never liked the concept, but now he despised it. The idea of denying the care of a mother to someone who hadn't even been born made him sick. Their design wasn't meant to protect them; it was meant to isolate them from the world and themselves.

He stood and shook his head, hoping she disliked the idea as much as he did.

"It's amazing, though." Her face lit up while her eyes turned to the sky. "I miss the little one in me."

Hayden crouched in front of her to listen better.

"Murllen lied to me." She fought her tears back. "I was so upset because he brought Chris's mother that I didn't think about what I was saying. I told him about you. That you are our rightful leader and I was expecting your successor." She paused and dropped the blanket to wrap her arms around herself. "I could feel the baby moving inside of me."

He had never contemplated the idea of having offspring before, and it shocked him how agonizing it was to have lost that baby. His baby. He felt even worse when he saw how much it hurt Genevieve and how little he could do for her. He leaned forward and touched her head. He held a loose curl between his fingers, enjoying how soft and smooth it was, just like he remembered.

"Do you regret it?" he said. "I'm sure your life would have been better if I had never—"

"I regret nothing about you." Genevieve looked straight into his eyes. "I was an idiot, and I messed it up, but not you..." She moved her hand towards his and stopped an inch away. "I'm so sorry I lost your baby. I wouldn't blame you if you hate me."

Hayden touched her face, and her tears made his fingers wet as he lifted her chin to look into her eyes. "Genevieve, the last thing I could ever do is hate you."

Careful not to hurt her, he pulled her close and tasted once again the sweetness of her lips. Between his arms, he felt her trembling and heard her sobbing against his shoulder.

"I'd give my life to see you smile like you did the day I met you." Hayden moved back so she could look at him. "I'm not stupid. I know there isn't much I can do for you." Genevieve touched his face, but he didn't let her talk. "What I'll do, though, is kill those freaking bastards, and not because of our race or our future. I couldn't give a damn about that. I'll do it because of what they did to you, what they took from you...from us."

He hugged her as tightly as he dared and felt glad no one could see him, not even her, when he rubbed his face in her hair to wipe the tears from his eyes.

~

It was night again when John came back. They were less than a day away from the fortress, and the place didn't expect visitors. The towers were empty, and they found no watchers or scouts. It did not surprise Chris. Murllen's arrogance had made him certain of his dominion over the swamp.

"In that case, we have to prepare for the fight," he said to John, and he sent a soldier to gather the other leaders.

"I know you need to rest, but I'd rather you stay for this one," he said.

"No problem, Commander."

"You mean general," Amanda said, almost running towards them. She stopped in front of John and checked his arm before giving him a quick perusal that made John and Chris chuckle.

"My apologies, General. I was just—"

"General?" John lifted his arm. "What did I miss?"

Donald and Lily approached them, looking somber.

"Let's go to the large fire," Chris said, loud enough that Charlie followed them, though his usual joy was missing. Right behind him, Hayden walked with Dunstan and Genevieve. Chris was still mad at him, but they had more important things to deal with.

"Major," Chris said, "explain to the lieutenant the change of rank and find Sara, please."

"Yes, sir," Amanda said and strode away with John.

Right before Chris followed the others, he saw John grabbing her hand, and she leaned against his shoulder. He sighed and shook his head. After he'd yelled at Sara, she'd made a point of not crossing his path.

By the fire, Hayden was sitting with Genevieve. There was an edge of danger radiating from her, and he didn't want to test it. Lily, on the other hand, looked defeated and sad.

"We need a map of the fortress," Chris said.

"Isn't that your dream, Christopher?" Hayden said, but he picked up a stick and traced a rough blueprint on the muddy ground.

The tension among them was difficult to ignore. Winning the battle meant winning the war, and the end of the war meant a new beginning for everyone.

"Where is Sara?" Donald said.

"She is coming." Chris kept his eyes on the uneven lines on the ground.

"There is another way in," Genevieve said. "The back of the asylum isn't protected by a wall."

Hayden looked at her with a hint of kindness in his eyes. "There must be a good reason for that."

"Two, actually." She sat straighter. "The foliage of the swamp behind the building is too thick, and the water is deep, taller than a person. However, there is a narrow path. Since I grew up looking out those windows, I can guide you there."

"What is the other reason?" Chris said.

"Well, the reisers in the asylum, of course." A smile spread over her face, but it wasn't a friendly one. "You would never survive crossing them. Luckily, they will be on your side… once I talk to them."

"I have questions about overconfidence," Charlie said.

Dunstan faced Charlie, and his disgust and anger were clear. "Isn't that a very…how did you call it, overconfident statement?"

Charlie let out a loud, fake laugh, and John, who had just walked in with Amanda, grabbed his arm before he could stand up.

"Let's put it this way," Hayden said while resting his hand on Genevieve's knee. "I wouldn't try to fight any of those reisers, and as my former prisoner, you should know what that means."

"I have no doubts," Chris said and his tone wasn't one to play with. "And this is more important than proving who is better than whom. I'm certain I don't have to remind anyone here what would happen if we lost this one."

"I wonder if Gemli knows about it, though," Sara said.

She walked around the fire and crouched by the map before pulling her hood down.

Chris wasn't sure if she noticed how her statement had intensified the group's tension.

"The first time I met him," Genevieve said, "he used the

front door…the same one he used the last… He never visited us."

Sara looked at her for a second and then turned to Chris. There was no kindness in her eyes, and suddenly the danger radiating from Genevieve was nothing compared to Sara's dreadful look.

"Did you finish the journal?"

Chris nodded, and she simply looked back at the ground.

"In that case, this won't be news to you." She stood. "Gemli was a reiser."

"That's impossible!" Hayden said, grabbing Dunstan's arm.

Chris found his hand looking for his sword, and Donald was standing by him, touching his arm.

"As impossible as it is to have a human as your leader?" Sara said, and both reisers looked away from her.

"In his journal, Gemli explains how he visited the asylum but something went wrong. His memory was intact when he left, and his leader sent him into exile and broke his armor."

"Wait a second," Donald said, staring at Sara. "That book—journal—is Gemli's?"

Sara nodded and pressed her lips together.

"And you have been studying it?" John said.

She just shrugged as if that was enough explanation.

"And you have known this for weeks?" Donald said. "Did you think it was—"

"Important to tell you?" Sara said, tilting her head and looking at Chris.

Chris crossed his arms and exhaled. "I guess I should ask if there is anything else that is important to learn now?"

Sara didn't have a chance to answer.

"His memory was intact when he left the asylum?" Genevieve said.

"Yes," Sara said. "He doesn't talk much about the place.

Instead, he explains how, after a few days of living in pain outside the fortress and without his armor, he—"

"He was in a rage because he fell for the lie?" Genevieve touched Hayden's arms and turned to him. "He mentioned something about this when he... Listen, if the sedative didn't work, it only means..." Her expression darkened. "Like you, Hayden, he was born to be one of our leaders."

Hayden shook his head and stood. "That monster! Why would he...? No. Not possible. It has to be a mistake."

Chris moved and was at Sara's side when Hayden turned to her.

"That's garbage, Sara. Why would he want to...? Why not just take the leader down? All this war and..."

Sara sighed and nodded. "I understand your anger. The other monster is my blood relative."

Hayden turned to Genevieve, who smiled at him and gestured for him to sit down. After he did, he grabbed her hand and kept it between his.

"Gemli is a sorcerer," Donald said, "and a perverted one. Who knows how many years he has been planning all of this! Revenge is fuel for sick souls."

"How did he end up...?" Dunstan said. "I get that the armor's protection is fake, but still, surviving out here, probably injured like Genevieve...how did he make it?"

Sara looked at the map on the ground. "Zhortas. They saved him, taught him how to become one of them, and then gave him access to all the knowledge of Hune."

Lily gasped and covered her mouth. "The library? All those...? He knows—"

"He is very smart." Sara wrapped her arms around herself. "And like Donald said, he is looking for revenge. That's why he destroyed the abbey the way he did and why he played with all the races. His motive is to break Hune's balance so he will be in charge once everything falls apart."

The silence was as dense as the fog. Chris had avoided thinking about Gemli's motive for the war. Murllen was easy, and it made sense to him: control the reisers and the humans. The sorcerer couldn't be that simple, but knowing this didn't make it better. He took a step closer to Sara.

"We have one chance," he said. "Let's not mess it up."

~

THE ADDED pressure improved the willingness of everyone to plan their next move. With every piece of information, Chris understood more about his enemy and the reason they had failed for so long. He was conscious of how close they were to winning this time, something he'd only dared to dream about as a child.

They would assault the fortress from two sides, and the reisers inside the asylum would fight with them.

"Charlie and John will lead part of our army to the rear of the fortress with Genevieve," he said. "The rest of us will wait at the entrance. This will give the troops in the rear time to reach the asylum. How long do you think you need?"

Genevieve looked at the map. "A day to get to the fortress and half to cross the swamp."

"What about convincing the reisers in there?" John said.

"That won't be a problem," she said. "As soon as they see me alive, they will figure out who the real traitor is."

Chris nodded and explained the rest of the plan.

"You'll leave by sunrise. We'll wait until sunset and camp right by the fortress the next night. We'll start the attack early in the morning once we have enough light."

Chris looked at Sara for a second. She had been sitting quietly away from the group. He thought he'd had it all planned for her, but after what he'd learned from Gemli, he'd changed his mind.

"Hayden, Donald, and Amanda will be in the front with me." He paused for a moment. "Donald?"

His friend looked up at him, and Chris didn't need to ask. The shadow crossing Donald's eyes let Chris know he understood the question, and he answered by nodding and grabbing Lily's hand.

"Lily, you'll be with us."

Lily looked up, and although she lost a bit of color, she smiled.

"Sara, you'll stay behind the soldiers. Hayden, where are you going to—"

"Lily in the front?" Sara said, and her blank expression only increased Chris's concern. "Why?"

As a commander, he wouldn't have had to explain his decision, and as a general, it was an insult to even ask. However, that wasn't what bothered him. It was the half-truth he needed to tell her.

"You have to remove Gemli's spell and then break the armor inside the fortress. I need to make sure you have the strongest protection; otherwise…we can't do much if something happens to you."

He knew it sounded cold and was not what he wanted to tell her, but he had no other option.

"So, you are just using Lily as a distraction?" Sara said loudly.

Lily cleared her throat and leaned forward. "I offered—no, I begged Chris to let me do this… I want to earn your forgiveness. At least, I hope that one day you—"

"And you agreed to this?" Sara turned to Donald.

He kissed Lily's hand and nodded, but he looked terrified.

Unlike his friend, Chris kept his face calm, but he had never been this scared in his life. He wanted to take Sara somewhere where they could talk, but it was too late for that.

"I'll be in the back, then." Sara shrugged and avoided looking at him.

The rest of the planning was hard but fast. Chris kept waiting for Sara to yell at him, but her silence alarmed him more. Aside from that, when he dismissed everyone, he felt content.

He was walking to Charlie and John to go over the last-minute details when Sara stood in his way.

"Sara," he said, "I have to get everything ready for—"

"This won't take long." She held up Gemli's journal. "When you got injured, when you almost died, Donald asked me to read a letter from your sack."

Chris took a step closer to her and touched her arm. "Did you...?"

She nodded.

"I don't think it was much help for you, right?"

Sara tilted her head and smiled for a second. Then she pushed the journal into his hand. "It gave me a good idea. If after the battle..." She bit her lip and sighed. "If for any reason Hune is out of control and you need help, read it."

Chris shook his head and tried to give the book back, but she stepped backward.

"My mother...you saw her when Cielthos showed us..." She cleared her throat and grabbed her arm. "She called the Great Wizard with it. If you need to, just say the prayer."

"Sara, I can't talk right now. A lot has to be made ready for tomorrow before the first group leaves."

When her eyes filled with tears, Chris realized how harsh he'd sounded. He took a step forward, but she moved back.

"I understand. I'm sorry. I'll let you get back to—

"No, wait. I wish I had the time to talk to you. I'd rather fight with you than—"

"I get it." She reached for his hand and smiled, but the tears rolling down her face made her look sadder. "I don't want to fight, though. There is nothing else to say, but…" Her expression brightened when she peeked at his eyes. "I'm going to sleep now. Will you stay with me later?"

Chris pulled her close and kissed her forehead. "Of course."

THE BATTLE

Although Chris kept his word and eventually Sara noticed him sliding in next to her, he didn't stay long. In the morning, she barely saw him, and too soon, they started their march.

It didn't matter that they rode in the dark over unknown and difficult terrain. The night moved to day deceptively and now, at Sara's feet, stood the massive stone structure of the reisers' secret home. She was thankful that Mulsh was with her, because the rest of the people she cared for were far away.

She shivered when she looked around. The thick fog made it impossible to see the full extension of the fortress's protective wall, making it seem never-ending. Someone had mixed the mud in that section of the swamp with a dense red liquid that, along with the pestilential odor surrounding them, worked like the tool of intimidation that the reisers meant it to be.

"What the hell is this place?" a soldier said behind Sara.

"It's bigger than the freaking palace in Tundra," Another one said.

"We're doomed!"

The soldiers dismounted, so she did, too, and when her feet touched the ground, she breathed faster. Her hands trembled while her mind seemed to have fallen into a nightmare. Although she was cold, her hands were sweaty, and a knot grew in her stomach. The air appeared to be too thick as her lungs screamed for more oxygen, and she stepped backward until she bumped into a dead tree.

She remembered her father's conversation about the saber, and as she watched the tall structure, she realized those walls would be the last place she would ever see. She put her hands on the dead trunk behind her and tried to swallow her tears. Her fate wasn't important. The lives of everyone around her depended on her strength to not run away.

"General!" a soldier said, pushing the others out of his way.

Her gaze followed the soldier until she found Chris. He was riding a black horse at the front, with nothing but the empty dead field between him and the fortress. Sara focused on his calm and steady posture and forced herself to control her breathing and slow her heartbeat.

Chris leaned down to listen to the soldier. Then, with a nod, he directed the soldiers to move forward.

Hate, rage, and retribution filled them. Their emotions were dangerous, powerful, and in that case, rightful. Sara remembered what Cielthos had told her before he'd died, and she tried to let her mind fill with the sweet memories of Chris. It wasn't easy. Panic threatened to overcome her, and she didn't want her anger to surface. The soldiers were far from her by the time she found peace within her, and with a deep breath, she walked towards the front.

"Well, well," a powerful voice said from the top of the

wall. "You stupid humans. Finally, you made it to our sweet home."

Her heart skipped a beat at the voice's resemblance to her dad's, and she froze for a second. However, when she saw him, the oversized, mutilated reiser staring at the soldiers looked nothing like her father.

A dark, tall figure, his head covered by a familiar hood, stood next to the reiser. Sara thought the temperature had dropped, and she had to hold her hands to stop them from shaking.

"According to Hune's laws and in the name of its races," Chris said, and his voice wasn't nicer or weaker than Murllen's, "I'm forced to give you the chance to surrender and avoid this battle."

The reisers on the wall yelled and pretended to laugh. However, the soldiers on the ground, reisers, humans, and valsings, growled, making the ground tremble.

"I hope you don't take it," Chris said.

Murllen lifted his claw, and the fortress became silent. "Who the hell are you? And which freaking races are you talking about? We, the reisers—"

"Only a complete idiot wouldn't know what Hune's races are. But maybe the twisted magic that your lover Gemli used on you burned your already sickened brain."

Sara forced herself to walk again.

"I'm General Christopher Riddley."

On top of the wall, Murllen turned to Gemli, and even from a distance, she could see the sorcerer lift his shoulders and raise his palms in the air.

"You were supposed to be dead."

"Of course you would believe that," Hayden said at Chris's side. "You like to imagine your enemies were murdered."

Hate resonated in Murllen's voice. "Colonel Green. You freaking bastard. You made it back to my house!" He leaned forward and softened his tone. "By the way, I heard you broke our magnificent rules during your last visit to the asylum. They forced me to wipe away the scum you left behind."

Chris had to move his horse to block Hayden's while Murllen's sick laugh filled the swamps.

Sara reached for Lily's horse and got her attention.

"Sara! No, no! You need to get back. You have to stay away from—"

"I just want you to know that no matter how many stupid things you said to me, you will always be my best friend, and I also think of you as part of my family." Sara smiled even though her sight blurred. "I appreciate what you are trying to do more than you can imagine, but you don't have to, silly. 'Sorry' has always been a good word for you to learn."

Lily dismounted and grabbed her hand. "Come on. You have to go back—"

"I wish you happiness, Lily." Sara touched the scar on Lily's face, and a sweet, warm feeling filled her palm. "If I can ask for something, though, would you be nice to Chris? He'll need someone."

As understanding dawned on Lily, she cried, and Sara hugged her tight until Murllen spoke again.

"It makes no difference how many traitors you bring with you, General." He clapped a few times. "Leonard's death suited you well. In any case, we were hoping for any member of your defeated army to show up. Personally, I'm thrilled it's you. But now…let me introduce you to one of my dearest friends."

From behind the fortress, the wind blew, and a loud growl echoed throughout the swamp. The soldiers shifted nervously, and fear showed in their expressions. Donald looked at Lily, and his eyes widened when he saw Sara.

"What the hell are you—"

Lily silenced her scream by covering her mouth, and Sara turned just in time to see the enormous dragon fly out from behind the castle wall.

"I didn't see that one coming," Hayden said.

Chris turned to his men, but he only seemed concerned when he saw Sara.

"I didn't think it was important enough to mention it," she said, standing beside Chris's horse. "Do you mind if I use this?"

She reached into his coat pocket, where the sweet aroma led her to the glacier orchid.

"Sara, what are you…?"

She turned, and the flapping of the dragon's wings seemed to slow down. A slight burn like the one she'd gotten with Cielthos made her focus, and as soon as her fingers touched the soft petals of the blossom, her surroundings changed.

Time stopped being important as Hune's power reached her. As though she were stretching, Sara stood taller while the world she loved opened to her will. Her hands, instead of trembling, twinkled, begging her to control the ground, the air, the fog, and to clear the poison in it.

Although all other Great Wizards had that power, she knew the difference. Her father had passed it to her by blood. Hune had just accepted her as its wizard. The flutter in her stomach made her smile and brought a sureness to her steps.

From the corner of her eye, she saw Chris dismounting and overheard him yell her name, but in front of her, the dragon opened its mouth. Flames formed inside it and then flew towards her and the army behind her. She pressed the orchid, and it exploded into countless pieces, covering the soldiers and protecting them from the fire. She let the flames touch her, though, and enjoyed their heat and energy.

"Sara!" Chris said louder.

The dragon turned, and this time it targeted her. She crouched and blew on the ground, opening the mud. Thousands of dry leaves grew up around her, forming the shape of another dragon.

Then the dragon changed directions and attacked the leaf dragon, but the leaves twisted, entangling the real dragon and forcing it to lie at Sara's feet.

"Hello, Brutus," she said, and flames covered her once more. "Cielthos was so worried about you, but he couldn't reach you. He told me you believe you must follow their orders, but you don't. He also wanted you to remember how much my father appreciated you… I know he did."

Brutus growled once more, but this time, there was no fire.

"Gemli lied to you. Neither my father nor I was dead. He tricked you into helping him."

"You are lying," Brutus said, and she had trouble understanding him.

"I'm not," she said. "But I'm sorry for your loss…and also sorry because I couldn't help Cielthos. He hopes you avenge his death."

Brutus stared at her, showing her all the horrible things Gemli had made him do and how they weighed on his soul. He lowered his head closer to her, and she touched it with her hands and rested her forehead on his scales, letting her tears roll down. After a few seconds, Brutus's eyes narrowed, and she moved back.

The dragon flew straight to the wall, where he let his fire out. The reisers on the top screamed as they burned—some even jumped down—but Brutus didn't care about them. Gemli was his target, and he grabbed the sorcerer in his claw and threw him in front of Sara.

She covered her face when a wave of heat washed over

her. It was gooey and dense, but it was the odor of putrefaction that made her step back and cough.

"Behind you!" Chris yelled, and something grabbed her ankle. By instinct, she pulled her leg up and took another step backward, which gave Gemli enough time to stand up.

"I'm difficult to defeat," he said while his eyes changed from deep black to red.

She looked straight at them, and a breeze whipped around him. As she stepped closer to him, she made the dead roots of the swamp rise and grabbed the sorcerer's feet. He hit the ground head first and groaned.

Sara bent down in front of him. "Funny thing. I have never been defeated."

He pushed himself up and looked up at her. As she tilted her head and smiled at him, recognition filled his eyes, and he crawled backward.

"Impossible!" he said.

"Impossible? No," she said. "Just highly unlikely."

"You are alive." He clawed at the roots around his feet. "There is no way you can be—"

"The Great Wizard?" At her words, the ground trembled, and the swamp water near Gemli boiled. "Once you killed my father, I took his place."

The sorcerer looked up at the wall, where Murllen was staring down at them. Sara followed his gaze and smirked. "That's right. His brother, Colonel Landford White. I'm sure he would have been sorry to miss this day."

Murllen growled and threw a knife at her, but Brutus incinerated it long before it landed.

"I guess your family doesn't like you," Gemli said. "No wonder you grew up alone in—"

Brutus landed beside Sara and unleashed his fire on Gemli.

A dark shadow emerged from the sorcerer and fought the

flames, pushing them down and consuming them until only smoke was left. Gemli stood. His clothes were ripped and burned in parts, but he was intact.

"You didn't think that would hurt me, did you?" he said, smiling, but his voice was unsteady. "You can't kill what is not alive...unlike you."

The dragon's wing covered Sara, and from behind it, she saw its dark skin thin down until it disappeared, and Brutus growled in pain.

"Enough!" She put her arms up.

The density of the swampy ground grew for a second, and Gemli fell to his knees again.

"You won't do more harm. Remember the prophecy, your prophecy?"

On top of the wall, Murllen laughed, but the sorcerer froze, and panic appeared in his eyes.

"Zhorta Gemli, it's your turn."

The ground around the sorcerer shaped itself into hundreds of hands that pulled the sorcerer down. Between agonizing screams and painful growls, Sara drained all the power out of him until only the man was left in front of her.

The years of unnatural life were now apparent: his hair was white and half-gone, his skin was wrinkled and saggy, and his bones had withered, shrinking him a few inches.

"No, please!" Gemli dragged himself to her feet. "You are a good person. I can see light in your soul. I'm begging you, have mercy."

"Good person?" Sara said as her blood seemed to burn and her heartbeat sped up. "Mercy?"

She stared at what remained of the sorcerer who had tortured her mother and father, only to kill them afterward, who had massacred the zhortas in the Soto Forest, manipulated Chris into finding her and the saber, and toyed with everyone in Hune for decades.

"It is a peculiar position, being the most powerful one in a battle," she said.

"What do you want to do with that?" Brutus said as Gemli trembled and cried on the ground.

Sara glanced at the dragon, and her hands flew to her mouth. His wing hung in pieces, like fabric bathed in blood, and half of his face had lost its scales, showing the muscles underneath.

She rested her palms on top of the rough scales. The poisoned heat emanating from him reduced at the same time as the wing grew back. Although it wasn't possible, she thought she perceived a smile from Brutus.

"You are right, Gemli," she said. "I'm a good person. Brutus deserves to live in peace. He can claim revenge for the members of our families that you killed." Then she stepped in front of the dragon. "This thing, it's all yours. You can do as you please with it."

She turned and walked back to the soldiers' line.

"You'll make your uncle proud," Gemli said.

Sara kept walking and heard screams, cracking, and tearing, which she didn't want to think about. Instead, she forced her eyes on the ground ahead and slowed her breathing. Her hands were shaking, and fear had nothing to do with it. Cielthos had warned her about anger, and the only thing she dreaded was hurting Hune by mistake.

Once she was a few steps from the soldiers, she knelt and blew on the land. The fog lifted at the same time that the swamp's waters cleared up. The essence of putrefaction was washed away by a fresh breeze, and though there wasn't much to be done for the dead foliage, the clean surroundings made the swamp look less sinister.

She pushed her hands together, and the pieces of the glacier orchid reshaped into the original beautiful blossom. Gemli's spell had died with him, so she only needed to open the armor. She closed her eyes and followed the same path she had with Hayden.

From inside the fortress, she overheard the sound of metal cracking, but afraid to hurt or weaken the already free reisers outside, she stopped short, knowing, this time, she hadn't opened all of them. She just hoped it was enough.

She wrapped the flower in Chris's handkerchief and took a deep breath before looking up.

Chris was struggling against Hayden and Donald, who were holding him back. The second he noticed her, he stopped.

"Thank you for allowing me to borrow this," she said, handing him the orchid.

"Sara." He pulled her into his arms and hugged her tightly.

The thud of the wooden gate hitting the ground, followed by the screams of reisers charging, made him stop.

"Stay behind," he said, looking her straight in the eyes with a hard expression.

Sara barely had time to move to the side before the soldiers passed her and the crash of metal on metal filled the swamp.

~

THE BATTLE around Sara kept going, but it was impossible to know for how long. She was only aware of how fast she needed to go from one wounded soldier to help a reiser out of his armor. She didn't even notice the moment she walked inside the fortress until she recognized Donald.

He froze and stared into the distance. Close to the castle entrance, a valsing was burying his sword in a human soldier. It was clear the valsing hadn't fought; he was only making sure the man wouldn't survive.

The sound of horseshoes approaching warned her, and

she barely had a chance to move before a reiser hit her. Sara rolled to the side and lay on her back, looking at the sky. Above her, Brutus flew past, reminding her of what she needed to do. Her vision blurred, but she stood with determination. It was time to find the saber and finish the war.

"Wait!" Donald ran towards her. "I have no idea where you think you are going, but you better be with someone else."

"That's right," Chris said marching towards her from the other side of the fortress. "You can't be here, much less alone."

She took a deep breath as she noticed the rips in Chris's sleeves and the dark spots on his uniform. She was about to move closer to him when, from the corner of her eye, she recognized the bigger shape of Murllen running away.

"You promised, Sara," Chris said, blocking Murllen from her sight. "Everything will be all right." He sounded sure of himself, but when she looked down, blood bathed his hand and sword, telling her something else.

"There is only one way to finish this, and you know it," she said.

"Listen to me." He lifted her face. "This is my job, Sara, and I'm damn good at it. It'll be done soon, and you won't need to do anything else. You took down the hard one for us." He stepped closer to her, and his voice softened. "I'm telling you, we will win. Please, Sara, trust me."

Sara's breathing eased as she stared into Chris's eyes. There was no hint of doubt in them, and it was easy to believe him. She nodded, and a huge weight lifted from her shoulders, allowing her to smile at him.

"I will get her out of here," Donald said.

Before she changed her mind, Sara turned to follow Donald, but then Chris grabbed her elbow, pulled her towards him, and kissed her. It wasn't a soft kiss. His desire to love and protect her was clear in it, and she responded with the same passion and longing.

All too soon, he moved away, and without taking his eyes from hers, he grabbed a lock of her hair and followed it down while he stepped back.

"Stay with Donald," he said, and his smile illuminated his face.

Donald didn't wait any longer and strode with her in the other direction. It wasn't easy to run against the battle, and they had to lean against the tower's wall to find a path to get out.

"Do you see any…?" Donald said, but a couple of Orson's valsings spotted them and walked towards them.

The only escape was to hide inside the tower.

Sara saw a valsing pull a sword from a dead reiser and race towards them. Donald helped her slam the heavy door closed behind them just in time.

As she leaned against the door, she noticed the smell of decay and the dark stains of a dripping liquid on the walls. The few torches in the place illuminated a circular stairway where chains, knives, hooks, dented traps, and saws hung all the way up.

"I don't think we should stay here," she said, but in answer, heavy pounding threatened to smash the door behind her.

Donald bolted it and shook his head. "I dislike this place, too, but we certainly can go back out." He climbed the stairs.

A dark chamber opened in front of them. More weapons and tools hung from its walls, but most were scattered on the floor. The smell of death was stronger, and the light coming from the window dared the visitors to look around.

"Sara!" a male voice said, making her jump. "My sweet girl, you are all right… You need to get out of here."

As if her feet had a life of their own, she approached the man.

He hung from the ceiling by his wrists, suspended just high enough by the chains to keep his feet from touching the floor. His hair was white and long, and bruises and scars covered his thin body. But his eyes were the same ones she had grown up looking at.

"Rafael?" she said. "I thought they killed you."

The zhorta looked at her. Pain and sorrow clouded his sight.

"Sara, I…" His voice broke in sobs.

Disgusted by what Murllen had done, Sara closed the gap between them. She abhorred Gemli and detested Leonard, but even when she remembered her mother and what they had done to her, Rafael was different. She might never forgive him, but she couldn't hate him, either.

"Donald, I need your help," she said and turned to look for him.

For the first time, she noticed the other prisoner. She was sitting on the floor with her hands chained to the wall. Her face was stained with dry blood, and like Rafael, she was pale and sick. Most of her hair was gray, but the light of the sun brightened the trace of red on it.

"We need to get you both out of here," Donald said.

"No!" the woman said. "You must leave now."

Sara knelt by her and touched her cheek. The second her gray eyes looked back at her, she recognized her.

"You are Chris's mother."

Donald stopped trying to open the chains on her wrists and glanced at Sara. "How do you…?" Then he saw the woman's eyes and nodded.

"I'm no one," Alleta said. "My son is dead."

"No, he isn't," Sara said. "He is going to win this war." A

smile crossed her face when she realized how certain she was about it.

The pounding on the door stopped, and the silence was frightening. Alleta grabbed Sara's hands tightly.

"Just kill me, then. I'm a hazard to him. Murllen will use me against—"

"I won't kill you," Sara said and looked up at Donald. "We'll get you out of here."

Terror contorted Alleta's face, and she pushed Sara away. "No, you won't." She pressed herself back against the wall, hiding the chains as much as she could.

Sara took a deep breath and turned to look at Rafael. He was also defeated, and he nodded at her. "She is right, Sara. Leave now."

Donald moved to the window and looked out. "We could use the chains to lower them down. But they need to—"

"No!" Alleta said. "Just go before he comes back."

Sara pushed herself up, knowing that without their cooperation, it would be impossible to get them out. The coldness of her pendant against her chest made her smile, and she knelt again and put her necklace in Alleta's hand.

"Chris told me you had something like this before."

Alleta's eyes shone as they filled with tears.

"I know it isn't yours," Sara said, "but it's a reminder that you have someone who loves you. You have to go back home with him."

"We need to move now," Donald said. "Can you break the chains? I'll get her down and come back for the zhorta."

Sara grabbed the chains above Alleta's head and solidified the metal until it shattered. The part around her wrist would have to wait until they were safe. As soon as Alleta was free, Donald picked her up with no trouble. She hold onto his neck while he used the chain to climb down the window.

"Just go, Sara," Rafael said when she reached for his hands.

"No," she said, and her voice betrayed her.

He tried to move closer to her.

"There is nothing I can tell you that could make a difference. I have hated myself since the moment your poor mom died. I swore to protect you then…to try to make up for what I did to her. To you."

She touched the metal and heated it fast. She wasn't sure if she wanted to hurt Rafael or not, but without something to hold him, he hit the floor and growled in pain.

"Sorry, I should have…" She knelt by him.

"No, my child. I'm the one who is sorry. I deserve this and more."

A scream reached them, and Sara ran to the window just in time to see Murllen.

He grabbed Donald and threw him against a wall on the other side of the yard. There were no signs of Alleta. His eyes looked up at her, and with a kick, the door broke down. She stepped back as the heavy steps of the reiser climbed up the stairs.

"Murllen," Rafael said. "Sara, the window. Go!"

"I'm not leaving you." She moved towards the zhorta. "You are the father I grew up with. I won't abandon you."

A similar fear to the one she'd had on the field overtook her, blurring her thoughts when she realized Murllen wasn't running up the stairs to catch them. He was making sure they heard him coming.

Rafael touched her cheek. His eyes were wet, but he was smiling. "My sweet girl, please—"

"Look who we have here," Murllen said at the top of the stairs. "Landford's daughter. You weren't leaving without meeting your uncle, were you?"

As Sara tried to help Rafael to his feet, to her horror, she realized that his legs were broken.

"Leave her alone." Rafael crawled between her and the reiser.

"Or what?" A cynical laugh escaped Murllen's mouth. "You'll bite my toes?"

She tried to push Murllen like she had Lily when she saved Donald's life, but the second her magic hit his armor, it bounced back, and she smashed into the wall behind her.

Murllen laughed louder. "I guess I have Gemli to thank for that."

Slightly dizzy, she looked around. The room was full of weapons, and though she didn't know how to use any of them, she grabbed the first one she could and threw it at Murllen. A heavy hammer hit its target harder than she could have hoped, and her uncle fell backwards on the floor.

She moved to help Rafael, but he pushed her away.

"I can't stop him for long, but Sara, you are my life and happiness. Please go."

He pushed himself on top of Murllen, preventing the reiser from getting up.

Between tears, Sara reached the window as horrible screams filled the room, along with the hard thumps of something hitting the wall. She grabbed the edge of the opening and pulled herself up. Her head pounded against her ears, and she was disoriented, incapable of controlling her breathing. There was no way she could turn into wind, but jumping was still an option.

"Like I said." Murllen grabbed her leg and pulled her down. "You are here to meet your family."

Sara's head bumped the window frame so hard that she didn't notice hitting the floor after. A sudden pressure on her brain made the room disappear for a few seconds, and there was no sound but an increasing buzz. The warmth of her blood dripped down her cheek, and she feared touching her face would increase the pain underneath her eye.

"Let's see." Murllen rolled her over to face him. "All that blood doesn't help, but…no, you don't look like Landford."

"Neither do you."

He snorted.

She needed to make time to find a way to get out of there.

"My father…he had a message for you."

He leaned on her, letting his weight press against her torso, and in her ear, she perceived his breath, warm and humid.

"Let me guess. He wanted me dead." He grabbed her neck with one claw. "Tell me, Sara. Do you think you can kill me?"

The lack of air and the growing pressure on her lungs made her lightheaded. Desperate, she grabbed his face. With all her will, she heated her palms until she started hurting herself.

Murllen let her go and jumped backward. He growled louder than before and clutched his face as a few pieces of metal fell from him.

She looked at her hands and, horrified, noticed the open blisters and burning scales, and she could swear her finger bones were visible. Ignoring all of that, she stood and moved towards the stairs.

"I'm not done with you!" He grabbed Sara's shoulder so hard that she thought he would crush it and pulled her against a wall. "Did you forget my message? You don't want to disappoint your daddy, do you?"

She stared at the monster in front of her, terrified and disgusted.

Murllen's armor wasn't like the other reisers'. He was part of it, and now pieces of flesh and metal hung from his face and chest. Severe scars that had never healed crisscrossed his body, and he was covered in blood.

"Tell me, sweetie," he said, looking at the zhorta's body, or what he'd left of it. "Who did my brother send to kill me? You or your little general?"

Sara tried to push him away, but this time, it was useless. She had weakened herself, and her fear wasn't helping.

"You know what?" He increased the pressure on her shoulder. "I like your silence. It'll be priceless to break it later."

A feeble scream escaped Sara's mouth when her blood pushed through her veins like thousands of needles scratching their way through her arm.

"Let me tell you a secret," Murllen said. "When I'm done with you, I'll teach your moronic soldier who is in charge of Hune and why."

Sara swallowed hard and shook her head.

Murllen brushed her hair.

"Poor sweetie, you don't think this is over, do you?" He grabbed her face and forced her to stare at him. "It doesn't matter what the hell happens to the reisers. As long as I'm alive, you'll never find peace, not for Hune and not for you or your freaking lover. That's the best part of this curse."

He took his black sword out and traced its tip along her body.

"Do you like it? A magnificent present from my new friends. But don't worry, you'll get time to admire it soon."

Sara didn't have a message for Murllen. Her dad had said little about her uncle. She knew her dad felt guilty for letting Gemli use his brother, and it was clear Murllen hated him. The betrayal had been mutual, though, and her life depended on her ability to make the reiser see that.

"He didn't want you dead," she said as firmly as she could. "He said you distrusted him."

"I distrusted him!" He pushed her against the wall. "Your bastard father declared war against me. Did he tell you how much he used me? Did he mention how he enlisted me in the army? And that he liked how it was me doing all the dirty jobs? I'm sure he avoided painting that unpleasant picture for his pure daughter."

Sara put her hands on top of his claw, and Murllen dropped it quickly, which made her stumble and fall. He didn't laugh but crouched in front of her.

"He never tried to change you," she said, pushing herself backward as far away from him as possible. "But you did. It was you who didn't accept him. You betrayed him when you chose Gemli. You knew he wouldn't have an option but to stop you, and even then…he tried to talk to you first, but you had made up your mind."

Murllen walked back a couple of steps and touched his jaw, remaining quiet for a moment.

Sara didn't waste time. Though still a bit clumsy, she stood and ran to the window on the other side of the room. She was a step away from it when something icy and sharp penetrated her side. Her blood gushed from her waist, down her leg, and over the floor. As the blade slid out of her body, an excruciating pain threatened to rip her apart.

She understood that her uncle was being compassionate because that wasn't an accidental mortal wound.

"Let's finish this," Murllen said, "and since you want some air, let me help you."

He grabbed a big hammer and threw it against the wall. The stones crashed, and sunlight illuminated the room. Sara was still trying to breathe when he tossed her out of the opening.

It took her a moment to realize that she was somewhere along the protective wall of the fortress. Sounds of the battle rose from below. A loud groan got her attention, and Murllen jumped at her. Her instinct to move was stronger than her pain, and she rolled onto her stomach.

For the first time in her life, she saw the saber. The only weapon that could stop Murllen, and it was just a few steps away from her, still in the ice that protected it. She held her breath and pushed herself forward.

She heard him say, "Where do you think you are—"

The crash of metal interrupted him, but she didn't look back until she heard her name.

"Sara," Chris said. "You promised me… One second. Please!"

"Chris…" she said, and the effort made her side burn, so she held her wound. The amount of wetness in her dress and the thickness of the liquid on her fingers made her cry. He was so close yet still a life away.

Behind Chris, Murllen stood up and charged him. Chris lifted his sword just in time to stop the black blade from cutting his head.

Chris retreated one step and stopped the next strike with both hands. In seconds, he changed his weight and attacked Murllen, but the reiser just charged again. It wasn't difficult to see how that battle was going to end.

Sara crawled as fast as she could until she knelt by the ice. The saber's dark shape was trapped inside, and her body temperature dropped when she looked at it. A strange energy traveled through her; it didn't hurt her, but it wasn't pleasant, either. A few images crossed her mind, and her heart dropped when she learned what they needed to do.

The sudden silence made her look up.

"Sara, no," Chris said, and Sara sighed. "I can finish this. Just don't… It doesn't matter if he survives."

She shook her head, but he kept talking, getting closer to her.

"Listen to me. The reisers won't keep fighting, and we'll stop the valsings."

"The valsings?" She held her breath and touched the ice.

Within a second, it melted, allowing her to pick up the sword.

"No, Sara."

"We didn't consider them before. Chris, it will matter if Murllen is alive... You know it." Tears rolled down her cheeks when she offered him the sword. "No one will be safe as long as he is around."

"But I'll lose you," he said and pushed her hand away.

Sara wiped her tears and stared into his eyes. "Chris, look at me... I'm dying."

She uncovered her side, and her blood rushed out, making her dizzy for a second.

"Sara, no! Damn it!" Chris moved closer and covered her wound with his hand. The warmth of his palm eased her pain and calmed her down. "I need to get you... You'll be fine."

Chris tried to stand, but she held his hand tighter and shook her head. He rested his forehead on hers, and his wet lashes touched her skin.

"You know what to do," she said and handed him the saber.

"Sara," he said, "I won't... I would never..."

"It won't hurt, but...I can't do it myself..." She held her breath again and, grabbing the sword's blade, placed its point against the center of her chest.

Chris's eyes were full of tears, which he tried in vain to fight back.

Behind him, she heard Murllen moving again as his fingers brushed her face. "Could you...please close your eyes."

Nothing could have prepared her for the suffering of having her soul torn apart.

She wanted to hug him, to rest in his arms at least one more time, at least for a second, but she just closed her eyes.

"I love you," she said. "I'll see you later, Chris."

Ice touched her, stopping all her pain, and bluebird songs filled her ears right before everything turned black

CHRIS'S HAND trembled as he forced the sword into Sara, but just as it touched her, a bright light surrounded it, countless birds sang, and a breeze passed through her as she vanished. The saber floated in the air, inches away from Chris's face, and when the light disappeared, the sword fell, and he caught it before it hit the floor.

At that moment, Murllen attacked him from the back, and Chris was surprised that he could block the blow.

If it hadn't been for the amazing sword in his hand, the reiser's lunge would have cut his arm off or killed him. He pushed Murllen back and stood up.

He took the luxury of a few seconds and swung the saber in the air. Never before had Chris used a weapon like this one, and he never would after. It anticipated all his moves as if responding to his thoughts like it was a part of him.

Murllen tried to attack him once more, and this time, he was looking for a fight. Chris lifted the sword and parried the blow, forcing the reiser to retreat. As he advanced, he pulled the saber down from his shoulder, using gravity to strengthen his lunge.

The curve of the sword struck Murllen's black blade, shattering it. The reiser growled and threw the handle at him, but Chris blocked it and advanced again. Using the guard around his hand, he punched the reiser in the face.

Murllen swung his claw at Chris's head, and Chris swung at it. Neither of them expected the saber to cut cleanly through Murllen's armor.

The reiser pulled the rest of his arm to his chest and looked at the sword with alarm.

"Poor sweetie!" Chris said. "You don't think this is over, do you?" He took another step forward, swinging the weapon in his hand. "It doesn't matter what the hell happens to the reisers, right?"

"Well, look who has been eavesdropping," Murllen said, but he stepped back. "Didn't your mother teach you it isn't polite?"

Chris didn't care what Murllen had to say, but the silence below got his attention. The battle was done. Everyone was watching them, waiting to see what their future would be. His jaw tightened when he realized how close he had been to being happy.

"You should have escaped when Hayden didn't kill you."

"Oh! Come on. I would not miss the party with my niece," Murllen sneered. "By the way, where did she go?"

Chris's rage didn't cloud his mind. Instead, he kept moving forward until he cornered the reiser between the edge of the wall and him.

"Such a waste," he said. "Hunting you would have been so much fun."

"Stupid human. You'll think of me for the rest of your life. I'll fill your nightmares."

Chris knew Murllen was right. Because of Sara, he'd think about the bastard every day, and his nights would be full of nightmares about what he'd done to her. However, there was no reason to let the asshole know this.

He snorted. "Is that all? You are about to die, and you can't come up with anything better?"

"You think you can—"

"Listen, Thornton." At the sound of his name, Murllen stiffened. "The only reason you got so far was because of Gemli's love for you. Face it. Without him, you are nothing but the mentally ill little brother of a real soldier. I won't waste my days thinking about such an insignificant person, and as for my nightmares, I've never feared you, and I will not start after I've killed you."

Murllen lunged at Chris, but he wasn't used to being wounded. As soon as the saber cut him, he retreated.

"You are nothing without that sword," Murllen said. "You want to face something? Face the fact that you are using a girl to protect you."

"Like you did for years?" Chris said. "Believe me, if it were up to me, I would have killed you."

Murllen opened his mouth, but Chris didn't let him finish. He lifted the saber over his head and allowed his hate to bring it down. Without effort, he cut Murllen in half.

The reiser's eyes dilated in front of him. There was no scream or growl. His body fell in two pieces down the wall until they smashed to the ground. Murllen's death was so easy that Chris became even angrier than before. If anyone in Hune deserved to suffer, it was that bastard.

~

CHRIS MOVED AWAY from the edge while cheers from below filled the air.

He lifted the saber and inspected it. No doubt, it was a dangerous and beautiful sword. He wasn't sure what material it had been forged from. Like water or ice, it had a blue tone, close to translucent, and the blade was thin and deadly sharp. Its handle felt as if it had been welded for his hand and weighed barely anything.

Regardless of the battle and the way he'd killed Murllen, the blade remained clean and reflected the light of the sun. Chris held it up and noticed the letters engraved in silver: wisdom and justice.

The saber heated until it got so hot that he had to let it go. Instead of falling, it floated in front of him. However, when it exploded in thousands of pieces, like the glacier orchid, Sara didn't come back.

Chris fell to his knees and hit the ground with his fits.

She had given everything for a world she would never see. He wasn't wise or just. His mind screamed at him, calling him a moron and a coward, while his soul wished he could use magic to go back in time. He only needed a few minutes.

Sara had been with him right before he'd noticed Hayden chasing Murllen. She had been leaving with Donald. Both were supposed to be safe, and Chris had no idea what had happened.

When he saw Hayden's battle, like the other reisers and soldiers, he'd stopped to watch. It was a difficult duel. Murllen wasn't a poor warrior and somehow was still protected.

Hayden was an outstanding soldier and finally knocked Murllen's sword from his hand and pushed him to the ground. The reisers applauded and cheered, claiming a new leader.

Murllen didn't surrender like an honorable soldier, though. He impaled Hayden through the back and, in the confusion, ran away.

The second Murllen crossed eyes with Chris, he marched towards him, but halfway there, he changed his direction and ran to a tower. He pulled someone from the ground just to throw him against a wall and walked inside.

It took him a second to realize that it was Donald lying on the ground, and in a panic, he ran to get him, conscious the monster was after Sara.

Murllen blocked the entrance.

From outside, Chris heard Murllen talking, and his soul froze when he also heard Sara's voice. His only option was to find another way in, so he rushed to the next tower, hoping he could cross the wall in time.

He was already at the top when the wall on the other side shattered, and his heart seemed to stop when he saw Sara falling onto the broken stone. It wasn't until she moved that he could breathe again.

Chris stopped Murllen just in time, blocking the reiser's sword right before it struck her. He had to fight Murllen, and it wasn't until he pushed him down that he turned to her. She was kneeling by the ice.

She was bleeding from a cut on her face, but Chris was more worried about the saber. Then she showed him her wound. The blood on her hand and the way it dripped from her dress told him a lot. Still, if he had tried harder, if he'd had more time, she might have survived.

His heart broke when she handed him the sword, but his soul ripped apart when he realized what he had to do. His nightmare rushed through his mind as understanding dawned on him. Murllen would never go away, and he would destroy their world.

Chris asked her not to look at him while he killed her.

After, he didn't explain to her how her eyes had cleared up. There was no black on them, just their beautiful bright blue. He never thanked her for what she had done for them. He didn't even say that he loved her and always would, whether or not she was with him.

On top of that broken wall, nothing mattered anymore. He let the time pass without moving because, if he stayed there, he could pretend Donald and Hayden were all right. He could imagine they were celebrating somewhere down there with John and Charlie, and he could believe that he had saved the only person who made him want to live.

He could dream that Sara was close and he would see her soon.

EVENHANDEDNESS

Although Genevieve had explained to Charlie what to expect in the asylum, he didn't get it until the moment he landed inside the broken window and found himself pinned to a wall with a knife to his neck. No sound or warning prepared him for the attack. If it hadn't been for Genevieve's order, he would have died. Unsurprisingly, the soldiers nearby were in similar positions.

Genevieve didn't even raise her voice or give an explanation. She only told them to wait for the fortress's gate to open before fighting. He realized as she guided them to the other side of the building how most of the reisers were children, but unlike the ones in Tundra, none of them seemed scared. He thought about asking Genevieve if they were going to fight in the battle, but then, to his immense relief, another two reisers walked into the room.

It had taken them a moment to reach the battle, since they had been at the far end of the fortress, but once they did, things moved fast. Not that Chris was losing, but the reisers on their side fought with precision and speed, even when their priority seemed to be to incapacitate their opponents instead of killing them.

He wanted to believe it had to do with their understanding of the armor and Gemli's missing spell, but he knew better, and he was thankful he did not have to fight against them.

Charlie struck down a valsing standing in his way and then noticed the battle on top of the wall. Everyone stopped and watched Chris cut Murllen in half.

A deep silence followed the reiser's fall, and it lasted until both parts hit the ground. Then cheers, screams, and applause filled the place while swords dropped.

For a couple of minutes, Charlie enjoyed the feeling of being done with the battle, but then he realized they'd ended the war, and he celebrated by jumping and yelling with everyone who had fought with them.

The reisers, just like the ones in the asylum, didn't have trouble celebrating Murllen's death, and it wasn't until later that Charlie learned that their former leader had broken their rules when he'd stabbed Hayden in the back after losing the duel to him.

His happiness stopped when he found Donald lying on the ground. He ran over to the valsing and knelt to check on him. He exhaled when he noticed Donald's stupid smile.

"You idiot!" he said, laughing. "I thought you were dead!"

Donald laughed weakly and then tried and failed to get up.

"Where is she?" he asked while Charlie helped him sit against the wall.

"Who?" Charlie looked around.

Behind a pile of rocks, he found Alleta.

It was easy to recognize her, and he rushed to check on her. She was unconscious and had trouble breathing, looking a lot like Amanda when Hayden had brought her to him the night the reisers had taken the soldiers as prisoners.

"Charlie," she whispered.

"Everything will be fine, Alleta. The war is over."

She looked up at him. "Jean?"

He smiled. "She is all right and safe."

Alleta closed her eyes and exhaled.

"Let me help you." He sat her next to Donald, who was holding the back of his head. "Don't touch it," Charlie said, noticing the dried blood on the valsing's neck. "You are going to infect the wound. I'll get someone here."

He stood and realized something was wrong. The soldiers and reisers, although happy, were going in all directions. No one had taken charge, and there was no sign of Chris anywhere.

"Listen up!" Charlie said, and the soldiers nearby stopped. "You, get a valsing over here with their medical stuff, and you, stay with them. The rest follow me."

Chris's words weighed in Charlie's mind as he took control of the situation.

The soldiers and the reisers on their side needed to help the injured ones and seat the reisers still in armor against the outside wall of the fortress. He had no idea how to remove it and hadn't found Sara, Genevieve, Hayden, or Chris.

"Commander," Amanda said, and her expression only concerned him more. "I need a few soldiers. We found the dungeon."

Charlie's stomach twisted. He could only imagine what they would find there.

"Take as many as you need to," he said, "and Major…be careful."

Not too long after, he encountered John and Hayden.

"Lieutenant, what happened?"

Hayden was laying on the ground, unconscious. His torso

was wrapped, and one of his arms had been tied against his chest.

"Murllen," John said, "that freaking coward, of course."

Hayden opened his eyes and stared at Charlie. "Where the hell is Chris?"

Charlie shrugged and turned to the top of the wall. He was about to go up to check when Hayden said, "We need to move. The swamp gets pretty cold at nighttime. It'll be too hard to start fires around here."

Charlie wondered about the possibility of staying in the building, but then he realized what state it was in. The massive structure that, in the morning, had been almost impenetrable now lay in ruins.

"I'll start sending groups with the injured ones. I have no idea how to remove the armor from some of them. What do you prefer to do with them?"

Hayden tried to sit up, but John held him down. "You are not going anywhere unless you want to bleed to death. Lily went to get something to help you."

"Just take them prisoner." Hayden closed his eyes and clutched his abdomen. "We'll deal with that later." His tone changed. "Have you seen Genevieve?"

Charlie put a hand on his shoulder. "Last time I saw her, she was taking—"

At that moment, Genevieve rushed over. "Did you take any antidote?" she said as she knelt by Hayden and placed a sack on the ground. "Murllen's sword was a valsing design. I just hope they didn't change the solution or that the blade was clean."

Hayden touched her hand, and when she looked at him, her expression was as serious as before. "Are you—"

"Hayden. Antidote, did you have some?"

"I don't think so," John said. "Lily and Dunstan helped me

wrap him, but we didn't give him anything. They went to find some medicine and, you know, medical stuff."

Genevieve nodded and took out a few bottles and wraps from the sack. "You won't have to chain or tie the reisers," she said without taking her eyes off Hayden while she unwrapped him. "If you tell them Hayden is alive and he needs them to stand still until we can help them out, they will follow the order."

"I'll do it," Dunstan said, approaching with Lily. "It'll help if one of your soldiers comes, too, though."

Charlie nodded and ordered a soldier to go with Dunstan. He stood up and looked around. Although things appeared organized, there was endless work ahead, and he had no idea what had happened to Chris. He didn't want to say it aloud, but he wondered if Murllen had fatally injured him and his friend had died hours ago.

"Charlie?" Lily said, touching his arm. "Are you all right?"

"I'm fine," he said and couldn't avoid staring at her. "Your scar…it's gone." It was such a big difference that it was impossible not to notice.

"I know." She covered where it used to be with her hand. "It was Sara."

"Of course." He realized what might be more important to her. "Have you seen Donald?"

The color drained out of her.

"No, don't worry. He is alive but got hurt. I left him by that tower with—"

She ran towards the tower.

The mention of Sara brought his best friend to his mind. It was time he climbed up there and looked for him.

"Have the valsings get everyone ready to leave," Chris's voice called in the distance, and Charlie stopped and relaxed. "We need to get out of here."

Chris was helping Donald walk, and Lily was right

behind them. He set Donald down by Hayden, Genevieve, and John.

"You think he'll be fit to go with the next group?" Chris said to Genevieve, and after she nodded, he turned to Lily. "You and Donald are leaving with them. Lily, make sure the camp has as many tents and fires as possible."

Chris didn't wait for her to answer before walking over to Charlie. "What happened to the prisoners? Did Amanda get them out?"

"I believe so."

"Let's be certain of that."

Charlie didn't need to ask. Chris's countenance was hard, and it was obvious who was missing.

"What are you waiting for?" Chris said, and when Charlie didn't answer or move, he added, "I'm fine, but there is no time. Orson is missing, and I'm not letting that bastard start anything. We have to find him."

Charlie kept his questions to himself and followed the orders.

As expected, Chris's judgment as a leader was as sharp as ever. It was a skill Charlie knew he didn't have and one he admired in his friend. But Chris was acting like he had when he'd just lost his father.

Charlie waited until no one was around to hear them and asked, "Did you see your mother?"

Chris didn't stop walking or look at him. "Yes, she was unconscious. I'm hoping she'll recover."

Charlie nodded, aware of the bitter tone in Chris's voice and concerned he might have lost a friend that day.

After that, they didn't have any opportunity to talk, and in no time, the sky turned red as sunset fell. Hayden had warned them about the temperature dropping, but he'd failed to mention that everything would freeze.

Charlie had lost the sensation in his hands hours ago, and

he could see his breath when exhaling. The snowflakes falling didn't surprise anyone. His head hurt because of the icy wind hitting him, and he couldn't feel his legs or feet, either.

"I know Hayden said it was going to be cold, but I don't think he meant freaking freezing," John said at Charlie's side.

"Good thing we are getting the hell out of here now," Charlie said.

Aside from the last few reisers still in armor, the soldiers walking with them, and Chris, whom they were waiting for, everyone had left already.

Chris had wanted to make sure they had left no one behind, so he'd gone into the fortress to check again. Charlie didn't need to ask who he was looking for, and he'd patiently waited with John by the entrance.

The second Charlie saw Chris's figure walking out, he gave the order to get going, and when he looked back, he saw Chris do something he never thought he would.

Chris stopped mid-step, turned back, and looked up. During the few seconds he stood like that, Charlie held his breath, sure his friend would not leave. He was about to get him when Chris took a few steps backward. The moment Chris crossed the threshold of the fortress, he looked like their general, and he strode toward them in silence.

~

CHARLIE WAS glad to see fires going. Even from a distance, he perceived the warmth coming from them. He didn't care that they'd set the camp up in a strange location and an awkward shape.

They didn't have enough tents, as they'd sent most of them with the civilians to Laconia. They had also added a bunch of reisers and a few prisoners that had survived Murllen's dungeon to their group. As a result, most soldiers in good health wrapped themselves in blankets and sat by the fires.

"Donald and Hayden are over there," John said as he dismounted.

"You should go ahead," Chris said, speaking for the first time during their brief trip. "I'll check the camp first."

He left without waiting for them to reply.

"I liked Sara," Charlie said before they reached the others, "but I may hate her now for what she did to him."

"I'm sure she didn't mean to die!"

Charlie looked at John. "I don't think so, either, but still I need to blame someone."

"Don't you have enough with Murllen or Gemli or the idiot Orson, whom now we have to find?"

Charlie shook his head. "Chris doesn't give a damn about them, but…he left his life with her. That's what I blame her for."

~

THE CAMP WAS LONGER than usual because of how they'd set it up. As Chris walked through it, he kept closing and opening his fist. Its setup not only made it hard to find anything or anyone, but it made it difficult to defend if someone attacked them, and Orson was a sick bastard with twisted ideas. It might seem like they'd ended the war, but he would not believe it until he found that valsing.

Lily's voice got his attention, and he walked towards her. He knew she wasn't with Donald and wondered what she was doing. Also, he wanted to see her. She was the only connection he had with Sara now.

"You need to rest and take this." She was looking inside a

tent, so he stopped and waited. "I haven't seen him, but I will ask."

The moment she saw him, her eyes filled with tears, and she took a deep breath to contain them.

"Chris! I was going to find you. Your…"

She didn't have to finish. His mom was smiling at him from the bed close to the entrance.

"Christopher!" Alleta said barely above a whisper.

"My sweet lady." He hugged her.

Behind him, he heard Lily leaving.

He moved back to look at his mother. The marks on her face and hands, along with her pale skin and the clear signs of the starvation she had gone through, told Chris how Murllen had kept her as his personal prisoner.

"I am so sorry I couldn't reach you before," he said, and his mom touched his face. "My dad would have—"

"I'm just thankful you are alive." She held his hand tightly to her chest. "Your friend saved me."

"Donald is a great guy." Chris nodded. "I'm very lucky to have met him."

Alleta shook her head and, with an immense effort, moved her other hand out from underneath the blanket. When she opened it, Chris saw the silver chain with Sara's pendant and had to fight the knot in his throat.

"She was with the valsing, Donald?"

Chris could only nod.

"Before he helped me down, she saved me."

He brushed his fingers over the pendant in her hand.

"I gave up, Chris. I was ready to die. Murllen…he did that much to me, but then…then she handed me this and reminded me of its meaning. I met her mother many years ago… She was my friend."

His hand trembled when he took it, and he didn't trust his voice.

"Chris, what happened?"

He didn't answer right away, and his mom just squeezed his hand. Once he could say something without breaking down, he looked at her again. "I know now how painful it is for you to live without Dad."

Chris didn't know how, but his mom sat up to hug him. This time, a few tears fell from his eyes. He hugged her back, conscious of not hurting her more. Then, in a whisper, he asked, "Do you mind if…? Just rest. I'll be back."

He kissed her forehead, helped her lie down again, and walked out of her tent holding Sara's necklace in his hand.

His steps were fast and sure, and though some soldiers looked at him, no one followed him. He reached the line of dead trees and kept walking until he found a fallen trunk. He let himself down to the ground and leaned against it.

The clouds covered most of the moonlight, but he forced his eyes to look at the map engraved on the pendant. He passed his fingers over the almost invisible letters: S and W.

The warmth from his tears rolling down his face felt uncomfortable against the cold. He closed his hand so hard that the metal cut his palm, but he didn't care. That pain was easy to suffer. The one inside his chest was devastating.

Losing his father had been hard, but he couldn't imagine anything worse than losing Sara the way he had. He blamed himself for killing her, but he couldn't be certain of it. The saber never really cut her. She just vanished in front of him, wounded and bleeding. If she showed up somewhere else, he wouldn't be there to help her. He would have abandoned her to die alone.

Heavy snowflakes fell on him, bringing a peculiar silence with them. Chris put his arms on his knees and let his head rest on his hands.

THE FROZEN WIND SPED UP, hitting Chris's back with more strength and howling over the swamp as a storm picked up. In the distance, he thought he heard someone call his name, but he just ignored it.

He closed his eyes and tried to let the exhaustion of the day take over his mind. In there, Sara's voice seemed clearer when he heard his name called again. He refused to move. After losing his father, he knew his voice was something he couldn't remember anymore, and he wasn't ready to forget Sara's.

The storm picked up, and the wind and the crashing of the branches hitting each other covered all other sounds. A strange buzz filled his ears, and as it increased, a pressure threatened to make his head explode. Chris covered his ears and rolled on the ground, incapable of opening his eyes even if he wanted to.

"I'm sorry." He thought he heard Sara, but his side burned like it had when the reiser stabbed him. Then the skin of his palms seemed to rip apart, like they had when he touched the glacier orchid, and his hand hurt the same way it had when he first met Gemli at the mountain.

Chris tried to sit up, but the pressure inside his head intensified, and memories whipped through his mind as if they were being ripped away.

"Help them," Sara's voice said.

The asylum showed up in his mind. Its windows and doors were destroyed, the rooms were torn apart, and everyone was running away from it. Orson's valsings carried boxes and sacks across the fortress's yard.

"Help them," she said again, and this time, he saw the swamp, full of valsings and tied-up children. Two bodies were lying on the ground. The third one was still moving, crawling towards the little ones.

The pain intensified inside his brain, and Chris held his head and groaned.

"I'm sorry." Sara sounded upset, and then Orson's face, smiling with pleasure and holding a device similar to the one Liam had made, appeared in Chris's mind.

"Chris!" someone said in the distance. "Help them!"

Everything stopped, and Chris lay on the ground, disoriented and nauseous.

"Chris!"

It took a huge effort, but he stood and rushed towards the voice.

In a few steps, he caught up with Cassandra, who crashed into him, looking frightened and out of breath.

"Thank the gods." She held his arms and bent over. "Orson, he got—"

"I know." He pulled her up and made sure she was looking at him. "The camp is right there. Tell Charlie and take them back to where you found Orson."

"Chris, he was marching fast. He won't be—"

"Charlie will track him."

He let her go and ran towards the swamp, knowing exactly where to find Orson.

~

WHETHER OR NOT IT had been Sara, Chris didn't want to think about it yet. He needed to find the opening in the swamp and stop Orson.

Even though they had been running, they were slower than him. They were carrying young reisers and weapons and pulling heavy wagons, and if Cassandra had reached the camp, they couldn't be that far. He hoped he could hold them until Charlie arrived.

The flowers' aroma hit him and almost made him stop,

and he noticed the bluebirds Sara had told him about in the trees. A few steps ahead, he saw the first valsing. He was trying to pick up a sack from the ground. If it hadn't been for the bloody blade at his side, Chris would have left him alone. But a rage he had tried to deny woke up.

Sara had decided to use the saber, because leaving Murllen alive with Orson somewhere would be dangerous. He was going to stop that danger.

By the time the valsing looked up, it was too late. Chris grabbed him by the face and snapped his neck. He crouched down and opened the sack. Jars of medicines and bottles of antidote poured out, along with things he didn't recognize.

The storm above him became a blessing, covering his steps. He stopped three steps later when he saw Orson.

As expected, Orson was hiding behind a few valsings, holding a needle in one hand and a sword in the other. Like in Chris's vision, the blade was dripping a black liquid, the reisers' poison. On the ground in front of him, a body convulsed, screaming, making Orson laugh.

"I told you, sweetheart," Orson said. "You could be the best warrior in Hune, and it won't matter. You are a reiser, and I know your weakness. Your race owes your existence to us."

Behind them, the smaller reisers cried and hugged each other while the slightly older ones stepped at the front.

"Grab them again!" Orson said. "And this time, keep the ropes tighter."

Chris slid as close to Orson as possible. He waited until most of his valsings moved towards the reisers and then jumped at the few standing by him.

The valsings raised their swords, but Chris was faster, and with no trouble, he incapacitated two of them. He noticed Orson running to the other side, looking for the other valsings and ignoring the reisers.

"Get him!" Orson said.

Chris swung his sword, and only one valsing managed to stop him for a second, but Chris just pushed him down and attacked him. One jumped on his back, so he reached over his shoulder and threw him against a trunk.

Two more jumped on him, pushing him to the ground. He felt a knife cutting the skin of his arm, and with a groan, he punched the valsing in his face, not only breaking his nose but his jaw as well.

The valsing tumbled backward, allowing Chris to stand up and face the other one, but that one ran away.

Chris saw movement among the dead trees and turned in time to stop a valsing's sword aimed at his head. He didn't waste time and struck the valsing in the stomach.

"Freaking coward!" Chris said. "Was this your plan all along? Steal the asylum and take over the reisers?"

Orson's eyes opened wide, and he froze for a second before pushing a valsing towards Chris.

"You should thank me for taking care of Murllen, then," Chris said just before the valsing Orson had pushed attacked him.

His sword looked like Murllen's, and it was stronger than the others. Chris used his size to press the valsing back, and he was ready to strike when another valsing hit his arm, making him lose his sword and balance.

It was a dangerous move, and when Chris saw the broken nose of the attacker on top of him, he understood it was personal.

"So many years, I've waited for this," the valsing said, and he tried to punch Chris, but Chris moved to the side, and the valsing's hand hit the ground.

The valsing growled, and Chris pushed him to the side and rolled up on his knees.

"Chris!" a female voice said, and almost at the same time,

something smashed into the side of his head, throwing him down again.

A loud buzz inside his mind blocked all the sound around him. He touched his head, and his hand came away wet. It took him more than a second to understand that blood was coming not only from his head, but from his ear. He looked up, and soldiers were running towards him, but he couldn't understand their shouts.

A shadow behind him covered the moonlight, and as his hearing started to return, a hysterical laugh and a scream replaced the buzz.

"Stop. You cannot—" the same voice said right next to him.

He turned just in time to catch Cassandra as Orson slid Chris's sword from her body.

The king stared at her daughter, and his laughter became louder. "You stupid—"

Chris grabbed his blade, not caring about his palm, and pushed it back against Orson. The pommel smashed his face, and Chris heard bones breaking, followed by a high-pitched scream.

Chris stood and, although dizzy, kicked Orson in the chest, sending him flying against a tree trunk.

He knelt by Cassandra, and although the front of her dress had only a small bloodstain, the ground beneath her had already turned darker.

"Hey," he said and held her hand when she offered it to him. "What were you—"

"I owed it to everyone…to Sara,"

She touched his face, and her breathing became erratic.

"Cassie," he said, called her by the name she'd told him the night they'd met, and it made her smile. "You shouldn't…"

She closed her eyes but tightened her grip on his hand. "I

should have been brave when he asked me. I should have left with Wilson when we could..."

Her head fell back, and Chris placed her carefully on the ground.

He looked at Orson, who was standing up, holding his face and whining about his pain.

The rising heat in Chris's blood gave him the strength to stand and walk over to the valsing. He kicked the back of his knees, and when Orson dropped, he grabbed him by his hair.

Something felt off inside Chris's head. His hearing was still buzzing, and the pressure seemed to blur his vision from time to time.

Donald stepped forward with a severe expression, one that Chris had never seen on him before. Behind Donald, some valsings cheered. Although Chris's sight kept getting worse, he recognized Charlie standing while John held the valsing with the broken nose. He guessed Genevieve was the red hair helping the little reisers.

He ignored everything and grabbed his sword from the ground. The silence made him look up again. The shape of a valsing approached him, and after he blinked and wiped his eyes a few times, he recognized Donald shaking his head.

The events of the day, along with all the years of losses, came to Chris's mind. He understood what Donald wanted. As a diplomat, he needed to foresee what he would do as a leader, but that wasn't his call.

Chris secured his sword in his hand. He forced Orson to his knees and turned to look at him. Orson's face was bloody and dirty. Panic shone in his eyes, and tears fell from them.

"You murdered your daughter," Chris said, "kidnapped innocent reisers, and killed their caregivers. Not to mention you broke into the asylum and stole from it. I'm positive your new leader wants to keep you alive."

Orson smiled as he looked at Donald.

"He is a good guy," Chris said. "He would be pretty fair with you."

Chris waited until the king's eyes reflected hope and relief. Then he raised his sword.

"But I won't." Without a second thought, he lopped off the king's head.

HUNE

"You just questioned my authority in front of the valsings!" Donald said in the tent, as if the fabric could stop his loud complaints from being overheard outside.

"It was the right thing to do," Chris said, covering one ear and fighting the increasing pressure inside his head. "I will not allow anyone to think they can do as they please."

Donald threw his arms in the air. "So, you just informed the valsings you can overturn my decision?"

"Gods be damn." Chris shook his head and cleared his throat, trying to get rid of the blur again. "I overturned nothing. Do I have to tell you what the hell happened? That bastard murdered his own daughter in front of everyone while he tried to kill me! All because I caught him kidnapping the young reisers! What did you expect me to do?"

He pushed Charlie out of his way. He wasn't getting anywhere with Donald, and he needed to lie down or take something, as his headache and sight were worsening.

"Justice had nothing to do with what you did!" Donald said.

"Donald," Lily said, "do not... You will regret it."

Chris noticed Donald's silhouette pushing her behind him.

"You did it because your wrath blocked your rationality. You just needed someone to get even with."

Chris snorted while John moved closer to him.

"I did it because you didn't have the courage to do it."

If Chris hadn't been half-blind and disoriented, Donald wouldn't have been able to push him. As he stumbled a few steps backward, he chuckled. Charlie moved to his side, undoubtedly to stop him in case he wanted to attack the valsing.

"Let me make this clear for you, little one," Chris said as he distinguished Lily's shape pulling Donald back. "I did it because I'm in charge here and I decide how and when to implement justice. Your former king needed to be stopped before he started another war. No one here needs to fight again, and that's fair."

Donald puffed and grabbed Lily's hand.

"You did it because you became a selfish bastard the second Sara died. I can only imagine how happy she would have been to watch you implement your first act of justice!"

Charlie blocked Chris while John pulled him back as he tried to grab Donald's neck.

"See," Donald said without moving, "just like an idiot. You were not the only one with something against Orson."

Chris stopped fighting. As his muscles relaxed, his brain pounded as if it were about to explode, and his vision became nothing but a blur of lights and shadows.

"I had the right to do whatever I wanted with him. You let Hayden do it with Murllen." Chris's eyes cleared just in time to see Donald touching Lily's face. "I never imagined you would not understand, but I guess we were never friends."

Donald stood in front of Chris, aware of his physical

state, and made sure to kiss Lily's hand in front of his eyes before he walked out of the tent.

Chris pushed Charlie and pulled his arm from John's grasp. He rubbed his face, but his sight didn't improve, and groaning didn't help, either.

"You need to stop doing that." Chris recognized Genevieve's voice, but he hadn't heard her enter.

"Stop what?" Chris said. "Yelling, fighting, talking to morons? What I need is to make sure we are ready to proceed before we get buried in snow. I have sent every single—"

Genevieve stepped into his range of vision and punched him, hitting his collar bone.

Chris bent over and heard someone moving towards him, but Genevieve forced him to sit down.

"Stop all of that," she said, crouching in front of him. "If you don't rest, you won't be able to do anything."

"You need me to get…" Charlie said and sighed.

"I got him," she said, talking in the other direction. "You two should go out and do your job."

Chris heard footsteps leaving, and for a while, the only sound came from things moving nearby.

"You saved my little ones," Genevieve said. "You killed Murllen. Thanks to you, my race will have a better life, and you saved me before all of that."

She pressed a hot wrap against the side of his head. It stung at first, but then the warmth soothed the pain.

"If it weren't for all of that, I would just let you become an idiot, like Donald said. With that injury, you would die in a few weeks, or even days."

Chris narrowed his eyes, but his head had become a living torment. After a while, Genevieve helped him to a cot, and he lay down on it. The storm kept hitting the tent, and it seemed to worsen, just like the pressure in his mind and chest.

"The medicine will work soon," she said. "I'll check on you later."

"How is Hayden?"

She stopped walking, and the few seconds she took to answer worried him.

"He is…I guess frustrated at having to rest and ready to get going. He'll be fine. I checked on your mom, too. She'll recover as well."

Chris nodded and closed his eyes. "Thanks, Genevieve."

THE SOUND of the ocean woke him up, and to his surprise, he was sitting on the cliff outside his house in Tundra. He didn't need to turn to realize someone was sitting next to him. It was Sara.

Although he hadn't been in one of her vivid dreams in years, this one seemed different, and its timing was too convenient. His head wasn't pounding, his ears weren't buzzing, and he had no trouble watching the waves hitting the rocks beneath them.

"I figured you would like to visit this place," she said. "But don't look back. The city isn't in the best shape."

Chris puffed and kept staring at the water. Such a simple view, but he had missed it for so long. He had no idea if the ocean would rise again, but he didn't ask her about it. He also didn't ask about the saber or what would happen after he used it…if she knew.

"I couldn't tell you," she said, and he accepted that she wasn't real, because she would never read his mind. "No one but my mom knew who my father was, not even Cielthos. Otherwise, Gemli would have—"

Chris nodded, and all his frustration echoed in his question. "So, how did you know?"

It took a while for his mind to make up a story that only confirmed she was a hallucination. Orson must have hit his poor brain really hard for him to come up with that.

"Do you remember the owl that upset the roots by the north side of the Soto Forest?"

"The one that almost killed us? Yes, I remember the stupid bird."

She sighed. "Right…well, that was my father."

"Unbelievable! The huge magician, the colonel of Laconia's army, was an owl?" He chuckled and shook his head. "Even Gemli would have trouble falling for that one."

When she didn't answer, he rested his arms on his knees, refusing to look at her.

"Should I expect a visit from him, yelling at—no, sorry, hooting at me for losing his daughter? I deserve it."

"He died." From the corner of his eye, he noticed her hand move towards him, but she stopped herself. "Gemli killed him the night you became conscious after the passage. He helped me fix the waterfall… I guess the ocean, too."

"Nice!" Chris pushed his hair back. "I can't wait to visit the stupid waterfall. Just don't break my brain next time."

"Chris, I'm…sorry about that. I'm too weak, and…well, now I'm barely aware of things. It was the only way to tell you about Orson."

"Oh, I understand. I suppose now you are going to tell me how I messed up everything? How I shouldn't have killed him?"

At his side, she sobbed, and he confirmed his decision of avoiding her eyes. The last thing he wanted was to visualize her bleeding to death or frozen somewhere in Hune.

"What did you wish for?" she said. "You made a wish to the bluebird, but…would you tell me now? Please?"

"Dear gods." Chris rubbed his face. "Wishes? Those are stupid things. What did I wish? I have no idea. But you should. After all, you are not here. This is only my head being stupid. Who knows, maybe I've lost it? That bastard hit me really hard."

"Hit you? Who? What are you...?" She stood and stepped back. "Really, Chris...after all of you have seen..."

Chris looked up.

She wore the same dress she'd had on during the battle. Like the last time she was with him, blood covered the side. Her cheek was swollen where it had been cut, and there was blood on the side of her head. She had been crying, and when she wiped her eyes, he noticed the deep burns on her palms.

However, the disappointment in her eyes was the hardest thing to see, and it pinched Chris's heart.

He reached for her, but instead of touching her hand, he woke up.

"General...Chris," Amanda said at his side. "Just lie down, relax. We need you to get better."

Chris tried to look around, but he only perceived blurs of light and shapes. He guessed he was in the same tent where Genevieve had left him. Outside, the wind remained loud, and from the brightness, he assumed it was daytime.

He inhaled, hoping to smell flowers, but only detected the odors of burned wood and medicine.

"How are you?" Amanda said. "I can get Genevieve if—"

"I'm..." Chris rested his head back and closed his eyes. "Last time I saw you, we were in Murllen's dungeon. What happened to those prisoners?"

Amanda sat and remained quiet for a while. Chris heard the tent door opening but didn't recognize the person who entered until Genevieve touched his forehead.

"Like you figured, we found our royalty and the members of the High Council, all dead... Leonard let them kill his own family."

"Not surprising," Chris said. "But did you—"

"The prisoners they took later in the war…most of them were dead already," Amanda said. "It looked like Murllen or Gemli made them…" She cleared her throat. "The few still alive are here, but…we don't have too much hope for them."

"The doctors had no hope for me, either, and here I am," John said from the entrance. "Chris, the scouts came back. They found the rest of the caravan. Major Baker sent a few soldiers with the wagons. Jean is in Laconia already, although, according to their message, the state of the city isn't promising."

Chris shook his head, and with Genevieve's help, he sat up. "How long until we can leave?"

"Less than an hour if we move now, but you can't—"

"Get everyone moving, then," Chris said. "How far are we from Laconia?"

"Two days, hopefully less," John said. "I'll tell Charlie your order."

The door opened again, letting the cold air enter, and the reflected light from outside hurt Chris's eyes. They were getting buried in snow.

"You need something else?" Amanda said to Genevieve. "Is the wound infected?"

"No," Genevieve said. "It isn't medicine that Chris needs. The faster we can have him in a warmer place and resting, the better."

She grabbed his hand, so he turned towards her. Only the surrounding red distinguished her from Amanda. "Take this. It'll help slow the pain during the trip. I can't give you more since you'll be riding and we don't want you unconscious."

"A wagon?" suggested Amanda.

"I'll be fine," Chris said, taking the medicine. "I'm not the only one who needs rest and a warm place."

Chris was lightheaded, and his arms and legs seemed to

become heavier. Now he knew how it was to be drugged by the valsings and the reisers.

For the next two days, the snow fell, making the march towards Laconia slow. The weather turned into a silent enemy, and if they didn't reach the city soon, it might kill more people than they'd lost in battle.

They were running out of provisions, and hunting had become harder. Even the valsings, who had been nomads, had grown worried about it. It wasn't natural.

His mind was also turning against him.

He needed to recover his energy, but his body was sore and tired. Even worse were the confusion and the constant headache. He wasn't dead yet because of Genevieve's medicine, but keeping his train of thought clear took a tremendous effort. Even talking had become difficult.

A horse approached him, and he waited until the rider stopped by his side.

"The city is visible now, Chris," Charlie said. "We will get there tonight, but I'm not positive we should stay. I didn't believe Baker at first, but he is right. That place looks…sinister. Dead."

"Is Donald still around?"

Chris hadn't asked about him or any of the valsings. He wasn't proud of what he'd said, and he hoped Donald's willingness to help had kept him around.

"Yes," Charlie said. "He's in the back with the valsings. They have been helping…a lot."

"He is a good guy." Chris thought about their adventures and smiled to himself. "His community is also an expert in construction. Check if he can send some of them to the city before the rest of us arrive."

Charlie cleared his throat. "You could order it."

Chris sighed and turned to his friend. Charlie was just a dark blur, and Chris swore again at his stupid, broken brain.

"Regardless of what he said, I want you to go with the advance group."

"I think John should go first. Just like usual, Chris."

"I'm not that lost yet, Charlie."

"No! I didn't mean—"

Chris chuckled, and though it felt good for a second, the effort made him grunt.

"And I even remember stuff." Chris rubbed his face. "Do you still want to be part of the army? You were never a fan of the idea."

"Chris, I don't... This isn't the time—"

"Why not? Unless you can stop the snow, I don't..." Chris sighed. "I get why you want to be with Jean. I don't want to have a reason to force you to stay away from her again. Who knows if anything else will happen? You may as well be with her."

Charlie led their horses off to the side and stopped, letting the soldiers get ahead of them.

"Chris, you aren't in the best shape now. You need help. I'm not saying you are useless or anything, but...I'm your second, and I won't abandon you."

"I know," Chris said. "We'll always be friends. I just want you to have something I can't have anymore."

The blur that was Charlie came into focus long enough for Chris to notice his conflict. "Look, I'm just asking if you still want that. If you do, what are you waiting for?"

"What about the army? And you? I can't leave you like this!"

"Like this! I'm not dying...yet, and imagine how happy John will be with your decision."

Charlie laughed at his side. "He deserves a higher rank."

"He had...for a while."

"Are you sure, Chris? Like you said, things have changed. It shouldn't be as hard, and—"

"You want to know a secret?" Chris rubbed the back of his neck. "I thought about leaving, too."

"What? When?"

Chris inhaled and closed his eyes. "I should have. If I had, she would still be here."

He felt Charlie's hand on his arm. "I think you would have had trouble making her stick to that plan."

"True. She thought I wouldn't like the idea after a while."

"You even talked to her about it? That's crazy." Charlie exhaled. "Is she really…?"

Chris shook his head, and after a moment, he told his friend everything that had happened on the wall. He kept a few parts between Sara and him, but he even told Charlie about his hallucinations in the vault and the last one he'd had just a few days ago.

It helped to maintain his credibility, the way she'd gotten rid of Gemli. Otherwise, Chris was certain Charlie would have declared him mentally unstable.

"Listen, Chris," Charlie said. "I understand nothing about magic and stuff, but once you get better and we've settled everything, I'll go with you to figure out what happened to her."

Chris puffed, but Charlie didn't let him answer.

"Like I said, I know little, but…Lily said the abbey is still there, and there must be something in those countless papers about it. We should find out."

Chris sighed as he tried to think about it, but his growing headache didn't make things easy, so he just nodded and changed the topic.

"I'll make John a colonel. Just to upset Hayden."

Charlie helped him ride back to the line. "I couldn't agree more, even though we will have to tolerate John every day. What about Amanda?"

"Well, she should be a colonel, too."

Charlie chuckled and started to leave. Then he turned back and, lowering his voice, asked, "Did you think about deserting?"

"Only every day after I realized who she was."

"You knew she was the Great Wizard?"

"No. I knew she was and is the love of my life."

~

DONALD SENT his valsings with Charlie to the city, and in the early morning hours, all the injured rested in a room inside the palace, which the valsings had declared safe enough to hold an infirmary. They placed the rest of the survivors in houses by the valley at the top of the city.

The valsings informed him that the buildings by the port and the ones close to the piers had structural damage. Once the weather improved, they would start fixing them.

At least for the night, they had a shelter stronger than the tents.

Chris was standing by the palace's entrance, waiting for John. He hadn't told him about his decision to increase his rank and was hoping to do it before the afternoon.

Everyone had to be wondering about their general's health, and he didn't want to jeopardize a rebellion. Hayden still wasn't strong enough to take over, although Genevieve shouldn't have trouble controlling the reisers.

"The infirmary is ready," Donald said, surprising Chris. "I am afraid to report that Murllen's prisoners did not make it...but the soldiers and reisers who were injured during the battle seem to be just fine."

Chris tried to look at him, but his sight was black against the dark sky. "How are your people?"

Donald stepped closer and pulled up a light, completely blinding him. "For the gods above! You look terrible."

"Thanks?"

"Genevieve said you were getting better, but…how is your head?"

Chris leaned against the wall and slid to the ground. "If I'm certain of something, it's that my head is still above my shoulders."

"That bad? Like a pressure or more lightheaded?"

"Both? I'm not sure. I can't think straight…or see."

"You cannot see? Chris, why did you not ask for…?" Donald sat next to Chris and exhaled. "I understand you are mad at me. I said things I should not have."

Chris pulled his handkerchief from his coat pocket and handed it to Donald.

"I am not crying."

Chris snorted. "I remember you wanted one of these for Lily. Just be careful. I have no idea who could clean your hands or hers now."

At his side, Chris heard the fabric moving, and the flower's scent made the knot in his heart tighter, making him wonder how it was possible it could still beat inside his chest.

"Oh, gods…this aroma. It reminds me so much of the abbey and the stupid roots." Donald cleared his throat. "Is she gone?"

Chris rested his head back and closed his eyes. "I thought so. Murllen stabbed her. That freaking coward—I don't think she would have survived if we had made it down…but then I had to… I used the saber on her. She vanished the second that thing touched her."

"You what? I cannot… It is horrible."

Chris nodded. "For a while, I believed the curse killed her. I killed her, but…she told me how to find Orson when she almost ripped my brain out."

"What? No, I saw Orson hitting you." Donald snorted. "Man, I was sure you were done right there."

Sunlight must have peeked above the horizon, because Chris's blur lighted. He liked the night more these days. In the dark, he could pretend his eyes weren't as bad, although he would give up his sight for his mind to work again and the pain to go away.

"Chris?"

"Right. Sorry..." He exhaled. "Before I found Orson, something happened. Kind of when we met Gemli in the mountain."

"She would not have hurt you!"

"I don't think she had an option. I'm sure I saw her, in a dream or something..." Chris held his forehead. "When she healed you, she lost part of her memories. Important ones, like the zhortas' names or how we met her. I'm afraid that if she survived, she won't remember who she is—was—and I won't see her again...but she may not be dead."

For a while, they remained quiet. The snow kept falling, but the wind had stopped.

"Did you know?" Donald said. "Did she ever mention who she was?"

Chris shook his head.

"I thought her wording was peculiar."

"What wording?"

Donald chuckled. "When she named you general...she said, 'by the power of Hune in my hands.' I thought she just said it wrong, but I guess she knew. I guess no one can really challenge your rank."

Chris puffed.

"An exile and a traitor," Donald said. "No wonder we did not figure it out before."

Chris chuckled. "Genevieve's sedatives are as bad as yours. But maybe you could check my eyes after everyone is—"

A loud rumble that reminded Chris of the Soto Forest

echoed around them, followed by an even louder blast that shook the ground.

He stood and tried to focus. A horse approaching made him take a step forward.

"General!" John said. "The freaking trees!"

"What trees?" Chris turned back towards the forest.

"Not those," John said.

"For the gods!" Donald said. "The roots are moving."

"The roots? What...?" Another loud rumble surrounded them, and Chris's memory of them leaving the abbey came to his mind. "The Soto Forest?"

"Yes!" John said. "We have to get everyone somewhere safe...if there is such a place. What the hell is happening?" He ran inside.

"Lily said they were by the desert, but—" Donald touched Chris's arm. "Come on. Maybe the basement...outside, at a high point. The waterfall? Hune is out of control, Chris."

"We need help." Chris turned around.

Everything he'd fought for was about to fall apart, and only he knew what to do. Sara had told him, and he'd ignored her. Now it was time to fix it.

"Where are you going?" Donald said, running behind him, but Chris stopped him.

"Those are roots, big ones, but just roots. Make sure you are in a place where you can see where they are landing."

Chris turned and stumbled, but then he stood and kept running.

"Where are you going?" Donald called back.

"To get help, Donald. Hune lost its Great Wizard. We need one."

Screams filled the streets as people ran out of the shelters, just like when Brutus had shown him the reisers taking the city years ago. Chris could only hope he could stop everything before a fire broke out.

Everything would be easier if his eyes and brain were working.

He made it outside the stables at the same time the rumble increased. The sound of ice cracking and the rush of water informed him the ocean was running free from the ice. It reminded him of how the glacier had ripped open. This time, it seemed the roots were winning the battle.

Inside the stable, he could only see the shapes of stalls, and he heard loud puffs and neighs while blows hit the wooden doors.

He couldn't concentrate beyond the urgency to find his sack. Chris inhaled and stopped to think. This annoyed him since, just a few days ago, he wouldn't have needed those seconds.

Against Charlie's opinion, Chris had ridden Mulsh to the city. The horse was calmer but also slower, which was why Chris had given him to Sara.

After a moment, he remembered walking his horse to the end of the stable. It was quiet there, and the poor animal had needed a long rest. A loud crack at his side made him duck, and only his instinct saved him from getting kicked by a horse, although a piece of the door got his arm.

"Gods be damn!" he said, but he found the last stall. His sight cleared for a second, and he found Mulsh in the next stall, and he raced over to him.

Mulsh's legs kept hitting the door, preventing him from leaving. Chris cursed his decision to leave his stuff in the stables. He stopped again, and the screams outside sped up his heartbeat.

"Hey, Mulsh," he said as calmly as possible. "I need you to relax."

The horse did everything but stop, so Chris groaned and hit the wooded door with his fist. The pain in his knuckles made him sear, but it also gave him an idea.

He unlocked the door and kicked it open. He barely had time to squish against the other side of the stables and cover his head before Mulsh ran out.

Chris jumped into the stall and searched with his hands until he found his sack. With no hesitation, he grabbed it and stopped before moving out to listen. All the horses kept making noises, but from the cold air and increased noise from outside, Chris guessed Mulsh had left.

He ran out, and his eyes flashed just in time to show him a big root moving towards him. Once again, his instinct made him leap out of the way.

Even with his poor eyesight, watching the massive shapes of the roots trying to land on the ground was dreadful. As the trees invaded the city, the sky closed, and the sunlight dimmed.

He knelt and opened his sack. Most of his stuff rolled down the street, but the book remained safely in his hand.

The letters and lines were a whitish blur to him. He moved it close to his face and turned the pages. This helped, but it was still hard to read.

A root crashed into the street near him, breaking the stones and pushing dirt out of the ground. Most of the light had disappeared, so he grabbed the book and ran over to where it seemed brighter.

A branch fell at his side, and he tumbled, rolling until he stopped on the frozen sand of the strange beach. Chris exhaled, grateful not to have lost the journal, and opened it again. A piece of paper fell from its pages, and Sara's conversation came to his mind.

It was his letter, the one that had given her the idea, so he left the journal on the ground and picked up the envelope.

It had something on the front that looked a lot like his name, but he didn't have time to look at it, so he just opened the envelope. He put the paper right in front of his eyes and turned towards the light. The letters became clearer, but it was still impossible to read them.

"Gods!" he said and moved the paper even closer. Behind him, the screams increased, and the light continued to vanish. "For once, a little of help would—."

A loud thump shook the ground, and he heard a familiar growl from the large presence approaching him. Chris looked in his pocket, but he didn't have the orchid anymore. The vast blur of the dragon bent down, and its scales touched Chris's head.

"I don't understand—"

Chris blacked out, and a second later, the letter in his hand became clear. He understood it was Brutus looking at the paper and, like before, the dragon allowed him to see through its eyes.

Everything made sense then.

Sara had written the prayer her mother had said before Gemli, Rafael, and Leonard had killed her. Chris hesitated for a second. He would call the Great Wizard, but he had no idea who that would be. Even if she looked like Sara, she might not be the same.

One of the few nights they were together, he talked to her about Stuart, Wilson, and Daniel. She swore to him she would never heal herself. He tried to make her see it could be different. After all, she didn't seem to have lost anything after she healed him or Genevieve. Still, she said she wouldn't risk it, since it would be a selfish act and could put Hune in danger.

He sighed and read the prayer.

When he finished, Brutus stepped back, and Chris's sight blurred again. The screams didn't stop, and the roots kept digging into the city grounds. The water flooded the streets, and the sunlight disappeared.

Chris closed his eyes and lowered his head, letting his

arm fall to his side. A soft breeze moved the paper in his hand, and a hint of flowers' scent passed by him.

HER BODY FELT numb and cold for a few seconds until a sharp pain made her bend over. She touched her side and almost threw up. Her hand shook when she realized it was wet and warm, and when she looked down, tears escaped her eyes.

That was too much blood.

Murllen returned to her mind, and her hand drifted from her wound. A soft breeze brushed the hair from her face, and the flowery scent that surrounded the abbey reached her. The song of birds got her attention, but the loss of blood made her lightheaded. She pushed her hand against her wound again, and although it nauseated her, it felt better.

She remembered her own warning and stopped before her weakness made her do something she didn't want to. Chris's face came to her mind. He looked as bad as he had when she'd seen him in Gemli's cave. A sob escaped her lips when she realized he'd said the prayer because he needed her.

Trembling, she moved her hand again and concentrated on her own needs. She heated her palm, and a peaceful healing sensation enfolded her. The breeze picked up, and the birds' song became louder.

Sara inhaled, and the roots of the Soto Forest's trees, moving past the waterfall, appeared in her mind.

Her memories seemed to flood into her head, but she held on to them. If Cielthos was right, as long as she didn't use her anger, all should work out, especially since Hune needed her. She concentrated on what had happened: Chris taking the saber, Murllen attacking her, Donald falling,

Gemli dying, the camps and the walks, all of it, along with the threat they were living with now.

As her body healed, she sighed and looked up at the top of the trees. Thousands of bluebirds sat on the branches, chirping loudly and happily, oblivious of how their simple magic had saved her life.

"You shouldn't be this far north." She smiled. "Let's go home."

She stood and, without trouble, turned into wind, and the birds followed her.

In almost no time, she reached Laconia. The high level of snow concerned her, as well as the enormous number of trees. She flew straight to the ocean and called the trees back.

It was easy to do when there was no evil magic stopping her. All of it had died with Gemli; even the zhortas' souls were free to reach the next life.

Freedom filled her heart, and smiling, she rushed among the roots, just like she had roomed by the abbey for years. She warmed up the city and allowed the snow to melt, and having the time, she called forth sprouts.

She flew to the beach and landed right by the water. A strange happiness filled her until she saw something at her side that made her crouch down.

~

"CHRIS!" Donald said while running towards him, but his eyes were stuck on the blurry shape standing by the water. "Do you see…? No, you cannot. It is Sara."

Chris put his hand on Donald's chest, stopping him.

"Of course. You can meet her first…I guess."

Chris exhaled, and for once, he was thankful to be half-blind. "I'm not sure she is actually Sara."

"What are you talking about?" Donald said. "I am telling

you she is Sara. The same dark hair, not very tall, zhorta coat—"

"It may look like her, but the person you see by the water is the Great Wizard. Sara's memories may not be part of her."

Chris took a deep breath and walked towards the figure. It seemed to him that she picked up something from the ground. This time, he felt her glance, and he stopped and let her walk the rest of the way to meet him.

Once she was closed enough, he bowed to her. "Your excellency."

"Excellency?" she said, and her tone took Chris's breath away for a second.

"I'm sorry. I have never talked to anyone as important—powerful—as you... I don't know what to call you. Thank you for your help."

"You shouldn't have waited this long."

Chris's shoulders dropped as he lost all hope. "I apologize. I'm sorry...again. It has been a tough couple of days for us—for me. I got injured, and my mind seems not to be—"

She walked so close that Chris could almost distinguish her face.

"They'll come here, Brutus" she said by his side.

"Who?" Chris said.

"The other dragons." She didn't explain more. "Here, I found it down there. It broke."

Chris moved his hand forward but then pulled it back. He couldn't see what she was trying to give him, and there was nothing more important than Sara's letter in his hand.

He feared he had offended her, as she stepped back, and he could hear Donald's disapproval. Someone who had just sent the Soto Forest's trees away and melted the surrounding snow shouldn't be upset.

"Your eyes..." She touched the side of his head.

The warmth of her palm soothed the pressure in his mind

and eased the pain that had threatened to drive him insane for days. He leaned against her hand, and the memory of her touch came to him.

She pulled away and put his father's compass in his free hand. He stared at it, shocked. The case was cracked, and the needle bent, but it looked clean, and it pointed at her.

"Like I said. It's broken. North is over there."

Chris looked up and found her bright blue eyes staring at him.

"What did you wish for?" she said and shook her head. "Never mind. It doesn't matter anymore. I guess we are… I'm done here."

She wiped her eyes before the tears in them fell. "Let me know if you need anything else, Admiral…General, whatever."

She turned and walked towards the water.

"Admiral?" Chris mumbled, and in two steps, he grabbed her arm and pulled her into his arms.

"I wished…I asked those birds to pay you back the favor. I wished they could protect you from the prophecy and Gemli's work on the war and what Rafael… How can you remember? Murllen…me…you must have closed your wound. Otherwise, you wouldn't… You know what? You are right. It doesn't matter."

He pulled her close and kissed her. He felt her knees weaken, and he just held her tight.

"I thought I lost you," he said without letting her go.

"You saved my life, Chris." She bit her lip and smiled. "The saber should have killed me, but…you made the perfect wish."

He leaned down and was about to kiss her, but then he stopped. "Is there anything else I need to learn about?"

"Um." Sara tilted her head as a growl rumbled behind him and the sky filled with dragons flying towards them. "Well,

Cielthos kind of left me in charge of them. I'll have to purify Reign Mountain and the valley and the abbey... Andromeda sank into the ocean, and Tundra needs a lot of work... I guess that means Laconia is the new capital..." She sighed. "And Lily is having twins. I think Amanda may—"

Chris kissed her, and for the first time, he realized there wasn't an upcoming threat. Smiling, he hugged her close.

"It'll be a hard job, Chris."

"You aren't reading my mind...are you?"

She shook her head against his shoulder.

He lifted her chin and stared into her eyes. "But you are here, and Hune will recover, and...who is having twins?"

Sara pulled him close, and he let himself get lost in the moment.

EPILOGUE

Standing in front of the fortress with Hayden and Donald brought unpleasant memories to Chris. However, their reason to be by those gates couldn't be more different than the last time they stepped on the swamps. Still, while they waited for Genevieve to finish gathering their stuff from the asylum, Chris kept Sara's hand on his, as he tried his best to look confident.

The weather over there had improved since Sara had come back. Just as Chris had figured out, Hune needed a Great Wizard. He was glad he had started to think in time.

"Are you sure you want to do this?" Sara said to Hayden once Genevieve joined them.

He glanced up.

The fortress was in bad shape, but not like how they'd found Laconia. One tower had fallen, along with most of the protective wall, but the main building and the asylum were intact.

"There is nothing left here for us," Hayden said, and he pulled Genevieve closer to him. "It was a prison for too many years and too many reisers. It had to come down."

Genevieve looked at him and smiled. It was a simple gesture, but it reaffirmed Hayden's decision. He took a step back and nodded at Sara.

"All right," Sara said.

"Wait, wait," Donald said. "Did you get everything out of the—"

"Yes, Donald," Genevieve said. "There is nothing important left inside."

Sara moved closer to the entrance. Chris's stomach twisted, and he found his hand looking for his sword. There was no danger anymore, but his worst memory lay in there.

"Do we need to be quiet, to not put anyone on edge here?" Sara said, making Hayden chuckle.

"No, I think an explosion will suit this time."

Sara smiled wider and knelt. Her hands stroked the ground, still wet but full of dry leaves and branches. A gust of wind crossed the yard, and the second it touched the building, the ground opened with a loud blast and, within seconds, swallowed all the stones that had formed the fortress.

Chris stepped closer, while the others took a few steps back. And he didn't relax until Sara stood up and the dust and dirt settled down.

She walked towards him, shaking her hands, and put her palms up when she stopped next to him.

"See? All good."

The only scar left on them was the one from his father's sword.

"Good." He kissed them. "Now we can get out of here."

Hayden walked Genevieve to her horse and helped her up. After making sure she was all right, he climbed onto his.

"It's strange," he said to Chris, "not having a home and being so relieved about it."

"You have a home," Chris said. "We just need to fix it."

There had been some discontent among the races. Just like Chris had suspected, once the fear of dying disappeared, overconfidence took over some minds. To his surprise, it wasn't only the humans; some reisers, and even valsings, were part of it, too.

However, it didn't worry him much. Hayden and Donald were great leaders, and together they would reshape their world.

"Let's go," Hayden said, and he set off on his horse without looking back.

"I guess he is happy to be out of here," Sara said, standing by Chris's horse.

"You are hurting Mulsh's feelings," Chris said.

"Mulsh? He is not even here!"

"Because you refused to ride. He told me he was ready to take you anywhere."

Sara shook her head and looked at Donald. "Don't get lost, you two. It wouldn't be the first time."

"You are not coming?" Donald narrowed his eyes. "I need your help with… Lily needs you in Laconia, Sara."

Sara stepped back, smiled, and vanished, but a soft breeze washed over Chris, filling the air with flowers' scent.

"Where…? Come on, Chris. You need to make her come to—"

"I agree, but Maximus is having a problem with something by the glacier, and Brutus wasn't helping." Chris laughed. "If someone had told me I was going to be talking about dragons with a valsing, I would have… Anyway, Lily should be fine, and Sara will be back in time. She won't leave you to suffer the demands of your wife."

LACONIA WAS in better shape already. They even had some ships to sail to Tundra. Chris was the only one who had seen that city, thanks to Sara. He wasn't looking forward to the job ahead, but he knew it needed to get done; it would give people things to do and their homes back.

"General," John said, catching up with him. "We are all set for next week's meeting, and the scouts came back. They didn't find any trouble by the Northern Forest."

"That is good news, Colonel," Chris said. "Are you getting used to it?"

"Hell, no!" John shook his head. "Sorry, I'm still waiting for something... I hope not, but..."

"I get it." Chris nodded. "See you and Amanda later?"

"Of course." John blocked his way. "You think I can talk to Sara first...in private? I want to ask if she knows—"

Chris pushed him to the side, laughing.

"She hasn't come back, but I doubt she would tell you anything." He turned and, stepping backward, yelled at John, "Isn't the surprise better? Just like Donald and Lily."

"For the gods above! She told you!"

Chris shrugged and walked down the street to the house where his mother had been staying with Charlie and Jean. It wasn't far from where Sara's parents had lived and, of course, where she had been living when she was in the city.

He was glad she wouldn't need to choose like her father, but that didn't take away how much he missed her when she was somewhere else in Hune.

"Don't forget your flower," Alleta said, walking outside the house with a small pot in her hand, behind a little girl and a man Chris recognized.

"Dunstan?" he said, but his mom's hug interrupted him. "My sweet lady, how are you? Is that fresh-baked bread?"

"Yes," Alleta said. "This young man and his little girl helped me make it."

"General," Dunstan said, standing straighter.

"Please don't." Chris waved his hand. "We aren't working."

"Christopher?"

"Sure," he said, "or Chris. Either is fine for someone who gets my mother to bake...and not for me!" The girl giggled and hid behind Dunstan's leg. "Who is this little one?" Chris said.

Dunstan looked down with a full smile, something Chris had never seen from the reiser, not even after they defeated Murllen.

"Well, this is Violet, my daughter," he said. "Genevieve introduced us to Alleta the other day, and she offered to help me—us—with cooking. I've never done it before, but we'll all need to know how soon."

Violet jumped and clapped her hands.

"Well, I hope she teaches you better than she taught me," said Chris.

Alleta nudged his arm. "So disrespectful. You never tried to learn." She looked down at Violet. "He just wanted to eat."

"Do you...?" Violet said to Chris, still half-hiding. "Can you do magic? Like the wizard? I have seen you with her and...can you?"

Chris was about to say no, but instead, he grabbed the flower pot from his mom and handed it to her. "What I learned from her is that if you take care of these things, magic may happen."

Violet narrowed her eyes as she gazed at the pot.

"You missed the dust," Sara said, walking down the street.

Chris hadn't heard her approach, so he guessed she'd just shown up, but it didn't matter. Every time he saw her, his world was full again, and somehow everything seemed possible and easy to enjoy.

Sara crouched in front of Violet and picked up soil from the ground. "Let me see your hand."

Violet hesitated, but then she offered her hand, and Sara gently poured the dirt onto her palm. "Now, put it in the pot."

Violet did, and her eyes opened wide when the little stick grew a couple of leaves and a sprout at the end. "That's amazing! Thanks!"

She half-hugged Sara before turning to Dunstan and showing the new plant to him. "Did you see? It is magic!" She kept looking at it, touching its leaves.

"Thank you," Dunstan said to Sara. "Hope that makes the walk back easy."

Sara stood. "I did nothing."

Dunstan stared at her, and Chris could have sworn he turned pale and shaky. "You didn't?"

"Nop. That's on her." Sara smiled at the girl, who kept playing, ignoring their conversation. "It's natural for Hune's magic to flow through more of its inhabitants now. She'll need to learn, but I'm happy to help her."

Sara looked at Dunstan, who seemed to be about to get sick. "What's wrong? It's nothing bad. You just—"

"No, I understand, but..." He lowered his tone so Violet couldn't hear him. "I'm barely getting a hold on this, and... she is amazing, but...how can I—"

"Good," Alleta said, wrapping her arms around his shoulder. "Now you sound like a father."

Chris laughed at the growing concern on Dunstan's face.

"What is it?" Violet said, and Dunstan cleared his throat. "Oh, no. Is it time to go?"

Dunstan nodded. "Genevieve will have dinner ready for you, and you can share our bread with them...and soon you won't have to do this again."

Genevieve explained to Chris how, without the asylum, she would introduce the young reisers to their parents. One of the reasons she asked to visit the asylum one last time, so she knew how to match the families.

If the reisers chose to, she would find them a home so they could live together; otherwise, the little ones would stay with her in one of the gigantic mansions in Laconia. She needed to make sure the ones leaving would be all right, though. Like Dunstan said, they were raised to be warriors, not care for children.

"All right." Violet's shoulders dropped as she reached for his hand.

"Thanks again," Dunstan said, and after Violet waved, they walked up the street.

"Come in," Alleta said, and she led Chris and Sara into her house.

The smell of his mother's kitchen brought back many memories. It wasn't the same house, but it was easy to see the resemblance. The same was true of his mom's mood. She was enjoying her life once again.

"Sara," Alleta said, grabbing her hand and walking her towards the kitchen table, "before anyone else gets here, I want to give you something."

Sara shook her head, but she sat where Alleta told her.

"Dear gods, you look so much like Elizabeth." Sara's eyes shone as Alleta touched her cheek. "She was a great friend of mine. And Landford...he was so funny. I have wonderful stories about them...when you are ready to listen...but here."

Alleta put a leather bracelet on the table in front of Sara. John had carried a similar one for years until he'd found Amanda. He'd told Chris it was how the people from Laconia proposed.

John had made one for Amanda, engraving all the important and special things they'd shared. He was teaching Chris how to make them.

"Xander went to Landford's funeral. If I had known your

mom had a baby I would have gone, too, and dragged her all the way back with me."

Sara cleared her throat and tilted her head. "Not even my dad knew…"

Alleta patted Sara's hand. "It makes sense. Elizabeth gave this to Xander. She told him things would get… Never mind that." Alleta exhaled and smiled at Sara. "Your dad made this for your mom when they got married."

"How…?" Sara said as her eyes flooded.

"Genevieve gave it to me. You see, I had it in my pocket when we left Tundra, and she found it the other day when you all went to the…that place. She didn't know what it was, but she brought it back."

Sara lightly brushed her fingers over it. "Thank you."

Alleta patted her one more time, and then the door opened, and Charlie stepped inside, carrying two heavy baskets. Jean followed with some flowers.

Chris greeted everyone, but he kept an eye on Sara, who walked out to the back of the house. He didn't need to say anything to his mom, who pushed him to follow her while she talked to Jean.

Sara was sitting on the ground, her legs bent, looking at the bracelet. When Chris sat by her, she wiped her eyes and leaned her head on his shoulder.

Chris kissed it and grabbed her hand. "My lady…"

"How did all get to be…so wrong?" She hugged his arm.

"You know, Sara," Chris said by her ear. "I'm more afraid now than in all the years I fought in the war. This," he moved their hands closer and looked behind them for a second. "This, I can't lose."

"I never met your father, but I can tell you…if he hadn't believed what he was doing was for the best, he wouldn't have done it. He would have never left your mom, and this would have been a different story."

He lifted her chin. "Maybe the reason I wanted to save Hune is because I always knew I was in love with its Great Wizard."

Sara touched his face and smiled the way he liked so much.

Being at peace was dreadful and threatening. Once they experienced what they wanted, the thought of losing it was unimaginable. Chris knew that very well. Sara was more than his reason to fight. She was his reason to live and was with him because of a simple wish in his beloved world founded on dangerous magic.

I HOPE YOU ENJOY MY BOOK,

DON'T FORGET TO JOIN MY MAILING LIST TODAY AND GET A HOLD TO

Saber, Seeds of Darkness

I was supposed to die in that fall, but I didn't.

I used to believe my precarious brother and abusive father were my biggest problem, but all changed.

Now, I can't trust anyone and if I don't control the power in me, everyone will be in danger. Especially my Elizabeth.

Discover how it all begins.

ALSO BY MONICA RED

Roots of Hope, Book 1

Most believe our colonel sent us back to protect Tundra, our last city, but I know better. My father send me to make sure my mother doesn't suffer when our enemy wins the war.

Now, in what it seems to be our last days of freedom, I face a decision. Do I betray my King and stand to face our enemy? Or should I follow a strange order into a quest to find hope in Hune?

Some believe there is magic left in Hune, but I don't trust it. After all, it was a prophecy that started the war.

The problem is, now I'm in charge and everyone is looking at me for answers and to be saved.

Shadows of Tomorrow, Book 2

Hune is not what it used to be.

As I expected, our enemy took over our last city, and although I'm thankful they didn't kill everyone as they had been doing, I can't stop but wonder why they took them prisoners and where are they taking them.

However, as much as I want to save them, this time I have no option.

Without an army, I can't chase them and free my people. I have to follow the misdirection of the prophecy to unveil the truth behind it all in a quest that is out of my control.

Also, I'm certain this path will put a person very important to me in danger, and I'm not willing to sacrifice her.

Could the shadows of the past lead us to tomorrow?.

Short Stories from blog:

Before the Devil Eats your Breakfast

Podcast: Birds On Topic

https://anchor.fm/monica-r9

ACKNOWLEDGMENTS

For your patience, support, belief in the cause, staying with me and tolerating the time that I took away from all of you to sit down and write. During these years I learned so much from all of you. For listening to my stories, complains, successes. For your help and critiques all of these and more.

Mom, Aunt Gloria, and Teddy. The amazing support and learning resources of Prowriting Aid Academy. My amazing editors from First Editing; Michael and Jefferson. Josephine Noel (I would need a book to tell you how much I thank you for) and You up there...

Thank you.

ABOUT THE AUTHOR

I was born in Mexico City a few years back when the internet wasn't a thing and we listened to music on FM radio. My parents decided to move to Toluca, the capital of the State of Mexico, which was a less crowded. It was a small town at the time, only between 1 to 2 million people!

I became an architect and worked for years on my career. Eventually I ventured to the northern end of the American continent and settled down in the Midwest, where nowadays I enjoy the brief summer and crazy winter of Minnesota.

As for writing? Well, I started to write my first novel when I was in high school. This manuscript developed and became a fantasy trilogy that you can find as Saber. I wrote many short stories, both Spanish and English, along with several manuscripts that maybe one day will see the light of day.

Besides reading, I love painting although I doubt my talent is worth sharing. I enjoy music, especially loud and although I complain about bugs, I enjoy hiking and exploring the great outdoors... or cities (must be the architect in me). See more of my work at monicared.com

Made in the USA
Columbia, SC
28 October 2023

25105056R00217